The Kept Woman

Also by Karin Slaughter

Blindsighted

Kisscut

A Faint Cold Fear

Indelible

Like a Charm (Editor)

Faithless

Triptych

Skin Privilege

Fractured

Genesis

Broken

Fallen

Criminal

Unseen

Cop Town

Pretty Girls

eBook originals

Snatched

Busted

The Kept Woman

Karin Slaughter

CENTURY

1 3 5 7 9 10 8 6 4 2

Century
20 Vauxhall Bridge Road
London SW1V 2SA

Century is part of the Penguin Random House group of companies whose addresses can be found at global.penguinrandomhouse.com

First published in Great Britain by Century in 2016

www.penguin.co.uk

A CIP catalogue record for this book is available from the British Library

9781780896953

Typeset in India by Thomson Digital Pvt Ltd, Noida, Delhi

Printed and bound in Great Britain by Clays Ltd, St Ives PLC

Penguin Random House is committed to a sustainable future for our business, our readers and our planet. This book is made from Forest Stewardship Council® certified paper.

To Georgina

Prologue

For the first time in her life, she cradled her daughter in her arms.

All those years ago, the nurse at the hospital had asked if she wanted to hold her baby, but she had refused. Refused to name the girl. Refused to sign the legal papers to let her go. Hedging her bets, because that's what she always did. She could remember tugging on her jeans before she left the hospital. They were still damp from her water breaking. The waist was baggy where it had been tight, and she had gripped the extra material in her fist as she walked down the back stairs and ran outside to meet the boy waiting in the car around the corner.

There was always a boy waiting for her, expecting something from her, pining for her, hating her. It had been like that for as long as she could remember. Ten years old: her mother's pimp offering to trade a meal for her mouth. Fifteen: a foster father who liked to cut. Twenty-three: a soldier who waged war on her body. Thirty-four: a cop who convinced her it wasn't rape. Thirty-seven: another cop who made her think he would love her forever.

Forever was never as long as you thought it was.

She touched her daughter's face. Gentle this time, not like before.

So beautiful.

Her skin was soft, unlined. Her eyes were closed, but there was a tremble behind the lids. Her breath whistled in her chest.

Carefully, she stroked back the girl's hair, tucking it behind her ear. She could've done this at the hospital all those years ago. Smoothed a worried forehead. Kissed ten tiny fingers, caressed ten tiny toes.

Manicured fingernails now. Long toes damaged from years of ballet lessons and late-night dancing and countless other events that had filled her vibrant, motherless life.

She touched her fingers to her daughter's lips. Cold. The girl was losing too much blood. The handle of the blade sticking out of her chest pulsed with her heart, sometimes like a metronome, sometimes like the stuck second hand on a clock that was winding down.

All those lost years.

She should've held her daughter at the hospital. Just that once. She should've imprinted some memory of her touch so that her daughter didn't flinch the way she did now, moving away from her hand the way she would move away from a stranger's.

They *were* strangers.

She shook her head. She couldn't go down the rabbit hole of everything she had lost and why. She had to think about how strong she was, that she was a survivor. She had spent her life running on the edge of a razor—sprinting away from the things that people usually ran toward: a child, a husband, a home, a life.

Happiness. Contentment. Love.

She realized now that all that running had led her straight to this dark room, trapped in this dark place, holding her daughter for the first time, for the last time, as the girl bled to death in her arms.

There was a scuffing noise outside the closed door. The slit of light at the threshold showed the shadow of two feet slithering along the floor.

Her daughter's would-be killer?

Her own murderer?

The wooden door rattled in the metal frame. Just a square of light indicated where the knob had been.

She thought about weapons: the steel posts in her high heels that she had kicked off as she ran across the road. The knife sticking out of her daughter's chest.

The girl was still breathing. The blade of the knife was pressed against something vital inside, holding back the torrent of blood so that her dying was a slow and labored thing.

She touched her fingers to the knife for just a second before she slowly pulled her hand away.

The door rattled again. There was a scraping sound. Metal against metal. The square of light narrowed, then disappeared, as a screwdriver was jammed into the opening.

Click-click-click, like the dry fire of an empty gun.

Gently she eased her daughter's head to the floor. She got on her knees, biting her lip as a sharp pain sliced into her ribs. The wound in her side gaped open. Blood slid down her legs. Muscles started to spasm.

She crawled around the dark room, ignoring the chalky grit of sawdust and metal shavings grinding into her knees, the stabbing pain beneath her ribs, the steady flow of blood that left a trail behind her. She found screws and nails and then her hand brushed against something cold and round and metallic. She picked up the object. In the darkness, her fingers told her what she was holding: the broken doorknob. Solid. Heavy. The four-inch spindle stuck out like an ice pick.

There was a final click of the latch engaging. The screwdriver clattered to the concrete floor. The door cracked open.

She narrowed her eyes against the coming light. She thought about all the ways she had hurt the men in her life. Once with a gun. Once with a needle. Countless times with her fists. With her mouth. With her teeth. With her heart.

The door opened a few more careful inches. The tip of a gun snaked around the corner.

She gripped the doorknob so that the spindle shot out between her fingers and waited for the man to come in.

Monday

ONE

Will Trent was worried about his dog. Betty was getting her teeth cleaned, which sounded like a ridiculous waste of money for a pet, but when the vet had explained to Will all the terrible things that poor dental hygiene could do to an animal, he had been ready to sell his house in order to buy the little thing a few more precious years.

Apparently, he wasn't the only idiot in Atlanta who was ensuring his pet had better health care than many Americans. He glanced at the line of people waiting to enter the Dutch Valley Animal Clinic. A recalcitrant Great Dane was bottlenecking the front door, while several cat owners gave each other knowing looks. Will turned back to the street. He wiped the sweat off his neck, unsure whether he was perspiring from the intense late August heat or from the sheer panic of not knowing whether or not he had made the right decision. He'd never had a dog before.

He'd never been solely responsible for an animal's well-being. He put his hand to his chest. He could still feel the memory of Betty's heart jangling like a tambourine as he handed her over to the vet tech.

Should he go back inside and rescue her?

The sharp beep of a car horn startled him out of his apprehension. He saw a flash of red as Faith Mitchell drove past in her Mini. She made a wide U-turn, then pulled up alongside Will. He was reaching for the handle when she leaned over and pushed open the door.

'Hurry,' she said, her voice raised over the whine of the air conditioning, which was set to polar. 'Amanda already sent two texts asking where the hell we are.'

Will hesitated before getting into the tiny car. Faith's government-issue Suburban was in the shop. There was a baby's car seat strapped into the back seat, which left approximately thirty inches of space up front into which he could wedge his six-feet-four-inch frame.

Faith's phone chirped with a new text. 'Amanda.' She said the name like a curse, which was how most people said it. Deputy Director Amanda Wagner was their boss at the Georgia Bureau of Investigation. She was not known for her patience.

Will tossed his suit jacket into the back seat then folded himself into the car like a burrito. He tilted his head into the extra few inches afforded by the closed sunroof. The glovebox pressed into his shins. His knees almost touched his face. If they were in an accident, the coroner would have to scrape his nose off the inside of his skull.

'Murder,' Faith said, letting her foot off the brake before he'd even closed the door. 'Male, fifty-eight years old.'

'Nice,' Will said, relishing the death of a fellow human being as only a law enforcement officer can. In his defense, both he and Faith had spent the last seven months pushing boulders up some very steep hills. She had been loaned out to a special task force investigating the Atlanta Public Schools cheating scandal, and he had been stuck in the particular hell of a high-visibility rape investigation.

Faith said, 'Atlanta nine-one-one got the call around five this AM.' She had an air of giddiness about her as she relayed the details. 'An unidentified male caller said there was a dead body near those abandoned warehouses off Chattahoochee. Lots of blood. No murder weapon.' She slowed for a red light. 'They're not releasing cause of death on the radio, so it must be pretty bad.'

Something inside the car started to beep. Will reached blindly for his seat belt. 'Why are we working this?' The GBI couldn't just walk on to a case. They had to be ordered in by the governor or asked in by the local cops. The Atlanta Police Department dealt with murder on a weekly basis. They didn't generally ask for help. Especially from the state.

'The victim is an Atlanta cop.' Faith grabbed his seat belt and buckled him in like he was one of her kids. 'Detective First Grade Dale Harding, retired. Ever heard of him?'

Will shook his head. 'You?'

'My mom knew him. Never worked with him. He was in white-collar crimes. Took early medical leave, then popped up doing private security. Mostly knuckle-dragging and knee-breaking.' Faith had been with the APD for fifteen years before she'd partnered with Will. Her mother had retired as a captain. Between the two of them, they were familiar with practically everyone on the force. 'Mom says that knowing Harding's reputation, he probably pissed off the wrong pimp or missed the vig with his bookie and got a bat to the head.'

The car jerked as the light changed. Will felt a sharp jab in his ribs from his Glock. He tried to shift his weight. Despite the frigid air conditioning, sweat had already glued the back of his shirt to the seat. The skin peeled away like a Band-Aid. The clock on the dash read 7:38 AM. He couldn't let himself think about how sweltering it would be by noon.

Faith's phone chirped with a text. Then chirped again. And again. 'Amanda,' she groaned. 'Why does she break up the lines? She sends three separate sentences in three separate texts. All caps. It's not fair.' Faith drove with one hand and texted back with the other, which was dangerous and illegal, but Faith was one of those cops who only saw infractions in other people. 'We're about five minutes out, right?'

'Probably closer to ten with traffic.' Will reached over to steady the steering wheel so they wouldn't end up on the sidewalk. 'What's the address on the warehouse?'

She scrolled back through her texts. 'It's a construction site near the warehouses. Three-eighty Beacon.'

Will's jaw clamped down so tight that he felt a lightning bolt of pain shoot into his neck. 'That's Marcus Rippy's nightclub.'

Faith gave him a startled look. 'Are you kidding me?'

Will shook his head. There was nothing about Marcus Rippy that he would kid about. The man was a pro basketball player who'd been accused of drugging and raping a college student. Will had spent the last seven months building a pretty solid case against the lying asshole, but Rippy had hundreds of millions of dollars to spend on lawyers and specialists and experts and publicists, who had all made sure that the case never went to trial.

Faith asked, 'What's a dead ex-cop doing inside Marcus Rippy's club less than two weeks after Rippy walks on a rape charge?'

'I'm sure his lawyers will have a plausible explanation by the time we get there.'

'Jesus.' Faith dropped her phone into the cup holder and put both hands back on the wheel. She was quiet for a moment, probably considering all the ways this had just turned bad for them. Dale Harding was a cop, but he'd been a bad cop. The hard truth about murder in the big city was that in general, the deceased rarely turned out to be a shining, upstanding citizen. Not to blame the victim, but they tended to be involved in activities—like pissing off pimps and not paying bookies—where it made sense that they would eventually end up murdered.

Marcus Rippy's involvement changed everything.

Faith slowed the car as morning traffic thickened like paste. 'I know you said you didn't want to talk about your case crapping out, but now I need you to talk about it.'

Will still didn't want to talk about it. Over a five-hour period, Rippy had repeatedly assaulted his victim, sometimes beating her, sometimes strangling her into unconsciousness. Standing beside her hospital bed three days later, Will could make out the dark lines where Rippy's fingers had gripped her neck the same way he would palm a basketball. There were other bruises documented in the medical report. Cuts. Lacerations. Tearing.

Blunt-force trauma. Bleeding. The woman could not speak above a whisper, but she still told her story, and she kept telling it to anyone who would listen until Rippy's lawyers shut her up.

Faith asked, 'Will?'

'He raped a woman. He paid his way out of it. He'll do it again. He probably did it before. And none of that matters because he knows how to handle a basketball.'

'Wow, that's a lot of information. Thank you.'

Will felt the pain in his jaw intensify. 'The day after New Year's Eve. Ten in the morning. The victim was found unconscious inside Marcus Rippy's house by one of the maids. The maid called Rippy's head of security, who called Rippy's business manager, who called Rippy's lawyers, who eventually called a private ambulance to take her to Piedmont Hospital. Two hours before the victim was reportedly found, around eight AM, Rippy's private jet left for Miami with him and his entire family on board. He claims the vacation was on the books all along, but the flight plan was filed half an hour before take-off. Rippy said he had no idea the victim was in the house. Never saw her. Never talked to her. Didn't know her name. They'd had a big New Year's Eve party the night before. A couple of hundred people were in and out of the residence.'

Faith said, 'There was a Facebook post of—'

'Instagram,' Will said, because he'd had the pleasure of trawling the internet for hours of party footage that people had filmed with their phones. 'Someone at the party posted a GIF of the victim slurring her words before she threw up into an ice bucket. Rippy's people had the hospital do a tox screen. She had pot, amphetamines and alcohol in her system.'

'You said she was unconscious when they brought her into the hospital. Did she give permission for Rippy's people to see her drug screen?'

Will shook his head, because it didn't matter. Rippy's team had paid off someone at the hospital lab and leaked the results of the blood test to the press.

'You gotta admit, he's got a great name for it. Rapey/Rippy.' Faith twisted her lips to the side as she thought it out. 'The house is huge, right?'

'Sixteen thousand square feet.' Will's head called up the layout he'd studied for so many hours that it was still imprinted in his brain. 'It's shaped like a horseshoe, with a swimming pool in the middle. The family lives in the main section, the top of the horseshoe. The two wings off the back have a bunch of guest suites, and there's a nail salon, an indoor basketball court, massage room, gym, movie theater, playroom for his two kids. You name it, they have it.'

'So, logically, something bad could happen in one part of the house without someone in the other part knowing.'

'Without two hundred people knowing. Without the maids and the butlers and the valets and the caterers and the cooks and the bartenders and the assistants and the whoever else knowing.' Will had been given a two-hour tour of the Rippy estate by the family's chief of security. Cameras were mounted at every possible angle around the exterior of the house. There were no blind spots. Motion sensors detected anything heavier than a leaf landing in the front yard. No one could go in or out of the estate without someone knowing about it.

Except for the night of the assault. There had been a bad storm. The power kept cutting in and out. The generators were state-of-the-art, but for some reason the external DVR that recorded footage from the security cameras was not jacked into the backup power grid.

Faith said, 'Okay, I saw the news. Rippy's people said she was a nutjob looking for a payday.'

'They offered her money. She told them no.'

'Could've been waiting for a higher number.' Faith drummed her fingers on the steering wheel. 'Is it possible her wounds were self-inflicted?'

That had been the contention of Rippy's lawyers. They'd even found an expert who was willing to testify that the giant finger marks around her neck and back and thighs were made by her own hand.

'She had this bruise here—' Will indicated his own back. 'Like a fist print between her shoulder blades. A big fist. You could see the finger marks, same as the bruises on her neck. She had a severe contusion on her liver. The doctors put her on bed rest for two weeks.'

'There was a condom with Rippy's semen—'

'Found in a hall bathroom. The wife says they had sex that night.'

'And he leaves the used condom in the hall bath, not the master?' Faith frowned. 'Was the wife's DNA on the outside of the condom?'

'The condom was on a tile floor that had been recently mopped with a cleaner that contained bleach. There was nothing we could use on the outside.'

'Any DNA found on the victim?'

'There were some unidentified strands, all female, probably picked up at her dorm.'

'Did the victim say who invited her to the party?'

'She came with a group of college friends. None of them can remember who got the initial invite. None of them knew Rippy personally. Or at least none of them claimed to. And all four of them immediately distanced themselves from the victim when I started knocking on doors.'

'And the victim positively ID'd Rippy?'

'She was standing in line for the bathroom. This was after she threw up in the ice bucket. She says she only had one drink, but it made her sick, like something wasn't right. Rippy approached her. She recognized him immediately. He was nice, told her there was another bathroom down the hallway in the guest wing. She followed him. It was a long walk. She was feeling a little dizzy. He put his arm around her, kept her steady. He led her into the last guest suite at the end of the hall. She went to the toilet. She came out and he was sitting on the bed with his clothes off.'

'And then what?'

'And then she woke up in the hospital the next day. She had a bad concussion from being punched or hit in the head. She'd obviously been strangled repeatedly, lost consciousness a few times. The doctors think she won't ever completely recover her memory of that night.'

'Hm.'

Will felt the full weight of her skepticism in the sound.

Faith asked, 'The hall bath where the condom was found?'

'Six doors down from the guest suite, so they passed it on the way there, and he passed it on his way back to the party.' Will added, 'There's video evidence from phones that show Rippy at the party off and on all night, so he went back and forth to work his alibi. Plus, half his team backed him up. Jameel Gordon, Andre Dupree, Reuben Figaroa. The day after the assault, they all showed up at the APD, lawyers in tow, each of them telling the exact same story. By the time the GBI caught the case, every single one of them declined to be interviewed again.'

'Typical,' Faith noted. 'Rippy said that he never even saw the victim at the party?'

'Correct.'

'The wife was pretty vocal, right?'

'She was a megaphone for his defense.' LaDonna Rippy had gone on every talk show and news program that would have her. 'She backed up everything that her husband said, including that she never saw the victim at the party.'

'Hm.' Faith sounded even more skeptical.

Will added, 'And people who saw the victim that night said she was drunk and falling all over every basketball player she could get her hands on. Which, if you look at the GIF of her puking and combine that with the tox screen, makes sense. But then you look at the rape kit and you know that she was brutally raped, and the victim knows that Rippy was sitting on that bed, totally naked, when she came out of the bathroom.'

'Devil's advocate?'

Will nodded, though he knew what was coming.

'I can see why it fell apart. It's he said/she said and Rippy gets the benefit of the doubt because that's how the Constitution works.

Innocent until blah-blah-blah. And let's not forget that Rippy is filthy rich. If he lived in a trailer park, his court-appointed lawyer would've pled him down to five years for false imprisonment to keep him off the sex-offender registry, end of story.'

Will didn't respond, because there was nothing else to say.

Faith gripped the steering wheel. 'I hate rape cases. You don't throw a murder case to a jury and they ask, "Well, was the guy *really* murdered or is he lying because he wants the attention? And what was he doing in that part of town? And why was he drinking? And what about all those murderers he dated before?"'

'She wasn't sympathetic.' Will hated that this even mattered. 'Her family's a mess. Single mom with a drug habit. No idea who the dad is. She had some drug issues in high school, a history of self-cutting. She was coming off academic probation at her college. She dated around, spent a lot of time on Tinder and OkCupid, like everybody her age. Rippy's people found out she had an abortion a few years ago. She basically wrote their trial strategy for them.'

'There's not much daylight between being a good girl and a bad one, but once you cross that line—' Faith blew out a stream of air. 'You can't imagine the shit people said about me when I got pregnant with Jeremy. One day I was a junior high school honor student with her entire life ahead of her, and the next day I was a teenage Mata Hari.'

'You were shot for being a spy?'

'You know what I mean. I was a pariah. Jeremy's dad was sent to live with family up north. My brother still hasn't forgiven me. My dad got forced out of his Lodge. He lost a ton of customers. None of my friends would speak to me. I had to drop out of school.'

'At least it was different when you had Emma.'

'Oh, yeah, a single thirty-five-year-old woman with a twenty-year-old son and a one-year-old daughter is constantly praised for her excellent life choices.' She changed the subject. 'She had a boyfriend, right? The victim?'

'He broke up with her a week before the assault.'

'Oh, for godsakes.' Faith had worked enough rape investigations to know that a defense lawyer's dream was an accuser with an ex-boyfriend she was trying to make jealous.

'He stepped up after the assault,' Will said, though he wasn't a fan of the ex-boyfriend. 'Stayed by her side. Made her feel safe. Or at least tried to.'

'Dale Harding's name never came up during the investigation?'

He shook his head.

A news truck sped by, dipping into the oncoming traffic lane for twenty yards before taking an illegal turn.

Faith said, 'Looks like news at noon has its lead story.'

'They don't want news. They want gossip.' Up until Rippy's case had been dismissed, Will couldn't leave GBI headquarters without some well-coifed anchor trying to bait him into a career-ending sound bite. He got off light considering the death threats and online stalking Rippy's fans lobbed at his accuser.

Faith said, 'I guess this could be a coincidence. Harding being found dead at Rippy's club?'

Will shot her a look. No cop believed in coincidence, especially a cop like Faith.

'Okay,' she relented, shuffling the steering wheel as she followed the news van's illegal dip and dash. 'At least we know why Amanda sent four texts.' Her phone chirped. 'Five.' Faith grabbed the phone. Her thumb slid across the screen. She hooked a sharp turn. 'Jeremy finally updated his Facebook page.'

Will took over the steering as she typed a message to her son, who was using the summer months away from college to drive across the country with three of his friends, seemingly for the sole purpose of worrying his mother.

Faith mumbled as she typed, bemoaning the stupidity of kids in particular and her son in specific. 'Does this girl look eighteen to you?'

Will glanced at a photo of Jeremy standing very close to a scantily clad blonde. The grin on his face was heartbreakingly hopeful. Jeremy was a skinny, nerdy little kid studying physics at Georgia Tech. He was so out of the blonde's league that he might as well have been a cantaloupe. 'I would be more worried about the bong pipe on the floor.'

'Oh, fer fucksake.' Faith looked like she wanted to throw the phone out the window. 'He'd better hope his grandmother doesn't see this.'

Will watched as Faith forwarded the picture to her mother to make sure this very thing happened.

He pointed to the next intersection. 'This is Chattahoochee.'

Faith was still cursing the photo as she took the turn. 'As the mother of a son, I look at that picture and I think, "Don't get her pregnant." Then I look at it as the mother of a daughter and I think, "Don't get stoned with a guy you just met, because his friends could gang-rape you and leave you dead in a hotel closet."'

Will shook his head. Jeremy was a good kid with good friends. 'He's twenty years old. You have to start trusting him sometime.'

'No I don't.' She dropped her phone back into the cup holder. 'Not if he still wants food, clothes, a roof over his head, health insurance, an iPhone, video games, pocket money, gas money—'

Will tuned out the long list of all the things Faith was going to take away from her poor son. His mind instantly went to Marcus Rippy. The basketball player's smug face as he sat back in the chair with his arms crossed and his mouth shut. His wife's hateful glares every time Will asked a question. His conceited business manager and his slick lawyers, who were all as interchangeable as Bond villains.

Keisha Miscavage, Marcus Rippy's accuser.

She was a tough young woman, defiant, even from her hospital bed. Her hoarse whispers were peppered with fucks and shits and her eyes stayed constantly squinted as if she were interviewing Will instead of the other way around. 'Don't feel sorry for me,' she'd warned him. 'Just do your fucking job.'

Will had to admit, if only to himself, that he had a soft spot for hostile women. It killed him that he'd failed Keisha so miserably. He couldn't even watch basketball anymore, let alone play it. Every time his hand touched a ball, he wanted to shove it down Marcus Rippy's throat.

'Holy crap.' Faith coasted to a stop several yards behind a news van. 'Half the police force is here.'

Will studied the parking lot outside the car window. Her estimate didn't seem far off. The scene was vibrating with people. A semi truck hauling lights. The APD crime scene investigation bus. The GBI Department of Forensic Sciences mobile lab. APD cruisers and unmarked cop cars scattered around like Pick-Up Sticks. Yellow crime-scene tape roped off a smoldering burned-out car with a halo of water steaming off the scorching asphalt. Techs swarmed the area, laying down numbered yellow markers by anything that could be evidence.

Faith said, 'I bet I know who called in the body.'

Will guessed, 'Crack addict. Raver. Runaway.' He took in the vault-like building in front of them. Marcus Rippy's future night-club. Construction had stopped six months ago when the rape charge had looked like it was going to stick. The poured concrete walls were rough and weathered, darkened along the bottom by several overlays of graffiti. Weeds had cracked up around the foundation. There were two giant windows, high up, tucked into opposite corners of the street side of the building. The glass was tinted almost black.

Will didn't envy the job of the techs who had to inventory every condom, needle and crack pipe on-site. There was no telling how many fingerprints and shoeprints were inside. The broken glow necklaces and pacifiers indicated that ravers had made good use of the space.

Faith asked, 'What's the story on the club?'

'The investors put construction on hold while they waited for Rippy's problems to go away.'

'Do you know if they're back in?'

Will muttered an expletive under his breath—not because of the question, but because his boss was standing in front of the building with her hands on her hips. Amanda looked at her watch, then looked at them, then looked at her watch again.

Faith added her own expletive as she got out of the car. Will blindly reached for the round door handle, which was roughly the circumference of an M&M. The door popped back on its hinges. Hot air rushed in. Atlanta was at the tail end of the hottest, most humid summer on record. Going outside was like walking straight into the mouth of a yawning dog.

Will unfolded himself from the car, trying to ignore the audience of cops standing several feet away. Their voices didn't carry, but he was pretty sure they were waging bets on how many more clowns would come out of the tiny vehicle.

Fortunately, Amanda's attention had been pulled away by one of the crime scene analysts. Charlie Reed was easily recognizable by his handlebar mustache and Popeye build. Will scanned the area, looking for other familiar faces.

'Mitchell, right?'

Will turned around to find himself looking at a remarkably handsome man. The guy had dark wavy hair and a cleft in his chin, and he looked at Faith with the eyes of an all-conquering frat boy.

'Hi.' Faith's voice had a weird, high pitch. 'Have we met?'

'Never had the pleasure.' The man ran his fingers through his boyish, floppy hair. 'You look like your mom. I worked with her when I was in uniform. I'm Collier. This is my partner Ng.'

Ng gave an almost imperceptible tilt of his chin to convey his coolness. His hair was buzz-cut, military style. He was wearing dark wraparound glasses. Like his partner, he wore jeans and a black APD POLICE T-shirt—in contrast to Will, who looked like the maître d' at an old Italian steakhouse.

'I'm Trent,' Will said, straightening his shoulders, because at least he had the height advantage. 'What've we got here?'

'A clusterfuck.' Ng looked out at the building instead of looking up at Will. 'I hear Rippy's already on a plane to Miami.'

Faith asked, 'Have you been inside?'

'Not upstairs.'

Faith waited for more, then tried again. 'Can we talk to the unis who found the body?'

Ng feigned a strain on his memory. He asked his partner, 'You remember their names, bro?'

Collier shook his head. 'Drawing a blank.'

Faith was no longer enamored. 'Hey, *21 Jump Street*, should we leave so you two can finish jerking each other off?'

Ng laughed, but he didn't provide any more information.

'For godsakes,' Faith said. 'You know my mom, Collier. Our boss is her old partner. What do you think she's gonna say when we have to ask her to catch us up to speed?'

Collier gave a weary sigh. He rubbed the back of his neck as he looked off into the distance. The sun picked out slivers of gray in his hair. There were deep lines at the corners of his eyes. He was probably in his mid-forties, which made him a few years older than Will, which for some reason made Will feel better.

'All right.' Collier finally relented, but not before doing the fingers-through-the-hair thing again. 'Switchboard gets an anonymous tip there's a dead body, this location. Twenty minutes later, a two-man uni rolls up. They sweep the building. Find the DB, male, upstairs inside one of the rooms. Stabbed in the neck. A real bloodbath. One of 'em recognizes Harding from choir practice—drunk, gambler, poon hound, typical old-school five-o. I'm sure your mom's got some stories.'

Ng said, 'We were working a domestic when we got the call. That was some violent shit. Chick's gonna be in surgery for days. Full moon always brings out the crazy.'

Faith ignored his war story. 'How'd Harding or whoever gain access into the building?'

'Looks like bolt cutters.' Collier shrugged. 'The padlock was cut clean, which probably took some muscle, so we're thinking a man did it.'

'You find the bolt cutters?'

'Nope.'

'What's the story on the car?'

'It was throwing off heat like Chernobyl when we got here. We called in AFD to hose it down. They say an accelerant was used. Gas tank exploded.'

'No one called in a vehicle fire?'

'Yeah, it's shocking,' Ng said. 'You wouldn't think all the junkies and whores squatting in these warehouses would pull a Kitty Genovese.'

Faith said, 'Look who knows his urban legends.'

Will scanned the abandoned warehouses—one on either side of Rippy's club. A construction sign advertised mixed-use housing coming soon, but the faded condition indicated that soon hadn't come soon enough. The buildings were four stories each, at least a block deep. Red brick from the turn of the century before last. Gothic arches with stained glass that had been broken out long ago.

He turned around. There was a matching office building across the street, at least ten stories tall, maybe more if it had a basement. Yellow signs posted over the chained doors indicated that the building was scheduled for demolition. The three structures were massive relics of Atlanta's industrial past. If Rippy's investors had gone all in now that the rape case had disappeared, the project could net them all millions, maybe billions, of dollars.

Faith asked, 'Were you able to pull the VIN off the car?'

Collier supplied, 'White, 2016 Kia Sorento, registered to one Vernon Dale Harding. AFD says it was probably burning for four or five hours.'

'So, someone killed Harding and torched his car, then someone else, or maybe the same guy, called it into nine-one-one five hours later.'

Will stared at the nightclub. 'Why here?'

Faith shook her head. 'Why us?'

Ng didn't understand that the question was rhetorical. He threw his hand out toward the building. 'This was supposed to be some kind of nightclub. Dance floor below, VIP rooms circled around the top, like an atrium in a mall. I thought there might be a gang involved, slinging up a dope club like this in the middle of Shitown, so I called my girl, she did a record check, Rippy's name came up and I was like, "Oh shit." So I kicked it up to my boss. He gives your ballbreaker a courtesy call and she's out here ten minutes later flossing her teeth with our short hairs.'

They all looked at Amanda. Charlie Reed was gone, and a tall, willowy redhead had taken his place. She was pinning up her hair as she talked to Amanda.

Ng gave a low whistle. 'Damn, son. Lookit that fine Girl Scout. Wonder if the paint matches the trim?'

Collier grinned. 'I'll let you know in the morning.'

Faith glanced down at Will's clenched fists. 'That's enough, guys.'

Collier kept grinning. 'We're just having fun, Officer.' He winked at her. 'But you should know I got kicked out of Girl Scouts for eating some Brownies.'

Ng guffawed, and Faith rolled her eyes as she walked away.

'Red,' Will told the detectives. 'Everybody calls her Red. She's a crime scene tech, but she gets in the way a lot, so keep an eye on her.'

Collier asked, 'She seeing anybody?'

Will shrugged. 'Does it matter?'

'Not a bit.' Collier spoke with the extreme certainty of a man who had never been rejected by a woman. He gave Will a cocky salute. 'Thanks for the four-one-one, bro.'

Will forced his fists to unclench as he walked toward Amanda. Faith was heading into the building, probably to get out of the heat. The red-haired woman was signing herself into the crime scene at the front gate. She saw Will and smiled, and he smiled back, because her name wasn't Red, it was Sara Linton, and she wasn't a crime scene tech, she was the medical examiner, and it was none of Collier's and Ng's God damm business what matched where because three hours ago she had been underneath Will in bed whispering so many filthy things into his ear that he had momentarily lost the ability to swallow.

Amanda didn't look up from her BlackBerry when Will approached. He stood in front of her, waiting, because that's what she usually made him do. He was intimately familiar with the top of her head, the spiral at the crown that spun her salt-and-pepper hair into a helmet.

Finally she said, 'You're late, Agent Trent.'

'Yes, ma'am. It won't happen again.'

She narrowed her eyes, dubious of the apology. 'That odor in the air is the smell of shit hitting the fan. I've already been on the phone with the mayor, the governor and two district attorneys who refuse to come out here because they don't want the news cameras capturing them anywhere near another case involving Marcus Rippy.' She looked down at her phone again. The BlackBerry was her mobile command post, sending and receiving updates from her vast network of contacts, only some of them official.

She said, 'There are three more satellite trucks on their way here, one of them national. I've got over thirty emails from reporters asking for statements. Rippy's lawyers have already called to say they'll be handling all questions and any indication that we're unfairly targeting Rippy could lead to a harassment lawsuit. They won't even meet with me until tomorrow morning. Too busy, they say.'

'Same as before.' Will had been granted exactly one sit-down with Marcus Rippy, during which time the man had remained almost completely silent. Faith was right. One of the more galling things about people with money was that they really knew their constitutional rights.

He asked Amanda, 'Are we officially in charge or is APD?'

'Do you think I would be standing here if I wasn't officially in charge?'

Will glanced back at Collier and Ng. 'Does Captain Chin Cleft know that?'

'You think he's cute?'

'Well, I wouldn't say—'

Amanda was already walking toward the building. Will had to trot to catch up with her. She had the quick gait of a Shetland pony.

They both signed in with the uniformed officer in charge of access to the crime scene. Instead of going inside, Amanda made Will stand just out of reach of the shade so that the sun would turn his skull into a kiln.

She said, 'I knew Harding's father when I was a rookie. Senior was a beat cop who spent his money on whores and the dog track. Died of an aneurysm back in eighty-five. Left his son his gambling habit. Dale took a medical retirement that ran out two years ago. He cashed out his pension earlier this year.'

'Why was he on medical leave?'

'HIPAA,' she said, referring to the law that, among other things, barred cops from making doctors tell them intimate details about their patients. 'I'm working some back channels to get the information, but this isn't good, Will. Harding was a bad cop, but he's a dead cop, and his body is lying inside a building owned by a man we very publicly could not put away for rape.'

'Do we know if Harding has any connection to Rippy?'

'If only I had a detective who could figure that out.' She turned on her heel and walked into the building. The electricity was still off. The interior was dank and cavernous, the dark tinted windows giving the space a ghostly cast. They both slipped on shoe protectors. Suddenly the generators roared to life. Xenon lights popped on, illuminating every square inch of the building. Will felt his retinas flinch in protest.

There was a cacophony of clicks as Maglites were turned off and stored. Will's eyes adjusted to find exactly what he expected to find: trash, condoms and needles, an empty shopping cart, lawn chairs, soiled mattresses—for some reason, there were always soiled mattresses—and too many spent beer cans and broken liquor bottles to count. The walls were covered with multi-colored graffiti that went up at least as high as a person's arm could reach with a can of spray paint. Will recognized some gang tags—Suernos, Bloods, Crips—but for the most part there were bubbled names with hearts, peace flags and a couple of gigantic, well-endowed unicorns with rainbow eyes. Typical raver art. The great thing about ecstasy was that it made you really happy until it stopped your heart from beating.

Ng's description of the layout was fairly accurate. The building had an upstairs atrium that opened to the bottom floor like in a shopping mall. A temporary wooden railing ringed the balcony, but there were gaps where a less careful person might get into trouble. The main floor was huge, multi-tiered, with concrete half-walls designating private seating areas and a large open space for dancing. What was probably meant to be the bar arced around the back of the building. Two grand, curved staircases reached to the second floor, which was at least forty feet up. The concrete stairs hugging the walls gave the impression of a cobra's fangs about to bite down on the dance floor.

An older woman wearing a yellow hard hat approached Amanda. She had another hard hat in her hand, which she gave to Amanda, who in turn gave it to Will, who in turn set it on the floor.

The woman offered no preamble. 'Found in the parking lot: an empty clear plastic bag with a paper label insert. Said bag contained at one time a tan canvas tarp, missing from the scene. The tarp is Handy brand, three-feet-seven by five-feet-seven, widely available.' She paused her tired drone to take a breath. 'Also found: a slightly used roll of black duct tape, outer plastic wrap not yet located. Weather report indicates a deluge, this vicinity, thirty-six hours previous. The paper label on the tarp bag and the edges of the tape do not show exposure to said weather event.'

Amanda said, 'Well, I suppose we have a window at least, sometime over the weekend.'

'Canvas tarp,' Will repeated. 'That's what painters use.'

'Correct,' the woman said. 'No paint or painter's tools have been located inside or outside the building.' She continued, 'The stairs: both sets are part of the scene and still being processed. Found so far: items from a woman's purse, what looks like tissue. The guts kind, not Kleenex.' She pointed to a scissor lift. 'You'll need to use that to go up. We've put out a call for an operator. He's twenty-five minutes out.'

'Are you shitting me?' Collier had sneaked up on them. 'We can't use the stairs?' He was warily eyeing the scissor lift, which was a hydraulic machine that lifted a platform straight into the air, kind of like a very shaky open-air elevator with nothing but a thin safety rail between you and certain death.

Amanda asked Will, 'Do you know how to operate that thing?'

'I can figure it out.' The machine was already plugged in. Will found the key hidden inside the auxiliary battery box. He used the tip of the key to press the tiny reset button on the bottom. The scissor lift stuttered a quick up-and-down and they were in business.

Will grabbed the safety rail and climbed up the two steps by the motor. Amanda reached for his hand so she could follow. Her movements looked effortless, mostly because Will did all the lifting. She was light, less than the weight of a boxing heavy bag.

They both turned around and waited for Collier. He glanced at the fang-like stairs.

Amanda tapped her watch. 'You've got two seconds, Detective Collier.'

Collier took a deep breath. He grabbed the yellow hard hat off the floor. He clamped it down on his head and scampered up the platform like a frightened baby monkey.

Will turned the key to start the motor. In truth, he had worked construction jobs during his college years and he could operate just about any machine on a work site. Still, he stuttered the platform a bit just for the pleasure of watching Collier white-knuckle the safety rail.

The motor made a grinding noise as they started their ascent. Sara was on the stairs helping one of the techs collect evidence. She was wearing khakis and a fitted navy-blue GBI T-shirt that flattered her in more ways than two. Her hair was still pulled back, but some of the strands had come loose. She'd put on her glasses. He liked the way she looked in her glasses.

Will had known Sara Linton for eighteen months, which was roughly seventeen months and twenty-six days longer than any other period of sustained happiness in his life. He practically lived at her apartment. Their dogs got along. He liked her sister. He understood her mother. He was scared of her father. She had officially joined the GBI two weeks ago. This was their first case together. He was embarrassed by how excited he was to see her.

Which is why Will made himself look away, because mooning over your girlfriend at a grisly crime scene was probably how serial killers got their start.

Or maybe he would just be a regular murderer, because Collier had decided to take his mind off his vertigo by staring at Sara's ass while she bent over to help the tech.

Will shifted his weight again. The platform shook. Collier made a noise halfway between a gag and a yelp.

Amanda gave Will one of her rare smiles. 'My first rollout was for a guy who fell off the top of a scaffolding. This was back before Hazmat and all those silly safety regulations. There wasn't much for the coroner. We hosed his brains off the sidewalk and into the gutter.'

Collier leaned over so he could use his arm to wipe the sweat from his face and still hold on to the railing.

The lift shook of its own accord as Will stopped the platform a few inches below the concrete balcony. The wooden railing had been pulled away. Across from the opening, half-inch slabs of moldy four-by-sixteen drywall were stacked chest-high. The thick layer of dust on the buckets of joint compound indicated they had been there since construction stopped six months ago. Graffiti dripped lazily across everything—the floor, the walls, the construction materials—with two more ubiquitous rainbow-eyed unicorns standing sentry at the top of each stairway.

Heavy wooden doors lined what Will assumed were the VIP rooms. The custom-carved mahogany had been stained a rich espresso, probably at the factory, but the graffiti artists had done their best to black out the finish. Yellow numbered crime scene markers dotted the entire span of the balcony, from one set of stairs to the other. Several Tyvek-clad techs were photographing and collecting evidence. Some of the VIP rooms were being sprayed down with luminol, a chemical that made body fluids glow an otherworldly blue when exposed to a black light.

Will didn't want to think about all the body fluids they'd find.

Faith stood at the far end of the balcony, her head back as she drank from a bottle of water. She was wearing a white Tyvek suit. The zip was undone. The arms were tied around her waist. She had obviously passed herself off as a tech so she could get up to the crime scene without having to wait for the scissor lift. Sealed evidence bags were piled in front of her, alongside neatly stacked boxes of gloves, evidence bags and protective clothing. The murder room was a few feet away, the wooden door opened out. Light strobed as the position and state of the body were documented by the crime scene photographer. They wouldn't be allowed inside until every inch was recorded.

Amanda pulled out her phone and read her new messages as she walked toward the kill room. 'CNN is here. I'm going to have to update the governor and the mayor. Will, you'll take point on this while I'm hand-holding. Collier, I need you to see if Harding has any family. My recollection is that there's an aunt on the father's side.'

'Yes, ma'am.' Collier's shoulder rubbed the wall as he followed at a distance.

'Take off that hard hat. You look like one of the Village People.' She checked her phone again. Obviously a new piece of information had come in. 'Harding has four ex-wives. Two are still on the force, both in records. Track them down and find out if there's a bookie or pimp whose name kept coming up.'

Collier stumbled to keep up as he left the hat on the floor. 'You think his exes were still talking to him?'

'Am I really getting that question from you?' Her words obviously hit their mark because Collier responded with a quick nod. She dropped her phone back into her pocket. 'Faith, run it down for me.'

'Doorknob to the neck.' Faith pointed to the side of her own neck. 'It matches the other doorknobs up here, so we can assume the killer didn't bring it for the purpose of murder. They found a G43 by the car. The action is jammed, but at least one round was fired. Charlie is running the serial number through the system right now.'

'That's the new Glock,' Collier said. 'What's it look like?'

'Lightweight, slim profile. The grip is rough, but it's pretty impressive for concealed carry.'

Collier asked another question about the gun, which was manufactured specifically for government use. Will tuned him out. The gun wasn't going to solve this case.

He stepped around some marked bloody shoeprints and bent down to get a closer look at the lockset in the door. The backplate was rectangular, about three-by-six inches and screwed to the door. It was cast, plated in polished brass with a heavily detailed raised design featuring a cursive *R* at the center. Rippy's logo. Will had seen it all over the man's house. He squinted at the latchbolt, the long metal cylinder that kept the door closed or, when turned, allowed it to open. He saw scrapes around the hollow square where the doorknob spindle was supposed to go. And then he looked down at the floor and saw the long screwdriver with the numbered yellow card beside it.

Someone had been shut inside the room, and someone else had used the screwdriver to gain entry.

Will stood back up to look at the kill scene. The photographer stepped across the body, trying not to slip in the blood.

There was a lot of blood.

Sprayed on the ceiling, spattered and splattered on walls, glistening against the nearly black criss-cross of competing graffiti. The floor was flooded, like someone had opened the spigot on Harding's carotid and let it run dry. Light danced off the dark, congealing liquid. Will could taste metal in his mouth as oxygen hit iron. Underneath it all he caught a whiff of piss that for some reason made him feel sorrier for the guy than the doorknob sticking Frankenstein-like out of the meaty hambone of his neck.

In policing, there wasn't a lot of dignity in death.

Dale Harding's body was in the center of the room, which was about fifteen feet square with a vaulted ceiling. He was flat on his back, a big, bald guy wearing a cheap, shiny suit that wouldn't close around his ample gut, more like a cop of his father's generation than his own. His shirt had come untucked on one side. His red and blue striped tie was split like the legs of a hurdler. The waistband of his pants was rolled over. His stainless-steel TAG Heuer had turned into a tourniquet on his wrist because his body was swelling with the various juices of decay. A gold diamond ring cut into his pinky finger. Black dress socks stretched around his waxy yellow ankles. His mouth was open. His eyes were closed. He obviously had some kind of eczema. The dry skin around his mouth and nose looked like it was speckled with sugar.

Weirdly, there was only a slash of blood on the front of his body, like a painter had flicked a brush at him. There were a few drops on his face, but nothing else, especially where you'd expect it, around the too-tight collar of his shirt.

'These were found on the stairs.'

Will turned back around.

Faith was rolling the evidence bag in her hands so that she could read the labels on the contents. 'BareMinerals. Mac. Light browns in the eyeshadows. Espresso-brown mascara. Chocolate eyeliner. The foundation and powder are a light medium.'

Amanda said, 'So, probably a white woman.'

'There's also a tin of lip balm. La Mer.'

'Rich white woman,' Amanda amended. Will knew the brand, but only because Sara wore it. He'd accidentally seen the receipt and nearly had a heart attack. The balm cost more per ounce than a brick of heroin.

Amanda said, 'So, we can assume a woman was here with Harding.'

'And now she's not,' Faith said. 'Doorknob to the neck sounds like something a woman would do.'

Amanda asked, 'Where's the purse?'

'Inside the room. It looks torn, like it got caught on something.'

'And only the make-up fell out?'

Faith picked up the other evidence bags and listed off the contents. 'One car key, Chevy, model unknown, no keychain. A hairbrush with long brown hair in the bristles—they'll get that to the lab ASAP. Tin of Altoids, spearmint. Various coins with purse fuzz. Pack of Puffs tissue. Plastic contact lens case. A tube of ChapStick, the poor woman's La Mer.'

'No wallet?'

Faith shook her head. 'The photographer says he didn't see one in the purse either, but we'll look when he's finished.'

'So, we have a dead cop and a missing woman.' Amanda read Will's expression. 'She hasn't left the house. I talked to her an hour ago and checked in with the sheriff's deputy who's parked outside.'

Keisha Miscavage, Marcus Rippy's accuser. Her name hadn't been released to the press, but nobody stayed anonymous with the internet. Keisha had been forced into hiding three months ago, and she still had twenty-four-hour police protection because of credible death threats from several of Rippy's fans.

Collier said, 'What about all these gang tags? I'm counting two up here, at least four downstairs. We should get the gang taskforce on this, round up some bangers.'

Faith asked, 'Should we round up all the unicorns, too?'

Amanda shook her head. 'This is about the woman. Let's assume that she was in this room. Let's also assume she had something to do with the disposition of the victim, if we can call Harding the victim.' She looked down at the contents from the purse. 'This is a white, fairly wealthy woman meeting a dirty cop in a bad part of town in the middle of the night. Why? What was she doing here?'

Collier said, 'Paying for it's easier than marrying it. Maybe she was an escort, only he didn't wanna or couldn't pay and she got mad?'

Faith countered, 'Strange place to meet up for a blow job.'

'That's a small tarp,' Will said, because Amanda didn't spend her weekends strolling the tarp section at her local hardware store. 'Standard would be a five-by-seven, six-by-twelve, but the package outside was for a three-feet-seven by five-feet-seven, which is forty-three inches by sixty-seven. Harding's at least a forty-inch waist, and around six feet tall.'

Amanda stared at him. 'I need that in English.'

'If the killer brought the tarp to the scene in order to dispose of a body, then the tarp he purchased was for a much smaller person.'

'A woman-sized tarp,' Faith said. 'Great.'

Amanda was nodding. 'Harding met the woman here to kill her, but she managed to get the upper hand.'

'She's injured.' Sara came up the stairs. Her glasses were hooked on her shirt collar. She used the back of her arm to wipe the sweat off her forehead. 'There are bloody bare footprints going up the left set of stairs. Likely a woman's, probably size seven or eight, with a heavy strike that indicates she was running.' She pointed back at the stairs. 'Second tread down, there's an impact point that indicates she fell and hit her head, likely at the crown. We found some long brown hair in the spatter, similar to what was found in the hairbrush.' She pointed to the other set of stairs. 'On the right, we've got more footprints, walking, and passive spatter leaving a trail toward the emergency side exit, then it disappears on the metal stairs. Passive spatter indicates a weeping wound.'

'Ran up and walked down?' Amanda guessed.

'It's possible.' Sara shrugged. 'There have been hundreds of people in and out of this building. Someone could have made the footprints last week and someone else could've left the drops of blood last night. We'll need to sequence DNA on every sample before we can definitively say what belongs to whom.'

Amanda glowered. DNA could take weeks. She preferred her science more instantaneous.

'Finished.' The photographer started peeling off his Tyvek suit. His clothes were soaking wet. His hair looked painted onto his head. He told Amanda, 'You can have the room. I'll get the photos processed and uploaded as soon as I get back.'

She nodded. 'Thank you.'

Sara pulled a fresh pair of gloves from her back pocket. 'These shoeprints here—' She pointed to the floor, which looked like it belonged in an Arthur Murray studio. 'They're from the first responders. Two sets. One went into the room, probably to see the face. The treads for both are nearly identical. HAIX Black Eagles. Police issue.'

Collier bristled. 'They said in their statements that they didn't enter the room.'

'You might want to go back at them.' Sara slipped on a fresh pair of shoe protectors as she explained, 'There's a lot of blood. They recognized the victim. He's a fellow officer. That's a lot to—'

'Hold on, Red.' Collier held up his hand like a traffic cop. 'Don't you think you should wait for the ME before you go traipsing in there?'

Sara gave him a look that had once presaged the two most miserable hours of Will's life. 'I'm the medical examiner, and I would prefer that you call me Sara or Dr Linton.'

Faith barked a laugh that echoed through the building.

Sara braced her hand against the wall as she walked into the room. Ripples spread through the pool of blood. She picked up the purse in the corner. The strap was broken. There was a long tear down the side. The bag was black textured leather with heavy brass zips and buckles and a padlock at the clasp, the kind of thing that could be very expensive or very cheap.

'I don't see a wallet.' Sara held up a gold tube of lipstick. 'Sisley, rose cashmere. I've got the same at home.' Her eyebrows furrowed. 'The gold is scratched off on the side, just like mine. Must be a manufacturing defect.' Sara dropped the lipstick back into the purse. She tested the weight. 'This doesn't feel like Dolce and Gabbana.'

'No.' Amanda peered inside the bag. 'It's counterfeit. See the stitching?'

'The ampersand is in the wrong font, too.' Faith spread plastic on the ground so they could do a more careful inventory. 'Why buy a fake D and G when you can afford Sisley and La Mer?'

Amanda said, 'Twenty-five-hundred-dollar purse versus fifty-dollar lipstick?'

Faith said, 'You can palm the lipstick, but not the purse.'

'Maybe a tester. The scratch could be from peeling off the label.'

Will tried to give Collier a conspiratorial 'us manly men have no idea what they're talking about' look, but Collier was already giving him an 'I want to shoot you in the face' look.

Sara went back into the room. This was her first opportunity to really examine the murder scene. Will had caught glimpses of this side of her before, but never in an official capacity. She took her time exploring the room, silently studying the blood patterns, the spray on the ceiling. The graffiti did not make her job easy. The walls were painted black in places from oversprayed logos and tags. She got close to everything, putting on her glasses so she could differentiate between the spray paint and the blood evidence. She walked around the perimeter of the room twice before beginning her examination of the body.

She couldn't kneel in the blood, so she squatted down at Harding's thick waist. She searched his front pants pockets, handing Faith a melted 3 Musketeers, an opened pack of Skittles, a wad of cash strapped by a green rubber band and some loose change. Next she checked Harding's suit jacket. There was a folded sheet of paper inside the breast pocket. Sara unfolded the page. 'Racing form. Online betting.'

'Dogs?' Amanda guessed.

'Horses.' Sara handed the form to Faith, who set it on the plastic alongside the other items.

'No cell phones,' Faith noted. 'Not on Harding. Not in the purse. Not in the building.'

Sara patted down the body, checking to see if she'd missed anything obvious in his clothes. She pushed open Harding's eyelids. She used both hands to force open his jaw so she could look inside the mouth. She unbuttoned his shirt and pants. She studied every inch of his bloated abdomen. She pulled back the unbuttoned cuffs of his shirtsleeves and looked at his forearms. She lifted his pant legs and pushed down his socks.

Finally she said, 'Livor mortis indicates the body hasn't been moved, so he died here, in this position, on his back. I'll need to get ambient and liver temp, but he's in full rigor, which means he's been dead for more than four but less than eight hours.'

'So we're talking a timeline of Sunday night into Monday morning,' Faith said. 'The fire department estimates the car was set on fire four to five hours ago, which brings us to three AM. today. The nine-one-one came in at five AM.'

'Sorry, but can I ask a question about that?' Collier was obviously still licking his wounds, but he just as obviously wanted to prove his usefulness. 'He's got mold around his mouth and nose. Wouldn't that take a lot longer than five hours to grow?'

'It would, but it's not mold.' Sara asked, 'Can you help me roll the body onto its side? I don't want him falling forward.'

Collier pulled two shoe protectors out of the box. He gave Sara a lopsided grin as he slid the booties over the old protectors he'd put on when he entered the building. 'I'm Holden, by the way. Like in the book. My parents were hoping for a disaffected loner.'

Sara smiled at the stupid joke, and Will wanted to kill himself.

Collier kept grinning, taking the gloves Sara offered, making a show of stretching out the fingers with his child-sized hands. 'How do you want to do this?'

'On my three.' Sara counted down. Collier grunted as he lifted Harding's shoulders and tried to roll him onto his side. The body was stiff and tilted like a hinge. The weight wouldn't transfer without sending Harding face down into a pool of blood, so Collier had to brace his elbows against his knees to keep the body raised.

Sara peeled up Harding's jacket and shirt so she could examine his back. Will gathered she was looking for punctures. She pressed her gloved fingers into the skin, testing for open wounds and finding nothing. The dark blood on the floor had made Harding look like he'd been dipped into a pan of motor oil.

She asked Collier, 'You okay for another minute?'

'Sure.' The word got mangled in his throat. Will could see the veins in his neck popping out. Harding was at least two-fifty, maybe more. Collier's arms were shaking from the effort of keeping him tilted up.

Sara changed into a fresh pair of gloves. She reached into Harding's back pocket and pulled out a thick nylon wallet. The

Velcro made a ripping sound when she opened it. She called out her findings. 'Ticket stubs, receipts for fast-food places, betting slips, two different photographs of a naked blonde courtesy of BackDoorMan.com. Some business cards.' She looked at Collier. 'You can put him down, but be careful.'

Collier groaned as he settled the body back to the floor.

'You're going to want to see this.' Sara passed one of the business cards to Faith. Will recognized the full-color logo. He had seen it countless times on documents turned over by Marcus Rippy's sports management team.

'Motherfuck,' Faith muttered. 'Kip Kilpatrick. He's Rippy's manager, right? I saw him on TV.'

Will looked at Amanda. She had her eyes closed like she wished she could wipe the man's name from her mind. Will felt the same way. Kip Kilpatrick was Marcus Rippy's manager, head lawyer, best friend and all-around fixer. There was no legal proof, but Will was certain Kilpatrick had used his thugs to pay off two witnesses from the New Year's Eve party and intimidated a third into silence.

Sara said, 'I hate to make things worse, but the doorknob missed Harding's jugulars and carotids. And his esophagus. And pretty much anything else that matters. There's no blood in his mouth or nose. There was very little bleeding from the spindle, just a trickle that's dried down the side of his neck. He doesn't have any other significant injuries. This blood, or at least this volume of blood, isn't from him.'

'What?' Amanda sounded more exasperated than shocked. 'Are you certain?'

'Positive. The back of his clothes wicked up blood from the floor, and the swipe of blood on his shirt is clearly from someone else. His major arteries are intact. There are no significant wounds in his head, torso, arms, or legs. The blood you see in this room is not from Dale Harding.'

Will felt surprised, and then he felt stupid for being surprised. Sara had read the scene better than he had.

'So whose blood is it?' Faith asked. 'Ms. La Mer?'

'It seems likely.' Sara stood up carefully so she wouldn't lose her balance.

Amanda tried to make sense of the information. 'Our missing woman hit her head on the stairs, then she left her bloody footprints as she ran across the balcony, and then what?'

'There was a violent struggle between two people in this room. There are signs of high-velocity spatter on the ceiling, which suggests that an artery was punctured, and as I said, it wasn't Harding's.' Sara walked over to the far corner. 'We're going to need some alternate light sources because the graffiti is so dark, but can you see this swipe along the wall? That's from someone's hand, and the hand was covered in blood. The shape and span are small, more like a woman's.'

Will had noticed the smeared line of blood before, but not that it ended with a visible set of fingers. They reminded him of the finger-shaped bruises on Keisha Miscavage's neck.

Amanda told Sara, 'There were no unsolved shootings last night. Are we talking stabbing, then?'

Sara shrugged. 'Maybe.'

'Maybe,' Amanda repeated. 'Wonderful. I'll tell the hospitals to *maybe* look out for an unexplained stabbing with a serious head injury.'

'I can do that.' Collier started typing into his phone. 'I got a buddy works the precinct at Grady Hospital. He can check with the ER pronto.'

'We'll need Atlanta Medical and Piedmont, too.'

Collier nodded as he typed.

Faith said, 'Sara, back up a minute for me. The doorknob didn't kill Harding, but he's obviously dead. So what happened?'

'His bad choices happened. He's morbidly obese. He's unusually bloated. His eyes show signs of conjunctival erythema. I'm guessing he has an enlarged heart, hypertension. There are needle marks on his abdomen and thighs that indicate he's an insulin-dependent diabetic. His diet was fast food and Skittles. He wasn't managing his condition.'

Collier looked skeptical. 'So Harding conveniently slipped into a diabetic coma during the middle of a death match?'

'It's more complicated than that.' Sara indicated the area around her own mouth. 'Harding's face. You thought it was mold, but mold usually grows in a colony or clump. Think about bread when it goes bad. My first guess was seborrheic dermatitis, but now I'm fairly certain it's uremic frost.'

Will said, 'I thought I smelled urine.'

'Good catch.' Sara handed Collier a bag for his gloves and shoe protectors. 'Urea is one of the toxins that's supposed to be filtered out through the kidneys. If the kidneys don't work for some reason—diabetes and hypertension are good reasons—then the body tries to excrete the urea through sweat. The sweat evaporates, the urea crystalizes, and that leads to uremic frost.'

Collier nodded like he understood. 'How long does that take?'

'Not long. He's been living with chronic end-stage renal disease. He was getting treatment at some point. He has a graft for vascular access in his arm. Uremic frost is very rare, but it tells us that for whatever reason, he stopped getting dialysis, probably within the last week to ten days.'

'Jesus,' Faith said. 'So is this a murder or not?'

Amanda said, 'It seems they both tried to kill each other and both likely succeeded.' She told Sara, 'Let's focus on the missing woman. You said there was a violent struggle in this room that Harding obviously lost, but not before he managed to do quite a bit of damage to his opponent, as evidenced by the blood. Given her wounds, could the woman walk out of here and drive herself away?' She amended, 'No maybes or possiblies. You're not speaking to the court, Dr Linton.'

Sara still hedged. 'Let's start with the impact on the stairs. If it's from the missing woman's head, then she took a pretty hard blow. Her skull was probably fractured. At the very least, she's concussed.' Sara looked back over the kill room. 'The volume of blood loss is the real danger. I'd estimate this is just over two liters, maybe a thirty to thirty-five percent loss. That's a borderline Class III hemorrhage. In addition to stopping the bleed, she'd need fluids, probably a transfusion.'

'She could use the tarp,' Will said. 'To stop the bleeding. The tarp is missing. There was a roll of duct tape found in the parking lot.'

'Possible,' Sara agreed. 'But let's talk about the nature of the injury. If the blood came from the chest or neck, she would be dead. It can't be from the belly because the blood would stay in the belly. So that leaves the limbs. A good gash in the groin could do this. She would likely be able to walk, but not without difficulty. Same with the medial malleolus, the inside of the ankle. She could still drag or crawl her way out. There's also this—' Sara held up her arms as if to protect her face, palms out. 'A horizontal cut to the radial or ulnar arteries, then the arms flail and blood sprays around the room like a garden hose, which is basically what the artery would be at that point.' She looked back at Harding. 'I'd expect him to have more blood on him if that was the case.'

Amanda said, 'Thank you, Doctor, for that litany of multiple choices. How much time do we have to find this woman?'

Sara took the dig in stride. 'None of those injuries are the type that can go untreated, even if she manages to stop the bleeding. Given the four-to-five-hour window on time of death and the volume of blood loss, I'd say that without medical intervention she might have two to three more hours before her organs start shutting down.'

'You work the dead, we'll find the living.' Amanda turned to Will and Faith. 'We've got a clock ticking. Our number one goal is to locate this woman, get her medical help, then find out what the hell she was doing here in the first place.'

Collier asked, 'What about BackDoorMan.com? Does that bring in Rippy?'

'That'll be Harding's kink,' Will said. 'Rippy has a definite type.'

Faith supplied, 'Dark hair, smart mouth, killer body.'

Collier said, 'His wife is a blonde.'

Faith rolled her eyes. 'I'm a blonde. She's a bottle.'

'You can discuss hair color after we find the woman.' Amanda told Collier, 'Get that partner of yours to run missing persons reports submitted within the last forty-eight hours. Women, young, Rippy's type.' Collier nodded, but she wasn't finished. 'I need at least ten uniforms to check both warehouses and the office building. Call in a structural engineer on the building; it looks iffy. I want feet, not just eyeballs, on every single floor, every nook and cranny, no stone unturned. Our victim-slash-murderer could be bleeding out or hiding right under our noses. None of us wants to read that headline in the paper tomorrow morning.'

She turned to Faith. 'Go to Harding's place of residence. I'll have the warrant signed by the time you get there. Harding called himself a private investigator. It makes sense that he was investigating a woman, possibly for Rippy. She could be another victim or she could've been blackmailing him for money, or both. Harding will have a file, photographs, notes, hopefully a home address for the girl.'

She pointed to Will. 'Go with her. Harding can't be living in luxury. There will be liquor stores, check-cashers, strip joints in his neighborhood. They'll probably sell burner phones. Cross the IMEIs with any security footage to see if we can pin a phone number to Harding, then cross-reference the numbers against any that are linked to Kip Kilpatrick or Marcus Rippy.'

There was a chorus of 'Yes, ma'am's,' all around.

Will heard metal scraping concrete. The scissor lift had brought Charlie Reed to the second floor. He had a grim look on his face as he approached them.

Amanda said, 'Spit it out, Charlie. We're already against the clock.'

Charlie fidgeted with his cell phone. 'I got back the info on the Glock 43.'

'And?'

Charlie kept his gaze glued to Amanda. 'Maybe we should—'

'I said spit it out.'

He took a deep breath. 'It's registered to Angie Polaski.'

Will felt a sudden tightness in his chest. He tasted acid on his tongue.

Dark hair. Smart mouth. Killer body.

There was a burning sensation on the side of his face. People staring at him. Waiting for his reaction. A bead of sweat rolled into his eye. He looked up at the ceiling because he didn't trust himself to look at anything else.

It was Collier who finally broke the silence with a question. 'What am I missing here?' No one answered, so he asked, 'Who's Angie Polaski?'

Sara had to clear her throat before she could speak. 'Angie Polaski is Will's wife.'

TWO

Sara watched Will brace his hand against the wall to steady himself. She should do something—comfort him, tell him it was going to be all right—but she just stood there struggling against the usual spark of rage that accompanied any mention of his erratic, hateful wife.

Angie Polaski had been flitting in and out of Will's life like a mosquito since he was eleven years old. They had grown up together at the Atlanta Children's Home, both surviving abuse, neglect, abandonment, torture. Not all of this had come at the hands of the system. Of all the pains visited down upon Will during his adolescence, nothing compared to the torments Angie had put him through. Still kept putting him through, because it made a cruel kind of sense that they were all assembled here in this building with a pool of blood congealing around her latest victim.

Dale Harding was collateral damage. Will was always Angie's primary target, the one she kept hitting again and again.

Was this finally the end of her?

'It can't—' Will stopped. His eyes scanned the murder room. 'She can't be—'

Sara tried to push down her anger. This wasn't just another one of Angie's peevish grabs for attention. She could see Will making the same connections: the violent struggle, the life-threatening injury, the veritable lake of blood.

Wounded. Dangerous. Desperate.

Angie.

'She—' Will stopped again. 'Maybe she's—' He slumped against the wall. His breathing was erratic. 'Oh God. Oh Jesus.' He put his hand to his mouth. 'She can't be—' His voice cracked. 'It's her.'

'We don't know that.' Sara tried to make her voice reassuring. She reminded herself that this wasn't about Angie. This was about Will. Seeing him in so much pain was like a knife twisting in her chest. 'Her gun could've been stolen, or—'

'It's her.' He turned his back to them and walked a few feet away, but not before Sara saw the anguished expression on his face. She felt overwhelmed by her own uselessness. Angie was someone they both desperately wanted to be rid of, but not like this. At least not that Sara would ever say aloud. She had to admit that she had always known that Angie would never gracefully bow out. Even in death—or near-death—she had found a way to drag Will down with her.

Amanda asked, 'Charlie, what's the address on the registration?'

'The same as on her driver's license.' Charlie looked at the screen on his phone. 'Ninety-eight—'

'Baker,' Will interrupted, still not turning around. 'That's her old address. What about the phone number?'

Charlie read off a number, and Will shook his head. 'Disconnected.'

Amanda asked Will, 'Do you know where she is?'

He shook his head again.

'When did you last see her?'

Will paused a moment before answering, 'Saturday.'

Sara felt the knife in her chest make a final, violent twist. 'Saturday?'

They had slept over at his house. They had made love. Twice. Then Will had told Sara he was going for a run and secretly met with his wife.

Sara's mouth could barely form words. 'You saw her two days ago?'

Will said nothing.

Amanda gave a quick, agitated sigh. 'Do you have a phone number? A place of employment? Any means to get in touch with her?'

He shook his head to every question.

Sara stared at his back, his broad shoulders that she had wrapped her arms around. His neck that she had kissed. His thick dirty-blond hair that she'd run her fingers through. Tears welled into her eyes. Had he been seeing Angie all this time? All of those late nights at work. All of those early meetings. All of those two-hour runs and pick-up games of basketball.

'All right.' Amanda clapped her hands for attention. Her voice was raised to fill the building. 'Crime scene people, take a fifteen-minute break. Get hydrated. Sit in the air conditioning.'

There was a groan of appreciation as the white-suited techs made their way toward the exits. They would probably start gossiping as soon as they were outside.

Sara wiped her eyes before her tears could fall. She was at work. She had to focus on what was in front of her, what she could control. She told Amanda, 'We can do blood typing in the mobile lab. Results are almost instantaneous.' She tried in vain to swallow the lump in her throat. 'It's not DNA, but we can use ABO typing as a rule-out against Angie. Or as a rule-in, depending what her blood type is.' She had to stop to swallow again. She couldn't tell if she was making any sense. 'We can establish a loose narrative. Does the blood type from the spatter on the stairs match the type of the bloody footprints that go toward the room? Do those samples match the blood type inside the room? Is it the same type as the arterial spray? The hand swipe?' Sara pressed together her lips. How many times was she going to say the word *type*? Someone could turn it into a drinking game. 'I'll need Angie's blood type. And we'll need to backstop all of this with DNA. But the blood typing could at least tell us something.'

Amanda gave a curt nod. 'Do it. Angie was a cop for ten years. I'll pull the blood info from her file.' She sounded uncharacteristically flustered. 'Faith, hit the phones. We need a current address, phone, employer, anything you can find. Collier, yours and Ng's orders haven't changed. I want you to get teams to search the ware—'

'I'll do it.' Will started toward the lift, but Amanda clamped her hand down on his arm, stopping him cold.

'Stay here.' He tried to pull away, but her fingernails dug into his shirtsleeve. 'That's an order.'

'She could be—'

'I know what she could be, but you're going to stay here and answer my questions. Is that understood?'

Collier coughed into his hand, like the teacher was scolding a student. Faith slapped his arm to shut him up.

Amanda said, 'Charlie, take Collier and Faith downstairs, then come back up for me.'

Faith squeezed Sara's hand as she walked by. They had a rule that they never discussed Will except in general terms. Sara had never wanted to break that rule more badly than she did right now.

'Amanda.' Will didn't wait for the audience to leave. 'I can't just—'

Amanda held up a finger to silence him. At least someone was worried about Sara being humiliated. Again.

Saturday.

Two days ago.

She'd had no idea Will was keeping something from her. What else had she missed? Sara tried to scan back over the last few weeks. Will hadn't been acting strange. If anything, he had been more attentive, even romantic, which could've been the biggest sign of all.

'Amanda,' Will tried again, his voice lowered as he struggled to sound reasonable. 'You heard what Sara said. Angie could be bleeding to death. She might have a few hours before . . .' His words trailed off. They all knew what would happen if Angie didn't get help. 'I have to look for her. I'm the only one who knows the kinds of places she'd hide.'

Amanda gave Will one of her steely glares. 'I swear on my life, Wilbur, if you take one step off this balcony, I'll have you in handcuffs before you see sunshine.'

His eyes burned with hatred. 'I'll never forgive you for this.'

Amanda made a show of pulling out her phone. 'Add it to the list.'

Will turned his back to her. His gaze skipped over Sara. Instead of speaking to her, or even acknowledging what was happening, he walked back toward the stairs. Sara expected him to go down anyway, but he turned back around, pacing the length of the balcony like a caged leopard. His teeth were so tightly gritted that Sara could see his jawbone working. His fists were clenched. He stopped again at the top of the stairs, shook his head, mumbled something under his breath.

Sara could read the word on his lips. Not an apology. Not an explanation.

Angie.

He didn't love Angie. At least not as a husband. At least not according to what he had told Sara. For almost a full year, Will had been searching for his wife in order to file divorce papers. Their marriage was a scam anyway, something they had literally done on a dare. Will had promised Sara that he was doing everything possible to end it. She had never once questioned how a special agent with the Georgia Bureau of Investigation was unable to find a woman who was apparently right in front of his face as recently as two days ago.

Had he met her at a restaurant? A hotel? Sara felt her tears threatening to return. Had he been with Angie this entire time? Had he played Sara for a fool?

'All right.' Amanda had waited until the lift settled on the ground floor. 'Saturday. Where did you see Angie?'

Slowly Will turned around. He crossed his arms. He looked somewhere over Amanda's head. 'Outside my house. Parked on the street.' He paused, and Sara hoped he was remembering what she had done to him before he left, because it was never going to happen again. 'I was heading out for a run, and I saw her car. It's a Chevy Monte Carlo SS, eighty-eight, black with—'

'Red stripes. I've already put out a five-state APB.' Amanda asked Will the question that was burning in Sara's mind. 'Why was she at your house?'

He shook his head. 'I don't know. She saw me and she got back into her car and—'

'She didn't speak to you?'

'No.'

'She didn't go inside?'

'No.' He caught himself. 'Not that I know of. But she lets herself in sometimes.'

Sara looked down at the evidence bags Faith had left on the ground.

The lipstick.

Sisley rose cashmere with a scratch down the side of the case. There was no manufacturing defect. This was Sara's lipstick. She had left it at Will's last month. In his bathroom. On the sink basin. They had gone out to dinner, and when she had looked for it later, it was nowhere to be found.

In Angie's purse. In her hand. Between her fingers. On her mouth.

Sara felt nauseated.

Amanda asked Will, 'Do you know why she was parked outside your house?'

He shook his head. 'No.'

Sara struggled to find her voice. 'Did she leave a note on my car?'

'No,' Will said, but how could Sara trust him? They had gone to breakfast after his run. They had spent the day on the couch together and ordered pizza and fooled around and he'd had a million opportunities to tell her that the woman he had spent a year trying to locate had been parked outside his house that very morning. It's not like Sara would have been angry. Irritated, maybe, but not at Will. She never blamed him for Angie's bullshit. He knew that because Angie had caused problems for both of them countless times before.

Which meant that the only reason for Will to hide the visit was because there was more to the story. Like that Angie had been inside his house. Like that she had stolen Sara's lipstick. What else was Sara missing? Some hair combs. A bottle of perfume. Sara had blamed herself for misplacing things between her apartment and Will's house, never once considering that Angie was stealing from her.

And that Will knew.

Amanda said, 'Walk me through it. You come out your front door. You see Angie inside her parked car.'

'Standing beside it.' Will spoke carefully, as if he needed to think before he answered. 'She saw me, knew that I'd seen her, but she got into her car and—' He glanced down at the evidence bags. The Chevy ignition key. The old kind that might fit an '88 Monte Carlo.

He said, 'I ran after the car, but she drove off.'

Sara tried to block out the image of Will chasing Angie down the street.

Amanda turned to Sara. 'What note were you asking about?'

She shrugged, like it was nothing, but it was everything. 'Sometimes she leaves notes on my car. They say what you'd expect.'

'Recently?'

'The last one was three weeks ago.' Sara was working her last shift as a pediatrician at Grady Hospital. A four-year-old had mistaken a bag of crystal meth for candy. The boy was in full cardiac arrest when the paramedics brought him in. She had tried for hours to save him. Nothing had worked. And then she had gone out to her car and found the words FUCKING WHORE written in dark eyeliner on her windshield.

There was no question the missive was from Will's wife. Angie had a disjointed cursive with *F*s that looked like *J*s and *E*s that resembled backward *3*s. The two letters appeared in just about every note she'd ever left, starting a year ago, the morning after the first night Will had spent at Sara's apartment.

Amanda asked Will, 'Angie never left notes for you?'

Will rubbed the side of his jaw. 'She wouldn't do that.'

Sara looked down at the ground. He knew her so well.

'All right.' Amanda sounded even more flustered than before. 'I'll give the two of you five minutes to talk, then you're back to work.'

'No.' Will almost shouted the word. 'I need to look for Angie. You've got to let me look for her.'

'And what happens if you find her dead body, Will? Your ex-wife you've been trying to divorce so you can be with your new girlfriend? And the medical examiner in charge of the crime scene just happens to be said new girlfriend? And your partner and your boss are working the case, too? How's that going to read in the paper? Or do you need me to read it for you?'

Sara could tell from Will's expression that he hadn't considered any of this.

Amanda continued, 'Your wife murdered—or didn't murder, according to your girlfriend—a cop who was on Kip Kilpatrick's payroll, in the service of Marcus Rippy, who you've just harassed with a false rape charge for the last seven months, and oh, by the way, this same wife was stalking your girlfriend.' She had her hands on her hips. 'Does that sound about right to you?'

'I just want to find her.'

'I know you do, but you're going to have to let me handle this.' Amanda told Sara, 'Five minutes.' Her low heels made a snapping sound as she walked toward the lift. Sara hadn't even heard Charlie bring the platform back up.

Will opened his mouth to speak, but Sara stopped him.

'This way,' she said, indicating that they should move away from the murder room. No matter how Dale Harding had lived, he deserved some respect in death.

Will's Tyveked feet shuffled across the floor. His shoulders were slumped, giving him the air of a kid being taken to the woodshed. He stopped behind the stack of Sheetrock. He rubbed his face with both hands, wiping off any expression.

Sara stood in front of him. She waited for him to say something—anything. That he was sorry he had lied or that he was sad or angry or that he loved her and they would get through this or that he never wanted to see her again.

He said nothing.

He stared over her shoulder at the space where the lift would return. His fists were still clenched. His body was coiled, ready to leap the second the platform was in sight.

'I'm not keeping you here.' Sara felt the words catch in her throat. Her tone tended to go soft when she was angry. She could barely raise her voice above a whisper. 'You can go over there and wait. I've got plenty of work to do.'

Will didn't move. They both knew Charlie wouldn't return until their five minutes was up. 'What do you want me to say?'

Her heart was pounding. Her mouth had gone dry. He sounded angry. He had no right to be angry. 'Why didn't you tell me that you saw her?'

'I didn't want to upset you.'

'Usually when people say that, what they really mean is they didn't have the guts to be honest.'

He gave a laugh that flipped a switch inside of her.

Sara had never wanted to slap him so badly in her life.

'Look at me.'

His reluctance was palpable, but he finally looked at her.

'You know she took my lipstick. That she went through my things.' Sara felt her tears return, this time from anger. Everything started to unwind from the lipstick, because Angie wasn't the type of person who stopped at just one violation. Sara thought about all of the private things she had left at Will's house. Picturing Angie finding them, touching them, made her sick with rage. 'Do you think she broke into my apartment?'

'I don't know.' He held out his hands in an open shrug, like none of this was his problem. 'What do you want me to—'

'Shut up.' Sara's throat strained around the words. 'She went through my things. *Our* things.'

Will rubbed his jaw with his fingers. He glanced back at the balcony.

'You changed the locks on your doors last year.' At least Sara knew this was the truth. He'd given her a new key. She had seen the new deadbolts. 'Did you give her a key, too?'

He shook his head.

'How long have you known that she's been breaking into your house?'

He shrugged.

'Are you going to answer me?'

'You told me to shut up.'

Sara tasted bile in her mouth. She had left her laptop at Will's. Her entire life was on that thing—patient files, emails, her address book, her calendar, photographs. Had Angie guessed her password? Had she gone through Sara's overnight bag? Had she worn Sara's clothes? What else had she stolen?

'Look,' Will said. 'I'm not even sure she was in the house. It's just that sometimes stuff was moved. Or maybe you moved it. Or I did. Or—'

'Really? That's what you thought?' Will was congenitally tidy. He always put everything back in its place, and Sara was careful to do the same when she was in his house. 'Why didn't you change the locks again?'

'For what? Do you think it's that easy to stop her? That I can actually control her?' He sounded baffled by the question, and maybe he was, because as stubborn as Will could be, as strong as he was, Angie was always the one who dictated the terms of their relationship. She was like an older sister who wanted to protect him. Like a twisted lover who used sex to control him. Like a hateful wife who didn't want to be married, but didn't want to let him go. Angie loved him. She hated him. She needed him. She disappeared, sometimes for days, sometimes for weeks, months, more than once for a full year. That she always came back had been the only constant in Will's life for almost three decades.

Sara asked, 'Have you really been looking for her?'

'I showed you the divorce papers.'

'Is that a yes?'

There was a flicker of anger in his eyes. 'Yes.'

'Have you seen her before without telling me?' A bitter panic filled her mouth. 'Have you been with her?'

The anger glowed white-hot, as if she had no right to ask the question. 'No, Sara. I haven't been fucking her behind your back.'

Was he telling the truth? Could she trust what he was saying? Sara had upended her life for this man. She had silenced her gut instinct. She had compromised her morals. She had taken this job. She had made a complete fool of herself in front of everyone she worked with. Not to mention what her family would think, because there was no way to hide this awfulness from them without turning herself into a bigger liar than Will.

He asked, 'Do you think she's still alive?'

'I don't know.' The truth had the benefit of a cruel uncertainty.

Will looked at his watch. He was actually timing this, waiting for the second the lift came back up so he could jump on his white horse and save Angie yet again.

They had looked at open houses yesterday, the day after he'd seen his wife. They were out for a walk, and they had joked that lookie-looing air-conditioned houses was a good excuse to get out of the heat. Unbidden, Sara had found herself thinking about coming down that particular set of stairs to kiss Will hello or planting flowers in that yard while Will cut the grass or standing in that kitchen eating late-night ice cream with Will when what she should've really been thinking about was what kind of lock she should put on her fucking bedside drawer.

'Christ.' Sara covered her face with both hands. She wanted to wash herself with lye.

'She wouldn't give up.' Will picked at his eyebrow, a nervous tic Sara had noticed the first time they'd met. 'Angie. She wouldn't give up. Even if she was hurt.'

Sara didn't respond, but he was right. Angie was a cockroach. She left disease wherever she went and nothing could destroy her.

Will said, 'Her car isn't here. But her key is. But she could have another one. A key.' He dropped his hand. 'She was a cop. She was the toughest girl at the home. Tougher than the boys. Tougher than me, sometimes. She knows how to handle herself. She has people, a network, who would help her if she was in trouble. If she was hurt.'

Every word he said was like a dagger.

'Right?' Will said. 'If anyone could survive this, it's Angie?'

Sara shook her head. She couldn't have this conversation. 'What am I supposed to do here, Will? Reassure you? Comfort you? Tell you it's okay that you deceived me? That you knew she was violating my privacy—our privacy—but you let it happen anyway?' Sara put her hand over her mouth, because sounding shrill would not get them through this. 'I know that part of you will always have feelings for her. She's been an important part of your life for almost thirty years. I accept that. I understand that you are connected to her because of what you survived, but you and I are together. At least I thought we were. I need you to be honest with me.'

Will shook his head as if this was a simple misunderstanding. 'I *am* being honest. She was parked on the street. We didn't talk. I guess I should've told you.'

Sara bit down hard on the *guess*.

Again he glanced back at the opening where the lift would come. 'It's been longer than five minutes.'

'Will.' What little remained of her pride drained away. 'Please. Just tell me what you want me to do. Please.' Sara grabbed his hand before she could stop herself. She couldn't stand the feeling that he was slipping away. 'Should I give you some time? If that's what you need, just tell me.'

He looked down at their hands.

'Talk to me. Please.'

His thumb stroked the back of her fingers. Was he trying to think of a way to leave her? Was there more that he hadn't confessed?

She felt her heart start to shake in her chest. 'If you need to work through this alone, then tell me. I can take it. Just tell me what you want me to do.'

He kept stroking her hand. Sara remembered the first time Will had touched her like this. They were in the basement of the hospital. The feel of his skin against hers had set off an explosion inside of her body. Her heart had fluttered in her chest the same way it was fluttering now. Except that time, she was filled with hope. Now, she was flooded with dread.

'Will?'

He cleared his throat. He tightened his grip on her hand. She held her breath as she waited for his words, wondering if this was the end of their relationship or just another giant mountain they had to scale.

He said, 'Can you pick up Betty?'

Sara's brain couldn't process the request. 'What?'

'She's at the vet and . . .' He took a stuttered breath. He held on tight to her hand. 'I don't know how late I'll be. Can you pick her up?'

Sara felt her mouth open, then close, then open again.

'They told me she would . . .' He paused. She saw his Adam's apple work as he swallowed. 'They said to come at five, but maybe you can call to see if you can pick her up earlier, because they said she'd be finished by noon, but the anesthesia—'

'Yes.' Sara didn't know what else to do but relent. 'I'll take care of her.'

He let out a long, slow breath, as if figuring out what to do with Betty was the most difficult part of this conversation. 'Thank you.'

Charlie Reed came up the stairs, his footsteps unnaturally heavy to announce his arrival. He carried two heavy-looking duffel bags, one in each hand.

He told them, 'Stairs are cleared, so no more deathtrap elevator.' His mouth went into a tight smile under his handlebar mustache. 'Will, Amanda's waiting in the car.'

Will's hand slipped from Sara's. He took the stairs two at a time, sidestepping Charlie as he made a quick descent.

Sara stared after him, not sure what had just happened or how she was supposed to feel about it. She pressed her hand to her chest to make sure that her heart was still beating. The quick taps were the same as if she'd just run a marathon.

'Goodness.' Charlie had reached the top of the stairs. He dropped both the duffels. He clasped his hands together as he walked toward Sara. 'I'm trying to think about how to make this more uncomfortable. Should I take off my pants? Burst into song?'

Sara tried to laugh, but it came out sounding more like a cry. 'I'm sorry.'

'Don't apologize to me.' Charlie's smile was genuinely kind. He pulled a bottle of water out of one of the many pockets in his cargo pants. 'You need to drink all of this. It's officially eleventy billion degrees in here.'

Sara made herself smile because he was trying.

'Option one,' Charlie began. 'Daytime drinking. It has its pros and cons.'

Sara could only think of the pros. She hadn't had an alcoholic beverage in over a year. Will hated the taste. 'Option two?'

He indicated the building, which was still an active crime scene.

'The drinking is tempting,' Sara told him, feeling every single word to her core. 'But let's talk about what we need to do. Harding's body can be removed. We'll need at least four people.'

'I asked for six because of the stairs. ETA is forty minutes out.'

Sara looked at her watch. Her eyes blurred. She could only guess at the time. 'They'll need a few hours to do the prep. I'll start the autopsy after lunch.' Betty's vet would not release her before five, especially to Sara. The man had a chip on his shoulder about not being a people doctor. 'I guess the ABO testing is at the top of my list. Do we have Angie's blood type yet?'

'Amanda said she'd text it to you as soon as she finds out. Meanwhile, I've asked one of the techs to collect samples from the blood. He'll probably take about half an hour. As you can see, the walls are practically black with graffiti, so I told him to just collect what's visible and triple-check his labels. He's slow, but thorough.' Charlie paused for a breath. 'Until then, you can help me set up the black lights and photograph the luminol reactions, or you can sit in the coolness of the crime scene van and wait for the samples so you can work your magic.'

Sara longed to be alone in the van, but she said, 'I'll help you.' She took a mouthful of water. Her stomach roiled at the cold liquid. It was the lipstick. She couldn't get her mind off Angie standing at the mirror in Will's bathroom, testing Sara's make-up, taking what she wanted. That's what Angie Polaski did. She took things that belonged to other people.

Charlie asked, 'You okay?'

'Absolutely.' Sara carefully screwed the cap back on the water bottle. She asked Charlie, 'What else?'

'We're still cataloging evidence. That should take three, maybe four days. Harding's car has cooled down enough to process, though I doubt we'll find much. The thing is toast.' He turned around as a tech made his way up the stairs. The young man was dressed in a hoodless Tyvek suit. He wore a hairnet, his ponytail sticking out like an arrow at the back of his head. There was an ornate red and blue cross tattooed on the side of his neck. His chin showed a smattering of a goatee and his eyebrow was pierced.

Charlie provided, 'Gary Quintana. He came straight to us from tech school. Super smart, really wants to learn. Don't let his crazy look fool you. He does foster care for rescue cats. And he's a vegan.'

Sara smiled and nodded as if she was actually following what Charlie was saying. She could feel her heart pulsing inside her throat. Her stomach had turned sour. She prayed she would not get sick.

Charlie clasped his hands together. 'So I've got all my fancy camera equipment and lights and—'

'I'm sorry,' Sara interrupted. She put her hand to her chest again, certain that Charlie could see her heart pounding underneath. 'Do you mind if I have a minute?'

'Absolutely. I'll start setting up in the first room. Just pop in when you're ready.'

Sara could barely choke out a thank-you. She walked across the balcony toward the far set of stairs. She passed the room where Dale Harding had died, feeling like she'd committed the worst kind of sin for letting her life melt down when the man was lying dead. She stopped in front of the rainbow-eyed unicorn at the top of the stairs. Her stomach pitched like a tiny ship in the middle of an ocean. Sara closed her eyes. She waited out the nausea. Then she took out her iPhone because it offered the only socially acceptable excuse to stand silently with her head bent down.

There was a text from her sister. Tessa was a missionary in South Africa. She'd sent a photo of her daughter building a mud castle with help from some of the local kids.

Sara pulled up the keyboard. She typed, ANGIE IS BACK, but didn't send the text. She stared at the words. She deleted the last two and wrote: ANGIE MIGHT BE DEAD. Her thumb hovered over 'send', but she couldn't press it.

Sara had testified at several murder trials where phone data came into play. She envisioned herself on the witness stand explaining to a jury why her little sister had sent back a smiley face at the news that Will's wife might be dead. She deleted the unsent text and stared at the photo of her niece until her stomach settled and she didn't feel like flinging herself down the stairs anymore.

Sara had never fully understood Will and Angie's screwed-up relationship. It was something she'd come to accept as one of those things you tolerated when you were in love with someone, like the fact that he refused to eat vegetables or that he was completely blind to the toilet paper roll being empty. Angie was an addiction. She was a disease.

Everybody had a past.

Sara had been married before. She had been deeply, irrevocably in love with a man with whom she would've happily spent the rest of her life. But he had died, and she had forced herself to move on. Eventually. Slowly. She had left the small town where she grew up. Left her family. Left everything she had ever known to move to Atlanta and start over. And then Will had come along.

Had it been love at first sight? Meeting Will was more like an awakening. At the time, Sara had been a widow for three years. She was working double shifts at Grady Hospital, going home, then going back to work, and that was her life. And then Will had walked into the emergency room. Sara had felt something stir deep inside of her, like a winter flower poking its head out of the snow. He was handsome. He was smart. He was funny. He was also very, very complicated. Will would be the first to admit that he had enough baggage to fill every airplane in the sky. And Angie was only part of it.

For most of her professional life, Sara had worked as either a pediatrician or a medical examiner. Between the two jobs, she had seen the countless reprehensible ways that people took out their rage on children. Not until Will did she truly understand what happened when these abused kids grew up. Will's scars were both emotional and physical. He didn't trust people—at least not enough. Getting him to talk about his feelings was like pulling teeth. Actually, getting him to talk about anything of true importance was like pulling the *Titanic* through quicksand. With a shoestring.

They had been together for three months before he would even acknowledge the scars on his body. Almost a year passed before he told Sara some of the causes, but not the details, and certainly not the emotions behind them. She had learned to take his cue and not ask questions. She ran her hands along his back and pretended the perfect square imprint from a belt buckle was not there. She kissed his mouth and ignored the scar where his lip had been busted into two pieces. She only bought him long-sleeved shirts because she knew that he didn't want anyone to see where he'd taken a razor to his forearm.

For Angie.

He had tried to kill himself for Angie. Not because she rejected him, but because as kids, they were both placed in a foster home with a man who would not keep his hands off Angie. She had cried wolf before. She wasn't the kind of girl the police listened to. At fourteen, she already had a record. So Will had taken a razor blade and cut open his forearm in a six-inch line up from his wrist because he knew that an emergency room visit was the one thing they couldn't ignore.

This wasn't the first or last time he had risked his life for Angie Polaski. It had taken Will years to break the hold she had over him. But was that hold really broken? Was he just understandably upset that someone he'd known for almost the entirety of his life was probably dead?

Sara could not stop going back to the lipstick. That's all she could focus on, because the additional violations the lipstick signified were too much to handle. Will knew that Angie was breaking into his house. He could lay down his life for her, but he couldn't be bothered to protect Sara's privacy.

She shook her head. At least she knew where she fell on his list of priorities: right behind Betty.

Sara put her phone back in her pocket. She unhooked her glasses from her collar. The lenses were smeared. The building was insufferably hot. Everything was covered in sweat. She found a tissue in her pocket and rubbed the lenses with purpose.

She supposed one good thing about picking up Betty was that Will would eventually have to come by and get her. Which was ludicrous. Why had Sara given him so much power? She was a grown woman. She shouldn't feel like she was waiting for some boy to check yes or no on a note that she had slipped inside his locker.

Sara checked the lenses. She squinted at a smudge, about to curse herself for ruining another pair of glasses when she realized the smudge was not on the lens. It was on the unicorn behind it.

She slid on her glasses. She took a closer look. The unicorn was life-sized, if you could assume a unicorn was the same size as a horse. His head was tilted slightly as he gazed down the stairs. The creature's rainbow eye was about her shoulder height. Centered on the green and blue stripe in his iris was a hole that was around the size of a dime. Specks of gray concrete were chipped out, which is what she had taken for a smudge on her lens. Sara looked down at the ground. Concrete dust covered cigarette butts and crack pipes. The dust had fallen recently.

'Charlie?' she called.

He poked his head out of one of the rooms. 'Yes?'

'Can you come over here with your camera and some tweezers?'

'That's the most interesting proposition I've had all week.' He went back into the room and came out with his camera in one hand and a CSU kit in the other.

Sara pointed to the unicorn's eye. 'Here.'

Charlie shuddered. 'Two things that have always freaked me out: unicorns and eyeballs.' He took a magnifying glass from the kit and leaned in for a better look. 'Oh, I see. Excellent catch.'

Sara stood by while Charlie photographed the pierced eye, using a small metal ruler to capture scale. He did the same with the dust below the unicorn, then changed lenses to get a wider view. When he'd finally documented the creature, he handed Sara a pair of needle-nose tweezers. 'You do the honors.'

Sara was mindful that she could do a lot more harm than good if she didn't take her time. She was also mindful that she had never lost a game of Operation. She rested the heel of her hand just below the unicorn's eye. She opened the tweezers just wide enough to still clear the sides of the hole in the iris. Slowly she inserted the blades until she felt something solid. Instead of opening the tweezers, she narrowed them, fairly certain that there would be something to grip. She was right. The tip of the blades caught the flattened rim of what turned out to be a hollow-point bullet.

Charlie said, 'They shoot unicorns, don't they?'

Sara smiled. 'Thirty-eight special?'

'Looks like it.' Charlie told her, 'The G43 was unfired. The clip and chamber had nine-mill American Eagle, full metal jackets.' Charlie's mustache twisted to the side in thought. 'This could be from a revolver.'

'Could be,' Sara agreed. A cop of Dale Harding's age might prefer a revolver to a nine-millimeter. 'You haven't found another gun?'

'Maybe it melted in his car. I'll let the techs know to look for it.'

Sara sniffed the spent cartridge, picking up the lingering odors of sawdust, graphite and nitroglycerine. 'Smells recent.'

Charlie took a sniff. 'I think so. No blood, though.'

'The bullet would've been hot enough to cauterize any bleeding as it went through the body, but there could be microscopic traces.'

'Kastle-Meyer?'

Sara shook her head. The field blood test was known for false positives. 'We should let the lab do a wash. I'd hate to be told we used the only viable sample and they can't test for DNA.'

'Excellent point.' Charlie looked down at the floor. 'I'm no doctor, but if the bullet hit anything big, like an artery, we'd be able to see blood somewhere in this area.'

'Agreed.' Sara found a small plastic evidence bag in the CSU kit. Charlie took over the labeling because his handwriting was better.

He said, 'Just so you know, Amanda authorized rushes on everything, including the DNA.'

'Twenty-four hours is better than two months.' Sara studied the bullet hole in the unicorn's eye. 'Does this hole look more oval to you?'

'I saw that when I was taking pictures. We'll call in the computer geeks to do a rendering, calculate the trajectory, velocity, angles. I'll let them know about the rush. We should have something back in a few days.'

Sara took a Sharpie pen out of the CSU kit and slid it into the hole. The clipped cap pointed back toward the balcony at a slight angle. 'Do you have two levels and some string?'

Charlie laughed. 'You're a regular MacGyver.'

Sara waited for Charlie to retrieve a ball of string from one of the duffel bags. He tied it to the end of the Sharpie. He took his phone out of his pocket and pulled up a spirit level app.

'Oh, good thinking.' Sara pulled out her iPhone. She thumbed through her apps until she found the level. 'The other side of the balcony is how many yards?'

'Twenty-eight.'

Sara said, 'An airborne projectile is subject to the forces of air resistance, wind and gravity.'

'No wind inside of here. Resistance would be negligible at this distance.'

'Which leaves gravity.' Sara placed her phone on top of the Sharpie. The app showed an old-fashioned Stanley level with a digital number below the bubble. 'I've got seven-point-six degrees.' She placed the phone against the side of the pen for the second reading. The number kept jumping up and down. 'Let's call it thirty-two.'

'Fantastic.' Charlie started walking backward, rolling out the string, keeping the line tight. Occasionally he stopped and checked the level on his phone against the top and side of the string to make sure he was still on target. As long as he kept the angles consistent, the string would roughly indicate the point at which the bullet had left the muzzle of the gun.

Charlie glanced behind him as he walked, stepping around yellow plastic markers. His hand was too high to reasonably assume an average person had held a gun and fired it from that level. He passed the murder room, the stacked drywall. His hand started to move lower. He didn't stop until he was at the top of the stairs.

'Wait.' Sara looked at the level on her phone. 'You're pulling way left.'

'I have a theory.' Charlie went down one stair, then another. He looked back at Sara. The hand holding the ball of string went lower, then lower still. Sara kept the pen steady. The string had moved away from the balcony, tensing in the open air like a tightrope, until Charlie's hand was at his ankle. He used the level to make an adjustment. His hand slid back until it was pressed against the wall. He checked the angles one last time. 'This is the end of the line, as it were.'

Sara studied the path of the string. Charlie's theory was as good as any. Whoever had fired the gun would've been standing somewhere on the stairs. Or not standing. Charlie's hand was low, about three inches away from the tread. Two stairs down was the impact point where the woman—likely Angie—had hit the back of her head.

Sara said, 'They struggled for the gun there.'

'Angie and Harding.' Charlie picked up her train of thought. 'Angie has a gun. She's running up the stairs. Harding grabs her, bangs the back of her head against the tread. She sees tweety birds. He reaches for the gun. Maybe he bangs the back of her hand into the concrete and she squeezes off a shot.'

'Angie is right-handed.' Sara hated that she knew this. 'If she was on her back, for your theory to work, the gun would have to be in her left hand, which means the bullet would be on that side of the stairs, not here.'

'She could've twisted to her side?'

Sara shrugged, because there weren't a lot of absolutes considering they were using a ball of string and a free app.

'Let's think about this.' Charlie started rolling up the string. 'Angie is running away from Harding, revolver in her hand because her Glock somehow got jammed out in the parking lot. She's almost at the top of the stairs. Harding catches her. The gun goes off. Angie gets away. She goes to the room. Shuts the door. To be continued.' He held up his finger. 'Problem is, how would the gun go off? A cop wouldn't have her finger on the trigger while she ran up the stairs. They're trained out the wazoo that you rest your finger on the guard until you're ready to shoot. You don't unlearn that when you take off your badge.'

'The footprints bother me,' Sara said. 'Why would her feet be bloody by the time she gets up the stairs?'

'No shoes?' Charlie guessed. 'There's a ton of broken glass down there, some of it covered with blood. Which reminds me, we found a small amount of dried blood on the floor downstairs. Looks like a bad nosebleed.'

'That could fit with the drug paraphernalia, but we should take a sample anyway.'

'Excuse me, sir.' Gary, the cat-rescuing tech, walked up behind Charlie. 'I couldn't help but overhearing, and I was wondering about the struggle for the gun. Like, if she was twisted on her side when they struggled on the stairs, wouldn't the muzzle of the gun be pointing up, more toward the ceiling?' He tried to approximate the pose, hands in the air like Farrah Fawcett in a TV show that had been off the air for years before he was born.

'More like this,' Charlie said, striking his own pose. 'And then the gun could turn this way . . .' He tilted his hand. 'I look like a Heisman Trophy, don't I?'

Sara's laugh was more genuine this time, because they both looked ridiculous. 'Maybe we should get the computer geeks in here.'

Gary picked up a tray of vials. 'I took samples from everywhere I saw blood. I also swabbed the trickle of blood on Harding's neck. Dr Linton, do you mind if I watch you type the blood? I've never seen it done before.'

Sara suddenly felt ancient. Forget Farrah Fawcett. Gary had likely been in diapers when O.J. Simpson's lawyers had educated America about DNA. 'I'd be happy to.'

Gary practically skipped down the stairs. Sara followed at a more careful pace. She tried not to think about earlier when she'd glanced over at Will working the scissor lift. The funny way he'd seethed at Collier for checking her out, as if Sara would ever give another man the time of day.

She asked Gary, 'What do you know about blood types?'

'There are four main groups,' he answered. 'A, B, AB and O.'

'Correct. For the most part, all humans belong to one of those groups, which are based on genetically determined antigens that attach to red blood cells. The ABO test determines whether or not the antigen is present by using a reagent that agglutinates when it comes into contact with the blood.'

'Yes, ma'am.' Gary looked lost. 'Thank you.'

She tried again. 'You basically drop blood on a pre-prepared card, mix it around, and it tells you what the type is.'

'Oh.' He took the clipboard from the cop standing inside the doorway and signed out. 'That's cool.'

He opened the door. Sara was blinded by a blast of sunlight, so she couldn't tell if Gary was really interested or just being polite. She scribbled her signature below his. Her eyes took their time adjusting as they walked across the parking lot. Gary took off his hairnet and tightened the band around his ponytail. He had already unzipped his Tyvek suit. His navy-blue GBI T-shirt had the sleeves tightly rolled up to his shoulders. More tattoos covered his arms. He wore a thick gold necklace with a medallion that caught the sunlight like a mirror.

She glanced around the parking lot and adjacent buildings, telling herself that she wasn't looking for Will or even Amanda, but still feeling disappointed when she didn't find either. Sara looked down at her phone to see if Amanda had sent her Angie's blood type. She hadn't yet, which was strange. Amanda was usually quick. Sara touched her finger to the phone icon. This would be a legitimate reason to call. She could ask Amanda about Angie's records and then casually question whether there was anything else going on, like had Will found Angie and carried her in his arms all the way to the hospital.

Sara returned her phone to her pocket.

She looked up, then quickly back down again. The sun was shining straight into her eyes. She guessed it was around ten o'clock, if she was remembering her Girl Scout training. The sunlight was so unrelenting that it brought tears into her eyes. She had to keep her gaze down as she made her way past Harding's burned-out Kia. The car was being thoroughly examined by two techs who were on their knees with magnifying glasses. The blackened frame had only slightly cooled down. Sara could still feel the heat radiating off the metal as she walked by.

The GBI's Department of Forensic Sciences mobile lab had been created inside a limousine bus that had been confiscated from a guy running a Medicare fraud. The seating had been torn out to accommodate a long desk with banks of computers and storage for various collection kits and evidence bags. Most importantly, the air conditioning had been left intact. Sara almost fell to her knees in relief when the cool air touched her skin.

Gary put the tray of samples down on the desk. He pulled out a chair for Sara, then took his own. She tried not to stare at his necklace. The medallion read SLAM.

He asked, 'Can you tell sex or race with the kit?'

She used a paper towel to wipe the sweat off her neck and face. 'With sex, you'd need a DNA test for the presence or absence of a Y chromosome.' She started searching the cubbies and drawers for the familiar EldonCard typing kits that she had ordered off Amazon because they were cheaper than the local supplier. 'For race, you can fall back on statistics, but it's not at all definitive. Caucasians have a relatively high number of As. Hispanics have a high number of Os. Asians and African Americans have a high number of Bs.'

'What about people who are mixed race?'

She wondered if he was asking the question because of Angie. She had Mediterranean features—olive skin and luxuriant brown hair and a curvaceous figure. The only time Sara had stood beside Angie, she'd felt like the proverbial gawky, redheaded stepchild.

She told Gary, 'Mixed race is a bit more complicated. Parents don't always match their children's blood type, but their alleles dictate the blood type. Two parents, type AB and type O, can have a child type A or B, but not O or AB. Two Os can only have an O, but nothing else.'

'Wow.' Gary scratched his goatee. 'Most of the stuff they taught us about blood in school had to do with DNA. Collecting, processing. This is blowing my mind.'

Sara wasn't sure whether or not he was being genuine. Nerds had it so much easier now. At Gary's age, she'd stuck out like a sore distal phalange.

She offered, 'I'll do the first typing. You'll do the second. I'll make sure you have the hang of it and then you can do the others.'

'Cool.' He flashed a smile. 'Thank you, Dr Linton.'

'Sara.' She sliced open the metal foil around the EldonCard. 'This is the test card.' She showed him the white index card with black print. At the top were four empty circles, or wells, each with a dot of reagent at their center. Beneath the circles were labels: ANTI-A, ANTI-B, ANTI-D, and a control.

'Anti-D?' Gary asked.

'D tests for the Rh factor.' Sara spared him another long lecture. 'The absence or presence of rhesus gives you the positive or the negative after the blood type. So, if you see blood clotting in the A circle and blood clotting in the D, that means your blood type is A-positive. If there's no clotting in the D, then it's A-negative.'

'Rhesus?'

She snapped on a pair of gloves. 'It's named after rhesus monkeys, because they were initially used to create the anti-serum for typing blood samples.'

'Oh,' Gary said. 'Poor monkeys.'

Sara laid out some clean paper towels and emptied the kit onto the counter. She set aside the alcohol swab and lancet because they weren't testing a live subject. She separated the four Eldon sticks—basically plastic Q-tips—and the tiny bottle of water that came with the kit. She told Gary, 'Write on the card where the first sample came from.'

Gary took a pen from his pocket and wrote LEFT STAIR TWO IMPACT, then the address for the building, date and time. His gold medallion tapped against the desk. Sara assumed he hadn't met Amanda yet. She had once slapped a ruler to the back of Will's neck to make sure that his hair was the regulation one inch off his collar.

Sara put on her glasses. She laid the card flat on the paper towels. She squeezed a pin drop of water onto the four separate reagents in each circle. Gary opened one of the test vials, which contained a glob of tissue, probably scalp. Sara used a glass pipette to collect some blood. She dabbed the blood at the bottom of the control well. She used the Eldon stick to mix the blood and reagent inside the margins of the printed circle.

Gary said, 'Would it be clotting already?'

'Not the control. It should always look smooth.' Sara dropped more blood onto the first circle, marked ANTI-A, and swirled it around with a fresh stick. Then she did the same for anti-B and -D. She told Gary, 'Next, you turn the card on its side, hold for ten seconds, then upside down for ten seconds, and so on until you make a full revolution to mix the blood with the reagent.'

Gary said, 'It looks like the B is clotting.'

He was right. There were patch-like red clumps inside the B circle.

'There's no clotting in the D circle,' Gary said. 'That means it's B-negative, right?'

'Correct,' Sara told him. 'Well done.'

'Do we know the blood type for Mrs Trent?'

Sara felt the name like a punch to her throat. 'She goes by Polaski.'

'Oh, sorry. My bad.'

'I haven't received her blood type yet.' Sara checked her phone to make sure a text hadn't come in from Amanda. She wondered again if something had happened. Will had a habit of agreeing with Amanda, then doing whatever he wanted. Sara used to find that attractive.

Gary asked, 'Is Mrs Polaski's DNA on file from when she was a cop?'

Instead of telling him they could probably find an intact sample on Sara's lipstick, she answered, 'It's unlikely unless she was a rule-out at a crime scene. She worked vice, so there probably wasn't a need.' Sara forced her thoughts to stay on the task at hand. 'DNA is the gold standard, but the typing is a significant finding. B-negative is found in only two percent of Caucasians, one percent of African Americans and well under a half a percent in the remaining ethnic groups.'

'Wow. Thank you. That there is some mad science, Dr Linton.' Gary took out his pen and filled in the next card without being asked. His letters were neat capitals that easily fit in the square provided. LEFT STAIR BLOODY FOOTPRINT A.

He said, 'So, the water first, right?'

'Just a pin drop.' She kept silent while Gary processed the next kit. He really was a fast learner. When he mixed the blood, his margins inside the circles were better than hers. He started to turn the card, holding it in place for ten seconds before turning it again, then again. As before, the blood clotted on B-negative.

She told him, 'Type the sample from Harding's neck.'

Gary had taken a swab because there wasn't a lot of blood. He had to use a blade to cut the cotton tip into sections, then use water to free the blood. He went through the same steps with the card. This time, only the circle for D clotted. He asked, 'Did I do something wrong?'

'He's O-positive, the most common blood type for Caucasians, but the important part is this makes Harding a definite rule-out for the footprint and the spatter on the stairs.' She handed him another kit. 'Let's try the sample of blood from the room where Harding died.'

There was a loud knock on the door. Both Sara and Gary jumped at the noise.

'Good Lord God.' Charlie held up his camera as he climbed into the van and slid down to the floor. 'I thought I was going to burst into flames inside that room.' He closed his eyes and breathed the cold air for a few seconds.

Gary started the next kit. Sara handed Charlie a paper towel to wipe his face. He was soaked through with sweat. They would need to get some fans in the building before they continued. It was August. Even tonight when the sun set, the temperature would only dip a few degrees.

'Okay.' Charlie tossed the paper towel into the trashcan. 'I've been activating the luminol inside the other rooms.'

Sara nodded. Luminol was activated by a black light that made the enzymes in blood glow an ethereal blue. The reaction lasted for a few seconds, and only happened once, which was why it was important to have a camera to record the process.

She asked Charlie, 'Anything good?'

'Oh yeah. I've got it right here.' Charlie switched on the LED on the back of the camera and started toggling through the pictures. 'By the way, I found some blood spray on the unicorn, which could mean the bullet went through somebody.'

'A lot of spray or a little spray?'

'More like a sneeze.'

'That's not enough to test with the EldonCard. We'll have to go with DNA.' For Gary's sake, she added, 'There's no time stamp on blood. Could be some raver sneezed out some blood three months ago.'

Charlie said, 'Nobody knows the trouble that unicorn has seen.' His thumb worked the scroll on the camera. Rorschachs of bright blue spatters and splatters flashed across the LED.

'Dr Linton?' Gary held up the card he'd just processed. 'More B-negative.'

Charlie asked him, 'By any chance, did you take a sample from the second room from the left stair?'

'Yes, sir.' Gary checked the vials. 'I found some blood on the floor, back right corner. And I triple-checked the label before I went to the next one, just like you said.'

'Good boy.' Charlie said, 'Type it for me, please.'

Gary waited for Sara to give him the nod to proceed.

She asked Charlie, 'What's going on? Did you find something?'

'Oh, I found something.'

Sara wasn't one for cliffhangers, but she let Charlie have his fun. For the most part, forensic work was the least glamorous part of policing. It wasn't like on television, where impeccably dressed, beautiful crime scene techs plucked clues from thin air, waved around guns, interrogated the bad guys, then carted them off to jail. Fifty percent of Charlie's job was paperwork and the remaining fifty percent had his eye to either a camera or a microscope. He had probably found an unusual pattern of spatter on a ceiling, or the forensic Holy Grail: a viable fingerprint left in fresh blood.

'There it is.' Charlie sounded triumphant. He held out the camera so that Sara could see for herself.

The display showed the familiar chemiluminescence—bright glowing blue against the dark graffitied background, almost like an X-ray. Instead of an unusual blood pattern or a clear fingerprint, there were two words written in blood: HELP ME.

'Dr Linton?' Gary had finished the test card. 'It says B-negative, just like the other two.'

Charlie verified, 'Gary, you're sure that blood was taken from the second room, which is where I found this note?'

'Yes, sir. Positive. Triple positive.'

'Sara?' Charlie waited. 'Did you get Angie's blood type from Amanda yet?'

She couldn't find it in herself to answer. Her eyes would not leave the glowing image on the camera. She stared at the two words, absorbing the familiar disjointed cursive like radiation into her brain.

Both of the *E*s were written like backward *3*s.

Amanda opened the back door. She held out her hand for Charlie to help her into the van. Gary stood to offer his chair. Amanda took in his tattoos and gold chain and scowled. 'Young man, wait for me outside.'

Gary quickly followed orders, gently clicking the door shut behind him.

Amanda sat in the vacated chair. She told Sara, 'Will is searching the office building across the street.' Her tone was accusatory, as if Sara could have stopped him. 'The structural engineer said the whole damn thing is about to fall down, but Will wouldn't listen. I can't send anyone in after him without risking a lawsuit if the building collapses.'

Sara handed Amanda the camera.

'What's this?' Amanda looked down at the screen. She stared at the words for a good long while. 'You recognize the handwriting?'

Sara nodded. She had gotten so many nasty notes over the last year that she knew Angie's handwriting almost better than her own.

Amanda said, 'For now, let's make sure this message goes no further than the three of us. Will doesn't need anything else to set him off.'

Charlie said, 'Yes, ma'am.'

Sara found she couldn't answer.

Amanda said, 'Records finally sent me Angie's file.' She let the camera rest in her lap. Her shoulders slumped. She seemed suddenly tired, older than her sixty-four years. 'Please tell me that none of the blood you found is B-negative.'

THREE

The front doors to the office building had been chained shut, but the junkies had pulled the boards off a window. The door to the basement and the doors to the elevator shafts were a different beast. The metal had been welded to the jamb. This hadn't put a damper on the party. The lobby was riddled with broken glass and pieces of steel from fractured desks and chairs. The building was old enough to be built from wood and not concrete. It was a wonder the thing hadn't burned down. Fires had been started on the asbestos tile floors and the smoke had blackened the asbestos tile ceilings. Urine stained the walls. Everything of any value had been broken or carted off long ago. Even the copper wires had been stripped out of the walls.

The structure was ten stories, almost perfectly square. Will gathered that each of the floors was divided into twenty offices, ten on each side, with a long open cubicle area down the center and two bathrooms at the back. The layout was less like a maze and more like an Escher drawing. Some of the rooms had makeshift stairs built from stacked crates and desks that led to rotted holes in the ceilings. These wobbly stairs led to locked doors or smaller rooms on different floors that needed to be searched after he finished the one below. Will felt like a pinball banging from one side of the building to the other, up some creaky stacked crates, down some shifting stacked desks, prying open cabinets and lifting downed bookcases and kicking over piles of paperwork that had been left to rot for decades.

Angie.

He had to find Angie.

Amanda had wasted almost an hour of Will's life, making him wait outside the governor's office while she briefed the man on what little they had so far in the Dale Harding murder investigation. Will had spent the time convincing himself that she was right. He couldn't look for Angie. He couldn't be the one to find her. The press would latch onto the story and Will wouldn't just see the end of his career, he would probably see the inside of a prison cell. He could ruin Amanda's life in the process. Faith's. Sara's. The damage would be irreparable.

Unless he found Angie alive. Unless she was able to tell the story of what had really happened inside Rippy's club.

That was when Will had walked outside the state capitol and hailed a cab.

Forty minutes had passed since then. If Sara was right, if Angie only had a few more hours, then he might be too late.

But he couldn't stop looking.

Will pushed open the last door to the last office on the third floor. There were no boards on the windows. Sunlight drenched the small room. Will pushed a desk away from the wall. A rat darted out. Will jumped back. His foot went through a rotted floorboard. He felt the skin along the back of his calf rip open like a zipper. He quickly wrenched his leg out of the hole, praying a stray needle or piece of broken glass hadn't infected him. His pants were torn. Blood streamed into his shoe. Nothing he could do about either right now.

A set of stairs was at the end of the hall. The concrete treads ran up the structure like a spine, broken windows on every other landing shooting blinding light into his eyes. Will grabbed the handrail and swung himself up to the next flight. His knee almost buckled on the landing. His leg might be hurt worse than he'd originally thought. He could feel blood pooling into the heel of his shoe. His sock made a squishing noise as he climbed to the next floor.

'Hey.' Collier was waiting for him. The yellow hard hat was back on his head. He was leaning against the door jamb. His arms were crossed over his chest. 'End of the line, buddy. You gotta get outta here.'

Will said, 'Move.'

'Your boss lady shit a brick when I told her you were here. I literally watched it pinch out between her legs.' Collier grinned. 'Guess she'll pinch out another one when she finds out I'm in here too.'

Collier didn't move, so Will shoved him aside.

'Come on, bro. This place ain't safe.' Collier had to jog to keep up with Will's longer stride. 'I'm in charge of the search teams. If you fall through the floor and break your neck, that's on my record.'

'I already fell through the floor.' Will strode up the hallway. He entered the first office. Dingy carpet. Broken chairs. Rusted metal desk.

Collier followed him, standing in the doorway, watching Will search the room. 'What's your deal, bro?'

Will saw the edge of a mattress. Newspapers covered the surface. He could make out a shape underneath. He used his foot to kick away the papers, breath caught in his chest until he saw that the shape was a blanket, not Angie.

Collier said, 'This is some crazy shit, man.'

Will turned around. Collier was still blocking the doorway.

Will asked, 'Where's your partner?'

'Ng's ball-deep in missing persons reports, plus he's waiting for our domestic from last night to get out of surgery. He won't see sunshine for days.'

'Why don't you go help him?'

''Cause I'm helping you.'

'No you're not.' Will towered over him. 'Move, or I'll move you.'

'Is this about before with your girlfriend? Mistress? Whatever?' Collier smirked. 'Lookit, dude, you should'a told me you were seeing her. Handle it like a man.'

'You're right.' Will reared back his fist and punched him in the side of the head—not just for Sara, but for being an asshole and being in the way.

Collier's hands went up a second too late. The blow was harder than Will intended, or maybe Collier was just one of those guys who couldn't take a punch. His eyes rolled back in his head. His mouth fished open. He dropped like a sack of shit thrown from wherever it is you throw sacks of shit from, knocked out cold before he hit the floor.

Will experienced five seconds of sheer bliss before he came back to his senses. He looked down at his hand, startled by his own sudden act of violence. He flexed his fingers. The skin had broken over two of his knuckles. Trickles of blood slid down his wrist. For a moment he found himself wondering if the hand had acted of its own accord, some kind of possession he couldn't control. This wasn't him. He didn't just haul off and punch people, even people like Collier, who deserved it.

This was Angie's real power over Will: she brought out the very worst in him.

Will untucked his shirt. He wiped the blood off his hand. He tucked the shirt back in. He leaned down. He grabbed Collier by the shoulders and propped him up in the doorway. Then he walked across the hall and continued searching for Angie.

Another office. Another desk. Another overturned bookshelf. A shopping cart with an old IBM Selectric. He turned around. There was a metal cabinet by the door. Every other office seemed to have one. Six feet tall. Three feet wide. Eighteen inches deep. Unlike the others, the doors were closed.

Will wiped the sweat off his palms. He wrapped his fingers around the handle. He tried to turn the latch. Rust kept it from moving. He put his shoulder into it, practically lifting the cabinet off the floor. There was a loud pop. The door squealed open.

Empty.

She might hide in a cabinet. Angie liked dark places. Places where she could see you but you couldn't see her. The basement at the children's home was her favorite retreat. Someone had dragged a futon downstairs and laid it on the cold brick floor. Kids would smoke down there. Do other things. Mrs Flannigan, the lady who ran the home, couldn't handle the stairs. Her knees were old. She carried a lot of weight. She had no idea what was going on down there. Or maybe she did. Maybe she understood that physical comforts were all they had to offer each other.

Will took out his handkerchief. He wiped the back of his neck.

He would never forget being down in the basement with Angie. His first time. He wasn't shaking so much as vibrating with excitement and fear and dread that he would do it wrong or too soon or backward and she would laugh at him and he would have to kill himself.

Angie was three years older than Will. She'd done a lot of things with a lot of boys, some other things with a lot of men, not always her choice, but the fact was that she knew what she was doing and he did not.

Just the touch of her hands made him shiver. He was clumsy. He forgot things, like how to unbutton his own pants. At that point in his life, the only people who had ever touched Will were either hurting him or stitching him up. He couldn't help himself. He started crying. Really crying. Not like the hot tears streaming down his face when his nose was broken or when he cut open his own arm with a straight razor.

Big, gulping, humiliating sobs.

Angie hadn't laughed at him. She had held him. Her arms around his back. Her legs wrapped with his. Will hadn't known what to do with his hands. He had never been held before. He had never been physically close to another human being. They had stayed in the basement for hours, Angie holding him, kissing him, showing him what to do. She had promised to never let Will go, but the truth was that things between them were never the same. She could never look at him again without seeing him as broken.

The next time Will had felt that close to a woman was almost thirty years later.

'Trent!' Collier was at the end of the hall, bobbing like a Weeble Wobble. He winced as his fingers touched his ear. Blood streaked down the side of his face and neck.

Will returned his handkerchief to his pocket. He pushed open another door, searched another room.

Angie, he kept thinking. *Where are you hiding?*

There was no use calling for her, because he knew that she would not want to be found. Angie was a wild animal. She did not show weakness. She slinked away to lick her wounds in private. Will had always known that when her time came, she would go off somewhere and die on her own. The same as the woman who'd raised her.

Or at least tried to raise her.

Angie was not even ten years old when Deidre Polaski injected her final not-fatal-enough overdose of heroin. The woman had spent the next thirty-four years in a vegetative coma inside a state-run hospice facility. Angie had once told Will that she wasn't sure which was worse: living with Deidre's pimp or living at the children's home.

'Trent!' Collier braced his hands against the wall. Spit drooled out of his mouth. 'Jesus Christ. What the fuck did you hit me with, a sledgehammer?'

Will struggled against his guilt, forcing himself not to apologize. He pushed open the next door. He felt his stomach clench as his eyes scanned what was left of the bathroom. The floor had rotted through. Broken toilets, sinks and pipes had crashed to the level below.

There was another metal storage cabinet on the other side of the hole. Doors closed. Could Angie be inside? Would she cling to the wall, edging her way to the other side of the room so she could close herself off and wait to die?

Collier said, 'You're not going in there.' He stood behind Will, his hand covering his bloody ear. 'No kidding, man. You'll fall to your death.'

Will took out his handkerchief and handed it to him.

Collier hissed a curse as he put the cloth to his ear. 'That cabinet's a foot wide, dude. How thin is this chick?'

'She could fit in there.'

'Sitting down?'

Will imagined Angie sitting in the cabinet. Eyes closed. Listening.

Collier said, 'Okay, this chick is hurt, all right? Real bad. She has all these other rooms to choose from, but this is the one she goes into, the one with the giant hole in it. How's she even gonna get over there?'

He had a point. Angie wasn't athletic. She hated sweat.

Will turned around. He went into the bathroom across the hall.

Again Collier watched him from the doorway, arms folded, leaning against the jamb. 'They told me you were a stubborn prick.'

Will kicked open a stall door.

'I guess you got your ass handed to you by the good doctor?'

'Shut up.' Will heard the echo of Sara saying the same two words a few hours ago. He'd never seen her that mad before.

Collier said, 'What's your secret, man? I mean, no offense, but Brad Pitt you ain't.'

Will grabbed Collier's shirt and moved him out of the way.

Angie wasn't on this floor. Six more to go. Will headed toward the stairs and started the climb to the next level. Was he doing this the wrong way? Should he have started at the top floor instead of the bottom? Was there an attic in this place? A top-floor C-suite with a panoramic view?

Tactically, higher ground was always better. The office building was right across the street from Rippy's club. Angie could've been watching the whole time. She would've seen the patrol car roll up, the fire department, the crime scene vans, the detectives, all of them spinning their wheels trying to figure out what the hell was happening while Angie was up on the tenth floor the entire time laughing her ass off.

Or bleeding to death.

Will passed the fifth floor, the sixth. He was winded by the time he saw a large *8* painted at the top of the next landing. He stopped, hands on his knees so he could lean over to catch his breath. The heat was getting to him. Sweat dripped onto the floor. His lungs were screaming. His hamstrings were aching. Blood dribbled down the side of his shoe. The cuts on his knuckles had opened up again.

Was this a mistake?

Angie wouldn't climb these stairs on a good day, let alone with a life-threatening injury. She hated exercise.

Will sat down on the stairs. He rubbed his face and shook the excess sweat off his hands. Was he sure that Angie was even in the building? Where was her car? Shouldn't Will be trying to find out where she was living instead of risking his life searching a condemned building?

And what about Sara?

'Holy Mother of Christ.' Collier had stopped a few flights down. He was panting like a locomotive. 'I think I need stitches in my ear.'

Will leaned his head back against the wall. Had he lost Sara? Had Angie, with this final, violent act, managed to do what she couldn't do for the last year?

Betty was his only saving grace. Early on in their relationship, Sara had kept volunteering to watch Betty while Will was working late. At first he thought it was because she wanted to know about his cases, but then he had slowly realized that she was using his dog to lure him over to her apartment. It had taken Will a long time to accept that a woman like Sara would want to be with him.

She wouldn't have agreed to pick up Betty if she wanted to end things now.

Would she?

'Trent.' Collier was like a broken record. His feet scuffed the stairs as he made it to the landing below Will. 'What's the point of this, dude? You think she's hiding under a typewriter?'

Will looked down at him. 'Why are you here?'

'It seemed like a good idea when I was outside. What's your excuse?' Collier seemed genuinely interested. 'Dude, you know she's not in here.'

Will looked up at the ceiling. Graffiti stared back.

Why was he here?

Maybe the better question was: where else would he be? There were no clues to follow. No leads to run down. He had no idea where Angie was living. Where she was working. Why she was in Rippy's building. How she had gotten herself tangled up in a rape case Will couldn't make against a man he despised.

Well, maybe he knew the answer to the last one. Angie always inserted herself into Will's business. She was stealth, like a cat tracking its prey then leaving the poor dead creature as a trophy on Will's doorstep so that he had to figure out what to do with the body.

There were so many unmarked graves in Will's past that he had lost count.

Collier said, 'I called around about your wife.' He leaned his shoulder against the wall. He crossed his arms again. The good news was the blood around his ear was drying. The bad news was that it had glued Will's handkerchief to his skin.

'And?' Will said, though he could guess what Collier had found out. Angie slept around. Frequently and indiscriminately. She was the worst kind of cop. You couldn't trust her to have your back. She was a loner. She had a death wish.

Collier was uncharacteristically diplomatic. 'She sounds like she's a real piece of work.'

Will couldn't disagree with him.

'I've known gals like that. They're a lot of fun.' Collier was still keeping his distance. He didn't want to get hit again. 'The thing is, they've always got people they can fall back on.'

Will had said the same thing to Sara, but it sounded shitty coming out of Collier's mouth.

'You really think she'd run across the street to this dump?' Collier slid down the wall so he could sit. He was still out of breath. 'Lookit, I never met the broad, but I've known plenty of broads like her.' He glanced up at Will, probably to make sure he wasn't coming down the stairs. 'No offense, bro, but they've always gotta backup plan. You know what I mean?'

Will knew what he meant. Angie always had a guy she could run to. That guy hadn't always been Will. She had different men she used at different times in her life. When it wasn't Will's turn, he went to work, he retiled his bathroom, he restored his car, and he convinced himself the whole time that he wasn't waiting for her to come back into his life. Dreading. Anticipating. Aching.

Collier said, 'My take is, the shit went down last night, she's injured, so she pulled out her phone—which we can't find—and she called up a guy and he came rushing over to help.'

'What if Harding was the guy?'

'You think she only had one guy?'

Will took a deep breath. He held on to it for as long as he could.

Collier asked, 'We leaving now?'

Will pushed himself up. Heat exhaustion put stars in his eyes. He steadied himself for a moment. He blinked away sweat. He turned around and resumed his climb up the stairs.

'Jesus Christ,' Collier muttered. The soles of his shoes hit the treads like sandpaper. 'You ask me, you oughta be running back down these stairs and telling ol' Red you're fucking sorry.'

Collier was right. Will owed Sara an apology. He owed her more than that. But he had to keep moving forward, because taking a step back, letting himself think about what he was doing and why, was a thread he couldn't let unravel.

Collier said, 'That's a good-lookin' woman you got there.'

'Shut up.'

'I'm just sayin', dude. Simple observation.'

Up ahead, Will saw a painted *9* marking the next landing. He kept climbing. The heat intensified with every step. He braced his hand against the wall. He went through the list again: he didn't know where Angie lived. He didn't know where she worked. He didn't know who her friends were. If she had friends. If she wanted friends. She had been the center of his existence for well over half of his life and he didn't know a damn thing about her.

'You got prime rib at home,' Collier said. 'You don't run out to McDonald's for a Happy Meal.' He laughed. 'I mean, not so prime rib ever finds out. 'Cause, shit, man, we all like a greasy cheeseburger every now and then, am I right?'

Will turned the corner at the *9*. He looked up to the next landing.

His heart stopped.

A woman's foot.

Bare. Dirty.

Bloody cuts criss-crossed the soles.

'Angie?' He whispered the word, afraid to say it louder because she might disappear.

Collier asked, 'What'd you say?'

Will stumbled up the stairs. He could barely carry his own weight. He was on his knees by the time he reached the landing.

Angie was lying face down on the floor. Long brown hair wild. Legs splayed. One arm underneath her, the other over her head. She was wearing a white dress he'd seen before. Cotton, see-through, which is why she wore the black bra underneath. The dress rode up her legs, showing matching black bikini underwear.

Blood radiated from beneath her still body, cresting in a halo over her head.

Will put his hand on her ankle. The skin was cold. He felt no pulse.

His head dropped down. He squeezed his eyes shut against the tears that came.

Collier was behind him. 'I'll call it in.'

'Don't.' Will needed a minute. He couldn't hear the call on the radio. He couldn't take his hand from Angie's leg. She was thinner than the last time he'd seen her—not Saturday, that was just a glimpse, but about sixteen months ago. It was the last time they were together. Deidre had finally died, all alone in the nursing home because Angie didn't see her anymore. Will was on a case when it happened. He had driven back to Atlanta to be with Angie. Sara was in the picture by then, like a blur at the edge of the frame that might be something or nothing at all, depending on how things developed.

Will had told himself that he owed Angie one last chance, but she had known the minute she looked into his eyes that all that weight between them—that Pandora's box of shared horrors that they both carried on their backs—had finally been lifted.

Will cleared his throat. 'I want to see her face.'

Collier's mouth opened, but he didn't say what he was supposed to say—that they should leave the body in situ, that they needed to call in forensics and Amanda and everybody else who would pick over Angie Polaski's lifeless body like carrion.

Instead, Collier climbed the stairs and went to the head of Angie's body. He didn't bother to glove up before he slipped his hands under her thin shoulders. He said, 'On three?'

Will forced himself to move. To get up on his knees. To wrap his hands around Angie's ankles. Her skin was smooth. She shaved her legs every day. She hated having her feet touched. She liked fresh milk in her coffee. She loved the perfume samples that came in magazines. She loved dancing. She loved conflict and chaos and all the things he could not stand. But she looked out for Will. She loved him like a brother. A lover. A sworn enemy. She hated him for leaving her. She didn't want him anymore. She couldn't let him go.

She would never, ever hold him like she held him in that basement ever again.

Collier counted down. 'Three.'

Wordlessly they lifted the body and turned her onto her back. She wasn't stiff. The arm over her head flailed, crossing itself over her eyes as if she couldn't face the fact that she was gone.

Her swollen lips were chapped. Dark blood smeared down her chin. White powder speckled her hair and face.

Will's hand shook as he reached out to move the arm. There was blood—not just from her mouth and nose, but from needle tracks. On her neck. Between her grimy fingers. On her arms.

Will felt his heart start to jackhammer. He was light-headed. His fingers touched her cool skin. Her face. He had to see her face.

The arm moved.

Collier asked, 'Did you do that?'

Unaided, the woman's arm slid off her face, flopped onto the ground.

Her mouth slit open, then her rheumy eyes.

She looked at Will.

He looked back.

It wasn't Angie.

FOUR

Faith sat in her car outside Dale Harding's duplex, taking a break from the unrelenting heat. She was sweating her balls off, to quote a post from her son's Facebook page that future potential employers would eventually find.

Maybe he could live with his grandmother. Faith had gotten a sunglassed smiley face back when she texted Evelyn the photo of Jeremy with the bong. This was certainly a radical departure from her mother's previous parenting techniques, which had come straight from the pages of *Fascist Monthly*. Then again, Jeremy wouldn't be here if fashioning yourself into your child's own private Mussolini was a strategy for success.

She took a long drink of water and stared at Dale Harding's duplex side of a well-maintained single-story bungalow nestled inside a sprawling gated complex.

Something wasn't adding up.

Faith hated when things didn't add up.

After hitting a series of brick walls trying to locate any contact information for Angie Polaski, Faith had burned through the remainder of the morning and part of the afternoon trying to track down Dale Harding's place of residence. Two dead ends had sent her to east Atlanta's shadier neighborhoods, where she was told by various neighbors and slumlords that Dale Harding was an asshole who owed them money. No one seemed surprised or sad to learn of his untimely death. Several expressed regret that they hadn't been there to witness it.

As Amanda had predicted, there were liquor stores, strip clubs, payday loan stores and all sorts of seedy dives where you'd expect to run into a slimeball like Dale Harding, and in fact many of the workers at these businesses recognized the dead man's photograph, though none could recall seeing Dale in the last six months. That was the story everywhere Faith went: Dale was bellied up to the bar every day until six months ago. He was shoving ones into G-strings every day until six months ago. He was buying loose cigarettes and three-dollar liters of whiskey every day until six months ago.

No one could tell her what had happened six months ago.

She was about to give up when she ran into a stripper who said Harding had promised her kid a hundred bucks if he helped move some boxes. Faith would've never found the quiet little duplex in north Atlanta if Harding hadn't stiffed the kid.

All of that made sense, from the slumlords to the strippers to cheating a fifteen-year-old boy out of a promised payday. What didn't make sense was the place that Harding had finally called home.

He hadn't lived in elegance so much as limbo. According to its website, the Mesa Arms was an active retirement community for the fifty-five-and-older set. Faith had drooled over the modern floorplans posted on the site. Everything was in italics with an exclamation point, like it wasn't exciting enough to live in a community that did not allow children under the age of eighteen to visit more than three days in a row.

Spa-style bathrooms!

Main floor masters!

Hardwoods throughout!

Central vacuum!

The place was a baby boomer's dream, if you could dream in half-a-million-dollar increments. Green lawns. Gently sloping sidewalks. Cute craftsman-style bungalows spread out like fans on tree-lined cul-de-sacs. There was a club lounge, gym, pool, and a tennis court that was currently occupied by two sporty seniors, even though the temperature had passed the one hundred mark.

Faith used the sleeve of Will's suit jacket to wipe the back of her neck. At this point, the thermometer might as well read HELL.

She finished the water and tossed the empty into the back seat. She wondered if Harding had found a sugar mama, then figured that was unlikely unless she had very, very low standards. It was possible. Cotton-candy-pink drapes were hanging in the front windows. There were three gnomes and a ceramic bunny in the front yard, all dressed in ill-sized pink jackets, which seemed incongruous with Harding's betting sheet and nudie pics from BackDoorMan.com.

Considering Harding had cashed in his chips both literally and figuratively, Faith found it odd that he'd chosen the Mesa to live out his dying days. Further, it was odd that the Mesa was allowing him to do so. The posted $1,200-a-month homeowners' association fee seemed well out of reach for a man who had bought out his pension for pennies on the dollar.

Then again, Harding had known he wasn't going to live long enough to take the full benefit, so maybe he was smarter than she was giving him credit for. Better to die in the Mesa Arms than some government-owned toilet of a nursing home.

Was it irony or just shitty luck that he'd ended up croaking in an abandoned nightclub with a doorknob stuck in his neck?

Not just any nightclub. Marcus Rippy's club.

She wasn't ignoring the timing of Harding's good luck so much as mulling it around inside her head. Marcus Rippy had been accused of rape seven months ago. Harding had hit paydirt approximately one month later. Then there was Angie Polaski caught in the middle. Had she been sent to the club to take out Harding, or had Harding been sent there to take her out?

Faith couldn't yet add it up, but she knew the math was there.

She fished around in the back seat for the bottle of water her mother had insisted she take with her this morning. It had been baking in the car since 6:30. The warm liquid slid down her throat like cooking oil, but the city was under a code black smog alert and she couldn't afford to get dehydrated.

Her time hadn't just been wasted in strip clubs and liquor stores. She had spent a good hour walking up and down the Mesa Arms knocking on doors that were never answered, peering through windows that showed well-appointed, otherwise empty homes. The sign outside the property manager's office said that they would be back at two, which had already come and gone.

The heat-resistant tennis players had shown up ten minutes ago. Faith was headed toward the courts when a wave of dizziness had sent her back to the car. She had tested her blood sugar under the roar of the Mini's air conditioning because Sara's lecture about badly managed diabetes had hit home.

Poor Sara.

'Okay,' Faith mumbled, psyching herself up for a return to the heat. She cut the engine. Before she could open the door, her phone chirped. She turned the engine back on so she could sit in the air conditioning. 'Mitchell.'

Amanda said, 'Will found a Jane Doe in the office building across the street. Junkie. Homeless. OD'd on a giant bag full of blow. Looks like it was on purpose. Her nose and throat collapsed. She's at Grady. Surgery should be two hours. Do what you can at Harding's, then go sit on her. I'd bet my eyeteeth she saw something.'

Faith silently repeated everything back in her head so that she could make sense of all the information. 'Do we know why she wanted to kill herself?'

'She's a junkie,' Amanda said, as if that was as good an explanation as any. 'I got your text with Harding's address. The search warrant is being faxed to the property manager.'

'No one's there. I called the emergency number, I knocked on doors. Not a lot of people seem to be home, which is weird, because it's some kind of retirement community. It's actually really nice. Nicer than Harding could afford, I would guess.'

'It's owned by a shell company. We're trying to trace it back, but we know Kilpatrick owns a lot of expensive real estate that he lets out well below market value.'

'Smart.' Faith had to hand it to Marcus Rippy's fixer. The guy knew how to squirm his way out of a legally binding financial entanglement. She told Amanda, 'Not a bad way to hide some money. Harding lives in old people Shangri-La for a nominal sum, Kilpatrick keeps him off the official payroll.'

'Incidentally, Harding bought the car brand new six months ago. Paid cash.'

'Harding did a lot of new things with money six months ago.'

'Tell me you have a lead.'

'Not yet.' Faith hedged her words so they didn't give false hope. 'I mean, I don't know what I have other than a feeling that something isn't adding up.'

Amanda sighed, but to her credit she never faulted them for listening to their instincts. 'Collier heard back from the hospitals. All the stabbing victims are accounted for. Two domestics. One bar fight. Another was self-inflicted, said the knife slipped into her side while she was cooking.'

Faith couldn't muster any surprise over the number of unrelated stabbings. She had worked this job too long. 'I should have Harding's bank accounts and phone records within the hour. I'll start going through everything as soon as it hits my email. Meanwhile, I guess I can interrupt the tennis players. So far, they're the only people I've seen.'

'Angie's blood is all over the crime scene.'

Faith bit her lip. This just kept getting worse. 'How did Will take the news?'

'He didn't hear it. And he won't. Hold on.' The phone clicked as Amanda took another call.

Faith picked at the stitching on the steering wheel. She thought about Will, the devastated look on his face when Charlie said the gun was registered to Angie. The only thing worse than his expression was Sara's. Amanda had sent them all away to give Will and Sara some privacy, but there had been a long line to sign out of the crime scene at the front door and Faith had managed to catch the gist of their discussion.

Sara was a better woman than Faith. If Faith had found out that her lover's ex was rifling through her things—not just rifling, but stealing—Faith would've burned down his fucking house.

'Faith?' Amanda had clicked back onto the line. 'Have you heard from Will?'

'Yeah, we had a long conversation about his feelings while he braided my hair.'

'I'm not in the mood for your humor.' Amanda had let an uncharacteristic edge of concern enter her tone. Will's weird, *Flowers-in-the-Attic-y* relationship with Angie paled in comparison to the dysfunctional freak show he had with Amanda. She was the closest thing he'd ever had to a mother, if you were constantly afraid that your mother would smother you in your sleep.

Amanda said, 'Will left after he found the Jane Doe. Just disappeared. I have no idea where he is. He's not at home. He's not answering his phones.'

Faith knew he didn't have a car at the scene. 'Did he get a ride from Sara?'

'She was already gone when the Jane Doe was found.'

'I suppose that's one small blessing.'

'Yes, well, I'm sure he's working on a new way to screw that up.'

Unfortunately, Faith was equally certain. 'Do you think Angie's dead?'

'We can only hope.' Amanda sounded like she meant it. 'I sent Collier to help you search Harding's place.'

'I don't need his help.'

'I don't care. Hold on again.' Amanda's voice was muffled as she barked an order to an unseen underling. She told Faith, 'I've managed to force a meeting with Kip Kilpatrick's team at four o'clock. Get Collier started at Harding's, then head over to the hospital. I don't want you spending too much time with him.'

Faith felt her hackles rise. 'What does that mean?'

'It means he's your type.'

Faith was too stunned to laugh. 'Does he drive a sixty-thousand-dollar truck and live in his mother's trailer?'

Amanda chuckled. The phone clicked again. She had hung up.

Faith stared at the phone. There was not much to recommend having your godmother as your boss. Actually, there was a lot that advised against it.

She set the alarm on her phone to go off in an hour. In her experience, the surgeons at Grady were always faster than they predicted, and Faith wanted to be standing by Jane Doe's bed when she finally came round. You only got one chance to surprise a witness, and considering how close this case cut to home, Faith wasn't going to blow it.

She put her hand on the car key but didn't turn off the engine. The air conditioning was too precious to cut a second too short. She looked at the tennis court, which, un-mesa-like, was over a hill and up several steps. She looked at Harding's front door, which was considerably closer. There was a fake-looking rock in the low-maintenance yard that likely contained a spare key. The search warrant was probably sitting in the fax machine inside the manager's office. She could go ahead and get started.

Faith was getting out of her car when Collier pulled up in a black Dodge Charger. Aerosmith leaked out of the closed windows. There was a figurine of a grass-skirted, half-naked Hawaiian girl stuck to the dashboard. His wheels skidded across the asphalt as he braked, threw the gear into reverse, and backed into the space beside Faith's Mini.

He gave her the once-over as he got out of the Charger, the same as he had this morning. He seemed appreciative, even though she was wearing her GBI regs—dark blue shirt, khakis and a thigh holster because the uniform was unflattering enough without adding two inches of Glock on her hip.

'What's that?' She pointed to the two round Band-Aids wrapped around the top of his right ear. Blood had dried into the crevices.

'Cut myself shaving.'

'With a machete?'

'My Epilady broke.' He glanced into the back of Faith's car, taking in the baby seat and scattered Cheerios.

She laid it all out in the open. 'I have a one-year-old and a twenty-year-old.'

'Uh, yeah. You were APD for fifteen years before you jumped ship. Never married. Graduated from Tech. Your mom was on the job. Your dad was an insurance agent, rest in peace. You live two streets over from your mom in a house your grandmother left you, which is how you can live in a nice neighborhood on a state salary.' He pushed up his sunglasses. 'Come on, Mitchell. You know cops gossip like bitchy little girls. I already know everything about you.'

Faith started up the sidewalk.

'I'm the second oldest of nine myself.'

'Jesus,' Faith muttered, thinking of his poor mother.

'Dad's a retired cop. Two brothers are with APD, another two are with Fulton County, another is in McDonough. I've got a sister who's a fireman but we don't talk about her.'

Faith picked up the fake rock, only to find that it was a real rock.

'Come on, Mitchell.' Collier was like a puppy nipping at her heels. 'I know you checked me out. What'd your mom say?'

Faith made an educated guess. 'That you're cocky and prone to mistakes.'

He grinned. 'I knew she'd remember me.'

Faith thought of something. 'Where did you take Will?'

He stopped grinning. 'What's that?'

'Will disappeared after he found the Jane Doe in the office building. Where did you take him?'

'That's some class-A detective work there, partner. But he didn't find her. Well, he did, but I was there too. So you could say we both found her.'

'I'm not your partner.' Faith knelt down and studied the rocks. All of them looked fake. 'Are you going to answer me?'

'I took him to his house.' Collier shoved his hands into his pockets. 'Don't ask me why, 'cause I can't tell you. My sister says I should'a been the fireman 'cause I'm the dumbass who runs into the burning building instead of running away from it.'

'Do you know why the Jane Doe tried to kill herself?'

He shrugged. 'She's a junkie.'

Faith picked up a suspiciously dull rock. This one was a real fake. She slid back the plastic cover, expecting to find the house key.

Empty.

Collier asked, 'Did your mom tell you I had a wrestling accident in high school?' He was leaning against the door jamb, his arms crossed. 'Testicular torsion.'

Faith tossed the empty rock back into the yard.

'Tragedy, really.' He ran his fingers through his hair as he squinted into the distance. 'I'll never be able to have kids.' He winked at her, because that was obviously in the script. 'Hasn't stopped me from trying.'

'Hello?' A hippy-looking woman in flip-flops and a belted yellow shirt dress was walking up the sidewalk. Her long gray hair was loose around her shoulders. She held a stack of papers in one hand and wore a loaded springy keychain on her wrist. 'Are you the police lady who called?'

'Yes, ma'am.' Faith pulled her ID out of her pocket. 'I'm Special Agent Faith Mitchell. This is—'

'Oh, I don't need to see that, hon. You've both got POLICE written on the back of your shirts.'

Faith put away her ID, skipping the lecture about how you could put POLICE on the back of anything these days.

The woman said, 'Can't say I'm surprised something bad happened to ol' Dale. He wasn't one for making friends.' Her shoes flip-flopped across the front walk. She banged her fist on Harding's door. The keys on the springy ring clattered around her wrist. 'Hello?' She banged again. 'Hello?'

Faith asked, 'Was he living with someone?'

'No. Sorry, force of habit. I do a lot of wellness checks, and I never enter a house without knocking.' She extended her hand. 'I'm Violet Nelson, by the way. The property manager. Sorry I was out so long. I got hung up at the library.'

'Were you involved in leasing this place to Harding?'

'That would be the responsibility of the owners, and the documents list them as a corporation based in Delaware, I'm assuming for the tax breaks.' She searched her keyring, checking the neat color-coded labels. 'Ugh, I need my glasses. Do either of you . . . ?'

Faith looked at Collier, because he was a hell of a lot closer to needing reading glasses than she was.

He gave one of his squinty smiles. 'I'm younger than I look.'

'It'll hit you soon enough. Both of you.' Violet laughed, but it wasn't funny. She kept going through the keys. There were at least fifty of them. Faith didn't offer to help, because Violet struck her as prone to idle chatter. 'I'll unlock this door and y'all can take as long as you want. Just slip the keys back through the slot in my office door when you leave.'

Faith exchanged another look with Collier, because this wasn't the usual attitude of a property manager. Then again, most of the property managers they dealt with worked behind cages or bullet-proof glass.

Faith said, 'I knocked on some of the neighbors' doors. Doesn't seem like anybody is home today.'

'It's busier on the weekends.' Violet tried to push a key into the lock. 'No one really retires anymore. They've all got part-time jobs. Some of the luckier ones volunteer. Come four o'clock, you'll find most of us down at the club house for cocktail hour.'

Faith would pass out if she had a drink at four in the afternoon. She asked the woman, 'Did you know Dale Harding?'

'I knew him well enough.' Violet didn't seem happy about it. 'He was a pain in my posterior, let me tell you.'

Faith rolled her hand, letting the woman know she should do just that.

'Let's just say that he wasn't the cleanest-living person.'

Collier guessed, 'Women? Booze?'

'Trash,' she said, then caught herself. 'Not like white trash. Like real trash—things that should be thrown away but aren't. I wouldn't call him a hoarder. It's more like he was just too lazy to walk to the trashcan. There were complaints about odors from Barbara. That's the gal next door. Spoiled food, she said, the stink of it just wafting through the walls to her side of the house. I smelled it myself. Disgusting. I've written about ten letters to the company in Delaware, with no luck. We've been talking to the HOA lawyers for months about what to do.'

'That's horrible,' Faith said, thinking that it never occurred to normal people that the smell of spoiled food was remarkably similar to the odor from a decaying body. 'What else?'

'They were constantly bickering.' Violet tried another key. 'Barb and Dale. Well, Dale and everybody, but especially Barb. They just rubbed each other the wrong way.' She jammed in another key, with no success. 'I had to step in a few times to help turn down the heat. I hate to speak ill of the dead, but Dale was . . .' She struggled for the word.

'An asshole?' Faith suggested, because that seemed to be the word of consensus.

'Yes, an asshole,' Violet agreed. 'So if this was like *Midsomer Murders* and you were asking if Dale had any enemies, the answer is that he went out of his way to make enemies.' She pointed to the windows. 'Those hideous curtains are a perfect example. The bylaws clearly state everyone should have white window coverings. When I sent him a letter about the pink curtains, he sent back a note on fake stationery from a fake law firm saying that I was discriminating against him because he's a homosexual.' She rolled her eyes. 'As if a gay man of that age would buy polyester curtains.'

Faith watched her try another key. She was going through the entire ring. 'What about Barb, the next-door neighbor? You said it got heated?'

'He taunted her. For no reason. Just picked and picked and picked.'

'For instance?'

Violet waved toward the front yard. 'These were her gnomes, and her grandson gave her that rabbit. We all knew that. She dressed them all in matching seasonal jackets. Red on Valentine's Day. Plaid for Armistice Day.' She shrugged. 'To each her own. But one day Barb comes to me and says the strangest thing has happened. All the gnomes and the rabbit are gone from her yard. We chalked it up to kids. Some of the grandchildren around here are a bunch of juvenile delinquents. Blood will out, as they say. But then two days later, Dale puts out the gnomes and the rabbit in his front yard and they're wearing pink jackets. And not even jackets that fit.' She tried another key. 'Actually, there were four gnomes, but he'd painted one of them in blackface, which is expressly forbidden in the homeowners' bylaws.' She lowered her voice, explaining, 'If we didn't have the rule, this whole place would be lit up with lawn jockeys.'

So much for Shangri-La. 'Did Harding have any regular visitors?'

'Nary a one that I ever saw.'

Collier asked, 'Did he keep a schedule?'

'He was home more often than not, which was extremely annoying, let me tell you. Gave him time to mess with people. As lazy as he was, he'd walk two streets over to yell at a grandkid having too much fun in the pool.'

'When did he move in?'

Violet tried another key. 'Six months ago, maybe? I've got the paperwork somewhere. Give me your email and I'll scan it to you. He's past due on his HOA fees.' She finally found the correct key. 'That's homeowners'—'

Collier stopped her hand on the doorknob.

Faith had her Glock in her hands before she completely processed what was happening.

There was a noise inside the house.

Rustling, like someone was trying to be quiet.

Faith looked at the fake rock. There was no key. Why have a fake rock when you didn't have a key?

Unless someone had already used the key to get inside.

Collier put his finger to his lips before Violet could ask for an explanation. He indicated for her to move back, then back some more, until she was standing on the other side of his car.

The noise came again. Louder this time.

Collier took out his phone and whispered a call-in for backup, then he motioned for Faith to take the lead.

Which meant that fifty years of feminism would probably end up getting Faith gut-shot.

She tapped her finger on the side of her Glock, just above the trigger, which is where they were trained to keep their finger until they had made the decision to shoot. She thought about her bulletproof vest in the car. The baby seat for her precious daughter. The bottle of water her thoughtful mother had given her this morning. The photo of her beautiful son on her phone.

Then she raised her foot and kicked in the door.

'Police!' Faith yelled, letting the word explode from her mouth.

She swiveled around, scanning the room. Kitchen. Table. Couch. Chairs. Clutter. Chaos. All of her senses had turned off but one. Her vision tunneled onto doorways and windows, searching for hands holding weapons. Collier checked the coat closet. Empty. He pressed his back against hers. He tapped her leg. They moved forward in unison, both crouched low, both swiveling their heads like gun turrets.

She remembered the Mesa Arms website. Harding lived in the Tahoe. Open concept. Two bedroom. One bathroom.

Doorway.

A separate powder room for your guests!

Doorway.

A well-appointed laundry room with optional storage cabinets!

Corner.

Faith put herself at an angle, letting the corner serve as a visual block to anyone standing in the hallway with a shotgun. If she couldn't see them, they couldn't see her. She had her weapon out in front of her, feet wide apart. Without any conscious thought, her finger slipped from the side of the gun and went to the trigger.

She forced herself to put her finger back along the barrel, to buy herself that extra second of hesitation in case it was a kid or an elderly deaf person standing at the end of the hall.

Now or never.

Slowly, a centimeter at a time, she rolled the upper part of her body to the side and peered around the corner.

Empty.

Faith took the lead down the hallway.

Doorway.

A central bathroom with walk-in shower and comfort seat toilet!

Closed doors.

Light-filled main-level bedrooms for you and your guests!

The bedrooms were on opposite sides of the hall, each taking up one side of the rear portion of the house.

Faith let Collier take the room on the right. Again she stood at an angle, covering him and the other closed door so his back would be protected when he breached the room. With an almost painful slowness, he reached down and turned the knob. The door opened. He slammed it back in case anyone was standing behind it. Pink curtains on a bay window to the backyard. A blow-up mattress on the floor. An open curtain where the closet door should've been.

Clear.

In the hall, Collier took position opposite the left bedroom and gave her the nod.

Faith kicked open the door so hard that the knob stuck into the drywall. More windows. More pink curtains. Another mattress on the floor, this one with a boxspring, dirty sheets. Cardboard box for a bedside table. Dangling cords. A lamp. The closet had a door and the door had a keyed deadbolt.

Faith made herself breathe, because she had been holding her breath so long that she was going to pass out. Her lungs would only half fill. Her heart was a stopwatch. Sweat dripped from her hands as she forced her grip on the Glock to loosen so the recoil wouldn't break her wrist if she had to shoot.

Collier stood with his back to the wall, covering the closet. She made herself move forward, blocking out the movie that kept replaying in her head: the closet door opens, a shotgun comes out, her chest is shredded to pieces.

With extreme deliberateness, Faith peeled her left hand away from her Glock. The bones inside her fingers felt like they were rattling together. Her shoulder pinched as she lowered her arm. She reached toward the egg-shaped doorknob. Her skin registered the cold metal. The joints in her wrist started the slow grind of rotating her hand.

Locked.

Faith opened her mouth. She inhaled.

Spacious walk-in master closet!

The hinges were on the outside. The door couldn't be kicked in.

She glanced back at Collier. He was still tensed, but he was facing away from her, toward the hallway. His chest heaved with each shallow breath. His Glock was pointed up at the ceiling.

The attic.

Optional storage for your precious keepsakes!

In the hall, a string dangled down from a set of folding attic stairs.

Faith started shaking her head. There was no way she was going up into that attic with just one person covering her.

A noise.

The scraping sound, this time heavier, like someone was inching across the attic.

Collier entered the hallway, knees still bent in a low crouch. Faith did the same, stopping in the doorway. He looked at her. She nodded, though every inch of her body was telling her that this was going to end badly. Collier reached up. He grabbed the string hanging from the stairs. The springs squealed so loudly that Faith's heart nearly detonated. Collier unfolded the steps with one hand, his Glock still pointing up with the other.

Both of them stood completely still, waiting for the other to move.

This wasn't about being scared. They were both terrified in equal measure. This was about trusting someone to have your back while you prairie-dogged your head into an open firing range.

Faith muttered a silent curse and took out her phone. Better to have her hand shot off than her face. She swiped through to the video camera and turned on the flash so that forensics would have a clear recording that explained the two dead cops in the hallway.

She forced her brain to unfreeze the muscles in her leg so that she could climb the stairs. Her foot was an inch off the ground when Collier snatched the phone out of her hand. He shot her a look like she was the crazy one. He planted his black sneaker on the first rung of the stairs. The springs groaned under his weight. He stepped up to the second rung.

Faith saw the movie in her head again, this time with Collier: a shotgun comes out, his chest is shredded to pieces.

Collier stopped on the second rung. Both of his hands were at chest level, one with his Glock, the other with her phone. He was listening for the sound, trying to gauge which direction it had come from, because he would only have one chance shining the phone's light into the dark attic space. Faith couldn't help him locate the direction. All she heard was blood rushing through her ears. She opened her mouth for more air. Her tongue felt like cotton. She could taste her own fear, sour, like rotted meat and sweat and acid.

Collier looked back for her go-ahead. She nodded. They both stared into the black expanse of the attic. His shoulders slumped. His head turtled down his neck. He raised his hand, using the phone as a digital periscope. They both looked at the screen. An image flashed up.

Faith felt her stomach punch into her chest.

Collier sighed out a low 'Fu-u-uck.'

A rat the size of a house cat stared back from the phone, its beady eyes glowing red in the light. It was sitting on its haunches. Its jaw was working as it chewed. Something was in its hands, which was even more horrific, because Faith didn't want to think about a rat having hands that could grab something.

Collier turned the phone in a three-sixty around the attic before holstering his Glock. He used his free hand to zoom in on the rat, then past it. There were two file boxes up against the shared wall of the duplex. They were resting precariously on separate joists because the attic floor didn't extend that far. An opened package of rotting ground beef was closer to the stairs. White maggots moved across the surface like waves breaking in the ocean. Flies buzzed. While they were watching, the rat's hands reached out and pulled the tray a few inches away from the stairs. The sliding sound felt like it was happening inside of Faith's skull.

The rat eyed them carefully as it pried away a chunk of meat with its thin, angular fingers. It drew the rotted meat back to its chest, took a couple of hops away, then bent down its head and stared at them as it chewed.

'Okay.' Collier stepped back down the stairs. He handed Faith the phone. 'I'm going to go throw up now.'

She thought he was kidding, because he seemed fine, but then two seconds later he was in the bathroom horking out the lining of his stomach.

Faith called out, 'Be sure to cancel backup.'

Collier retched in the affirmative.

She ran her hand along the dusty top of the closet door jamb. No key. She took a pen out of a pocket in her cargo pants and poked around the box Harding had used as a bedside table. She checked above the windowsills and the hall door. No key.

Collier sounded like he was finished in the bathroom, but then he gagged so loudly that her ears ached. Faith shivered, not because of the sound but because the attic stairs were still open. She could picture the rat lumbering its way down, tiny thumbless hands holding on to the thin handrail. She put her back to the wall as she slid past the open stairs. She waited until she was safely in the living room to play back the video on her phone.

The rat was a grayish blue with round ears and a thick, dirty white tail the color of the string on a tampon. The creature stared at her through the screen, mouth working. There was no sound, but she swore she heard lips smacking. A streak of blood trailed behind the tray where the rat had been pulling the meat away from the stairs and toward something. Probably a giant nest.

Her whole body shuddered at the thought.

Faith hit 'play' again. She remembered a pop-up book someone had given her daughter at Christmas. Emma was clearly terrified of the zillion-eyed housefly that popped out of the centerfold, but she couldn't stop herself from opening the book and screaming. Faith felt the same way when she watched the video again. She was disgusted, but she couldn't look away.

The toilet flushed. Collier wiped his mouth with the back of his hand as he joined her in the living room. 'So,' he said, brushing a smattering of vomit off his shirt. 'Rat burglar alarm?'

Faith made herself look away from her phone. The only words that came to mind were the ones she had been hearing about Dale Harding all day. 'What an asshole.'

'Could you tell if those file boxes were labeled?'

Faith held out the phone so he could check for himself.

'Uh-uh.' He held up his finger, like he needed a moment to decide. 'Okay, it passed.'

'You sure?' His face was the color of an envelope.

'No.' He walked over to the kitchen sink and turned on the faucet. He had to move a stack of dishes so he could stick his head under the tap. He gurgled, then spat into the sink, which was disgusting but Faith had a feeling that Harding had done worse things in that sink.

'Officers?'

Faith had forgotten about Violet.

'Good Lord, it smells like ammonia and trash in here.' The woman stood just outside the doorway. She pinched her nose closed. 'Is everything all right?'

'There's a rat up there,' Collier said. 'Big one. Maybe pregnant.'

'Is he gray with white ears?'

Faith showed her the paused video on her phone.

'I'll be damned.' Violet shook her head. 'Barb's grandson brought his rat over last weekend. He swore up and down that he put the top back on the cage. They looked everywhere for that stupid thing.'

'I'm pretty sure this isn't a pet.' Collier waved away a fly. 'I mean, it's huge. Like, unnatural.'

Violet offered, 'I can show you the MISSING poster Barb posted on the message board.'

Collier clamped his mouth shut and shook his head.

Faith thought about the package of ground beef near the attic stairs. 'Was the rat inside Barb's house when it went missing?'

'No. The kid put the cage on Barb's screened porch for about half an hour. Apparently they like fresh air. He came back and the top was pushed up and the rat was gone.' Violet frowned as she took in the room. 'I'm sure Mr Nimh was more comfortable in this squalor.'

Faith asked, 'Is Barb home much?'

'Now that you say that, she normally is. She'll be devastated she missed all this action. Bit of a busybody.'

Faith loved busybodies. She handed Violet her business card. 'Could you have Barb call me? I'd just like a general idea of Harding.'

'I'm not sure she can tell you much beyond what a bully he was.'

'You'd be surprised what people can remember.'

Violet tucked the card into her bra strap. 'As I said before, just slip the key back through the mail slot in my office door when you're finished.'

Faith listened to her flip-flop her way down the sidewalk.

'A pet.' Collier waved away another fly.

'That explains why it wasn't scared of us.'

'I still want it to die. Like, immediately. With fire.'

'Look for a key,' she told him. 'We need to get into that closet.'

'We need to call animal control,' he countered. 'Dude kept a rat in his attic. No telling what's in that closet.'

Faith wasn't going to wait for animal control. She took in the filthy living room and kitchen, wondering where somebody like Harding would hide a key. Nothing jumped out except an overwhelming sense of disgust. *Squalor* was a word that seemed custom-made for the way Harding lived. There were Styrofoam plates and cups all over the open-concept living/dining/kitchen area. The moist-looking brown velvet couch and scarred coffee table were overflowing with abandoned KFC takeout bowls. Gnawed chicken bones with green mold, cups of Coke with thick skins on the surface, browned sporks where he hadn't gotten off all the mashed potatoes.

Then there was the smell, which suddenly hit her like a hammer to the bridge of her nose. Not just ammonia, but rot, likely from Dale Harding's bad habits, if Sara's assessment of his final days proved to be correct. Faith hadn't noticed the stench when they broke down the front door. Adrenaline had a way of focusing your priorities, and her main priority had been not to get killed. Now that her terror had abated, her other senses had returned, and they were immediately assaulted by the stink.

And flies, because there were at least two dozen of them taking advantage of all the trash.

Faith said, 'In this heat, maggots can hatch in eight to twenty hours. It takes about three to five days for them to pupate.'

Collier guffawed. 'Sorry, *pupate* is a funny word.'

'I'm saying that it tracks that the meat was put in the attic this weekend, probably to feed the rat. Or keep him up there.' Faith forced open one of the windows to help dissipate the smell. Then she pushed out the screen to take care of the flies.

Collier belched loudly, then asked, 'You got any breath mints?'

'Nope.'

Faith turned away from Collier. She thought about the breath mints in her car, and how nice it would be to go outside and take a five-minute break from Harding's greasy, disgusting house. Her sense of smell had definitely returned. The rancid odor was biting into the back of her mouth and nose. She would've bet her life savings that the rotting meat in the attic was nothing compared to what was underneath the piles of wet-looking newspapers and magazines Harding had scattered around the floor. Violet was right. The trash was born of sheer laziness. If Harding had finished eating a bowl of macaroni and cheese when he came through the front door, he just dropped the bowl where he was standing and moved on.

'It's weird, right?' Collier was watching her. 'The way freaking out takes away your sense of smell?'

'How can you not smell this?' Faith opened another window. She wasn't going to bond with this jackass. 'Where's the TV?'

Collier ran his finger along a low console table, separating the dust like the Red Sea. 'There was a TV here, but it's gone. Looks like it was big.'

'No computer.' Faith opened a drawer in the table beside the couch. She used her pen to poke around the takeout menus. 'No iPad. No laptop.' She opened another drawer. More crap. No key to open the closet.

Collier said, 'Harding strikes me as a paperwork kind of guy.'

Faith coughed as a new smell infiltrated her nostrils. She pushed open another window. 'There were charging cables beside the bed in the master.'

'I'm detecting that was for his phones.' Collier had his arms crossed again. He stood with his feet wide apart, probably because he was used to carrying fifty pounds of equipment around his hips during his patrol days. He said, 'So, this thing you've got going on with Trent. Are you his work wife, or do you got something else on the side?'

Faith watched an Atlanta police cruiser pull up behind her Mini. They had probably been en route when Collier canceled the call for backup and decided to come check it out anyway. The two men looked young and eager. Their necks craned as they stared at the house. The driver rolled down his window.

Faith waved them off, calling out the window, 'We're fine.'

The driver put the gear in park anyway.

'Lemons into lemonade,' Collier said. 'We'll send one of the unis into the attic for the boxes, don't mention the rat, and see what happens.'

'Two weeks of rabies shots is what happens.' Which she knew was exactly what Dale Harding was hoping for when he shoved the boxes up into the attic with the packet of ground beef and some weird kid's stolen rat. Just one more way for the guy to wipe his ass on the toilet paper of his life. Harding knew that he was weeks away from death, whether by someone else's hand or his own shitty life choices. He also knew that someone would have to empty his house, and that they would likely get a face full of rat in the process.

Faith walked out the front door. The sun cut open her eyeballs. She wasn't sure whether she had tears or blood streaming down her face. She didn't care. Harding had been a cop. He knew what you risked when you pulled your gun and busted into a house. And he had set them up anyway.

She held up her hand to block the sun. The unis were standing by their cruiser, heads down, staring at their phones.

She told the driver, 'Give me your tire iron.'

He said, 'My tire iron?'

Faith leaned into the car and popped the trunk. The tire iron was snapped into a kit mounted inside the rear quarter panel. She hefted the weight of the long, heavy metal bar in her hand. It was the single-handle type, L-shaped with a socket on the end to loosen the wheel lugs.

Perfect.

Collier was watching from the window when she went back into the house. Faith grabbed a chair from the cheap dining set and dragged it down the hallway. Collier followed, asking, 'What are you doing?'

'I'm beating this asshole.' She stood on the chair and swung the tire iron into the ceiling. The socket end lodged into the Sheetrock. She shoved the bar in farther, turned it at an angle and pulled down. A chunk of ceiling dropped to the floor. She took another swing with the tire iron. She thought about the Mesa Arms' website, how it promoted its energy-efficient upgrades, like the spray foam in the attic that made it possible to break open the ceiling without getting a face full of pink insulation.

Faith dropped the tire iron, pleased that her guesstimate had worked out. The two file boxes were within arm's reach. All she had to do was fight the flies to get to them.

'Hey, lady,' one of the unis called from the hall. 'You know there's some stairs right here.'

'There's a rat,' Collier told him. 'Like, Godzilla's brother.'

'You mean Rodan?'

'Chibi, man. Rodan was a surrogate. Chibi was blood.'

'Goro,' Faith said, because she had spent three years of Saturdays watching Godzilla movies when Jeremy went through a phase. 'Collier, help me with these boxes.'

'She's right,' Collier said. 'It definitely looked like Gorosaurus.' He bared his teeth and made his hands into claws. 'Like it was out for blood.'

Faith let the first box drop on his head.

Annoyingly, Collier still managed to catch it. He put the box on the floor and waited for her to pass down the second one.

The uni said, 'You need us for anything else, man?'

Collier shook his head. 'I'm good, bro.'

'The closet,' Faith reminded him.

'Oh, right.' Collier motioned for them to follow him into the other room. Faith took a precarious step down with the heavy second box in her hands. She put it on the floor beside the first. From the other room she heard a discussion about the best way to pull pins from the hinges, like they had never seen a hammer and a flat-head screwdriver before.

Faith clapped dust from her arms and ran her fingers through her hair to get rid of the grit. The rotting meat smell was so pungent that she had to open the bedroom windows. And push out the screens because the flies were starting to swarm. Ripping down the ceiling probably hadn't been her best idea, but logic tended to go out the window when she was pissed off, and she was really pissed off at Dale Harding.

At the GBI, Faith had investigated her share of bad cops, and the one trait that they all had in common was that they thought they were still good guys. Theft, rape, murder, extortion, racketeering, pimping—it didn't matter. They still thought the crimes they had committed were for the greater good. They were taking care of their families. They were protecting their brothers in blue. They had made a mistake. They would never do it again. It was annoying how they were all the same in their insistence that they were still basically good human beings.

Harding hadn't just embraced his badness. He had forced it on others.

And now she had to go through even more of his crap.

Faith dragged the chair over to the window. She kicked the boxes in the same direction, then she sat down. She tried not to think about why the lid on the first box felt damp, but her mind still conjured up the useful fact that rats leave a trail of urine wherever they go.

She shuddered before digging into the stack of neatly labeled files.

Dale Harding had been a private eye, and the first box contained the sort of glamorous work done by PIs the world over: photos of cheating spouses in cheap motels, photos of cheating spouses in parked cars, photos of cheating spouses in alleyways and roadside gas stations and inside a kids' play house in the backyard.

Harding's record-keeping was meticulous. Receipts for gas and meals and developing photos were stapled to expense reports. Daily logs followed the movements of his targets. He wrote in tiny block lettering and his spelling was exactly what you'd expect from a guy who probably went from high school to the police academy. Not that Faith hadn't done the same, but at least she knew the difference between *you're* and *your*.

Collier stood in the doorway. 'Closet's clear.'

'You probably should've had the bomb squad check it.'

Finally he registered something other than cocky self-assuredness as they both realized that considering Harding, it wasn't exactly a joke.

He said, 'Something was in the closet at some point. There's an impression in the carpet. Round, like a five-gallon bucket.'

Faith stood up so that she could see for herself. The two unis were back on their phones, heads down, thumbs working. She could probably murder Collier with the tire iron right in front of them and they wouldn't notice.

The closet door had been propped up against the wall. Faith used the flashlight app on her phone to examine the inside of the four-by-eight walk-in closet. It was just as Collier had said. In the back corner, a circle impression was imprinted into the brown carpet. She scanned the rest of the closet. The rods had been removed. Wires dangled down where the light fixture should have been. The white walls were scuffed at the bottom. The enclosed space had a lingering odor of raw sewage.

Collier said, 'We see this a lot. Drug mules come up from Mexico with pellets or powder heroin in their stomachs. They shit them out in a bucket, take their money, then head back to Mexico to fill up again.'

'You think a place like this, where they have to specifically ban lawn jockeys in the yards, wouldn't be lighting up nine-one-one if they saw a bunch of Mexicans going in and out of Harding's house?' She told the unis, 'Turn the door around.'

'We gotta boot. Dispatch called.' Neither looked up from their phones as they walked out of the room.

Collier seemed impressed. 'Good guys, right?'

Faith wrapped her hands around the edges of the door. Of course it was solid wood. She tilted it onto its corner and swiveled the door around. She lost her grip at the last minute. The top edge of the door slammed into the wall, leaving a gash. Faith stepped back to look. There were scratch marks low on the wood. She double-checked the hinges, making sure she was looking at the side that faced into the closet.

'The rat?' Collier guessed.

Faith took a photo of the scratches. 'We need to get forensics in here.'

'My guys or your guys?'

'Mine.' Faith sent the photo to Charlie Reed, who would likely be open to a change of scenery after processing Marcus Rippy's nightclub for the last seven hours. She texted him the address and told him to process the closet first thing. She wasn't a scientist, but a five-gallon bucket and a locked closet door with scratches on the back probably meant that someone had been kept inside.

Or it could be more of Harding's bullshit waste of their time.

Collier said, 'The closet door was locked when we got here. Why lock the door when there's nothing in there?'

'Why did Harding do anything?' Faith went back into the other bedroom. She sat down in the chair and started putting the cheating spouse files back into the first box. Collier stood in the doorway again. She told him, 'There's nothing here, at least not the kind of thing you'd hide behind a rat.'

'I don't care what Violet said. That thing looked pregnant.' Collier sat down on the mattress. It made a farting sound. He gave Faith the exact look that she expected him to give. He pushed the lid off the second box. There were no file folders, just a stack of pages with lots of nude photos on top.

Collier took the pictures. He handed Faith the papers.

She thumbed through them quickly. Hospital admittance records. Arrest warrants. Rehab. Rap sheet. They were all for one person. Delilah Jean Palmer, twenty-two years old, current address the Cheshire Motor Inn, which was a known hangout for prostitutes. There was no family listed. From birth, Palmer had been a ward of the state.

She was also a current model for BackDoorMan.com. Palmer's most recent booking photo showed the same woman from the racy pictures Sara had found inside Dale Harding's wallet. Her hair was different in each photo, sometimes platinum blonde, sometimes her natural brown, sometimes purple or pink.

'It's her.' Collier leaned over, his shoulder pressed against Faith's arm. He showed her a larger image of the wallet-sized photos: Delilah Palmer leaning over a kitchen counter, her head turned back toward the camera, mouth open, approximating sexual excitement. He said, 'I'm gonna guess she's not a real blonde. See, I'm a fast learner, Mitchell. You should keep me around.'

Faith knew that the GBI's computer division was already looking into BackDoorMan.com, but she told Collier, 'Why don't you check the website?'

'Good idea.' He took out his phone. With any luck, he would waste the next hour looking at porn so that she could get some work done.

So, basically like every romantic relationship Faith had ever had in her life.

She returned to the documents for a more careful reading. She realized she was holding Delilah Palmer's juvenile records, which was strange, because juvenile records were usually sealed. Palmer's first arrest was at the age of ten for selling OxyContin at John Wesley Dobbs Elementary in east Atlanta. Faith had spent quite some time at Dobbs while helping the state build a RICO case against the Atlanta Public Schools system for widespread cheating on standardized tests. Some of the faculty had hosted a fish and grits sit-down dinner where they erased and changed the answers on students' Scantrons. Meanwhile, 99.5 percent of their struggling student body qualified for free or assisted lunch.

Faith studied Palmer's first booking photo from twelve years ago. The girl's hands were so small that she couldn't hold the reader board straight for the camera. The top of her head didn't reach the first line in the ruler painted on the wall behind her. There were scabs on her face. Her short brown hair was unwashed. She had dark circles under her eyes, either from lack of sleep, lack of food, or lack of belonging.

Delilah would've been an oddity at Dobbs, and not just because she had entered the drug trafficking trade at such an early age. Last month, when Faith was preparing documents for the RICO trial, she had to explain to the district attorney that she hadn't made a mistake in her charts. In 2012, Dobbs did not have a 5 percent white student body. They had a total of five white students. Had the demographics been reversed, there was no way the city would've allowed that level of corruption to go unchecked for so long.

Faith flipped to Delilah's next arrest. More Oxy sales at age twelve and then again at fifteen. By sixteen, Delilah had dropped out of school and was slinging heroin, which was what happened when you couldn't afford Oxy anymore. A single 80 milligram, pill could run sixty to one hundred dollars, depending on the market. The same money for a bag of heroin could keep you high for days.

She flipped ahead to the charging sheets. Parole. Diversion treatment. More parole. Rehab.

Despite her criminal history, Delilah Palmer had never spent more than a night in jail.

Her first prostitution arrest came at the end of her sixteenth year. There were four more arrests for solicitation, two more for selling pot and heroin respectively, all accompanied by a free one-night accommodation in the Fulton County jail.

Faith scanned the names of the arresting officers. Some of them were familiar. Most of them were from zone six, which made sense because criminals were like everybody else. They tended to stay in their own neighborhoods.

Dale Harding had also worked in zone six. He had obviously kept an eye on Delilah Palmer for most of her life. Reading between the lines, Faith guessed that he'd called in every favor he had to keep the girl from doing serious time.

Collier said, 'You gonna share or do I have to guess?'

'You smell like vomit.'

'I just threw up. Didn't you hear me in the bathroom? It, like, echoed.'

She handed him Delilah Palmer's rap sheet. 'Two bedrooms, two beds. Someone was staying here with Harding.'

'You think it was this Palmer chick?' He frowned. 'She ain't much, but she could do better than Harding.'

Faith thought about the locked closet, the bucket, the sewage smell. Harding could've been doing his own rehab. Cold turkey in a closet was a hell of a lot cheaper than fifteen grand for in-patient treatment. Again. That might better explain the squalor. This place certainly looked like a junkie was living here.

'Didja see over there?' Collier nodded toward a retainer on the floor. 'My sisters all wore those after they got their braces off. Like, not the same retainer, different ones, but they were all small, just like that one. Meaning it's sized like what a girl would wear in her mouth.'

Faith couldn't understand why he used so many words to say just one thing. 'What about the website?'

'Nothing popped out.' He laughed. 'Pun intended. I'm more of a front-door man myself. Especially the knockers.'

Faith felt the strain of her eyes rolling.

'You know what, Mitchell? When I first met you, I figured we'd end up in a bedroom looking at porn.'

Faith started to stand.

'Hold on.' He grabbed a stack of photographs from the box. 'Lookit these. Delilah's been modeling for a while. The BackDoorMan.com ones, I'd say they started when she was around sixteen. The earlier ones don't have a website or identifying marks, but I'd put her closer to twelve, maybe thirteen.'

Faith put the photos side by side with the mugshots from Delilah's various arrests. Collier's estimate was off by a few years. Faith could pin down the age back to the girl's first arrest at ten years old. The illicit image was heartbreaking. Delilah was dressed in lace panties and a bra that must have been clipped in the back so it wouldn't slide down to her feet. She didn't have a waist yet, or curves, or anything but baby fat that the heroin would eventually wear away. Faith looked at her dull, lifeless eyes. Everything about the girl reeked of abandon.

Why was Harding, who by all accounts didn't give a shit about anyone or anything, so interested in this abandoned girl? What did she mean to him?

Collier asked, 'What's next, Kemosabe?'

'I'll be right back.' Faith stood up. She went back into the kitchen. Again Collier followed her. He was like a kid, always underfoot. She longed for Will's quiet self-containment. 'We can be apart for longer than two seconds.'

'Then how will I know what you're up to?'

She opened the freezer door. Ice cream and alcohol filled the shelves, but there was also a quart-sized Ziploc bag with a stack of papers shoved into the back. Freezer burn had melded it to a box of fish fingers. Faith had to hit the box on the side of the fridge to break away the bag.

People with chronic or end-stage diseases were told to leave valuable documents like medical directives in their freezer so that paramedics could easily find them. As horrible a man as Harding was, he had managed to follow the guideline. Except his directive explicitly stated that all possible measures should be taken to preserve his life.

'Je-sus,' Collier said, because of course he was reading over Faith's shoulder. 'The guy's got a death warrant, but he wants the paramedics to keep him alive for as long as possible?'

'This was filled out two years ago. Maybe he forgot about it.' Faith found the contact information on the second page.

Next of kin: Delilah Jean Palmer.

Relationship: daughter.

'She was his kid,' Collier said, because he had forgotten that Faith had eyes in her head. 'Her juvie rap sheet listed her as an orphan.'

There were three phone numbers beside Delilah's name, two of which had lines drawn through them. All of them were in different shades of ink. Faith used Harding's landline and dialed the most recent number. It went straight into a pre-recorded message from the phone company informing Faith that the number had been disconnected.

She tried the other two numbers just to be sure.

Disconnected.

Collier took out his cell phone. 'My turn to work some magic?'

'Help yourself.'

Collier started to follow her back to the bedroom, but she put her hand out to stop him. 'We don't have to do everything together.'

'What if the rat comes back? With its babies?'

'Scream really loud.'

She headed down the hallway again, glancing up the attic stairs because the rat was still up there, possibly giving birth to triplets, because that was the kind of day she was having. Thank God Faith had made more holes in the ceiling in case the thing decided it wanted to expand its territory.

She sat down in the chair and made herself look at the photos of Delilah again.

Putting aside how disgusting it was that a father kept pictures of his naked daughter, age twelve, bending over a stick riding horse, there was something off about the girl. Faith couldn't articulate what made the photos different from the hundreds of similar photos she had seen throughout her law enforcement career, but it was there.

Exploitation had a common theme: misery. Delilah's eyes were glassy, likely from the heroin that had either been given or withheld so that she would pose for the camera. Her thighs were red where someone had been rough with her. A thin powdering of make-up barely concealed the bruising around her neck. There was lipstick on her teeth. None of this was new or particularly surprising.

It was that same feeling Faith had been having all day: something wasn't adding up.

Faith hated when things didn't add up.

'It's weird that they're pictures, right?' Collier was hovering in the doorway again.

Faith said, 'You mean like some fathers keep school pictures of their kids, only Harding kept naked photos?'

'No, I mean why doesn't he have videos? Porn is the sole reason for the internet. It ruined the nudie pic industry. Even *Playboy* gave up the ghost.'

'You're asking why Harding was looking at naked pictures of his daughter instead of naked videos?'

'Basically. Shit.' He clapped his hand to his throat. He coughed. 'I think I swallowed a fly.'

'Try keeping your mouth shut.'

'Ha-ha.' He sat down on the mattress again. It made the sound again. He gave her the look. Again. 'I asked my girl in records to run a priority background on little Delilah. We'll see what she's been up to lately. With Harding dead, she'll wind up in jail soon, and there won't be anybody to get her out.'

'She could know something,' Faith said. 'We have to figure out what Harding was up to over the last week or so of his life. That's going to tell us why he ended up in Rippy's nightclub.' She tried to talk through what was bothering her. 'Was he a pedophile or a bad father?'

'My vote goes for both.'

'He must'a broken his piggy bank over this chick.' A cop's currency was knowing who to call, and also knowing that when that person called you back, you did what they wanted, no questions asked. 'This isn't asking a uni to lose a speeding ticket. These are high-level favors, lieutenants and parole officers and judges, even. No way he could pay all of that back. He worked white collar. He didn't have the juice. There was probably nobody left on the force who would answer his calls.'

'You know the story about the dad who stopped going to work. He couldn't leave his little girl's behind.'

Faith shook her head, wishing Collier would shut the hell up. Will's sense of humor could be irreverent, but he would never, ever joke about a man molesting his own child.

Miraculously, Collier finally picked up on her mood. 'Harding doesn't have a computer or a printer.'

Faith checked the paper stock on the photos. 'These weren't printed at a lab. Somebody did them privately.'

'You think someone printed them out for him?'

'For what? Blackmail?' She thought about Harding's windfall six months ago. He moved into the Mesa Arms. He bought a new car. 'It would be the other way around. Harding's the one who came into some scratch. I have a good mind to call the lottery board and run his name.'

Collier's phone buzzed. His finger slid across the screen. 'Attachment.' He waited for the download. 'Oh man. This keeps getting better and better.' He held up the phone. The screen showed a scan of an official marriage license.

Faith squinted at the words. She had to read them twice before their meaning came through.

Five and a half months ago, Vernon Dale Harding had married Delilah Jean Palmer. It was his fifth marriage and her first.

Faith put her hand to her mouth, then thought better of it.

'Damn,' Collier said. 'Dude married his own daughter.'

'That can't be right.'

'You can see it right here. Processed and everything.'

'He listed her as his daughter two years ago. You saw it on the forms.'

Collier didn't seem as confused as she felt. 'The DNR forms aren't official, at least not unless somebody finds them and takes them to the hospital.'

Faith felt her head shaking in confusion. She wanted to go back and look at the papers again, but she knew she hadn't read them wrong. 'How did that even happen? You can't marry somebody you're related to. You have to fill out a license. They run the—'

'She was always an orphan in the system. Harding probably never had parental rights. They could do all the background checks they wanted and the relationship wouldn't show up.'

Faith had let the pornographic photos fall out of her hands. She looked down at the scattered images and tried not to think about why Dale Harding had kept them over the years. 'Good God, this poor girl never had a chance.'

'He wasn't sleeping with her.' Collier stopped Faith's protest. 'Not recently, at least. There's no Viagra in the bathroom, and considering what that guy had going on, there was no farmer left in the dale.' He laughed. 'Like, the tractor wasn't up to plowing the fields.'

'We need to find this girl.' Faith started typing a text to Amanda to put out an APB. 'She's Harding's legal wife. Harding was found dead or murdered in a room full of blood. If I'm his killer, then I'm looking for anyone Harding might have confided in. Whether she's his wife or daughter, she has to know something. Just by virtue of the fact that she was living with him.'

'Did you notice she's not here?' Collier's mood had shifted. He was getting it now. 'The TV's gone. There's no computer. Maybe she heard that he was dead, knew that there was a target on her back, so she sold his shit and got out of Dodge.'

'Violet, the property manager, never met Delilah. There's the weird closet thing. Why would you keep a girl hidden away from everybody in the neighborhood unless there was a reason to keep her hidden?'

Collier said, 'She's a whore, so she knows the streets. She was probably working Harding the same as he was working her. Maybe she's the one who got him killed. I can see that happening—girl crosses the wrong guy, Harding swoops in to protect her and gets a doorknob for his troubles.'

'Either way, she's in danger.' Faith asked, 'Did records give you her last known address?'

Collier went back to his phone. 'Renaissance Suites off I-20. My girl already called the manager, texted him a photo from Delilah's last booking. He says he don't know nothin' about nothin'.'

Faith heard her phone chirp. She read the text. 'Amanda's put out the APB on Delilah. You need to work your back channels in the APD for information on the girl. Knock on every door to every building or house she's ever lived in. Check into her juvie record, go by her school, whatever it takes to find out who her friends were.'

Collier had a weird look on his face. 'Anything else, boss lady?'

'Yeah, she was busted for soliciting, so she'll have a pimp. Find him. Talk to him. Run him in if you have to.' The alarm went off on Faith's phone. She started shoving the files and photographs back into the boxes. 'We need to find Delilah before someone else does.'

Collier asked, 'What are you going to be doing while I pound out this awesome amount of shoe leather?'

'I've got to go to the hospital and talk to the Jane Doe that Will found. She might have seen something last night.'

'Uh, technically we found her, as in Will and me.'

'Will and I.' She muscled up the boxes. They were heavier than she'd anticipated. 'I should have Harding's banking and phone information by the time I get to Grady. I'll go through these files and cross-check them against—'

'Wait.' Collier was trailing her down the hall. Again. 'Your Jane Doe—she knows me. She'd be more likely to talk to a friendly face.'

Faith stopped. Collier bumped into her from behind. She told him, 'Charlie Reed, our crime scene guy, will be here any minute. Wait for him, then go look for Delilah. If she's out there, we need to talk to her. If Angie and Harding were killed for a reason, she might know the reason, and that reason could get her killed too.'

'You really think she's in danger?'

'Don't you?'

'You're not much of a feminist, are you?' Collier grinned at what must have been the shocked look on her face. 'Could be Delilah's the one that went after both of them. Angie and Harding. Ever think of that? Women are capable of murder too, partner.'

'If you call me partner again, you'll find out exactly what women are capable of.'

For once, Collier took her seriously. 'I'll get Ng started, join him as soon as your guy gets here. Should I call you later?'

'If you find Delilah or have valuable information, yes.'

'What if I want to look at some more porn with you?'

Faith shouldered open the front door. She kept her head down so her retinas wouldn't ignite. At her car, she balanced the boxes on one knee and fumbled with the door handle until she nearly dropped everything. She finally managed to yank back the handle with the tip of her pinky finger. She used the toe of her shoe to pry open the door. She threw the boxes into the passenger seat. She got behind the wheel. All the while, Collier stood in the open front doorway, not bothering to offer any help whatsoever. He was up her ass when she didn't need him and she couldn't get him to move a muscle when she did.

'God dammit,' Faith muttered.

Amanda was right.

He was exactly her type.

FIVE

Will stood in the lobby of the gleaming Tower Place 100 office building. The twenty-nine-story skyscraper was part of the Tower Place complex, which anchored the corner of Piedmont and Peachtree Road and was only partially responsible for the dense line of Jaguars and Maseratis that clogged Buckhead morning, noon and night.

He hadn't planned on being here so much as followed the breadcrumbs Angie had left. First he'd gone home to change and get some documents from his safe, then he'd gone to Angie's bank, which led to the store where she kept her post office box, which led him to this office building, where he stuck out like a country rube because he'd forgone his usual suit and tie for something more comfortable. He couldn't even pass for a tech billionaire. His jeans were Lucky, not Armani. Sara had bought his long-sleeved polo from a store he had never heard of. His old running sneakers were splotched with the French-blue paint from his bathroom.

He had painted the walls a lighter color because he had realized one morning that the chocolates and dark browns he had chosen for his house were too masculine for Sara.

Sara.

Will felt his chest rise and fall with a deep, calming breath. Just the thought of her name had drained away some of his anxiety. He allowed himself a moment to remember how good it felt to wake up in the middle of the night and find Sara's body draped across his. She fit him like the last piece of a complicated puzzle. He had never met anyone like her before. She woke him up sometimes just to be with him. Her hands on him. Wanting him. Angie had never wanted him like that.

So why was he here?

Will looked down at the thick gray envelope in his hands. The multi-colored logo for Kip Kilpatrick's management company was in the corner. Angie's name was typed above a PO box number. The box was located in a midtown UPS store. There were actually two envelopes inside the box, but the one with the colored logo was the one Will saw first, and his heart had stopped like a train smashing into a brick wall.

He had stood motionless in the UPS store, staring at the envelope, not touching it, trying to get over his shock. Here was a concrete link between Angie and Kip Kilpatrick and, by extension, Marcus Rippy. He should've called Amanda immediately, got in a forensic team for fingerprints and to run the security footage. But Will hadn't done any of this, because among other things,

Amanda would want to know how he had tracked down the post office box number in the first place.

Angie's bank had given Will copies of her statements showing her mailing address. He'd offered the manager his marriage certificate to prove that he was still legally married to Angie. The woman hadn't needed to see it. All she'd needed was his driver's license. Will's name was still on Angie's checking account, the same as it had been for the last twenty years.

He had not told Sara about the account.

Angie's recent bank statement had shown an unusually large balance. She had always lived paycheck to paycheck. Will was the saver, the one who was terrified of running out of money and living on the streets again. Angie spent money as soon as it was in her pocket. She had told Will that she was going to die young so she might as well have fun.

Had she died young? Was forty-three middle-aged anymore?

The two-to-three-hour window to find Angie alive had closed hours ago. Sara was a good doctor. She knew how to read a crime scene and she knew how much blood was supposed to be inside of a body. Still, Will could not accept that Angie was dead. He wasn't one for cosmic signs, but he knew that if something really bad happened to her, he would feel it in his gut.

Will folded the envelope in half, then shoved it into his back pocket as he headed toward the bank of elevators. He passed on two cars before realizing there was no way he would find one that wasn't already packed with people from the parking deck. He looked at his watch. At 3:30 in the afternoon, the office workers should be pushing the clock to go home, not returning from late lunches. The elevator he finally jammed himself into was filled with the lingering odor of alcohol and cigarettes. Buttons were pressed. Will looked at the panel. They were going to stop on almost every floor.

He had been to Kip Kilpatrick's office only once, during the brief and uneventful interview with Marcus Rippy. Will could still recall the opulent details inside the offices, because it was the sort of place specifically designed to stick in your head.

110 Sports Management took up the top two floors of the building, seemingly so that they could build a fancy floating glass staircase connecting the two levels. There were life-sized Fathead stickers all over the walls showing players dunking basketballs, rushing the net and throwing game-winning touchdowns. Framed jerseys with familiar numbers were in a straight line outside the conference room like photos of past CEOs, which was appropriate because sport was a billion-dollar business. God-like athleticism wasn't enough to pay the bills. You had to have lifestyle brands and sneaker endorsements and your own clothing line to prove that you'd really made it.

Behind all of those billion-dollar deals, you also had to have a team of lawyers and managers and agents and brokers who all got their cut. Which was great, but it also created problems. Coca-Cola was a billion-dollar industry too, but there were lots of cans of Coke and bottlers who could make more of it. If a can of Coke exploded, you could get another one out of the fridge. If an athlete got pulled over going 100 miles an hour down I-75 while snorting cocaine with a hooker in his lap, then your entire business was dead the second TMZ posted the mugshot.

There was only one Serena Williams. There was only one Peyton Manning. There was only one Marcus Rippy.

Will forced out the image that came to mind when he thought of Marcus Rippy. Not the many photos of the athlete standing by his three-hundred-thousand-dollar car or on board his private Gulfstream or with his hand resting on the massive head of his pure-bred Alaskan Husky. The one of him at home with his family, acting like a happy father and caring husband while Keisha Miscavage, the woman Rippy had brutally raped, had around-the-clock protection because of the death threats from his fans.

One word from the ballplayer could stop those guys. One line in an interview or post to his Twitter account would make it possible for Keisha Miscavage to go home and start putting her life back together.

Then again, Rippy probably got a kick out of knowing she was still imprisoned.

A bell dinged. Fifth floor. The elevator doors opened. A handful of people got off. Will stood with his back pressed against the wall. He put his hand to his neck, remembering a second too late that he wasn't wearing a tie.

After Collier had dropped him at the house, Will had assumed he was on some sort of leave, if not outright fired. He remembered thinking that men who were unemployed did not have to wear a suit and tie. It was kind of the point of being unemployed. Now, he regretted his clothing choices, but when he set off from his house a few hours ago, he'd assumed he was going to be chasing down leads on Angie, not confronting Kip Kilpatrick.

The elevator stopped at the twelfth floor. Half of the people got off. No one else got on. Will kept his back to the wall. The car stopped two more floors up. One person got on and took the ride to the next floor. By the time the car left the fifteenth floor, Will was finally alone. He watched the display flash as the elevator took an ear-popping ascent toward the top floor.

Each time the number changed, he thought, *Angie. Angie. Angie.*

Was he deluding himself? Was she really dead?

Will had made his share of death notifications, steeling himself before knocking on a door, offering a shoulder to lean on or a face to scream at when he told a mother, father, husband, wife, child that their loved one would never come home again.

What was it like to be on the other side? Would Will get a call in an hour or a day or a week? Would he be told that a patrol car had rolled up on Angie's Monte Carlo and found her lifeless body slumped over the wheel?

Will would have to identify her. He would need to see her face before he believed that she was gone. In the unrelenting summer heat, what would she look like after all that time? Bloated, unrecognizable. He had seen bodies like that before. They would have to run DNA, but even then, Will's brain would always battle over whether or not that swollen, discolored face belonged to his wife or if Angie had managed to cheat death the way she always cheated everything else.

She was a survivor. She could still be out there. Collier was right. Angie always had a guy. Maybe one of those guys was a doctor. Maybe she was recovering right now, too frail to pick up the phone and let Will know that she was alive.

Not that she would ever call him so long as Sara was around.

Will pressed his fingers into his eyes.

The elevator stopped on the twenty-ninth floor. The doors slid open. White marble gleamed from every surface. A gorgeous, model-thin blonde looked up from her computer at the reception counter. Will recognized her from before, but he was certain she would not remember him.

He was wrong.

'Agent Trent.' Her smile dropped into a straight line. 'Take a seat. Mr Kilpatrick is still in his meeting. He'll be five or ten minutes.'

Kip Kilpatrick was smart, but he wasn't clairvoyant. Last Will had heard, Amanda was meeting with Marcus Rippy's agent/lawyer first thing tomorrow morning. Up until half an hour ago, even Will didn't know he was going to be here. Or maybe Kilpatrick wasn't expecting Will to show up so much as waiting for him to. It made sense. Marcus Rippy was Kilpatrick's biggest client, his only can of Coke. The slimy agent had already scuttled a rape charge. Explaining away a dead body was a comparative cakewalk.

'There.' The woman pointed to a seating area.

Will followed her order, walking across the lobby, which was the same square footage of his entire house. There was a frosted-glass door that led to the offices and one that led to a bathroom, but other than that, the lobby was completely closed off from the rest of the business.

From the sparse decor, you'd never know that you were standing right outside one of the top sports agencies in the country. Will supposed that was by design. No prospective client wanted to sit in the lobby staring at the smiling face of his on-court rival. Conversely, if your star was fading, you didn't want to see that some hot Young Turk's picture had taken your place on the wall.

Will sank into one of the comfortable chairs beside an expanse of floor-to-ceiling windows. Everything in the lobby was chrome and dark blue leather. The view outside stretched all the way to downtown. The light gray walls had *110%* printed over and over again in a glossy clear varnish like wallpaper. There was a sign that hadn't been here the last time: giant gold-leafed letters mounted on what looked like a nickel-plated quarter-inch sheet of metal that was taller than Will.

Will studied the letters. There were three lines of text, each at least eighteen inches tall. He watched the letters float around like sea anemones. An *M* crossed with an *A*. An *E* morphed into a *Y*.

Will had always had trouble reading. He wasn't illiterate. He could read, but it took some time, and it helped if the words were printed or neatly written. The problem had plagued him since childhood. He'd barely graduated high school. Most of his teachers assumed he was just lazy or stupid or both. Will was in college when a professor mentioned dyslexia. It was a diagnosis he did not share with anyone else, because people assumed that slow reading meant you had a slow mind.

Sara was the first person Will had ever met who didn't treat his disability like a handicap.

Man.

Age.

Ment.

Will silently read the three words from the sign a second, then a third time.

He heard the sound of a toilet flushing, then a faucet running, then an air hand dryer. The bathroom door opened. An older, well-dressed African American woman came out. She leaned heavily on a cane as she walked toward the seating area.

The receptionist turned on a smile. 'Laslo will come for you in another minute, Mrs Lindsay.'

Will stood up, because he had been raised by a woman old enough to be his grandmother, and Mrs Flannigan had taught them manners more suited to the Greatest Generation.

Mrs Lindsay seemed to appreciate the gesture. She smiled sweetly as she sat down on the couch opposite Will.

She asked, 'Is it still hot as the dickens outside?'

He took his seat. 'Yes, ma'am.'

'Lord help us.' She smiled at him again, then picked up a magazine. *Sports Illustrated.* Marcus Rippy was on the cover palming a basketball. Will looked out the window because seeing the man's face made him want to throw his chair across the room.

Mrs Lindsay tore out a subscription card and started to fan herself.

Will crossed his leg over his knee. He sat back in the deep chair. His calf was throbbing. There was a dot of blood on the leg of his jeans. He felt like a lifetime had passed since his foot had broken through the rotted floor of the condemned office building. At home, he'd wrapped his bleeding calf in gauze, but apparently that hadn't solved the problem.

He looked at his watch. He ignored the dried blood on the back of his hand. He checked his phone, which was packed with threats from Amanda. The only sound in the room was Mrs Lindsay turning an occasional page in her magazine and the sporadic clattering of the receptionist's long fingernails hitting her keyboard. *Tap. Tap. Tap.* She was far from proficient.

Will couldn't stop himself from duplicating the mantra from the elevator.

Angie. Angie. Angie.

She disappeared all the time. Months would go by, sometimes an entire year, and then one day Will would be eating dinner over the kitchen sink or lying on the couch watching TV and Angie would let herself into the house and act like only a few minutes had passed since the last time she'd seen him.

She would always say, 'It's me, baby. Did you miss me?'

That's what she was doing now. She had disappeared, and she would be back, because she always came back eventually.

Will uncrossed his legs. He leaned forward, hands clasped between his knees. He twisted the cheap wedding ring around his finger. He'd bought the gold band for twenty-five bucks at a pawnshop. He had wanted to look legitimately married for the bank manager. Will could've saved the cash. The manager had barely glanced at his ID before giving him access to Angie's entire financial life.

He picked at the ring. The gold was chipping off. It was nicer than the one Angie had given him.

Will dropped his hands. He wanted to stand up and pace, but he felt instinctively that the receptionist would not like that. Neither, he imagined, would Mrs Lindsay. Nothing was worse than watching someone else pace back and forth, plus it was a giant tip-off that you were nervous about something, and he didn't want Kip Kilpatrick to know that he was nervous.

Should he be nervous? Will had the upper hand. At least he thought he did, but Kilpatrick had blindsided him before.

Will picked up a magazine. He recognized the *Robb Report* logo. There was a Bentley Bentayga SUV on the cover. Will paged to the article. Numbers had never been a problem for him. He found the car's specs and traced his finger under the text. The words were easier to make out because they were familiar from other specs in other magazines, because he loved cars. Twin turbo 6.0 liter W12. 600 h.p. and 664 lb-ft of torque. Top speed of 187 m.p.h. The interior photographs showed hand-embroidered leather seats and delicate reeding around the chrome gauges.

Will drove a thirty-seven-year-old Porsche 911, but the car was no classic. His first mode of transportation had been a Kawasaki dirtbike, a sweet ride if you could show up for work covered in sweat or soaked in rain. One day Will had spotted a burned-out chassis abandoned in a field near his house. He'd paid some homeless guys to help him carry what was left of the Porsche back to his garage. The car was drivable after six months, but lack of money and a daunting technical schematic meant that it took Will almost ten years to fully restore it.

Sara had taken him to test-drive a brand-new 911 at Christmas. The trip to the dealership had been a surprise. Will had felt like an imposter standing in the showroom, but Sara had been right at home. She was used to being around money. Her apartment was a penthouse loft that cost north of a million bucks. Her BMW X5 had every bell and whistle. Sara had that confidence that came from knowing she could afford to buy what she wanted. Like the way she had stood in those open houses yesterday, looking around the large open spaces, silently thinking about the things she would change to make it more suited for her tastes, completely missing the fact that Will's hands were shaking as he held the flier and counted the number of zeroes in front of the decimal.

Will's Social Security number had been stolen by a foster parent when he was six years old. He didn't find this out until he was twenty and tried to open his first bank account. His credit was in the toilet. He'd had to pay cash for everything until he was twenty-eight, and then the only credit card he could use was the one attached to his ATM. Even his house had been paid for with cash. He'd bought it at a tax foreclosure auction on the courthouse steps. For the first three years, he'd slept with a shotgun beside his bed because crack addicts kept showing up expecting to score some rocks from the gang that used to squat there.

Will still couldn't get a credit card. Because of his cash-only policy, he had gone from bad credit to no credit. He literally did not show up with any of the ratings agencies. If Sara thought they were going to be able to buy a house together, she'd better be prepared to exchange her million-dollar penthouse loft for a shoebox. After ignoring Amanda all day, Will probably didn't have a job anymore.

'Are you a ball player?'

Will looked up from the magazine. Mrs Lindsay was talking to him.

'No, ma'am,' he told her, and then because as far as he knew, it was still technically true, he said, 'I'm a special agent with the Georgia Bureau of Investigation.'

'Isn't that interesting?' She played with the pearls around her neck. 'Now, the GBI is the state police?'

'No, ma'am. We're a statewide agency that provides assistance with criminal investigations, forensic laboratory services and computerized criminal justice information.'

'Sort of like the FBI, but to the state?'

She had picked it up quicker than most. 'Yes, ma'am, exactly.'

'All kinds of cases?'

'Yes, ma'am. Every kind.'

'How interesting.' She started to rummage inside her purse. 'Are you here for your job? I hope no one is in trouble?'

Will shook his head. 'No, ma'am. Just some routine questions.'

'What's your full name?'

'Will Trent.'

'Will Trent. A man with two first names.' She took out a small notebook with a church glass pattern on the vinyl cover. She picked at the pen inside the spiral.

Will leaned up so he could get his wallet. He fished out one of his business cards. 'This is me.'

She studied the card. 'Will Trent, Special Agent, Georgia Bureau of Investigation.' She smiled at him as she tucked the card into her notebook and returned it to her purse. 'I like to remember people I meet. How long have you been married?'

Will glanced down at the pawnshop ring on his finger. Was he a widower? What did you call yourself if your wife died when you no longer wanted to be married to her?

'I'm sorry,' Mrs Lindsay apologized. 'I'm being nosey. My daughter is always telling me I'm too curious for my own good.'

'No, ma'am. That's all right. I'm kind of nosey, too.'

'I should hope so, considering your job.' She laughed, so Will laughed too. She told him, 'I was married for fifty-one years to a wonderful man.'

'You were a child bride?'

She laughed again. 'You're very kind, Special Agent Trent, but no. My husband passed away three years ago.'

Will felt a lump come into his throat. 'And you have a daughter?'

'Yes.' That was all she said. She clutched her purse in her lap. She kept smiling at him. He smiled back.

And then he saw her bottom lip start to quiver.

Her eyes were moist.

Will glanced at the receptionist, who was still typing on her computer.

He lowered his voice, 'Is everything all right?'

'Oh yes.' Her teeth showed in a wide smile, but the lip would not stop its tremble. 'Everything is wonderful.'

Will noticed that the receptionist had stopped typing. She had the phone to her ear. Mrs Lindsay's lip had not stopped quivering. She was obviously upset about something.

He tried to sound conversational. 'Do you live around here?'

'Just up the street.'

'Buckhead,' Will said. 'My boss lives down the road in those town homes near Peachtree Battle.'

'That's a nice area. I'm in the older building at the curve across from the churches.'

'Jesus Junction,' Will supplied.

'The Lord is everywhere.'

Will wasn't religious, but he said, 'It's good to have somebody looking out for you.'

'You're so right. I am truly blessed.'

Will felt like he was trapped inside a plasma globe with little sparks of electricity arcing back and forth between him and Mrs Lindsay. They kept staring at each other for at least another ten seconds before the door behind the receptionist's desk opened.

'Miss Lindsay?' A bullet-headed thug wearing a tight-fitting black shirt and even tighter black pants stood in the open doorway. His Boston accent was as thick as his neck. 'Let's bring you back, sweetheart.'

Mrs Lindsay gripped her cane and stood, so Will stood too. 'It was nice meeting you.'

'You too.' She offered her hand. He shook it. Her skin was clammy. She bit her lip to stop the tremble. She leaned on her cane to get herself started, then walked through the open door without turning back around.

The thug eyeballed Will a fuck-you before shutting the door behind him. Will took a wild shot in the dark and guessed this was Laslo, and that Laslo worked for Kip Kilpatrick. Behind every fixer was a sleazeball eager to get his hands dirty. Laslo struck Will as the type who came pre-dirtied.

The receptionist said, 'Mr Kilpatrick should be about five or ten minutes.'

'More.' She looked confused, so Will explained, 'Because you said five to ten minutes before, so now it's—'

She started pecking on her computer again.

Will stuck his hands into his pockets. He looked at the couch, feeling like Mrs Lindsay might have left something for him. A breadcrumb, maybe.

Nothing.

He walked toward the bathroom door, turned around, and walked back toward the drink sign. He'd been right about the pacing. The receptionist kept giving him annoyed looks as she picked away at her computer keyboard. He wondered if she was updating her Facebook page. What exactly was required of a receptionist if she wasn't in charge of answering phones? Will considered this as he paced, because the other things he had to consider were too much to bear. He was on his sixth revolution when a loud *ding* pierced the air.

The elevator doors slid open. Amanda stepped out.

Her expression quickly changed from surprise to fury to her usual mask of indifference. 'You're early,' she said, as if the fact that he was standing in the lobby hadn't shocked the hell out of her. She turned to the receptionist, 'Can you find out how much longer Mr Kilpatrick will be?'

The girl picked up the phone. Her fingernails spiked the keypad.

'Thank you.' Amanda's tone was polite, but her shoes gave her away. The heels stabbed into the marble floor like knives. She sat in the chair Will had abandoned. Her feet didn't reach the ground. She teetered a bit as she tried to keep her balance. Will had never seen Amanda sit all the way back in a chair, but the problem was that this particular chair had been built for someone with a basketball player's long legs. No wonder Will had been so comfortable.

He told her, 'Sorry I was early.'

She picked up the *Robb Report*. 'I think I prefer you without testicles.'

The receptionist hung up the phone with a clatter. 'Mr Kilpatrick said he'll be five or ten minutes.' For Will's sake, she added, 'More.'

'Thank you.' Amanda stared at the magazine with a sudden interest in luxury watches.

Will figured he couldn't piss off Amanda any more than he already had. He resumed his pacing back and forth between the bathroom and the sign. He thought about the second envelope he had found in Angie's post office box. White, nondescript, more shocking than the first. There was no stamp. Angie had left it for him, and Will had left it locked inside his car. The Kilpatrick envelope was evidence. The second was nobody's business.

He asked Amanda, 'Did you find anything?' She stared at him blankly. 'At the crime scene?'

Amanda turned to the receptionist. 'Excuse me?' She waited for the girl to look up. 'The last time I was here, I was served a lovely mint tea. Do you mind making some for me again? With honey?'

The receptionist forced a smile. She slammed her hands on the desk and rolled back her chair so she could stand. She opened the door to the offices and closed it hard behind her.

Amanda told Will, 'Sit down.'

He sat on the couch.

She said, 'You've got until the girl comes back to explain to me why I shouldn't fire you on the spot.'

Will couldn't think of a good reason, so he settled on coming clean. He pulled the 110 envelope out of his back pocket. He tossed it onto the glass coffee table.

Amanda didn't touch it. She read the return address, which was for the office they were sitting in. Like the wallpaper in the lobby, the *110%* was repeated in clear ink across the front and back. Instead of asking what was inside the envelope, she said, 'How did you get Angie's PO box number?'

'I went to the bank. I'm on her checking account. The PO box is inside a UPS store off—'

'Spring Street.' She gave him a withering look. 'Your phone belongs to the GBI, Will. I could track you to the bathroom if I wanted to.' She motioned for him to continue. 'So, you went to the store and?'

Will let the information about the tracking sink in. 'I showed the manager the bank statement with our names on it and my driver's license and he gave me access to the post office box.' He left out the hundred dollars cash that had exchanged hands, and the veiled threats he had made to the store owner about the GBI's fraud investigation division, but something about the look Amanda gave him said that she knew.

She studied the envelope again, still not touching it. 'Who did you hit?'

He looked at the broken skin on the back of his hand. 'Somebody who probably didn't deserve it.'

'Are they going to be a problem?'

Will didn't think Collier was the type. 'No.'

'You need to take off that wedding ring before you see Sara. And I wouldn't tell her you're still listed on Angie's bank account, because she might wonder how you can find that post office box in two hours when you haven't been able to find one single viable lead off Angie in the last year and a half.'

Will didn't hear a question, so he didn't give an answer.

'Why are you still on her account?'

'Because she needs money sometimes.' He looked out the window. The truth was, he didn't know why he hadn't tried to track down Angie through the bank statement before. 'She'll text me sometimes that she needs help.'

'Which means you have her phone number?'

'The last time she texted me was thirteen months ago for a couple hundred dollars.' It was actually five hundred, but Will didn't want to overshare. 'The phone number that Charlie found is the same number she texted from. It's been disconnected.' He added, 'And it's the same number on her bank account.'

Amanda finally picked up the envelope. She pulled out the five-thousand-dollar check written from Kip Kilpatrick's personal account. Proof that Angie had been working for Kilpatrick. Amanda let her hand fall to her lap. 'This is why she didn't need to borrow money. If you can call it borrowing. I'm assuming she never paid you back.'

Again, he did not answer the question that was not asked. 'For the last three months, Angie has shown a five-thousand-dollar deposit every two weeks, the same amount that's on that check. She was working for Kip Kilpatrick.'

'For what reason do you think Kilpatrick was paying her ten thousand dollars a month out of his private account?'

Will shrugged, but he could think of a lot of illicit things Angie would do. She'd had a pill problem on and off from childhood. She didn't mind doing bad things or looking the other way when people did bad things for her. She had also dipped into legal enterprises, so Will went with the least of her sins. 'She was registered with the state as a private investigator. Maybe Kilpatrick had her investigating people, doing background checks on potential clients. She worked security part-time when she was a cop. Maybe she did that for him too.' He asked her again, 'What did you find at the crime scene?'

Amanda ignored the question a second time. 'Tell me the reason you didn't call me half an hour ago when you found this check.'

Will looked down at his hands. He was twisting the wedding ring again. He didn't know why he had developed an attachment to it. The ring meant about as much as the one that Angie had put on his finger at the court house.

Amanda said, 'The blood in the room is type B-negative, which is a very rare blood type. Angie is type B-negative. That's all I have for you.'

'All the blood was B-negative?'

'The majority of the blood, yes. The volume.'

Will heard Sara's words echo in his head.

The volume of blood loss is the real danger.

Amanda said, 'Jane Doe is still in surgery. We have a lead on a gal named Delilah Palmer. Ever heard of her?'

Will shook his head.

'White female, twenty-two years old. Her sheet has prostitution and drugs times eight. Harding was her guardian angel. She's been on the game for a while.'

'Angie worked vice when she was a cop.'

'Did she really?' Amanda put on a bad show of sounding surprised. 'We've put out a high alert. This Delilah Palmer likely knows why Dale and Angie were killed, which either makes her our top suspect or our next victim.'

Will twisted the ring on his finger. He forced himself not to look at his watch, to do the math for how much time had passed since Sara had said that Angie didn't have much time.

She would come back. Angie always came back. That's how he would get through this. He would treat this time like every other time she disappeared, and a year would go by, two years, and Will would find a way to accept that he had watched Amanda pretend to read a magazine while Angie had died alone. Just like she always said she would do. Just like Will had wished she would do because he wanted things to be easier with Sara.

He looked out the window. He tried to swallow. He felt that familiar tightness in his chest. The last thing he had said to Angie was that he didn't love her anymore.

Then he had gone back to Sara.

Amanda put down her magazine. She stood up. She walked around the coffee table and sat on the edge of the couch. She smoothed out her skirt. She stared at the wall in front of her. Her shoulder touched his, and it took everything Will had inside of him not to lean against her.

She said, 'You know my mother hanged herself in our backyard when I was a child.'

Will looked up. She had spoken matter-of-factly, but the truth was that he hadn't known.

She said, 'Every time I washed dishes, I would look out the window at that tree and think, "You are the last person who is ever going to make me feel this way ever again."'

Will didn't ask which way she meant.

'And then Kenny came along. I'm sure Faith has told you about her uncle.'

Will nodded. Kenny Mitchell was a retired pilot who'd flown test engines for NASA.

'Kenny was a stone-cold fox, as we used to say.' She smiled her secret smile. 'I couldn't understand why he chose me. I was such a plain, silly girl. Very naive. Desperate to please my father. Wouldn't say boo to a ghost.'

Will couldn't picture Amanda being any of those things.

'Kenny was like a drug. At first in the exciting way, then in the bad way. The way that led your Jane Doe to vacuuming up two ounces of coke.' Amanda's tone said she wasn't exaggerating. 'I lowered myself for him. I did things that I never thought I would ever, ever do.'

Will glanced back toward the closed office door. How long did water take to boil for tea?

Amanda said, 'The hardest part was that deep down inside, I knew it. I knew he would never marry me. I knew he would never give me children.' She paused. 'I could spot a lying perp from fifty yards, but I chose to believe everything that came out of Kenny's mouth. I'd invested so many years of my life in him that I couldn't admit that I was wrong. I was terrified of looking like a fool.'

Will sat back on the couch. If she thought that was how he was with Angie, then she was wrong. Will knew from the beginning that Angie was the wrong person for him. As for looking like a fool, everybody knew that she cheated on him.

Used to cheat on him.

Amanda continued, 'Kenny and I had been together for nearly eight years when I met Roger.' Her voice softened when she said the name. 'I'll spare you the details, but let's just say he caught my eye. He wanted to give me everything I didn't have with Kenny, but I said no, because I didn't know how to be with a man who wanted to be with me.' The softness had drained away. 'I was addicted to Kenny's uncertainty, that niggling little doubt in my gut that made me wonder if I could survive without him. I thought I could fix the pain inside of him. It took me a long time to realize that the pain was inside of me.'

Will rubbed his jaw. That hit a little closer to home.

Amanda turned toward him, her hand resting on the back of the couch. 'We had this kitten when I was a little girl. Buttons. She kept clawing the couch, so my father bought me a water pistol and told me to shoot her every time she got near it. And I remember that first time I squirted her, she panicked and ran to me for comfort. She clung to me, and I petted her until she calmed down. That's how I was with Kenny. That's how you were with Angie.' Amanda said this with conviction. 'It's the curse of the motherless child. We seek comfort from the very people who do us harm.'

Her words splayed him open like a razor.

She said, 'I think you never checked Angie's bank statement because you were afraid that she'd closed the account. That she'd cut off that final tie with you.'

Will looked down at his hands, the broken skin from punching Collier, the fake ring that signified his fake marriage.

'Am I right?'

He shrugged, but he knew that she was right.

Angie had left him a letter. That was what was inside the second envelope inside her post office box. This one had Will's name written on the outside in capital letters, clear so that he could easily read it. The letter inside was a different matter. Angie had deliberately written him a note in her cursive chicken scratch because she knew that Will would not be able to read it. He would have to find someone else to read it for him.

Sara?

He cleared his throat. 'What made you finally leave Kenny?'

'You think I'd ever give up?' She laughed deep from her belly. 'Oh no. Kenny left me. For a man.'

Will felt himself startle.

'I knew he was gay. I wasn't *that* naive.' She shrugged. 'It was the seventies. Everybody thought gay people could change.'

Will tried to get over his shock. 'Was it too late with Roger?'

'About half a century too late. He wanted a stay-at-home wife and I wanted a career.' She looked at her watch, then at the closed door. 'At least he showed me what an orgasm was.'

Will put his head in his hands and prayed for self-immolation.

'Oh stop it.' Amanda stood up, indicating that sharing time was over. 'Wilbur, I have known you for more years than I care to admit, and you have always been a raving idiot in your personal life. Don't screw things up with Sara. She *is* too good for you, and you'd better find a way to keep her before she figures that out.'

She grabbed his hand and slid the ring off his finger.

He watched her stomp over to the desk and toss the ring into the trashcan. The metal made a dinging sound, like the hammer hitting the bell at the end of round one. 'And don't tell any of this to Faith. She has no idea her uncle is gay.'

The door opened. The receptionist said, 'Mr Kilpatrick will see you now.'

'Thank you.' Amanda waited for Will to stand up and follow her.

Will put his hands on his knees and pushed himself up from the couch. His head was spinning through the slide show of everything Amanda had just told him, but he forced himself to stop the carousel and put it on a shelf. None of what she'd said mattered. Angie wasn't dead. She was off somewhere, the same place she always went to, and eventually one day his front door would open and he would hear those familiar words.

It's me, baby. Did you miss me?

A loud rebel yell shocked Will's attention back to the present. Two young guys in sharp suits high-fived each other as they celebrated something agent-y. The quiet of the lobby was gone. Phones were ringing. Secretaries were murmuring into their headsets. The floating glass stairs were filled with people who looked like they had stepped out of a magazine spread. Overhead, a giant LED sign counted up the number of millions the company had made for their players so far this year.

Except for the staggeringly high number, not much had changed in the four months since Will had been here. The life-sized stickers were still on the walls. Every office door still had a beautiful young woman stationed at a desk outside. There were still photos of agents looking like Tattoo next to Mr O'Rourke as they stood by their star players signing multi-million-dollar contracts.

The surly receptionist handed them over to another blonde, this one a few years older, probably with an MBA from Harvard, because hot blondes who worked in offices like this weren't just for show anymore.

The new blonde told Amanda, 'I put your mint tea in the conference room, but Kip wanted to talk to you first.'

Will realized he should've asked Amanda what she hoped to accomplish here. It was normal procedure to talk to a building's owner when a dead body was found on their premises, but this wasn't Kip Kilpatrick's first rodeo. There was no way he'd let them interview Marcus Rippy, even off the record.

It was too late to ask Amanda now. The blonde knocked on the office door, then let them in.

Kip Kilpatrick was sitting at a massive glass table in the center of his light-filled corner office. The ceiling soared twenty feet overhead. The dull marble slabs on the floor were broken up with heavy wool rugs shot through with strings of silk. The deep couches and chairs in the seating area had been designed for giants. Kilpatrick was not a giant. His small feet rested on the edge of the table, scuffing the backs of his bespoke leather loafers. He was leaning back in the chair, tossing a basketball into the air with both hands, talking into the Bluetooth earpiece stuck in his ear because he wouldn't look douchey enough speaking into a regular phone.

Kilpatrick had other clients—a top-seeded tennis player, a soccer player who had helped the US take home the World Cup, but it was clear from his office who the real superstar was. It wasn't just the regulation NBA Marcus Rippy backboard mounted high on the wall. They might as well have been standing in a Marcus Rippy museum. Kilpatrick had framed jerseys going back to Rippy's youth league days. Signed basketballs lined the window ledge. Two Rippy bobbleheads sat on opposite corners of his desk. Championship trophies were on a specially designed floating shelf that had a pin light wrapping every inch of gold. There was even a pair of bronzed size-fourteen basketball shoes that Rippy had worn when he helped his college team win the Final Four.

Will had always assumed that Kilpatrick was a failed player. He was not too short, but not tall enough, the kind of guy who puppydogged the team, trying to be friends with the players while they walked all over him. The only difference now was that he at least got paid for it.

'Heads up,' Kilpatrick said. He passed the basketball to Will.

Will let the ball hit him in the chest and bounce across the room. The sound echoed in the cold office. They all watched the ball dribble into the corner.

Kilpatrick said, 'Guess you're not a player?'

Will said nothing.

'Have I met you before?'

Will had spent seven months hounding Kilpatrick and his people over the Rippy investigation. There was probably a dartboard in the break room with his face on it. Still, if Kilpatrick was going to pretend they had never met, that was fine with Will.

He said, 'Drawing a blank.'

'Me too.' Kilpatrick bumped the glass table as he stood. The bobbleheads nodded. 'Ms Wagner. Can't say that I'm happy to see you again.'

Amanda didn't tell him that the feeling was mutual. 'Thank you for moving up our meeting. I'm sure we'd all like to get this straightened out as soon as possible.'

'Absolutely.' Kilpatrick opened a small refrigerator packed with bottles of BankShot, an energy drink that tasted like cough syrup. He twisted off the cap. He took a mouthful and swigged it around before swallowing. 'Tell me, what's "this" again?'

'"This" is a murder investigation that is currently taking place at Marcus Rippy's nightclub.' When he didn't respond, Amanda said, 'As I told you on the phone, I need information about the development.'

Kilpatrick chugged the drink. Will glanced at Amanda. She was being unusually patient.

'Ahh.' Kilpatrick tossed the empty bottle into the trashcan. 'What I can tell you right now is that I've never heard of this Harding guy.'

'So the name Triangle-O Holdings Limited means nothing to you?'

'Nope.' Kilpatrick grabbed the basketball off the floor. 'Never heard of it.'

Will had no idea where Amanda was going with her question, but for her benefit, he explained to Kilpatrick, 'The triangle offense was made famous by Michael Jordan's Chicago Bulls under coach Phil Jackson.'

'Jordan, huh?' Kilpatrick smiled as he palmed the basketball. 'I think I heard of that guy. Like a really old Marcus Rippy.'

Amanda said, 'Dale Harding was living in a very nice home owned by Triangle-O Holdings.'

Kilpatrick threw the basketball toward the hoop. It hit the backboard and he took the rebound for another shot. 'Nothin' but net,' he said, like he couldn't simply walk up and touch the bottom of the net with the tips of his fingers.

Amanda said, 'Triangle-O Holdings is registered in Delaware to a company that is registered in St Martin, then St Lucia, all the way through to a corporation held in Copenhagen.'

Will felt a tickle in his brain. The construction signs outside Rippy's nightclub had a Danish flag in the logo.

Amanda had obviously noticed the same detail, but earlier and when it could better serve her purpose. 'I've got the state department making an official inquiry into the names of the corporation's board and shareholders. You could make this a lot easier if you would just tell me.'

'No idea.' Kilpatrick tried to spin the basketball on the tip of his finger. 'Wish I could help you.'

'You could let us talk to Marcus Rippy.'

He coughed a laugh. 'Not a chance, lady.'

Will sneaked a glance at Amanda again, wondering what she was up to. She had to know they had lost their one shot at Marcus Rippy.

She asked, 'What about the name Angie Polaski?'

Kilpatrick finally got the ball to spin. 'What about it?'

'Have you ever heard of her?'

'Sure.' He slapped the basketball to make it spin faster.

'In what capacity?'

'Uh, let's just say she provided a service.'

'Background checks? Security?'

'Snatch.' Kilpatrick got a look on his face that made Will want to punch him straight out the window. 'She provided girls for some of my parties. Nothing was expected of them. I just asked that they be experienced.' He paused, and added, 'Conversationalists. Experienced conversationalists. Like I said, nothing sexual was expected of them. They were all adults. They were paid for their conversation. Anything else was their choice.'

'Choice,' Will repeated, because he knew for a fact that Marcus Rippy preferred women who didn't have a choice.

Amanda summed it up. 'So you're saying that Angie Polaski provided escorts for your parties?'

Kilpatrick nodded, his eyes on the spinning ball.

Will had to admit there might be something to what he was saying. Angie had loved working vice. She was always more comfortable walking the line between cop and criminal. She also knew her share of prostitutes, and she never had any problems with women making money any way they knew how.

Kilpatrick said, 'My clients are high-profile celebrities. Sometimes they want a little discreet company. It's hard for them to meet women.'

Amanda asked, 'You mean other than their wives?'

Will thought about the working girls that Angie knew. They were low-level streetwalkers, drug addicts, some of them toothless, all of them desperate, none of them more than a few years away from a prison cell or a grave. Will might be able to imagine a world in which Angie pimped out some girls and told herself that she was doing them a favor, but the girls she knew were not the kind of ladies that Kilpatrick's clients would want to meet.

Kilpatrick said, 'So, that's what you wanted to know? What Polaski was doing for me?'

'Do you have her current address?'

'Post office box.' He picked up the phone, punched in some numbers, and said, 'My office.' He hung up the phone. 'My guy Laslo can give you the details.' Laslo again. Will was right to assume the bullet-headed Boston thug was an extra pair of dirty hands.

Amanda asked, 'How did you meet Ms Polaski?'

Kilpatrick shrugged his shoulders. 'The way you meet these kinds of people is, they're just there. They know what you're looking for and they offer to take care of it for a price. Easy.'

Will said, 'Like bribing witnesses in a rape trial.'

Kilpatrick looked at him. Something like a snort came out of his nose. 'Yeah, now I remember who you are.'

Amanda asked, 'What about a phone number?'

'Laslo will have it. I don't deal with tradespeople.'

'Right,' Will said. 'You just mail them the checks from your personal bank account.'

Amanda shot Will a daggered look. She told Kilpatrick, 'We found a check written to Angie Polaski, drawn from your bank account.'

'The agency only pays for drinks and dinners. Anything else is on us.' Kilpatrick explained, '"Business development" is what we call it on our taxes.'

Amanda said, 'Let's talk about another development. The one where we found a dead body this morning.'

He started to spin the ball again. 'I'll let you get that from the horse's mouth.'

Amanda said, 'Does that mean that everything you've told us thus far has been from the horse's other end?'

Kilpatrick took a beat to get her meaning.

There was a knock at the door. Laslo said, 'Boss, they're ready.'

Kilpatrick dribbled the basketball as he walked across the office. 'Get these people Polaski's deets. They're cops. They're looking for her.'

'Big surprise.' Laslo grabbed the ball and shot it toward the hoop on the wall.

Kilpatrick started to go for the rebound.

Amanda snaked the ball and put it down on the closest chair. 'We're ready when you are, Mr Kilpatrick.'

He eyed the basketball, but thought better of it. 'This way.' He started down the hallway. 'The development is scheduled to break ground next week. We're calling it the All-Star Complex.'

She asked, 'We?'

'Yeah, that's thanks to you guys.' Kilpatrick led them past a bunch of closed office doors. 'Funny thing about that jacked-up rape charge you laid on Marcus. The other investors were looking for someone else to step in, and we realized we were missing a larger opportunity.'

'Meaning?'

'We pitched the investment to some of our higher-end clients. We realized we could expand the complex into a live/work community.'

Amanda said, 'So like Atlantic Station, but in an area that is historically more crime-ridden.'

Will smiled. She had a point. Atlantic Station had been pitched to the city as a dream development that would turn an area of blight into a thriving tax base. As with most dreams, reality had come crashing down in the form of a spike in sexual assaults, muggings, carjackings and vandalism. At one point, a couple of more enterprising bank robbers had strapped a chain around an ATM machine and pulled it out of the wall with their truck.

Kilpatrick had obviously handled the Atlantic Station question before. 'Those were growing pains. It happens. The whole thing's been turned around, as I'm sure you know. And also, the developers didn't have the benefit of eight of the most talented, tremendous athletes the world has ever known, ready to promote the project to make sure it succeeds.' He threw his hands out like a carnival barker. 'Think about it. Marcus Rippy alone has over ten million Facebook fans. His Tweets and Instagram reach twice as many as that. He puts up one post about a dope club or a hip shop he's excited about and within the hour the place is flooded. He's a taste-maker.'

Kilpatrick turned the corner and they were facing a vast glass-walled conference room with a table that could accommodate fifty people. Will forced himself not to flinch in disgust when he noticed the four lawyers already in the room. Kilpatrick must have called in the big guns the minute Amanda had requested a meeting.

Will recognized them all from the Rippy rape investigation. The interchangeable Bond villains: two old white men, each with a gorgeous thirty-ish woman dressed to kill sitting beside him. Kilpatrick ran through the introductions, but Will had already designated their Bond status from before. Auric Goldfinger was at the head of the table, his patches of Chia-like gold hair and thick German accent earning him the name. Obviously his blonde underling was Pussy Galore. Then there was Dr Julius No, a man who for some reason always kept his hands under the table. His sidekick was Rosa Klebb, named not for her looks, which were fantastic, but because her pointy high-heeled shoes seemed like the type that would have poison-tipped knives inside of them.

Goldfinger said, ‘Deputy Director, Agent Trent, thank you both for coming. Please sit.’ He indicated a chair with a cup of tea in front of it, two seats away from Rosa Klebb.

Will pulled out two chairs from the opposite end of the table, about half a mile away from the Bond quartet, because he knew that’s how Amanda would want to play it. She glanced up at Will as they sat down, her eyes going to his bare neck, and he got the feeling that she was really annoyed that he wasn’t wearing a suit and tie.

Will was annoyed too. He could’ve at least worn his gun on his hip. He needed some armor against these people. They didn’t roll out of bed for less than three thousand bucks an hour. Each.

The combined receipt for this meeting was probably more than Will's take-home pay.

He looked at Kilpatrick, but Kilpatrick was obviously no longer in charge. He had slumped into a chair, rolling an unopened bottle of red BankShot between his hands.

'So.' Amanda chose to forgo subtlety. 'I'm trying to understand why it takes four lawyers to answer one simple question.'

Goldfinger smiled. 'It's not a simple question, Deputy Director. You asked for details on the property in which the victim was found. We are simply here to give you the larger picture of the situation.'

Amanda said, 'In my experience, there's always a larger picture where murder is concerned, but again, it's never taken so many lawyers to draw it for me.'

Will watched them carefully. No one spoke. No one moved. Despite her question, Amanda didn't seem displeased to find herself talking to the lawyers. If someone had asked Will for his opinion, he would've guessed that she'd somehow contrived to put them all in this room.

The only question was why. Amanda set aside the tea bag and drank some tea.

Finally Goldfinger looked at Dr No, who in turn nodded to Rosa Klebb.

Klebb stood up. She stacked together some folders. She walked around the conference table, which was about the width of a sequoia. Will could hear her pantyhose scratching against her tight skirt. He looked down at her extremely high-heeled shoes. The soles were red because they could stop a man's heart. Sara had a pair from the same designer. He preferred them on Sara.

'This is a packet on the development,' Goldfinger told them. 'It's the same presentation we shared with the mayor and governor last month.'

Amanda would've already heard about the project. She had talked to the mayor this morning and was briefing the governor at the capitol when Will had given her the slip. She didn't volunteer this information. Instead she glanced at the folder, which had a massive star logo in the center. She handed her packet to Will. He put it on top of his packet and placed both at his elbow.

Dr No leaned over, his hands still tucked under the table. 'We'll have to ask you to keep this information to yourselves. There's a press embargo until the official announcement. You can read the details about the development in the packet.'

Amanda waited.

Goldfinger explained, 'The All-Star Complex will have a sixteen-screen movie theater, a thirty-story hotel, a twenty-story condominium complex, a farmers' market, an outdoor shopping mall with high-end boutique and chain stores, exclusive town homes, a members-only nightclub and of course a full-sized basketball court adjacent to what we're calling the All-Star Experience, an interactive museum showcasing all that is wonderful about NCAA basketball.'

Amanda asked, 'How will this be financed?'

'We have several private investors whose names I'm currently not at liberty to release.'

'And foreign investors?' Amanda prodded.

Goldfinger smiled. 'A project of this scope requires many, many investors, some of whom wish to remain behind the scenes.'

'Including yourselves?'

He smiled back a non-answer.

She said, 'The construction company is LK Totalbyg A/S, based in Denmark.'

'That is correct. As you know, Atlanta is an international city. We reached out to international investors. It's a win–win for everyone involved.'

Will thought about the people who actually lived in Atlanta who would be investing whether they wanted to or not. The perks that the government handed out for these kinds of projects were phenomenal. City-funded bond initiatives, decades-long state and local tax deferments, new roadways, new infrastructure, new traffic lights and cops to keep the area safe—basically all the cold, hard cash that always made these developments possible for the rich guys who touted the glories of private enterprise and talked about pulling themselves up by their bootstraps.

The American Dream.

'Deputy Director.' Dr No leaned toward Amanda as if they weren't separated by an ocean of hardwood. 'As both the mayor and governor have repeatedly expressed, both the city and state are very excited about the development. The proximity to the Georgia Dome, Georgia Tech, Centennial Village and SunTrust Park means the complex will be a mecca for tourists.'

Will thought that Chattahoochee Avenue was a bit far out to be a mecca for anything, but he had to assume these guys had seen a map.

Goldfinger said, 'We're hoping that the All-Star Experience will rival downtown's College Football Hall of Fame. I don't have to tell you what it would do for the city's economic opportunities if we could secure more vital slots in the March Madness rotation.'

'Sounds impressive.' Amanda didn't have to know about sports to understand that this was big business. She looked down the table, expectant. 'And?'

Dr No took over. 'And we would hope that you would understand that this is a delicate undertaking.'

Pussy Galore chimed in. 'It's not just the nuts and bolts of building such an impressive complex. We've put a lot of time and effort into making the announcement about the project's existence. You only get one opportunity to make that first big splash. We've got all of our all-star investors lined up to attend. We're flying in reporters from New York, Chicago and LA. We've booked suites and restaurants. We have a massive two-day party planned, culminating in a ground-breaking at the site. We've worked the press into a frenzy. It's very important that none of this is tainted by lingering doubt about any of the investors.'

Goldfinger added, 'Or about the site.'

Amanda said, 'If that means you're worried we're going to charge your client with rape again, I can put your minds at ease.' She smiled. 'This is a murder case, so if we make any charges, it will be for murder.'

The room lost all of its air.

Goldfinger smiled, and then the smile turned into a laugh.

Dr No joined in, his hands still below the table so that he looked like a lemming caught in a blender.

Amanda asked, 'When is this party planned?'

'This weekend.'

'Ah,' she said, as if she finally understood, but Will would've bet his life that she knew about the launch before she walked through the door. The mayor and the governor would've both been pressuring her harder than the lawyers to wrap up the investigation so the project could get under way. The city needed the jobs. The state needed the money.

Amanda told them, 'The fact remains that a dead man was found inside the nightclub. We've got a large crime scene to process. Even with overtime, it will take at least until Saturday to catalog and photograph all of the evidence.'

Not for the first time, Will admired Amanda's lying skills, because there was no way that crime scene would take that long to clear. She was playing the long game here. He just couldn't see the end point.

Goldfinger said, 'This is the problem at which we have arrived. Saturday is a bit of a difficulty for us.'

'Not just a bit.' Galore supplied, 'We promised an early peek of the club to the *LA Times*. They're scheduled for first thing Friday morning. They want to do a before-and-after kind of thing with Marcus, take some photos of him behind the bar, maybe standing on the balcony, then the later photos will show the same shots after the club is finished.'

'Can't you postpone that?' Amanda asked.

Galore wrinkled her nose. 'The word *postpone* is catnip to reporters. We'd be looking at a lot of bad press.'

Amanda told them, 'I was inside that club this morning. It looked more like a crack den than the anchor to a two-point-eight-billion-dollar project.'

None of them seemed to notice that she had the price tag at her fingertips.

Galore supplied, 'We had cleaners scheduled to go in this morning to start making the club more presentable. Obviously that was well after your crime scene people arrived.' She added, 'But still, we'd need at least two days, balls to the walls, to get that place spiffed up.'

'You realize the press has already gotten wind of the murder?' Amanda said. 'They know that a body was found inside the club.'

'Yes, they know that a body was found,' Galore said. 'They don't know that the man was anything other than a vagrant.'

'Both the GBI and the Atlanta police were on scene. The media is going to assume that we wouldn't put that much effort into solving the murder of a vagrant.' She smiled at them. 'Not that any death isn't a tragedy, but the local police normally don't ask the state for help in such circumstances.'

'So it's a drug deal gone bad, or two homeless men fighting over a forty,' Galore suggested. 'That would only serve to highlight another positive aspect of the All-Star development, taking an area that is prone to crime and turning it into a safe, clean, family-friendly neighborhood.'

'But he wasn't a vagrant. He was a retired Atlanta police detective.'

No one had an answer for that.

Amanda said, 'I'm sorry, folks, I understand the dilemma, but I can't rush a murder investigation for your grand opening. I have to think of the victim's family. The detective had a wife. She's only twenty-two years old.'

Will worked to keep the surprise off his face. Because of the age, he had to assume that the wife was Delilah Palmer. He had no idea why Amanda hadn't shared this detail with him. There was a big difference between Harding being Delilah's guardian angel and being her husband. Wives knew things. They had access to information. If Harding was targeted for knowing too much, then Delilah would be the next person on the list.

Amanda continued, 'Harding and the girl were married for only a few months. I already had to tell her that she's a widow. Am I supposed to go back now and tell her that her husband's death takes a back seat to a press event?' Amanda shook her head as if the very thought made her sad. 'And speaking of the press, Mrs Harding is incredibly photogenic. Blonde hair, blue eyes, very pretty. The press will be all over her.'

'No, no,' Dr No said. 'We wouldn't want any of that, Deputy Director. We're not trying to impede your investigation.' He shot Goldfinger a look, because of course they were trying to impede the investigation.

And Amanda would've known this already, so again Will had to wonder what she was angling for.

'Deputy Director,' Goldfinger began. 'We would just ask that you do all you can to speed things along.' He held up his finger. 'Not speed, of course, because that would imply rushing. I would just say that you could please handle this expeditiously.'

She nodded. 'Of course. I'll do what I can. But I can't have my people cleared out by Saturday. There are simply not enough hours in the day.'

Dr No asked, 'Is there anything we can do to help expedite the process?'

Will felt an invisible zap come off Amanda. Dr No's question was exactly what she had been waiting for.

'I wonder if—' She stopped herself. 'No, never mind. We'll do all we can.' She started to stand. 'Thank you for your time.'

'Please.' Goldfinger motioned for her to sit. 'What can we do?'

She sat back down. She gave a heavy sigh. 'I'm afraid it all comes back to Marcus Rippy.'

'Fuck no!' Kilpatrick had jumped to attention. 'You're not talking to Marcus. No fucking way, no fucking how.'

Amanda spoke to Goldfinger. 'Look at this from my perspective. I have a highly decorated, much respected ex-police detective found murdered inside a building that is under construction. In the course of a normal investigation, the first thing I would do is talk to the building owner to eliminate him or her as a suspect and to generate a list of people who would have access to the building.'

'I can give you a fucking list,' Kilpatrick sputtered. 'You don't need to talk to Marcus.'

'I'm afraid I do.' She held out her hands in a helpless shrug. 'I just need a few moments of his time, and a promise that he'll have an open and honest conversation with us. It would go a long way toward repairing his reputation if he was shown to be helping a police investigation. On the record.'

'Are you fucking kidding me? On the record?' Kilpatrick had jumped to his feet. He told Goldfinger, 'You can get five to ten years in this state for lying to a cop.'

Amanda asked, 'What is your client planning to lie about?'

Kilpatrick ignored her, telling Goldfinger, 'This fucking spider is trying to trap Marcus into saying something that—'

'Kip,' Dr No said, and Kilpatrick's mouth shut like a trout.

Goldfinger told Amanda, 'Deputy Director, perhaps you and I could speak in private?'

The three other lawyers stood in unison.

Amanda touched Will's arm, releasing him. He headed toward the door.

Kilpatrick threw his hands into the air. 'This is bullshit, man. Bullshit!' The trio of lawyers had already dispersed. Will watched Kilpatrick from the hallway. He said 'bullshit' two more times before leaving the room. He tried to slam the glass door behind him, but it was on a pneumatic closer.

Like magic, Laslo appeared at Will's elbow. Kilpatrick jabbed his finger at both of them, red-faced, furious. 'Walk this peckerhead to the lobby, then come back to my office. Pronto.' Kilpatrick punched the wall. The Sheetrock flexed but didn't puncture. He kicked it to the same effect before stalking away.

'Hey, peckerhead.' Laslo indicated the long walk back to the lobby. 'This way.'

'Laslo.' Will looked over the guy's head, taking advantage of the half-foot difference. He wasn't going to leave without Amanda, and something about the thug had rubbed him the wrong way. 'You gotta last name?'

'Yeah, it's Go Fuck Yourself. Now start moving.'

'Laslo Go Fuck Yourself.' Will didn't move. 'You gotta card?'

'I got my size ten up your ass if you don't get movin', buddy.'

Will forced a chuckle. He put his hands in his pockets like he had all day.

'What the fuck are you laughin' at?'

Will couldn't tame the thing inside of him that wanted to piss this guy off. He thought about the old lady from the lobby, the way her bottom lip had trembled. Was that because of Laslo? Kip Kilpatrick? Will felt instinctively that something was there.

He told Laslo, 'Mrs Lindsay warned me you're a pistol.'

Laslo's expression darkened, which meant Will had hit a nerve. Will wondered what the guy's rap sheet looked like back in Boston. He imagined there was some weight to it. He had prison ink on the side of his neck and the look of a man who could take a beating and still win the fight.

Laslo warned, 'You stay away from the old lady or I will fuck you up.'

'You'd better bring a ladder.'

'Don't think 'cause you're a cop I won't take you down.' Laslo put his hands on his hips, which Will thought was only appropriate for a man if he was standing on the sidelines at a game. Laslo's tight shirt gaped open. The material was stretched so thin that he could've saved his dry-cleaning bill and painted it on. He glared at Will, asking, 'What're you lookin' at, faggot?'

'That's a nice shirt. Does it come in adult sizes?'

The conference room door opened.

'Thank you so much,' Amanda called to Goldfinger. She smiled at Will, triumph putting a twinkle in her eyes. Marcus Rippy was important, but not as important as a two-point-eight-billion-dollar deal that everyone wanted a piece of.

Amanda asked Will, 'Ready?'

Laslo jabbed his thumb down the hall. 'This way.'

'Thank you, Mr Zivcovik.' Amanda took the lead toward the lobby. She asked Laslo, 'Did you manage to find the phone number for Ms Polaski?'

He didn't look away from Will as he passed her a piece of folded notepaper.

Amanda glanced at the number, then handed it to Will.

It was for the same disconnected line that was on everything.

Laslo yanked open the lobby door. 'Anything else I can do for y'alls?' He put on a hick accent that, layered on top of his Boston accent, made him sound like he was recovering from a stroke.

Amanda said, 'Young man, surely you've lived down here long enough to know that y'all is a second-person-plural pronoun.'

The comment was meant to be the last, but Will had a question for Laslo. 'Did you know Angie?'

'Polaski?' A toothy grin spread across his round face. 'Sure, I knew her.' He gave Will a knowing wink. 'She had a cunt like a boa constrictor.'

'Had?' Amanda asked.

He slammed the door in their faces.

SIX

Faith sat in an uncomfortable plastic chair across from the nurses' station inside the Grady Hospital ICU. There were armed guards at either end of the hall. The ward was full. Grady was Atlanta's only public hospital, a level one trauma center that saw most of the bad cases the city had to offer. At any given time, at least a quarter of the patients were handcuffed to their beds.

She glanced up at the whiteboard behind the desk. Olivia, the head nurse, was updating the status of one of the patients. Grady admitted a lot of Jane Does, but Faith only cared about her potential witness, Jane Doe 2. She was still marked critical. The junkie's surgery had taken four hours longer than planned. They'd had to rebuild her nose and throat. So much blood had been replaced that they'd basically put her into rapid detox from the coke. And now she was pumped full of morphine. She would be out of it for at least another hour, minimum.

At least Faith hadn't let her time go to waste. She had tackled Dale Harding's financial documents and phone records. Not that the task got her anywhere closer to a solution, let alone a clue to follow. Harding's phone calls were all for pizza or Chinese delivery, so he must have used a burner phone for business. As for his bank records, it didn't take a forensic accountant to understand the figures. Harding kept less than one hundred dollars in his checking account, a number that hadn't fluctuated much over the last six months, because he had used a gold MasterCard to charge everything, from his gorditas at Taco Bell to the support hose that kept the circulation going in his legs. The cumulative balance on the card for the last six months was forty-six thousand and change. Harding had stopped making payments on the bill. Faith assumed this was by design. He'd stopped dialysis, basically signing his own death warrant. He'd obviously planned to screw as many people as he could on his way out.

The question was, had one of those people been Delilah Palmer? Faith couldn't stop thinking about the porn photos, the dead look in the girl's eyes. Even back to ten years old, Delilah seemed to show the resignation that it was her fate to be used by every man who crossed her path. Not just any man, but Dale Harding. A cop. A father. The one person she should have been able to trust, and he kept nasty photos of her in his attic and married her because—why?

Delilah had to be the key to both Harding's and Angie's murders. Faith didn't buy Collier's feminist theory that the girl was behind their deaths. Harding had always taken care of Delilah. She would have known that he didn't have much time left. Why kill the guy when she could just wait a few days and dance on his grave?

Faith could think of a lot of people who would want Angie Polaski dead, so she kept the focus on Dale Harding. He was a gambler. He took risks. He had likely taken a final risk before his death, something with a big payout, which meant that Delilah, his legal wife, would be the beneficiary. Unless there was something illegal about the payout. That made more sense. And it also explained why Delilah's life would be in jeopardy.

And Faith had put that imbecile Collier in charge of finding her.

She scrolled through the sixteen different texts Collier had sent her since she'd left him at the Mesa Arms. If he was over-talkative in person, he was a freaking bible in the printed word. He peppered his texts with so much useless information about the weather, the songs on the radio and his dietary habits that Faith felt the need to distill the information into bullet points before her head exploded.

She reached into her cargo pants pocket and found her spiral notebook and pen. She flipped to a fresh page. At the top, she wrote four headers: PALMER, HARDING, POLASKI, RIPPY.

She tapped her pen on the blank columns underneath the names. Connections. That's what she needed to see. Delilah was married to Dale Harding, possibly his daughter. Harding worked for Rippy. According to the briefing Faith had gotten from Amanda, Angie worked for Kip Kilpatrick, which meant she really worked for Rippy.

Faith tapped the pen again. Angie probably knew Harding from way back. Bad cops stuck together. They told themselves they were outsiders because they were the only ones who could get the job done, but the truth was that good cops wanted nothing to do with them.

Faith turned to the next page and wrote QUESTIONS at the top.

1. Why did Angie and Harding meet at Rippy's club?
2. What does Delilah know?
3. Who would want to kill Harding?
4. Who would want to kill Angie?

If Harding and Angie knew each other from before, it made sense that one would tap the other for a job with Kip Kilpatrick. Harding had moved into the Mesa Arms six months ago, so Faith could reasonably assume that's when he'd started working for Kilpatrick. Angie's bank account had big checks coming in four months ago, so that meant she had worked for Kilpatrick at least four months.

Faith flipped back to the first page.

All of the arrows pointed to Marcus Rippy.

Her phone buzzed. Another lengthy text came in from Collier. Faith skimmed the lines for meaning, skipping over a report about the indigestion he'd gotten from a gas station hot dog. On Saturday, the day before the murder, Delilah Palmer had rented a black Ford Fusion from a Hertz location on Howell Mill Road. No security footage existed of the transaction. She had used her Visa card. Collier had put out a BOLO on the rental car. He'd also reiterated his heroin-mule theory, pointing out that dealers rented cars because they knew that their own rides would be seized by the cops if they were caught dealing out of them.

Again Faith tapped her pen against the notebook. She didn't buy Collier's drug angle. He was a hammer looking for a nail.

Delilah had rented the car Saturday, not Sunday or Monday, which implied that she had lined it up before Harding was murdered. Which could also imply that she knew ahead of time that Harding was in jeopardy and that she might need an escape. But she had used her own license and credit card to book the car. Delilah had been on the streets for years. She was too savvy to use her own name for a getaway.

Faith's phone vibrated again. Another text, blissfully short.

GIRLZ SAY SOUZA OD'D 6 MOS AGO. DEAD END. DEAD, GET IT?

Faith had to scroll back through her texts to remind herself who Souza was. She found the pertinent missive time-stamped two hours ago. According to some of Collier's sources in zone six, Virginia Souza was another whore for whom Harding had called in a handful of favors. She worked Delilah's street corner. She was fairly violent, considering she had been twice charged with assault against a minor. Faith wondered if that minor had been Delilah Palmer.

She looked at the text again. Collier's sign-off was to say that he was going to talk to the younger whores, who might know something or someone who could point him toward Delilah Palmer's whereabouts. Or he was talking to young whores because he was Collier. He had signed off with a series of eggplant emojis that, going by Jeremy's Facebook page, were a stand-in for a bunch of penises.

Faith returned to her notebook. Lots of arrows connecting back to Rippy. Lots of questions. No answers. She should've let Collier rot here at the hospital while she tracked down Delilah Palmer. That was the problem with murder cases. You never knew which lead would take you to the solution and which one would sink you into a black hole. Faith was getting the feeling that she had given Collier the good lead. She was going to throw herself off the roof of this building if he ended up lucking into their bad guy.

Her phone vibrated again. She didn't want to read another dissertation from Collier's awesome gumshoe file, but ignorance was a luxury she did not have. She looked at the screen. CALL FROM WANTANABE, B.

Faith stood up and walked down the hall for privacy. 'Mitchell.'

'Is this Special Agent Faith Mitchell?' a woman asked.

'Yes.'

'I'm Barbara Wantanabe. Violet told me you wanted to talk?'

Faith had almost forgotten about Harding's next-door neighbor. 'Thanks for getting back to me. I was wondering if you could tell me about Dale Harding.'

'Oh, I could give you an earful,' she said, and then she proceeded to do just that, complaining about the smell from his house, the way he sometimes parked his car with the wheels on the grass, his foul language, the loud volume on his television and radio.

Faith followed along as best she could. Barb was even more verbose than Collier. She had a way of saying something, then contradicting herself, then restating the first thing she had said, then equivocating, and by the fifth time she'd wound herself into a rhetorical knot, Faith started to understand why Harding had hated her so much.

'And don't even get me started on the music.'

Faith listened as she started on Harding's music. The same rap album, morning noon and night. Her grandson said it was Jay Z, something called *The Black Album*. Faith was familiar with the record, which her own son had played loudly behind the closed door of his room because it was the perfect backdrop to his white male privilege and early acceptance to one of the most prestigious universities in the country.

Faith tuned back into Barb, looking for a chance to jump in. Finally the woman had to stop to take a breath. 'Did he have visitors?'

'No,' Barb said, then, 'yes. I mean, I think so, yes. He might have had *a* visitor.'

Faith covered her eyes with her hand. 'I sense some uncertainty.'

'Well, yes. That's true. I am uncertain.'

She had to float Collier's drug-mule theory. 'Did you see people coming in and out? Like a lot of people who looked like they didn't fit in with the neighborhood?'

'No, nothing like that. I would've called the police. It's just that I thought there might be someone else, another person, over there at some point.'

'At which point?'

'Recently. Well, no, that's not right. Last month.'

'You thought someone was visiting at Dale's house last month?'

'Yes. Well, maybe staying there? Visiting might not be the right word.'

Faith gritted her teeth.

'I mean to say that there could've been someone living over there. I think. When Dale was gone. Now, he was usually not there during the day when he first moved in, but later, he was always there. Which was when the problem started. When he was there. Which sounds mean, but there you go.'

Faith tried to wrap her brain around all the information. 'So, when Dale first moved in six months ago, he was never home, but then you noticed that changed last month?'

'Exactly.'

'And around the time that changed, you heard sounds from next door that indicated someone other than Dale might be living there?'

'Yes.'

Faith waited for the contradictory no, but it never came.

'I heard sounds, you see.' Barb paused before the next hedge. 'Not sounds, per se. I mean, they could've been from the television. But who watches television and plays a rap album at the same time?' She immediately went back on herself. 'Then again, some people might do that.'

'They might,' Faith said. Especially if they wanted to cover up a noise, like a junkie beating on the closet door demanding to be let out. She asked, 'Did you ever hear any banging?'

'Banging?'

'Someone banging on a wall or banging on a door?'

'Well . . .' She took her time considering the question.

Faith called up a mental image of the Tahoe floorplan at the Mesa Arms. The guest room was against the shared wall of the duplex. The master was to the outside, which gave the room more windows, but it also afforded more privacy.

Large master closet ideal for keeping women!

Barb said, 'I guess you could say the noise sounded like a hammer.'

'Like a hammer pounding something?'

'Yes, but repeatedly. Maybe he was hanging pictures.' She paused. 'No, that would've been a lot of pictures. Not that it was constant—the noise—but it was long enough. I suppose he could've been assembling some furniture. My son does that for me. But only when he can find the time. My daughter-in-law, you see. But really, with Dale, the excrement was the real problem.'

Faith felt her mind boggle. 'Say what, now?'

'Excrement. You know . . .' she lowered her voice, 'doo-doo.'

'Waste?'

'Human.'

Faith had to repeat the two words together. 'Human waste?'

'Yes. In the backyard.' She sighed. 'You see, Dale would rinse out this bucket every evening, and at first I thought that he was painting inside, which made sense, because you would listen to music while you paint, yes?'

Faith threw out her hand. 'Sure.'

'And so I assumed that he was painting his walls, and not a very nice color, but then my grandson went into the backyard one day looking for twigs for Mr Nimh to chew on. Their teeth grow constantly, you see. Oh!' She sounded excited. 'Thank you, by the way, for finding him. I was persona non grata with my daughter-in-law for that particular crime. Believe me, she keeps a list. Now, I wasn't a big fan of my own mother-in-law, but you do what you have to do, yes? It's called respect.'

Faith tried to get Barb back on track. 'Let's go back to the excrement.' There were six words she never thought she'd say. 'You saw Dale cleaning out the bucket every night?'

'Yes.'

'Starting when?'

'Two weeks ago? No.' She doubled back. 'Ten days. I would say ten days ago.'

'A large bucket, not the kind you'd use to mop your floor?'

'Right. Yes. For paint. Or I suppose solvents, but that size. Big.'

'And one day your grandson went into the backyard and he found something? Smelled something?'

'Yes. No. Both. He smelled something, and then he walked over. It was a slime, sort of? Whatever it was, it got all over the bottom of his shoe.'

The rat must have been thrilled.

Barb said, 'I had to wash the sole with the hose. It was disgusting. And his mother was furious at me. Now, she's my daughter-in-law, and I know that I have to play by her rules, but honestly—'

'Did you ask Dale about the excrement?'

'Oh no. I couldn't talk to Dale about anything. That would be pointless. He would just curse at me and walk away.'

Faith understood why. 'Did you ever see a different car at Dale's house other than his white Kia?'

'Not that I recall.' She showed an unusual certainty. 'No, I'm sure I never did.'

'Are you home much?' Faith tried to tread carefully, because a lot of times even well-meaning people stretched the truth. 'I'm asking because you weren't home this afternoon.'

'I've been volunteering more at the YMCA. I fold towels, help keep things straightened up. I'm very clean, you see, which is why I had some issues with Dale. I don't like things messed up. There's no reason not to pick something up and put it right back where you found it, yes?'

'Yes.' Faith covered her eyes with her hand again. The woman never met a tangent she didn't travel. 'So you stepped up your volunteering to get away from Dale?'

'Correct. At first volunteering was just a way to get out of the house for a few hours. And to help people. Of course to help people. But then it became my only respite away from the noise. And the odor. You smelled the odor, yes? I couldn't live with it all day, you see. It was unbearable.'

Faith wondered if Barb's absence had been the very thing Harding was pushing for all along. If he was keeping Delilah locked in the closet to dry her out, he would want to make sure no one would hear her screaming and call the police.

Faith asked, 'When did you start spending more time away?'

'Last week.'

'So, seven days ago?'

'Yes.'

Which meant that Dale had managed to drive her out after three days of relentless torture.

Barb said, 'I just gave up. It was getting worse and worse. The smell. The noises. I couldn't take it anymore, and I'm not the type to complain. Violet can verify that.'

Faith had the feeling Violet would do no such thing. 'Well, I'm very sorry that you had to go through that, Ms Wantanabe. I appreciate your talking to me. If you think of anything else—'

'It's sad,' she interrupted. 'When he first moved in, I thought he was just a lonely old bachelor. He was obviously having health issues. He didn't seem very happy. And I thought to myself, *This is a good place for him*. We're a community here. We all have our differences. As Violet would say, some of us are to the right of

Genghis Khan and the rest are to the left of Pluto, but we look out for each other, you know?'

Faith felt her phone vibrate. 'Yes, ma'am. It seemed like a nice place. I need to—'

'You get to a certain age, you learn to look past people's quirks and idiosyncrasies.' She gave a long sigh. 'But I'll tell you what, honey. There's no looking past human poop in your backyard.'

'Well, okay.' Faith's phone vibrated again. There was a text from Will. 'Thank you, ma'am. Call me if you think of anything else.'

Faith ended the call before Barb could toss out another bon mot. She opened Will's text. He'd sent her a photo of the front of Grady, which was Will's way of saying he was at the hospital looking for her. Faith texted back an emoji of a dinner plate and a smiling pile of shit, meaning she would meet him in the food court.

She checked the patient board as she walked past the nurses' station. Jane Doe 2 was still critical. Faith didn't bother to ask the nurses for an update. They had her card. They had promised to text the minute the patient was coherent enough to talk.

Faith started down the stairs. She tapped the pockets of her cargo pants, making sure her blood testing kit was still there. She had two insulin pens left. She had used a third half an hour ago, so she needed to eat. The problem was that Grady only offered fast-food restaurants. This was great for their new cardiac wing, but it was awful if you were trying to control your diabetes. Not that she felt like controlling anything right now. Faith longed for the days when she could eat herself into a stupor that drowned out her stress.

Will had beaten her to the food court. He was sitting at a quiet table in the back. She didn't recognize him at first because he was in jeans and a beautiful long-sleeved polo that Sara had obviously sneaked into his wardrobe. He was a nice-looking guy, but he had a habit of blending in, which made him unlike every other cop she had ever met.

Will asked, 'Is this okay?'

He meant the salad he'd ordered for her. Faith stared at the wilted lettuce and white chicken strips that looked like fingers on a dead man. Will's tray had two cheeseburgers, large fries, a large Frosty and a Coke.

'Looks good.' Faith sat down, fighting the urge to unhinge her jaw and swallow everything on his tray. 'Thanks.'

He said, 'Amanda scheduled an on-the-record interview with Rippy tomorrow.'

'I know. She caught me up on everything.'

'Everything?'

'I know about the bank account you shared with Angie. And I agree that you shouldn't tell Sara about it.'

Will didn't answer. He had never been one for unsolicited advice. 'I got Laslo Zivcovik's sheet out of Boston. He's got some misdemeanors—open bottle, speeding, an assault against a woman and a felony manslaughter for a bar fight. He stabbed a guy twenty-eight times and left him to bleed to death. Laslo pulled a dime in big-boy prison.'

'Felony manslaughter?' Faith said. 'He must've had a good lawyer.'

'I'm assuming he was mobbed up, or was working for the Boston version of Kip Kilpatrick.'

'Does it bother you what he said about Angie?'

'I'm more worried that he knows what a snake's vagina feels like.'

Faith stared at him.

He shrugged. 'It's like living with an alcoholic. You're not surprised when somebody tells you they're at a bar.'

Faith had dated an alcoholic for years. Worrying about your partner choking on his own vomit or killing someone in a DUI was not the same as knowing he was out there fucking everything that moved.

Which, in retrospect, should have also been one of the things she worried about.

Will said, 'I met this woman outside Kilpatrick's office. Mrs Lindsay. African American, really put together. She had pearls around her neck. Probably in her seventies. She gave me a lot of information about herself. I got the feeling she was in a bad place.'

'Could be she's the mother of one of the players, worried her son's going off the deep end.'

'She talked about a daughter, but tangentially. Not the way you'd talk about your kid if she was good enough to play at that level.'

Will's gut instinct put Faith's to shame. She asked, 'What's bothering you about her?'

'Her lip quivered.' He touched his own lip. 'She seemed nervous. Upset.'

'She knew you were a cop?'

'Yes.'

'Did you get a first name?'

'No, but she told me that she lives in that apartment complex at Jesus Junction.'

'That's pretty detailed.'

'Not detailed enough. I called the building. There's no Mrs Lindsay there.'

Faith found it interesting that he'd bothered to call. 'A woman that age will have a church. You should try the AME on Arden.'

He nodded.

'Who was she there to see?'

'Kilpatrick, I'm assuming. Laslo fetched her. Called her Miss Lindsay.'

That threw up a flag. Calling a woman of that age Miss was just plain disrespectful. Unless it wasn't. 'Lindsay could be her first name. An older Southern woman like that might go by Miss as a form of respect, like *Driving Miss Daisy*.'

'I hadn't thought of that.' Will shrugged. 'It's probably nothing.'

'It's more than I've got to go on. You should make some calls in the morning.' She was aware that the errand sounded like busywork to keep him off Angie's case, so she tried to put a better spin on the task. 'Harding shows up dead at Rippy's club. Angie is working for Kilpatrick. Laslo is Kilpatrick's bulldog. Miss Lindsay shows up a few hours after the murder. Laslo takes her back into the offices, probably to Kilpatrick. You know where I'm going with this. There's no such thing as a coincidence.'

'She wasn't in his office,' Will said. 'Miss Lindsay. I didn't see her anywhere, actually. She might have been downstairs. She could've been seeing somebody else.'

'Or they could've been hiding her from you.'

'Yeah, maybe.' He started back in on the Frosty. 'Catch me up on your day.'

'It was like Whac-a-Mole without the hammer.' Faith picked at her salad as she ran down what she'd found out about Harding's life—the battles with Barb Wantanabe, the rat, the smell, the excrement, the naked photos of Delilah Palmer and the marriage certificate.

The last part caught Will's attention. 'He lists her as his daughter, but two years later she's his wife?'

'Yep.'

'And it's the same young woman from the nudie pic in his wallet?'

'He's got nudie pics going back to her elementary school days.'

He put down the Frosty. 'Harding was a pedophile.'

'Yes. Maybe.' She sounded like Barb Wantanabe. 'Here's what's bothering me: for the most part, pedophiles have age groups. If you like preteens, that's your thing. If you like them in between or after puberty, that's your thing. I know it happens, but it's very rare for them to stick with one victim as she ages.'

'It's rare to stick with just one victim, period. A guy Harding's age would have hundreds of victims. You didn't find any other photos?'

Faith shook her head as she forced down a piece of rubbery chicken. 'There was a second girl Harding called in favors for. Virginia Souza. Harding didn't have any pictures of her, nothing was in his files. She's dead. OD'd six months ago.'

'The magic six months,' Will said. 'You're thinking Harding was keeping Delilah at his house to dry her out?'

'Locked in his closet with nothing but a pot to piss in, as it were.' She thought of something. 'Maybe he had Angie locked in there?'

'No way. She would've clawed through the Sheetrock and killed him.'

Faith knew that he was not speaking metaphorically. 'Collier thinks Harding was running drug mules.'

Will gave her a skeptical look. 'Mexican cartels don't use doorknobs to send a message.'

She laughed, mostly because he'd made Collier look like an idiot. 'Okay, so we'll assume Delilah was the only woman Harding kept in his closet. Why did he lock her up?'

'Because he cared about her.' Will held up his hands to stop her protests. 'Harding chose to go off dialysis. He knew he was going to die, and soon. This is literally how he planned to spend the rest of his life—drying her out.'

'Maybe he felt responsible for fucking her up.' She remembered the dental device by the bed in the guest room. 'Somebody also sprang for an orthodontist. She was sleeping with a retainer.'

'We could get Collier's partner on that. Call all of the orthodontists in the area to see if she's a patient.'

Faith picked up her phone and started typing. 'I'll pass that through Amanda,' she said, but she suggested that Collier and Ng did the shitwork together.

Will waited until she had sent the text. 'You said Palmer's first big arrest was for slinging Oxy. Where was she getting the pills, do you think?'

Faith considered the question. 'She was living in the 'hood, attending elementary school. Adderall, Concerta, Ritalin—that's what you'd expect to find floating around. ADD/ADHD drugs. Valium and Percocet come along in middle school. Oxy is more high school, more of a suburban white people problem.'

'So who was supplying Delilah with Oxy to sell when she was ten years old?'

'Harding was white collar. He wouldn't have access.' Faith thought it through. Her mother had run the drug squad out of zone six. The evidence lockup would've looked like a pharmacy. 'Harding might know somebody who had access. Maybe he located a cop with a pill problem and Harding pressured him into sharing the take.'

'Zone six?'

She nodded.

Will's demeanor changed.

'Do you know somebody who worked zone six and had a pill problem who might've been connected to Harding?'

'Yeah,' he said, and he didn't have to tell her that it was Angie. 'She takes care of kids like that. At least she used to.'

'Kids like Delilah?' Faith felt her stomach turn. It was one thing for Angie to pimp out other women for high-end parties, but exploiting orphaned little girls was beyond the pale.

Will said, 'Angie worked vice. The young ones—she kind of took them under her wing.'

'And gave them pills to sell?'

Will rubbed his jaw. 'Angie knows what it's like to be stuck in that kind of situation with no one looking out for you.'

'You've lost me,' Faith said. 'I don't see the compassionate side of turning a ten-year-old into a drug mule.'

'Which is worse: selling Oxy or selling sex?'

'Those are the only two choices?'

'For kids like that, stuck in the system, changing schools and foster homes five times a year, never knowing where they're gonna sleep from one night to the next?' He sounded emphatic. 'Yeah, those are the choices.'

The mother side of Faith wanted to argue him down. The cynical side, the one who'd been a cop for fifteen years, could see the logic. Kids like that didn't live the lives they wanted. They survived the lives they had.

Will asked, 'How many strings did Harding have to pull to keep Delilah out of trouble?'

'More than a harp player.'

'Who did the favors?'

'That's not how favors work. You don't talk about them. That's kind of the point.' Faith heard her voice echo in the food court. She sounded pissed off, and maybe she was. Sure, kids like Delilah Palmer had it bad, but teaching them how to successfully enter the criminal underworld was not the solution. 'Jesus, Will. Do you really think Angie was giving little girls pills to sell?'

Will drummed his fingers on the table. He stared over her shoulder, which was probably one of his most annoying recurrent tactics.

Faith speared a piece of chicken. The tension over Angie's possible bad good deeds sat on the table between them. Faith forgot sometimes how rough Will's life had been. This was entirely his own fault. From the outside, he seemed like a normal guy. And then you noticed the scars on his face. Or the fact that he never rolled up his sleeves, even in ten-thousand-degree heat. He never talked about any of it. Actually, he never talked about anything. Like that the open cuts on his fist meant that he'd recently punched somebody. Like that his wife was probably dead. Or that his girlfriend's heart was broken.

'Faith?' Will waited for her to look up. He tried to smile. 'I feel like I need to see the rat.'

She let out a long breath that she didn't realize she'd been holding. She pulled the video up on her phone and slid it across the table. 'Collier threw up. Epically. The godfather of vomiting.'

Will laughed appreciatively. He played the video. Twice. Faith could hear Collier's panicked breathing through the speaker. It got better each time. Will finally put down the phone. 'That's a Russian Blue.'

'The rat?'

'I raided a pet store once. The guy was selling exotic animals out of the back, but the front was filled with rats. Amanda made me catalog all of them.' He slid the phone back her way. 'Dale could've gone after Angie to protect Delilah. Clean up the mess before he clocked out.'

She shrugged, but the theory made sense.

He said, 'If there's a drug angle, that opens this up.'

'You mean we'll have to tell Amanda.'

Will nodded.

'God dammit,' Faith muttered. 'Collier wanted to track down those gang tags in the club. I'm going to kill myself if he was right.'

'Let's not get ahead of ourselves,' Will said. 'It's a theory, right? We don't know for sure what Angie was up to.'

'Except getting paid ten grand a month by Kilpatrick.'

'Maybe she was hooking him up with drugs.'

'I'd buy that if they were growth hormones or steroids.'

'He wouldn't need Angie for that. He'd have doctors writing legal scripts.' Will sat back in his chair. 'Let's say we find Delilah and she's never heard of Angie. Then what?'

'Then she tells us what the hell is going on.' Faith didn't give Will time to laugh in her face, because they both knew that was very unlikely. Girls like Delilah didn't talk to cops. They waited out their time, then they disappeared.

Faith took out her notebook. He couldn't read her scrawl, but she pointed to the headers. 'Palmer was married to and possibly related to Harding. Harding lived in a house owned by a company that probably traces back to Kip Kilpatrick. Angie was working for Kip Kilpatrick. Harding hit the jackpot six months ago. Angie started getting her payday four months ago.' She pointed to the last name. 'They all tie to Rippy.'

Will took the notebook. He studied the names. Faith saw his eyes move, but she didn't know how quickly he could take it in. She knew that he was better with words he had seen before, but there were new names on the paper.

Will put the notebook down. He asked, 'What if we were building a case right now? Palmer is in the wind for whatever reason. Rippy is Teflon. The only two people we know for sure about are Harding and Angie. They were both at the same location, the club. One of them died there. The other died because of something that happened there. Probably died.'

Faith let the 'probably' slide by.

He said, 'These arrows to Rippy look good on paper, but we don't really have a direct connection, because all of them go through here—' He tapped his finger on Kilpatrick's name. 'He's the intermediary, the thing standing between Rippy and everybody else. Let's say by some miracle we have a solid murder charge with evidence and all that other good stuff and the judge gives us an arrest warrant. It won't be Rippy we charge. It'll be Kilpatrick. That's what Rippy pays him for. And if you're thinking we can build a conspiracy charge, you're dreaming. Harding's dead. Angie's probably dead. Rippy walks away just like he always does.'

She couldn't accept that he was right, even though every single word made absolute sense. 'Jane Doe could've seen something. She was in the office building across the street. She would've had a bird's-eye view.' Faith looked at the time on her phone. 'She should be coming out of her morphine stupor soon. We can talk to her.'

Will didn't look hopeful.

Faith closed her notebook. She couldn't look at it anymore. 'Why do you think she tried to kill herself?'

'Maybe she was lonely?' He laid his arm across the back of the empty chair beside him. 'It's hard being homeless. You don't know who to trust. You never really sleep. There's nobody to talk to.'

Faith realized that Will was the first person who had actually tried to answer the question. 'How much coke did she have?'

'I'd guess about two ounces.'

'Jesus Christ. That's almost three grand's worth of coke. Where the hell did she get it?'

'We can ask her when she wakes up.' He put his hand to his chest. He winced in pain. 'I feel like I'm having a heart attack.'

Panic shook her into action. She started to stand, but he stopped her.

'Not for real. Just this tightness.' He rubbed his chest with his fingers. 'Like a shaking, almost. Do you ever get that, where your heart shakes in your chest?'

Faith got it all of the time. 'That sounds like stress.'

Will kept rubbing his chest. 'Sara sent me a picture of Betty. She was in her bed at Sara's place. That's good, right?'

Faith nodded, but she had no idea. Will had his own way of communicating with people.

He said, 'I checked online. That lipstick costs sixty bucks.'

Faith nearly choked on a piece of lettuce. The most expensive thing she had ever put on her face was a New York strip after a perp had punched her in the eye.

Will said, 'All the colors looked the same to me. Can you pull the product number from the evidence log?'

'Will.' Faith put down her fork. 'Sara doesn't care about the lipstick.'

He shook his head, like she had no idea. 'She was really, really pissed off.'

'Will, listen to me. It's not about the money. It's about Angie stealing it.'

'That's just how Angie is.' The excuse seemed to make sense to him. 'When we were growing up, none of us had anything. If you saw something you wanted, you took it. Otherwise you never had anything. Especially anything nice.'

Faith struggled for a way to explain it to him. 'What if one of Sara's ex-boyfriends broke into her apartment and stole the shirt that you sleep in?'

'Wouldn't it make more sense for him to steal Sara's shirt?'

Faith groaned. Men had it so easy. When they got mad at each other, they fought it out. Women cut themselves and gave each other eating disorders.

She said, 'Remember that suicide last year at the women's detention center?'

'Alexis Rodriguez. She cut her wrists.'

'Right. And when we asked the other inmates why she did it, they said that girls had been stealing her stuff. Not just her commissary. She'd put down a pen and the next thing she knows, it's missing. She'd take off her socks and they'd disappear. They even stole her trash. Why do you think they did that?'

He shrugged. 'To be mean.'

'To make her understand that nothing belonged to her. That no matter how important or inconsequential, they could take away anything at any time, and she couldn't do anything about it.'

He looked dubious.

'Why else would Angie leave those notes on Sara's car?'

'She was mad.'

'Sure, she was mad, but she was fucking with Sara.'

Will shifted in his seat. He still wasn't seeing it.

'Angie was a bully, Will. And she wanted Sara to know that she could take you back anytime she wanted. That's why she stole the lipstick. That's why she left the notes. She was marking her territory.' Faith had to say the next part. 'And you let her get away with it.'

Will sat back in his chair. He did not stand up and leave. He did not tell her to mind her own business. He rubbed the side of his jaw. He stared at the trashcan by the door.

Faith waited. And waited. She tried to finish her salad. She checked to make sure that there were no new messages on her phone.

'She left me a note,' Will said. 'Angie.'

Faith kept waiting.

'Amanda doesn't know. At least I don't think she does. It was in the post office box.' He stared at his hands. 'She printed my name on the outside, but the letter is in cursive.'

Faith knew that Will had trouble reading cursive. Angie would know this too, which to Faith's thinking made her an even bigger bitch than before.

He said, 'I can't let Sara read it. The letter.'

'No, you can't.'

'It's what she wanted. For Sara to have to read it. Out loud. To me.'

'It is.'

'So . . . ?'

Faith felt her throat work. He had never asked her to read anything for him. It had always been a point of pride. He took his turn writing up their reports. He was the only man she had ever worked with who didn't try to turn her into his private secretary.

Faith said, 'All right.'

He reached into his front pocket and pulled out a piece of folded notebook paper. The edge was tattered from being ripped away from the spiral. He unfolded the letter and smoothed it out on the table. Angry words filled the page, crossing the margins, spilling onto the back. Things were underlined. The pen had actually torn through the paper.

Faith's eyes picked up the word *Sara*, and she cringed inside. 'Are you sure?'

Will didn't say anything. He just waited.

Faith didn't know what to do but turn the letter around and start to read. '"Hey, baby. If someone is reading this to you, then I am dead."'

Will put his head in his hands.

'"I hope it's Sara, because I want that cu—"' Faith cursed Angie under her breath. '"I want that cunt to know that you will never, ever love her the way that you love me."' She glanced up at Will. He still had his head in his hands.

Faith returned to the letter.

'"Remember the basement? I want you to tell your precious Sara about the basement because that will explain everything. She will understand that you have only been fucking her because she is a poor substitute for me. You have been lying to her about everything."' Faith squinted at the scrawl, trying to decipher the next few words. '"You like her because she's safe, and because she'll—"' Faith stopped. Her eyes had skipped ahead. She told Will, 'I don't think—'

'Please.' His voice was muffled by his hands. 'If you don't read it, I'll never know.'

Faith cleared her throat. Her face burned with embarrassment. For herself. For Sara. '"You like her because she's safe and because she'll go down on you and you never see her spit because that is part of her scam. She is your lapdog for a reason."' Faith silently scanned ahead, praying it wouldn't get worse.

It did.

'"Needy bitches like Sara want the white picket fence and the kids in the yard. How would that be, having a bunch of little monsters with your fucked-up genes inside of them? Loser retards like you who can't read their own fucking names."'

Faith had to stop again, this time to tamp down her own fury.

She continued. '"Ask yourself this: would you ever risk your life for her? Sara Linton is a boring bitch. That's why you can't let me go. That's why you found this fucking letter. She will never excite you like I do. You will never want her like you want me. She will never understand who you really are. The only person on earth who ever got you was me, and now I am dead, and you didn't do a God damm thing to stop that from happening."' Faith felt a palpable relief as she read the last line. '"Love, Angie."'

Will kept his head in his hands.

Faith folded the note back into a square. This was evidence. Angie had suspected that she was going to die, which meant her murder was premeditated. Faith let that play out in her head. If and when they caught the killer, there would be a court case. The letter to Will would become part of the public record. This was Angie's final swipe at Sara. The blow would be a knockout.

Faith said, 'You need to destroy this.'

Will looked up. His eyes glistened in the overhead lights.

Faith tore the letter in two. Then she tore it again, then another time, until Angie's hateful words were ripped into a million pieces.

Will said, 'Do you think she's dead?'

'Yes. You saw the blood. You heard what Angie wrote, that she knew she would be dead soon.' Faith culled the tiny shreds of paper into a pile. 'Don't tell Sara about the letter. It will destroy everything. Exactly what Angie wanted.'

He started rubbing his chest again. His face was pale.

She tried to remember the signs of a heart attack. 'Does your arm hurt?'

'I feel numb,' he said, and he seemed as surprised as Faith that he had admitted as much. 'How do people get through this?'

'I don't know.' Faith dragged her finger through the torn pieces of paper, then piled them back up again. 'When my dad died, my world turned upside down.' She felt tears well into her eyes, because fifteen years was still not enough time to get over the loss. 'The day of the funeral, I didn't think I could do it. Jeremy was a wreck. My dad worked at home. They were extremely close.' Faith took a breath. 'So, we get to the funeral and Jeremy just loses it. Sobbing like I hadn't seen since he was a baby. He wouldn't let go of me. I had to hold him the entire time.'

She looked up at Will. 'I remember standing on the stairs to the chapel, and I felt this click, like, "Okay, you're the mom. Be strong for your kid and deal with this when you're alone and you can handle it."' Faith smiled, but the truth was that she was never alone. If she was lucky, she had thirty minutes in the morning before Emma woke up, and then the phone started ringing and she had to get ready for work and the world started crashing in. 'How people do it is they don't have a choice. You get out of bed. You dress yourself. You go to work, and you just do it.'

'Denial,' Will said. 'I've heard of that.'

'It has made me the woman I am today.'

He drummed his fingers on the table. He studied her the way he did when he was trying to figure out what was wrong. 'Delilah Palmer. You're worried because you gave Collier the good lead.'

Hearing him guess what was wrong made her realize what was wrong. 'It's not because I want the collar. I mean, hell, yeah, of course I want the collar, but there's something about Collier that—'

'I don't trust him either.'

Her phone chirped. The nurse had finally texted her. 'Oh for fucksakes.' Faith had to read the message twice before she believed it. 'Jane Doe was taken back into surgery. If she makes it, we won't be able to talk to her until tomorrow morning.'

Will laughed, but not because it was funny. 'Now what?'

'I'm going home.' Faith swept Angie's shredded note into her open palm. She handed the pieces to Will. 'Flush this down the toilet, then go talk to Sara.'

SEVEN

Sara lay on the couch with Betty on the pillow beside her. The little dog had managed to wrap her entire body around Sara's head. Her two greyhounds, Bob and Billy, were draped across her legs.

She had started out the evening at her dining-room table researching uremic frost while she drank a cup of herbal tea. Then she'd moved onto a glass of wine at the kitchen counter while she edited a paper for a journal. Then she had looked around the apartment and decided that it needed to be cleaned. Sara always cleaned when she was upset, but this was one of those rare occasions when she was actually too upset to clean. Which is how she'd ended up lying on the couch, drinking a Scotch and covered in dogs.

She sipped her drink as she watched the laptop propped up on a pillow on her stomach. As with the rest of the evening, her lesser demons had won out. She'd started out with a documentary about Peggy Guggenheim and ended up watching *Buffy the Vampire Slayer*. Or trying to. The plot wasn't that complicated—obviously, Buffy was going to slay a vampire—but between the alcohol and her other problems, Sara couldn't focus.

Will hadn't called. He hadn't texted, even when she'd sent him a picture of Betty. He had spent all day looking for Angie, and even now, when Angie was almost certainly dead, Will still hadn't made the effort to get in touch with her.

If Sara had been the type to force a choice, she would've taken Will's lack of communication as an answer.

She paused the computer. She took off her glasses. She closed her eyes.

Sara let her mind drift back to Saturday morning, ignoring the part where Will had seen Angie. Friday night, they had decided to stay at Will's house because he had a fenced-in backyard and a dog door in the kitchen, which meant that the animals would be able to take care of themselves while the humans slept in.

Sara had awakened at 4:30. The curse of the on-call doctor. Her brain wouldn't shut down long enough for her to go back to sleep. She thought about doing some work, or calling her sister, but she had found herself watching Will sleep, which was the silly kind of thing you only saw in movies.

He was on his back, head turned. A sliver of light from underneath the window shade played across his face. She had stroked his cheek. The roughness of his skin had kindled an interest in further exploration. She let her fingers travel along his chest. Instead of continuing down, she placed her palm over his heart and felt the steady beats.

This is what she remembered from that morning: the overwhelming joy of ownership. His heart belonged to her. His mind. His body. His soul. They had been together for only a year, but every day that passed, she loved him more. Her relationship with Will was one of the most meaningful connections she'd had in her life.

Not that Sara had been in that many relationships. Her first boyfriend, Steve Mann, had elicited all of the excitement possible for a third trombone in the high school band. Mason James, whom she'd met during medical school, had been more in love with himself than any woman could ever hope to be. The first time Sara had introduced him to her family, her mother had quipped, 'That man needs to build a bridge to get over himself.'

Then there was Jeffrey Tolliver, her husband.

Sara opened her eyes.

She took another sip of her drink, which was more water than Scotch at this point. She checked the time. Too late to call her sister. Sara wanted to talk to someone, to work through the grand explosion that had shattered her life, and Tessa was the only safe haven. Faith had to be on Will's side because she was his partner and their unquestioned loyalty was what kept them both safe. Calling her mother was not an option. The first thing out of Cathy Linton's mouth would be a giant 'I told you so.'

And God knows her mother had told her so. Many times. Countless times. Don't date a married man. Don't fall in love with a married man. Don't ever think that you can trust a married man. Sara had thought there was more nuance to their story than her mother was picking up on, but now she was having second thoughts. The only words worse than 'I told you so' were 'Yes, Mother, you were right.'

Sara looked at the time again. Not even a minute had ticked by. She weighed the consequences of waking up her sister. Tessa was in South Africa. It was two in the morning on her side of the world. She would panic if the phone rang so early. Besides, Sara knew exactly how the conversation would go. The first thing out of Tessa's mouth would be 'Show him how you feel.'

What she meant was that Sara should break down in front of Will, let him see that she was a basket case and couldn't live without him. Which was a lie, because Sara could live without Will. She would be miserable, she would be devastated, but she could manage it. Losing her husband had taught her at least that.

But Tessa wouldn't let Sara hide behind Jeffrey's death. She would likely say something about riding a high horse into the lonely sunset. Sara would remind her that one of the things Will liked about her was her strength. Tessa would say that she was confusing strength with stubbornness, and then she would do what she always did: allude to what her family called the Bambi incident. The first time they had watched the film, Tessa had wept uncontrollably. Sara had mumbled an excuse about needing to study for a spelling test because she hadn't wanted anyone to see her crying.

Tessa's final point would be delivered in a tone reminiscent of their mother: 'Only a fool thinks she can fool other people.'

On the contrary, Sara had made a career out of fooling people. If you were a parent with a sick kid, the last thing you needed was a doctor who couldn't stop bawling. If you were a terrified patient, you didn't want to see your doctor break down at your bedside. The skills transferred. There was nothing to be gained by turning into a mess in front of Will. It was a cheap way to win an argument. He would comfort her, and she would feel horrible for manipulating him, and in the morning nothing would've changed.

He would still be in love with his wife.

Sara took a mouthful of Scotch and held it before she swallowed.

Was that the truth? Did Will really love Angie the way a husband loved his wife? He had lied to Sara about seeing her on Saturday. He was probably lying about other things. Death had a way of focusing your emotions. Maybe losing Angie had made Will realize that he didn't want Sara after all.

There was no need for him to call or text if there was nothing left to say.

The dogs shifted. Bob jumped down from the couch. Billy followed. Sara heard a soft knock at the door. She looked at the door as if it could explain how someone had gotten into the building without using the intercom system. Sara was on the penthouse floor. She had only one neighbor, Abel Conford, who was on vacation for the month.

There was another soft knock. The dogs ambled over to the door. Betty stayed on the pillow. She yawned.

Sara put her laptop on the coffee table. She forced herself to stand up. And to not get angry, because the only reason the dogs weren't barking was because they recognized the man knocking on the door.

She had given Will a key last year. It was cute that he'd still knocked on the door the first week after. Now, it was annoying.

Sara opened the door. Will had his hands in his pockets. He was wearing jeans and the gray Ermenegildo Zegna polo she had slipped in with his Gap T-shirts.

He saw the laptop. 'You're watching *Buffy* without me?'

Sara left the door open and went back to retrieve her drink. The loft was open-concept, the living room, dining-room and kitchen taking up one large space. Sara was glad to be able to put some distance between them. She sat down on the couch. Betty stood from the pillow. She stretched and yawned again, but didn't go to Will.

He didn't go to the dog either. Or Sara. He stood with his back against the kitchen counter. He asked, 'She did okay? At the vet?'

'Yes.'

His hands were gripped together the way he used to do when he twisted his wedding ring around his finger. The skin over the knuckles of his index and middle fingers was broken open.

Sara didn't ask about the injury. She took another drink from her glass.

'There's a girl,' he said. 'She might know what Harding knew. What got him killed. That could get her killed.'

Sara feigned interest. 'This is the Jane Doe you found in the office building?'

'No, another girl. Harding's wife. Daughter. Maybe. We don't know.'

Sara drank her Scotch.

'I cut myself.' Instead of holding up his hand, he turned and showed her the back of his right leg. There was a dark patch of blood. 'I slipped through some floorboards.' He waited. 'There's a couple of splinters.'

'If it's been longer than six hours, it's too late for sutures.'

Will waited.

Sara waited too. She wasn't going to make this easy for him. If he was going to break up with her, then he had to be a man about it.

He said, 'Have you had much?' He paused. 'To drink?'

'Not nearly enough.' Sara got up from the couch. She passed Will on her way into the kitchen. Her stomach wouldn't like a second drink on top of the earlier glass of wine, but she poured herself one anyway.

Will stood on the other side of the counter. He watched her top off the glass. He had a physical aversion to alcohol. His shoulders squared. His chin lifted. She wasn't even sure if he noticed. She had to assume it was muscle memory from all the drunks who had abused him when he was a child. As with most things, Will did not talk about it.

She asked, 'Do you want one?'

He nodded. 'Okay.'

Sara had seen him drink alcohol once, but that was under duress. She had forced a trickle of Scotch down his throat because he couldn't stop coughing.

He asked, 'Do you have gin?'

She leaned down to search the cabinet, which, until tonight, she hadn't opened for months. Dust covered the foiled corks in the wine. There was a full bottle of gin in the back, but something told her that gin was Angie's drink, and Sara was not going to toast her boyfriend's dead wife in her kitchen.

She stood up. 'No gin. There's wine in the fridge, or do you want Scotch?'

'That's what I had before?'

She took down a glass and poured him a double. When he didn't move to take it, Sara slid the glass across the counter. He still didn't take it.

She said, 'Amanda told me not to tell you, but there was a note from Angie.'

The color drained from his face. 'How did she . . . ?'

'You already knew?'

He opened his mouth again, but nothing came out.

Sara said, 'I'm glad it's out in the open. I wasn't going to lie, or pretend that I didn't know. That would make me the worst kind of hypocrite.'

'How . . .' He hesitated. 'How does Amanda know?'

'She's in charge of the investigation, Will. It's her job to know everything.'

He spread his hands palms down on the counter. He wouldn't look at her.

Sara thought back to the crime scene bus, Charlie's glee when he'd shown her the glowing HELP ME on the wall. Angie's injuries had been severe, life-threatening, but she had stopped to write the words in her own blood, knowing that Will would see them. That Sara would see them. That everyone would know that Angie would always have her claws in him. She might as well have written FUCK YOU, SARA LINTON.

Will asked, 'Did you read it? The note?'

'Yes. I'm the one who recognized her handwriting.'

Will kept staring at his hands. 'I'm sorry.'

'For what? You said it before: you can't control her.'

'What she said . . .' His voice trailed off again. He sounded distraught. 'It doesn't matter. Not to me.'

Sara didn't believe him. The fact of Angie's death hadn't yet sunk in. 'It mattered to her. It's probably the last thing she wrote before she died.'

He lifted the glass of Scotch. He threw back the drink, and then he almost coughed it all back up.

Sara pulled a paper towel off the roll and handed it to him.

His eyes were watering. He wiped the mess off the counter. He was sweating. He looked shaken. And he should be. Angie was dead. She had begged him for help. He hadn't been able to save her, not this time when it really mattered. Thirty years of his life was gone. He was probably in shock. Alcohol was the last thing he needed.

Sara took the glass away from him and put it in the sink. 'Wait for me in your bathroom.' She didn't give him time to respond. She found her glasses on the couch and walked down the hall to her office. She pulled down her medical bag from the closet shelf. She turned around.

She did not want to leave the room.

She stood by her desk, holding the bag, willing herself to calm down.

There was no way to fix this. She couldn't stitch together their relationship like she could stitch together his leg. Talking around the problem was only delaying the inevitable. And yet she didn't have it in her to confront him. She was frozen in place, terrified of what might come if they really talked about what had happened, what was coming next. Sara couldn't guess the future. There was just a blank expanse of unknown. All she could do was stand in the darkened office listening to the blood rushing through her ears. She counted to fifty, then one hundred, and then she made herself move.

The hallway seemed longer than it ever had before. More like an arduous journey than a stroll. Will's bathroom was in the spare bedroom. Sara had designated a separate area for Will for the benefit of their relationship. When she finally rounded the corner, he was waiting for her in the doorway.

She said, 'Take off your pants.'

Will stared at her.

'It's easier than trying to roll up your jeans.' She emptied her medical bag into the sink. She laid out the tools she would need. 'Take off your pants. Take off your socks. Stand in the tub. I need to clean the wound.'

Will obeyed the orders, giving a slight wince when he peeled the jeans away from his leg. He had bled through the bandage, which was little more than an oversized Band-Aid. He stood in the tub.

'Take off the bandage.' Sara looked for a pair of gloves, then thought better of it. If Angie had given Will a disease, Sara already had it. She put on her glasses. 'Turn sideways.'

Will turned. The leg was worse than she'd expected. This was more than a few splinters. He had a deep two-and-a-half-inch laceration down the side of his calf. Debris had crusted into the blood. It was too late for sutures. She would be sewing in an infection.

She asked, 'Did you wash it?'

'I tried in the shower, but it hurt.'

'This is going to hurt more.' Sara unwrapped the bottle of Betadine. She closed the toilet lid so she could sit down. She didn't give him any warning before she blasted a steady stream of cold antiseptic directly into the wound.

Will grabbed the curtain rod, almost ripping it from the wall. He hissed air between his teeth.

'Okay?' she asked.

'Yep.'

Sara jetted out a chunk of debris. He'd done a poor job of cleaning the site. Caked blood dropped onto the white porcelain tub. Will lifted up onto his toes. He had braced his hands on the curtain rod and shower head. His teeth were clenched. So much for the Hippocratic Oath. Sara had gone from being a caring doctor to a passive-aggressive bitch. She put down the bottle. Will's leg was shaking. 'Do you want me to numb you?'

He shook his head. His shirt had ridden up. He was holding his breath. She could see every single clenched muscle in his abdomen.

Sara felt the full weight of her transgression. 'I'm sorry. I don't want to hurt you. I mean, obviously, I did, but I—'

'It's okay.'

'No, it's not okay, Will. It's not okay.'

Her words echoed in the bathroom. She sounded angry. She *was* angry. Both of them knew that Sara wasn't talking about his leg.

He said, 'I know why Angie took your lipstick.'

Sara waited.

'She was trying to bully you. I should've stopped her.'

'How?' Sara genuinely wanted to know. 'It's like the note she left for you on the wall at the club. She knew that Charlie or somebody would luminol the area. That I would see it. That it would be a public thing. She does what she wants to do.'

'The wall.' Will nodded, as if that explained everything. 'Yeah.'

'Yeah,' Sara agreed, which brought them right back to where they had started.

She wet some gauze under the tub faucet and used it to wipe off the Betadine. Will eventually lowered his heel. She scooped warm water onto his leg and foot, rubbing away the iodine stain. She'd made a mess of everything. Even the hand towel she used to pat him dry showed streaks of yellow-brown from the antiseptic.

Sara told him, 'The hard part's over. I can still numb you. Some of the splinters are deep.'

'I'm fine.'

Sara took a flashlight out of the drawer. She found the tweezers from her bag. There were several tiny black splinters just below the surface of his skin. She counted three that were deeper, more like shards of wood. They would've been jabbing him every time he took a step.

She folded the hand towel and knelt on the tile floor so she could get at the splinters.

Will flinched before she touched him.

'Try to relax the muscle.'

'I'm trying.'

She made the offer again. 'I have some lidocaine right here. It's a tiny needle.'

'I'm fine.' His death grip on the curtain rod said otherwise.

This time, Sara tried to be gentle. As a pediatric intern, she'd spent hours sewing sutures onto peaches in order to train a softer touch into her hands. Still, there was no way to get around some types of hurt. Will remained stoic, even as she worked a piece of wood the size of a toothpick out of the open gash.

'I'm sorry,' she repeated, because she hated the thought of hurting him. At least she hated it now. 'This one is really deep.'

'It's okay.' He allowed a breath, but only so he could speak. 'Just hurry.'

Sara tried to hurry, but it didn't help that Will's calf was a concrete block. She remembered the first time she'd seen him in running shorts. She'd felt a rush of heat at the sight of his lean, muscular legs. He ran five miles a day, five days a week. Most of the time he took a detour to the local high school, where he sprinted up and down the stadium steps. There were sculptures in Florence with less definition.

'Sara?'

She looked up at him.

'I could've gotten stronger locks for the doors. A Flip Guard. An alarm. I'm sorry I didn't do that. It was disrespectful to you.'

Sara carefully worked out the last splinter. Now that he was talking about it, Sara didn't want to have the conversation. She sat back on her heels. She put down the tweezers. She hooked her glasses on her collar. Will was standing in front of her in his boxers. His arms were still raised over his head. The alcohol inside of her suggested that there was an easy way to get them through the night.

Will said, 'Everyone's been telling me what it's like to lose somebody.'

Sara reached into the sink for the bandage roll and some fresh gauze.

'Faith told me about her dad dying. Amanda told me about her mother. Did you know she hanged herself?'

Sara shook her head as she tied the bandage around Will's leg.

'I'm just going to tell myself that Angie's where she always goes when she leaves me. Wherever that is.'

Sara stood up. She washed her hands.

Will pulled on his jeans. 'I think I'll be okay if I can do that. Just tell myself that she's not really gone. That way, when she doesn't come back, it won't matter. It'll just be like all the times before.'

Sara turned off the water. There was a tremble in her hand, more like a vibration that was working through her body, as if a tuning fork had been touched to her nerves.

She asked, 'Do you want to know what it was like when my husband died?'

He looked up from buttoning his jeans. Sara had told him the story, but not the details.

She said, 'It felt like someone had reached inside of my chest and ripped out my heart.'

Will zipped his pants. His expression was blank. He really had no idea what Angie's death was going to do to him.

She said, 'I felt hollow. Like there was nothing inside of me. I wanted to kill myself. I *did* try to kill myself. Did you know that?'

Will looked stunned. She had told him about the pills, but not her intentions. 'You said it was an accident.'

'I'm a doctor, Will. I knew what to do. Ambien. Hydrocodone. Tylenol.' Tears started to fall. Now that the words were coming out, she couldn't stop them. 'My mother found me. She called an ambulance and they took me to the hospital, and people I worked with, people I've known since I was a child, had to pump my stomach so that I wouldn't die.' Her fists were clenched. She wanted to grab him and shake him and make him understand that death wasn't the kind of thing you could just pretend away. 'I begged them to let me go. I wanted to die. I loved him. He was my life. He was the center of my universe, and when he was gone, that was it. There was nothing left for me.'

Will slipped on his sneakers. He was listening, but he wasn't hearing.

'Angie's dead. Brutally murdered.' He didn't flinch from her words. Four years ago, if someone had said the same thing about Jeffrey, Sara would've been on the floor. 'She was the most important person in your life for thirty years. You can't just tell yourself that she's on a vacation, that she's going to come back from the beach with a tan. That's not how it works when you lose somebody. You see them on street corners. You hear their voice in the other room. You want to sleep all the time so you can dream about them. You don't want to wash your clothes or your sheets so you can still smell them. I did this for three years, Will. Every single day for three years. I wasn't living. I was going through the motions. I wanted to be just as dead as he was until—'

Sara caught herself at the last second.

'Until what?'

Her hand went to her throat. She felt like she was dangling over a cliff.

He repeated, 'Until what?'

'Until enough time had passed.' Her pulse jumped under her fingers. She was angry. She was terrified. She was breathless from the rawness of her words and she was a coward for not telling him exactly what had turned her life around.

She just couldn't do it.

She said, 'You're going to need time to grieve.' What she really meant was, *You're going to need time away from me, and I don't think my heart can take it.*

Will carefully lined up his socks. He folded them in two. 'I know you can never love me the way that you loved him.'

Sara felt blindsided. 'That's not fair.'

'Maybe.' He tucked his socks into his back pocket. 'I think I should go.'

'I think you should too.' The words came unfiltered from her mouth. Sara recognized her voice. She just didn't know why she had said it.

Will waited for her to step aside so he could pass.

She followed him into the living room. Her equilibrium was gone. Everything had shifted, but she couldn't figure out how.

'I don't know if I have a job anymore.' He was talking to her as if nothing had changed. 'Even if I do, Amanda won't let me near the case. Faith's following up on the Palmer angle with Collier.' He scooped up Betty. 'I'll probably be stuck at my desk processing paperwork.'

Sara struggled for composure. 'I won't have the tox screen back on Harding for another week.'

'Probably doesn't matter.' He took Betty's leash off the hook and snapped it onto her collar. 'Okay. I'll see you later.'

He shut the door behind him.

Sara leaned against the wall for support. Her heart was battering her ribs. She felt light-headed.

What the hell had just happened?

Why had he left?

Why had she let him?

Sara put her back to the wall. She slid down to the floor. She looked at her watch. It was still too late to call Tessa. Sara didn't even know what she would say. Everything had escalated so quickly. Was Will having some sort of mental breakdown?

Was Sara?

She had said too much about Jeffrey. Sara had always walked a fine line with memories of her husband. She didn't want to deny their time together, but she didn't want to rub Will's face in it either. Did Will really think she was telling him that she couldn't get over losing her husband? Four years ago, Sara would have believed that was true.

Until she'd met Will.

That was what she'd stopped herself from saying in the bathroom: that Will had changed everything. That he had made her want to live again. That he was her life and the thought of losing him terrified her. The shame of her cowardice was equal to her regret. She had been scared because there was no point in telling him that she loved him if he was just going to leave.

Sara leaned her head back against the wall. She stared at the dark sky out the windows. She'd seen death too many times to believe that there was such a thing as angels, but if there were demons in the afterlife, Angie Polaski was out there cackling like a witch.

This was the revelation that finally moved Sara; not love or need or even desperation, but the absolute conviction that she was not going to let Angie win.

Sara stood up. She found her purse. The dogs stirred, hoping for a walk, but she brushed them aside as she left the apartment.

She didn't bother with the lock. She pressed the elevator button. She pressed it again. She looked up at the lighted panel. The car was stuck on the lobby level. She turned toward the stairs.

Will was standing by her door.

Betty was beside him.

He asked, 'What's wrong?'

Of all the idiotic questions. 'I thought you left.'

'I thought you wanted me to.'

'I only said that because you said it.' She shook her head. 'I know that sounds stupid. It *is* stupid. Was stupid.' She wanted to reach for him. To hold him. To make the last ten minutes go away. 'Why are you still here?'

'It's a free country.'

'Will, please.'

He shrugged. He looked down at his dog. 'I don't have a lot of quit in me, Sara. You should know that by now.'

'You were just going to wait out here all night?'

'I knew you would have to take out the dogs before you went to bed.'

A bell dinged. The elevator doors opened.

Sara was fixed in place. She felt the tingling in her nerves again. She was back on the cliff, her toes dangling over. She took a deep breath. 'I don't love you less than him, Will. I love you differently. I love you . . .' She couldn't describe it. There were no words. 'I love you.'

He nodded, but she couldn't tell if he understood.

She said, 'We have to talk about this.'

'No, we don't.' He reached out to her. He cupped his hand to her face. His touch was like a balm. He smoothed her brow. He wiped her tears. He stroked her cheek. Her breath caught when his thumb brushed across her lips.

He asked, 'Do you want me to stop?'

'I want you to do that with your mouth.'

He gently pressed his lips to hers. Sara kissed him back. There was no passion, just the overwhelming need for reconnection. Will pulled her close. Sara buried her face in the crook of his neck. She wrapped her arms around his waist. She felt him relax into her. They clung to each other, standing outside the open door to her apartment, until her cell phone chimed.

Then chimed again.

And again.

Will broke away first.

Reluctantly Sara picked up her purse from the floor.

They both knew that Amanda sent rapid-fire texts, just as they both knew there was only one reason she would be reaching out to Sara after eight o'clock at night.

She found her phone. She swiped her finger across the screen.

AMANDA: NEED YOU NOW ANGIE'S CAR FOUND 1885 SOMMERSET.

AMANDA: CADAVER DOG FOUND SCENT IN TRUNK.

AMANDA: DON'T TELL WILL.

Sara told him.

EIGHT

Will sat beside Sara in her BMW. She was being strong for him. Silent, but strong. They hadn't talked about more than logistics since she'd read Amanda's texts.

Do you know where this is? Do you want me to drive?

Sara turned onto Spring Street. Night had fallen. The instrument panel cast her face in white tones. Will gripped her hand as tightly as he could without breaking something. He still felt numb, except for the places where he didn't. There was an elephant standing on his chest. The pain was physical, suffocating. His arm hurt. Or maybe it only hurt because Faith had asked him before if his arm was hurting. Or maybe he was unraveling because that was what everyone kept saying he was going to do.

Cadaver dogs were trained to find the scent of decomposition. They had alerted on Angie's trunk. That meant that everyone was thinking that Angie was dead.

Was it true? Was Angie dead?

The most important person in his life for thirty years.

Angie had been the *only* person in his life for thirty years.

That was the only incontrovertible fact.

Will tried to summon that moment in the basement, all those years ago, when Angie had held him, comforted him. Nothing. He tried to remember the one time they went on a vacation together. They had argued about directions. They had argued about where to eat. They had argued about who was being more argumentative.

You dumbass was the last thing she'd said to him that night, and the next morning she was gone.

Angie was awful to live with. She was constantly breaking things, borrowing things, never putting his stuff back where it belonged. Will's mind strained for one single good memory but all he saw was static, the fuzzy white and black patches that used to show on TV when the station went off the air.

Sara squeezed his hand. He looked down at their intertwined fingers. One of the first things he'd noticed about Sara was how long and graceful her fingers were. He didn't know if that came with being a surgeon or if it was simply because everything about her was beautiful.

He studied her face. Her sharp chin. Her button nose. Her long auburn hair that was pinned up into a swirl at the back of her head.

She usually took her hair down after work. Will knew this was for his sake, that it drove her crazy when her hair fell into her eyes. She was constantly pushing it back and he never told her to pin it up because he was selfish.

Every relationship, romantic or otherwise, had a certain level of selfishness. It went back and forth depending on who was stronger or who needed it most. Amanda sucked up selfishness like a sponge. Faith gave it away too easily. Angie reached down your throat and grabbed it and then kicked you in the balls for thinking you could have it in the first place.

Will had always thought that he and Sara shared an emotional equivalence, but was Will taking all the selfishness for himself? He had lied to her about what had happened with Angie last Saturday. He had lied to her about the letter Angie had left for him in the post office box. He had lied about his and Angie's joint bank account. He had lied about not doing everything he could do to find her.

Angie. Angie. Angie.

She was dead now. Maybe. Most likely. He would have a clean slate. For the first time in thirty years, Will's confidante, his torturer, his source of support and source of pain was gone.

He shivered.

Sara turned down the air conditioner. 'Are you okay?'

'Yes.' He looked out the window so she could not see his face. The elephant shifted its weight. Will could almost feel his ribs flex from the pressure. His vision strobed. He opened his mouth and tried to fill his lungs.

They were in midtown. The bright lights outside the window hurt his eyes. His ears buzzed with the fan blowing out cold air from the dash. Underneath the sound, there was music. Soft women's voices harmonizing over a steel guitar. Sara never turned off the radio, she only turned the volume down low.

She released his hand so that she could put on the blinker. They were at 1885 Sommerset. Instead of a building, there was a house, a sprawling English Tudor that took up half a city block. The lawn sloped toward the street, neatly trimmed grass and well-manicured flowers led up to stone steps.

Angie's car had been found at a funeral home.

Sara pulled into the parking lot. An old pickup truck with a yellow Lab in the passenger's seat was leaving the scene. A patrol car was parked on the grass. The officer was sitting behind the wheel typing into the laptop mounted onto the dash. Will recognized Amanda's Suburban and Faith's red Mini. Charlie Reed was there in his white crime scene van, but for some reason he was sitting behind the wheel instead of processing Angie's car. The black Dodge Charger belonged to Collier and Ng. The GBI was still in charge, but Angie's car had been found in the Atlanta city limits and there was still an active murder investigation.

The two detectives were sitting on the hood the same as they'd been this morning. Ng still had on his wraparound sunglasses. He did the chin nod thing when Will got out of the car. Collier waved, but Amanda must have put them under strict orders to keep their distance, because neither of them approached.

Angie's Monte Carlo SS was parked in a handicapped space in front of the building. She would park in a handicapped space because that's what she did. Yellow crime scene tape roped off the area. The trunk was open. The driver's door was open. Even from twenty yards, Will could smell the sickly sweet odor of death. Or maybe it was like his arm hurting. He only smelled death because someone had planted the idea in his mind.

Amanda came out of a side door. Unusually, her BlackBerry wasn't in her hand. She had a lot of things she could yell at Will about right now, but she didn't. 'Uniformed patrol spotted Angie's car an hour ago. The funeral home closed at six, but there's an intern who sleeps here for overnight calls.'

'An intern?' Will tried to ask the question that a cop would.

'From the local mortuary school.' Amanda crossed her arms. 'He was picking up a body at a nursing home when the uni found Angie's car. Faith is talking to him in the chapel.'

Will studied the house. He guessed the large two-story structure at the end was the chapel.

Amanda said, 'The uni smelled an odor. He popped the trunk using the latch inside the car. He called in the cadaver dog. It hit on the scent immediately.'

Will looked at the car again. Parked at an angle. Hastily abandoned. The windows were down. His vision flashed up an image: Angie slumped over the wheel. He blinked and it was gone.

'Will?' Sara said.

He looked at her.

'Why are you rubbing your chest?'

Will hadn't realized he was rubbing his chest. He stopped. He told Amanda, 'There are license plate scanners on Spring and Peachtree.'

She nodded. Scanners all over the city tracked the movement of traffic and searched for the license plates of stolen or suspect vehicles. 'The data is being sent to the computer division for analysis.'

Will looked out at the street. Sommerset and Spring was a busy corner. Midtown was heavily monitored. Every major intersection had a camera.

Amanda said, 'We've requested footage from GDOT and APD. We'll comb through it as soon as it's in hand. Search teams are on the way.'

Will said what she already knew. 'Someone left the car here. They would need to drive away or—'

'I've got everybody in the state looking for Delilah Palmer.'

Will had forgotten about Dale Harding's wife or daughter or both. Palmer was a young prostitute with a drug problem. She had grown up in the system. The only parent she'd ever known had exploited her. She could've been Angie twenty years ago, except that Angie had managed to pull herself out. Or at least make it seem that way. Will wasn't so sure she had managed to escape anything.

Sara's hand pressed against the small of his back. 'You okay?'

Will walked toward the car. The smell grew more pungent as he got closer. You didn't need a bloodhound to know that something bad had happened here. He stopped at the crime scene tape. The trunk of Angie's car was lined with a scratchy charcoal-colored carpet that he'd gotten from a roll at Pep Boys. He had leaned over the trunk for hours lining up the seams, gluing it in place.

Amanda shined a police-issue Maglite into the trunk. There was a dark stain in the carpet, just a little off from the center. The only thing in the trunk was a red plastic bottle of transmission fluid.

Will knelt down. He examined the pavement under the car. The transmission was leaking. The car was probably his now. He would have to fix it before he sold it.

'Will?' Sara put her hand on his shoulder. She knelt beside him. 'Look at me.'

He looked at her.

'I think we should go. There's nothing here.'

Will stood up, but he didn't go. He went to the driver's side of the car. The door was wide open. A half-empty bottle of tequila was in the footwell. A joint was in the ashtray. Candy wrappers. Gum. Angie had a sweet tooth.

He asked Amanda, 'It was like this when the uni rolled up?'

She nodded.

The open door would act like a flag to whoever drove by, which meant the car was left to be found sooner rather than later. Will took the flashlight from Amanda. He shined the light into the car. The interior was light gray. The shift for the manual transmission jutted out from the floor between the seats. He saw blood on the steering wheel. Blood on the driver's seat. Blood on the white circle on top of the black shifter knob. It was an 8-ball. Angie had picked it out of a magazine. This was before the internet. Will had gone to three different stores to find an adapter so it would screw onto the stick.

He turned the flashlight, examining the back seat. More blood, almost black from baking in the sun all day. There was a smear near the door handle. Too small for a handprint. Maybe a closed fist punching out. Maybe a desperate last move to get away. Someone had lain bleeding in the back seat. Someone had lain bleeding in the trunk. Someone had been bleeding or covered in blood when they drove the car away.

He asked Amanda, 'Two bodies and the driver?'

Amanda had obviously considered this. 'She could've been moved from the back seat to the trunk.'

'Still bleeding?' he asked, meaning still alive.

'Gravity,' Sara said. 'If there was a chest wound, and she was on her side, depending on how she was positioned, you might expect that amount of blood to seep out post mortem.'

'She,' Will said. 'What about Delilah Palmer?'

'I had someone at Grady run down her blood type. She had an admit for an OD last year. She's O-positive. Angie was B-negative.' Amanda's hand was on his arm. She had tried to let him work this out on his own, leaving Charlie in his van, calling off Collier and Ng, but now she was going to give him the truth. 'Wilbur, I know this is hard to hear, but everything points toward Angie.' She laid it out for him. 'Angie's blood type was all over the crime scene. We found her purse, her gun. This is her car. Charlie already typed the blood for me. The back seat, the trunk and the front seat are all B-negative. We've got the DNA on rush, but given the rarity of the blood type, the likelihood that it's not Angie is slim to none. And it's a hell of a lot of blood, Will. Too much blood for her to walk away.'

Will mulled over her words. The stain in the trunk was in the area you would expect from a chest wound. Arterial spray was found on the walls of the room where Dale Harding died. Arteries were in the heart. The heart was in the chest.

Will tried to play out a likely scenario. Angie in the back seat, bleeding to death. The driver some guy she'd called because she always had a guy she could call. He would be desperately trying to get her help, and then he would realize that it was too late. And then he would put her in the trunk because he couldn't drive around the city with a dead woman in the back seat of the car. And then he would wait until sundown and drive the car here.

'The manager is on the way.' Faith came walking down a lighted path. An open spiral notebook was in her hand. She looked at Will, then looked at him again.

Amanda said, 'And?'

Faith referenced her notes. 'Inside, we've got Ray Belcamino, twenty-year-old male Caucasian, no record. Mortuary student at Gupton-Jones. He clocked into work at approximately five fifteen for a five-thirty shift. His call-in sheet has him three times off the premises, once to Piedmont Hospital at six forty-three, another to the Sunrise Nursing home at seven oh two, and a third, a false alarm, at eight twenty-two.' She looked up. 'Apparently it's a thing for interns to call in fake deaths to prank each other.'

'Of course it is,' Amanda said.

'All three times, Belcamino used the commercial entrance near the chapel, behind the fence. There's a service elevator that goes down to the basement. He can't see the parking lot over the fence. He drove in from the west each time, so he didn't pass the parking lot and he didn't see the car.'

Amanda asked, 'Closed-circuit cameras?'

'Six, but they're all trained on the doors and windows, not the parking lot.'

Will asked, 'Did you check the Dumpster?'

'First thing. Nothing.'

He asked, 'Were any of the doors tampered with?'

'No, and there's an alarm system. Every door and window is wired.'

'How is the elevator accessed?'

'There's a keypad.'

Will asked, 'Can the keypad be seen from behind the fence?'

'Yeah. And it turns off the alarm, too.'

Amanda asked, 'Where are you going with this?'

'Why bring a car that has a dead body in a trunk to a funeral home?'

They all looked back at the building.

Faith said, 'I'll go. Wait here.'

Will didn't wait. He didn't run, either, but his stride was twice as long as Faith's. He reached the chapel before she did. He opened the door before she did. He passed the pews and walked onto the stage and found the door that led to the back half of the funeral home before she did.

Behind the scenes was scuffed and utilitarian. Drop ceiling, peeling linoleum. There was a long hallway running the entire back of the building. Two massive elevator doors stood sentry at one end. Will knew that there was likely an identical set of elevator doors to the outside and that this was where the bodies were transported down to the basement. He headed toward the elevator, assuming there would be stairs. Faith was right behind him. She was jogging to catch up, so Will started jogging so that she couldn't.

The metal stairs were old and jangly. His footsteps jarred the railing. At the bottom, there was a landing with a swinging door. Will pushed through to a small office, more like a vestibule. There was another set of double doors behind a wooden desk, and at the desk sat a young man who could only be Ray Belcamino.

The kid jumped up. His iPad clattered to the floor.

Will tried the double doors. Locked. No windows. 'How many bodies do you have in here?'

Belcamino's eyes darted to Faith as she came through the swinging door

She was out of breath. 'I need your logs. We have to match each body to a name.'

The kid looked panicked. 'Is one missing?'

Will wanted to grab him by the collar. 'We need a body count.'

'Seven,' he said. 'No, eight. Eight.' He picked up the iPad. He started tapping the screen. 'The two tonight, three more from this week, one being processed, two awaiting cremation.'

Faith grabbed the iPad. She glanced through the list. She told Will, 'I don't recognize any of the names.'

'What names?' Belcamino had started to sweat. He either knew something or suspected something. 'What's wrong?'

Will pushed him back against the wall. 'Who are you working with?'

'Nobody!' Panic cracked his voice. 'Here! I work here!'

The swinging door banged open. Amanda, then Sara, then Charlie, crammed into the small vestibule.

Amanda asked Belcamino, 'Where do you store the bodies?'

'There's a buzzer.' His eyes darted toward the desk. Will let him go. The kid reached underneath the desk and found the button. The rear set of doors arced open.

Light green tiled walls. Dark green linoleum floor. Chemical smells. Bright lights. Low ceiling. About the size of a school classroom. There was a body at the front of the room. Elderly man. Wrinkled skin. White tufts of hair. A cloth covered his genitals. Tubes went out of his neck and connected him to a machine with a canister.

The walk-in freezer was in the back. Large stainless-steel door. Reinforced glass window. Amanda was already there. Her hand hovered over a green lighted button to open the door.

Will traversed the room. This was the second time today he'd walked toward an unknown, thinking that he was going to find Angie's body. His vision sharpened. His ears picked up every sound.

The freezer door made a heavy clicking sound. Cold air seeped out from around the edges. An automatic arm opened the door at a glacial pace. Will had worked in a grocery store once. The walk-in where they kept the frozen foods was not dissimilar. Shelves on each side. Six tiers evenly spaced floor-to-ceiling. About fifteen feet deep, maybe ten feet high. Instead of bags of peas on the shelves, there were black body bags.

Four on one side. Four on the other.

'Fuck me.' Belcamino ripped a clipboard off the wall. He ran into the freezer. He checked the labels on the bags against the list. He was on the last body when he stopped. 'There's no tag.'

Will started to go inside. Sara caught him by the wrist. 'You know you can't be the one to find her.'

He *had* found her. He had figured out why the car was at the funeral home. He had led them into the basement. He couldn't stop now. The bag was less than ten feet away. The shelves were tight. Angie's nose would be less than half a foot from the corpse above her. She was claustrophobic. She was terrified of tight spaces.

'Will.' Sara's hand moved to his arm. 'You need to let them take care of her, okay? Let Charlie do his job. He has to take photographs. The bag needs to be preserved for fingerprints.

There could be trace evidence on the floor. We have to do this the right way, or we'll never be able to find out why she was left here.'

He knew all of this was true, but he couldn't move.

'Come on.' She pulled at his arm.

He stepped back, then back again.

Charlie opened his duffel. He slipped on a pair of shoe protectors, then gloves. He put a fresh card in his camera. He checked the batteries, confirmed the date and time.

He started outside the freezer, slowly working his way in. He photographed the bag from every angle, kneeling down, leaning over the other bodies. He used his ruler for scale. He left marked cards on items of interest. It felt like an hour had passed before he finally told Ray Belcamino, 'Get a gurney. The space is too tight. We'll need to move her so we can open the bag.'

Belcamino disappeared into another room. He returned with a gurney. A white sheet was folded on the center. He kicked the wheels straight and forced the gurney up the small ramp that led to the freezer.

Charlie handed him a pair of gloves.

Obviously moving bodies was a job that Belcamino had done on his own before. He muscled the black bag onto the gurney like he was moving a rolled carpet. Will had to look away, because he was going to hit the kid if he had to watch him a second longer.

He heard the gurney being rolled out, the freezer door shutting with a *thunk*.

Amanda said, 'Thank you, Mr Belcamino. You can wait upstairs.'

Belcamino offered no protest as he left the room.

Charlie took more photographs. He dragged over a step stool that was against the wall. He stood over the bag and took more photos. He used the ruler again to document scale.

Will stared at the contours of the black bag. He couldn't make sense of what was underneath. And then he realized that the body was on its side, that whoever had taken it from the trunk had left it in the same position in which it had died.

Angie always slept on her side, close to him but not touching him. Sometimes at night her breath would tickle his ear and he would have to turn over so that he could go to sleep.

'Faith?' Charlie held out an extra pair of gloves. The fingers dangled in the air for a second before Faith finally took them.

Her hands were obviously sweating. She struggled to pull on the gloves. Her jaw was clamped tight. She hated dead bodies. She hated being in the morgue. She hated autopsies.

She grabbed the zipper and started to pull.

The sound was like a rip. Something tearing apart. Something breaking. The body was turned away from them. Will saw dark hair. Brown, the same color as Angie's. The woman's bare shoulder was revealed. The curve of her spine. The arc of her hip. Her legs were bent. Her hands were between her knees. Her toes were curled, the feet sickled.

Faith gagged. The smell was noxious, putrid. The body had been in the trunk for hours in the broiling sun. Heat had accelerated the decomposition. The skin was desiccated. The human body was made up of the same fiber and tissue as any other mammal. Both had the same reaction to heat, which was to release fluids.

Charlie spread open the bag. A trickle of blood turned pink by cholesterol splattered onto the floor.

Faith gagged again. She put the back of her hand under her nose. She squeezed her eyes closed. She was standing on the opposite side of the gurney. She had seen the face. She shook her head. 'I can't tell if it's her. She's just—'

'Beaten,' Charlie said.

Will looked at her back, blackened with patches that looked like soot. The same pattern was on her legs. On the soles of her feet.

'Bleach,' Sara said. The odor steamed off the bag.

'She wasn't scrubbed clean, though. It looks like the bleach was poured. Almost sloshed.'

'Her clothes are gone,' Amanda noted. 'Someone was worried about trace evidence.'

Faith said, 'She was somewhere other than the car.'

'Her face looks like someone took a bat to her.' Charlie did a cursory examination. 'Contusions and lacerations on the face and neck. Fingernail scrapes. It looks like bones were broken.' He knelt down with the camera, zooming in on the head, neck, chest, torso. 'Multiple stab wounds.' He asked Will, 'Does she have any identifying marks? Tattoos?'

Will shook his head.

Then he remembered.

Time moved in double frame, as if someone had pressed the fast-forward on his life. Will was pulling away from Sara. He was walking around the gurney. He was pushing Charlie aside. He was looking at the body, the deep black bruises, the cuts, the mottled skin, and there it was: a single mole on her breast. Was it in the same place? Why couldn't he remember where the mole was supposed to be?

He found himself on his knees. He looked at her face.

Bloated. Unrecognizable.

Her head was swollen to twice its size, black and red marks criss-crossing her face. Her lips were leaking fluid. Her nose was twisted to the side. More like a Halloween mask than a face.

Was it Angie?

Did it *feel* like Angie?

The numbness inside of Will had never really gone away. He felt nothing looking at this woman. He noticed the things he would notice on any case. Domestic homicide. Battery. Assault. Mouth open. Teeth broken. Lips chapped and swollen like too-ripe fruit. Her eyelids were thick, the consistency of wet bread. Blue veins and red arteries shot through almost translucent skin. Her cheek had been sliced with a very sharp knife or a razor. The skin flapped back, hanging open like a page in a book. He saw tissue, sinew, stark white of bone.

He looked at her hands. They were balled together between her bent knees. The heat had curled her fingers. Decomposition had cracked open the skin. Clear liquid seeped out from the joints of her knuckles. The ring around her finger had broken apart.

Angie's wedding ring.

Green plastic with a bright yellow sunflower. Will had wasted three quarters on a bubble gum machine before the ring had come out. The dare had been that Angie would marry him if it took less than four quarters. She never backed down from a dare. She had married him. She had lasted ten days before he came home from work and found that all of her clothes were gone.

Will opened his mouth. He breathed in and out.

Amanda asked, 'Will?'

Will shook his head. This wasn't right. Someone had planted the ring. He would know instinctively if this was Angie. He stood up. He said, 'It's not her.'

Faith asked, 'What about the ring?'

Will kept shaking his head. More looks were being exchanged. They clearly thought he was in denial, but they were wrong. Maybe when he was outside looking at the bloodied car, hearing Amanda run down the evidence, he had let himself think it might be Angie, but now that he was in the same room with this body, this stranger, he was certain that she was still alive.

It was what Sara said. He did not feel the hollowness. He did not feel an absence of the heart.

Charlie said, 'I have a mobile fingerprint scanner.'

'Her finger pads are cracked open. It'll be hard to get a print.'

'We can still try, but we'll have to go upstairs to get a signal.'

'She's in full rigor.'

Will looked at the woman's face again. It was like trying to read a book. He could see pieces but not the whole. The eyelashes were clumped together. The lip was torn apart. The jaw was set, roped like a cable on a suspension bridge. Rigor mortis. The coagulation of muscle proteins. It started in the eyelids, neck, jaw. All the muscles of the body stiffened, fixing the corpse in place.

Faith asked, 'That means she's been dead for three to four hours?'

'Longer,' Sara said, but she didn't say how much longer.

Amanda asked, 'How do we get fingerprints when her hands are curled?'

'You'll have to break the fingers.'

'Would it be easier if she were on her back?'

'I'll need help turning her.'

Will walked away from them to the other side of the room. The elderly man was still lying on the gurney. Will tried to figure out the machines. Yellow fluid lurched around inside the canister. An orange tube came out of the bottom. There was some kind of pump working. He heard the motor turning, the *shhh* of a bellow moving air. One liquid being pushed out. Another liquid being pushed in. He followed the tube to the man's carotid. The liquid passed through a heavy-gauge needle. There was another tube dropped over the side of the table, resting on the rusted edge of a floor drain.

Snap.

Like a twig being broken.

Snap.

Will kept his back to them. He didn't want to know who broke open the fingers.

Snap.

'Okay,' Charlie said. 'I think that's good.'

'Her fingers are a mess,' Sara said. 'I don't think the scanner will be able to pick up the ridges.'

'Try,' Amanda told them.

There was a rustling sound, a click, three rapid beeps. The mobile fingerprint scanner. Biometrics. There was an injection-molded dock with a 30-pin iPhone connector. The dock had a silver pad. The pad scanned the fingerprint. An app on the phone processed the scan into a 256-bit grayscale, 508 dpi image, then transmitted the data to the GBI's Live Scan servers, where the print was compared against the hundreds of thousands of prints stored in the system.

The only thing required was the dock and a phone with a signal.

Charlie was holding both in his hands as he walked toward the vestibule. He told Will, 'It's iffy because of the damage, but we might be able to get a hit.'

Will didn't know why this information was directed specifically to him. He looked at his watch. Violent crimes tended to peak around ten p.m. The servers would be processing thousands of requests. Even on a slow day, the results could take anywhere from five minutes to twenty-four hours, and then the GBI required that the prints had to be peer-reviewed by a group of human beings who could reach a consensus on whether or not the computer match met the threshold for a legal level of certainty.

Faith said, 'Sara?'

Something about her tone of voice made Will turn around.

Faith was standing at the foot of the gurney. She was looking down. The dead woman's feet were raised off the table, frozen by rigor mortis. Her hands between her knees had opened her legs and her open legs gave a clear view of what was between them.

Rape, Will thought. The woman who could not be Angie had not just been strangled and beaten and stabbed. Sara was going to tell him that she had been raped.

'Will?' Sara waited for him to look at her. 'Did Angie ever have a child?'

He couldn't understand the question.

Sara said, 'She has an episiotomy scar.'

Will had never heard the word before. 'From an assault?'

'From having a baby.'

He shook his head. Angie had been pregnant before, but not by Will. 'She had an abortion eight years ago.'

Faith said, 'That's not how you get the scar.'

Sara said, 'It's a surgical incision made in the perineum during a vaginal birth.'

Faith translated, 'They cut you open down there so the baby can come out.'

Will still didn't understand. It was like looking at the dead woman's face. He recognized the words, but not the sense.

Sara asked, 'Does your chest feel tight?'

Will looked down. He was rubbing his chest again.

Faith said, 'He wasn't feeling well before.'

'You're wrong,' Will said. 'I don't think it's her.'

Sara was pushing him backward. The double doors opened. They stuttered closed. They were in the vestibule. Will was sitting at the metal desk. All three of them were hovering over him like in his worst kind of nightmare.

Sara said, 'Take some deep breaths for me.'

Amanda said, 'I have some Xanax.' There was an enamel pill case in her hand. Pink base, roses on the lid. It was the sort of thing an old lady would use for her sniffing salts.

Sara said, 'Put this under your tongue.'

Will complied without even thinking. The pill tasted bitter. He could feel it melting under his tongue. Saliva filled his mouth. He had to swallow.

'It'll take a few minutes.' Sara started rubbing his back like he was a kid at the hospital. Will didn't like it. He hated being fussed over.

He leaned over, putting his head between his knees, pretending like he was dizzy. Sara rubbed his back some more. He palmed the pill.

'Just breathe.' Sara's fingers went to his wrist. She was taking his pulse. 'You're okay.'

Will sat up.

Sara was watching his every move. Amanda still held the open pill case in her hand. Faith had disappeared.

Sara asked, 'Okay?'

'I don't think it's her,' Will repeated, but if anything, saying the words a second time made him question whether or not they were true. 'She never had a baby.'

'She did,' Amanda said. Will watched her mouth move. Her lipstick was smudged. 'Twenty-seven years ago, Angie disappeared from her foster placement. Three months later, she showed up at the hospital. She was in labor. She delivered a girl. She left before social services could arrive.'

The news should've hit him like a lightning strike, but nothing about Angie could surprise him anymore.

Sara asked, 'How old was she?'

'Sixteen.'

1989.

Will was stuck at the children's home. No one wanted a teenage boy around, especially one who was taller than all of his teachers. Angie was living with a couple who took in kids for a living. They had anywhere from eight to fifteen kids at a time, stacked into bunk beds four to a room.

Will asked Amanda, 'How did you find out about this?'

'The same way I find out about everything.' Amanda's voice was hard. They never talked about the fact that she had followed Will from infancy, that throughout his life she had been the invisible hand that had redirected him whenever he got off course. Had she corrected Angie, too, steering her away from Will?

He asked, 'What did you do?'

'I didn't do anything.' Amanda dropped the pill case back into her pocket. 'Angie disappeared. She abandoned her child. None of this should surprise you.'

Sara asked, 'Did the baby survive?'

'Yes. I never found out what happened to her. She was lost in the system.'

Their marriage application.

Angie had filled out the form. They were sitting outside the probate office. The sunflower ring was already on her finger. Angie had read the questions aloud. *Over the age of sixteen? Sure. Ever been married before? Not that you know of. Father's name? Who the fuck knows. Mother's name? Doesn't matter. Related to the intended spouse—uh-oh.* Her pen scratched the paper as she scribbled in the answers. *Children? Not me, baby.* She had laughed her deep, husky laugh. *Not that I know of, anyway . . .*

Amanda said, 'The daughter was born in January. She would be twenty-seven now. Delilah Palmer is twenty-two.'

Sara cleared her throat. 'Do you know who the father is?'

Amanda said, 'It's not Will.'

Will wondered if that was true. That time in the basement. They hadn't used a condom. Angie wasn't on the pill. Then again, Will wasn't the only boy she took into the basement.

Sara's fingers were on his wrist again. 'Your pulse is still thready.'

Will pulled away his hand. He stood up. He looked at the closed double doors. He did not need to see the body again to know the truth.

The sunflower ring. The car. The blood.

Her ring. Her car. Her blood.

Her baby.

Angie would abandon a baby. For some inexplicable reason, Will accepted this as proof above everything else. Angie did not have the capacity or the desire to care for something every single day for the rest of her life. Self-survival, not empathy, had always been her guiding principle. Will had seen it last Saturday and he could easily see it happening twenty-seven years ago. Angie went to the hospital. She'd had the baby. She'd left as soon as possible.

And now she was dead.

Will asked Sara, 'Can we go home?'

'Yes.' She put her keys in his hand. 'Go wait for me in the car. I'll be right there.'

Amanda worked her BlackBerry. 'I'll tell Faith to wait with him.'

Will understood that a conversation was going to take place between Sara and Amanda, and that he would be the subject, but he didn't have the wherewithal to fight it. His chest was still caught in a vise. There was a rock inside his stomach.

He climbed the stairs. He shoved his hand in his pocket to wipe it clean. What was left of the pill had melted into chalk. Some of the Xanax had gotten into his system. He was dizzy by the time he reached the end of the hall. His mouth tasted gritty.

He tried three doors before he found the chapel. The lights were off, but between the large windows and the downtown glow, the rows of pews were easy to see.

He looked up at the arched ceiling. Huge chandeliers hung down like jewelry. Gray carpet lined the aisle between the pews. The stage was flat, a lectern to the side. He guessed it was as non-denominational as a chapel could be. Will had been to church twice with Sara, once at Easter and once on Christmas Eve. She wasn't religious, but she loved the pageantry. Will could still recall his surprise when she sang along with the congregation. She knew all the words by heart.

Angie despised religion. She was one of those arrogant assholes who thought all believers were mentally deranged. She had been driven here in the trunk of her car. She had been carried down to the freezer. Her wedding ring was still on her finger. Had she been alive when the ring was put on? Had she asked the person with her to make sure that she wore it even in death?

Will felt a burning sensation in his chest. He was rubbing his skin raw. What were the symptoms of a panic attack? He didn't want to ask Sara because she would probably shove another pill in his mouth.

Why had she done that? She knew he hated anything stronger than aspirin. He hated it even more that she had seen him upset. He'd acted like a pathetic kid. She would probably never want to have sex with him again.

Will sat down on the steps to the stage. He fished his phone out of his back pocket. Instead of Googling 'panic attacks', he lay back on the carpet. He looked up at the crystals sparkling in the chandelier. The weight started to lift off his chest. His lungs filled with air. He was floating. This was the Xanax. Will didn't like it. Nothing good ever came out of losing control.

Delilah Palmer. She could've been at Rippy's club when Harding died. She could've tried to save Angie. She could've driven Angie's body here. She could've called in the false alarm to get Belcamino to leave, then watched him work the security panel at the elevator. One trip down to the basement. Another trip back up. She leaves Angie's car here. She walks to her rental car and never looks back.

Will's eyes would not stay open. He realized his head was where the casket would go during a funeral service. He would have to plan Angie's funeral. It would be easier to have it here. She would want to be cremated. Belcamino could take care of that—put it on his form, process her for the crematorium.

Who would come to the funeral? Amanda and Faith, because they would feel obligated. Sara? He couldn't ask her, but she would probably volunteer. What about her mother and father? They were good country people. Cathy would probably bake a casserole. Or would she? Will knew that Sara's mother didn't trust him. She wasn't wrong. He hadn't told Sara about Saturday. He hadn't told her about a lot of things.

Cops would come to the funeral. That's what you did when another cop died, no matter whether or not that cop was a good cop or a bad cop or retired. Lovers would attend—plenty of those. Old friends—not so much. Enemies, maybe. The father of her child. Maybe her child. Twenty-seven years old. Angry. Abandoned. Wanting answers that Will could not give.

He felt his eyelids relax. His face. His shoulders. An eerie silence settled in.

He was in a quiet chapel. It was the middle of the night. Angie was dead. This is when he should feel it: the overwhelming loss, the hollowness that Sara had described. She had been so angry at him for not being more devastated. Maybe something had broken inside of him. Maybe that was Angie's last piece of vengeance: she had turned off the thing inside of Will that was capable of feeling.

His phone buzzed in his hand. Faith was probably looking for him. He answered, 'I'm in the chapel.'

'Really?' Not Faith. Another woman, her voice low and cool.

Will looked at the screen. The caller ID was blocked. 'Who is this?'

'It's me, baby.' Angie gave her deep, husky laugh. 'Did you miss me?'

One Week Earlier

MONDAY, 7:22 PM

Angie Polaski stood up from her desk. She closed her office door. Muffled voices bled through, some asshole agent bragging to another asshole agent about money. Her hand stayed wrapped around the doorknob, strangling it. She hated this place with its stupid rich kids. She hated the perfect secretaries. She hated the pictures on the wall. She hated the athletes who'd built this place.

She could go blind listing all the things she hated.

She sat back down at her desk. She stared at the screen on her laptop, feeling like actual fire was coming out of her eyes. If the damn computer hadn't cost so much, she would've thrown it on the floor and crushed it with her heel.

She's got his past. I've got him.

Angie checked the date on the email that Sara had written to her sister. Eight months ago. By Angie's calculation, Sara had been screwing Will for only four months when she wrote the words. Pretty arrogant for her to think that Will was hers for the taking.

Angie arrowed up to reread the paragraph.

I never thought I could feel this way about another man again.

Sara sounded less like a doctor and more like a stupid teenage girl. It seemed appropriate. Sara Linton was the exact kind of simpering, clueless girl you'd find at the center of a kids' novel—the one who stared moodily out the rain-streaked window and couldn't decide whether or not to date the vampire or the werewolf. Meanwhile, the so-called bad girl, the girl who was fun at parties, the one who would give you the best fuck of your life, was relegated to the corner, bound to end up seeing the error of her bad-girl ways just before taking a stake to the heart.

I've got him.

Angie slammed the laptop closed.

She shouldn't have cloned Sara's laptop. Not because it was wrong—fuck that—but because it was torture reading the slow process of Sara falling in love with Will.

There were literally hundreds of emails from the last year and a half. Sara wrote to her younger sister four or five times a week. Tessa wrote back just as often. They talked about their lives in mind-numbing detail. They complained about their mother. They joked about their absentminded father. Tessa gossiped about the people living in Dirt Town, or wherever the hell she was a missionary. Sara talked about her patients at the hospital and new outfits she had bought for Will and how she had tried a new perfume for Will and that she had to get a doctor friend to write her a prescription because of Will.

If not for anything else, Angie despised Sara because she'd made her have to Google the words 'honeymoon cystitis'.

Angie hadn't been able to stomach the gooey, lovestruck bullshit for long. She had skimmed ahead through the emails, looking for clues that the new car smell was wearing off. Will was far from perfect. He had a habit of picking up everything you put down, putting it away before you were finished using it. He had to immediately fix anything that was broken, no matter what time of day it was. He flossed his teeth too much. He would leave one sheet of toilet paper on the roll because he was too cheap to waste it.

Had the most perfect night last night, Sara had written last month. *My God, that man.*

Angie stood up from her chair. She went to the window. She looked down at Peachtree. Evening rush hour. Cars were shuffling along the clogged roadway. She felt a pain in her hands. She looked down. Her fingernails were digging into her palms.

Was this what it felt like to be jealous?

Angie hadn't expected Sara to stick around. Women like that didn't like messy things, and Angie had repeatedly made it clear that Will's life was messy. What she hadn't anticipated was that Will would fight for Sara to stay. Angie had assumed the other woman was a trifle, something Will had been coerced into trying but would never enjoy, like the time Angie had talked him into buying a pair of sandals.

Then she had seen them together at Home Depot.

It was early spring, so maybe five months ago. Angie was at the store buying light bulbs. Will and Sara had walked through the entrance, so up each other's butts that they hadn't seen Angie standing five feet away. They were holding hands, swinging their arms back and forth in a wide arc. Angie had followed them to the gardening section. She had stood in the adjacent aisle listening to them talk about mulch, because that's how tedious their lives were.

Sara had offered to get a shopping cart. Will had picked up the bag and thrown it onto his shoulder.

Babe, Sara had said. *Look at how strong you are.*

Angie waited for Will to tell her to get the fuck out, but he hadn't. He had laughed. He had hooked his arm around her waist. Sara had nuzzled his neck like a dog. They had shuffled off to look at flowers and Angie had broken every single light bulb she had in her basket.

'Polaski?' Dale Harding stood in the doorway. His suit was wrinkled. The buttons of his shirt strained around his gut. She felt the usual disgust she always felt around Dale—not because of his weight or his sloppiness or that he had sold his own daughter to feed his gambling habit, but because Angie could never hate him as much as she wanted to.

He said, 'Party's about to start.'

'Your eyes are yellow.'

He shrugged. 'It's what happens.'

Dale was checking out. They both knew this. They didn't talk about it. 'How's Dee?'

'She's all right. Out of the closet.'

They both smirked at the double meaning. Delilah had busted out of her last rehab facility, so Dale had decided the quickest way to dry her out was to lock her in his closet.

He said, 'I gotta line on a doc who'll give her a legit script for the Suboxone.'

'Good,' Angie said. The maintenance drug was the only thing that kept Delilah off heroin. Because of government regulations, it was hard to come by. Angie had been scoring it through a dealer she didn't quite trust, banking on Dale dying soon so that she could stop aiding and abetting his worthless junkie of a daughter. Wife. Whatever. 'Did you talk to that lawyer?'

'Yeah, but I—'

His answer was cut off by loud cheering. Champagne corks popped. Rap music pulsed through every speaker in the office. The party had started.

They both knew that Kip Kilpatrick would be looking for them. Dale stepped aside so that Angie could go first. She smoothed down her skirt as she walked. Her high heels were killing her feet, but she would be damned if she wasn't going to go toe-to-toe with the young bitches in the office. They were all so clueless, their unlined faces and pouty lips contorting into confusion when Angie had to lean over the sink in the bathroom so she could get close enough to the mirror to reapply her eyeliner. There was no joy in telling them they were going to be forty-three someday, because when that day came, she would already be in a nursing home.

Or dead.

Maybe Dale had it right. Much easier to go out on your own terms. He probably would've done it a lot sooner if not for his worthless daughter. There was something to be said about living child-free.

'There's my girl.' Kip Kilpatrick was standing at the top of the floating glass staircase. As usual, he had a basketball in his hands. The guy couldn't go anywhere without the damn thing. He said, 'I need you after this. My office.'

'We'll see.' Angie brushed past him. She checked the room, looking for a familiar face. None of the big names had arrived yet. It was mostly twenty-somethings in skinny suits drinking Cristal like it was water.

She saw a large-scale architectural model underneath the LED sign. This was what the party was all about. The last pieces of the All-Star deal had finally come together. They were going to break ground in exactly two weeks. Angie looked down at the glass-enclosed model. Converted warehouses. Open-air shopping. Grocery store. Movie theater. Farmers' market. Chic restaurants. Marcus Rippy's abandoned nightclub.

Abandoned no more. The team would go in a week from now to spiff the place up. The club anchored the All-Star Complex, an almost-three-billion-dollar venture that all the agency's big stars had invested in. And some of the little stars, too. Kilpatrick was in for ten million. Two other agents had invested half that. Then there was the team of lawyers, an international cavalcade of leeches who, as far as Angie could see, were worth every freaking dime.

Will had tried to crack the lawyers a month ago and come out the loser. Angie had been rooting for him. She really had been. He had faced them all across the weirdly large conference table, doing his best to get any kind of answer. Marcus and LaDonna Rippy were almost secondary. Every time Will opened his mouth, Marcus looked at the lawyers and the lawyers spun the answer into a kind of beautiful gibberish that only a Martian or a politician could understand.

Angie had watched the entire thing from her office one floor down. Will had no idea that everything in the conference room was recorded. He sure as shit didn't know she was close by. On her screen she could see him looking more and more frustrated as the lawyers threw out more and more obstacles. All Angie could do was shake her head. Poor thing. He was asking Marcus questions when he should've been talking to LaDonna.

'Hey, doll.' Laslo was leaning against a desk. A flute of champagne was in his hand. He was wearing his usual tight black pants and shirt. The look wasn't bad. He had a fantastic body. And a bitchy nose for fashion. He glanced down at her shoes. 'How much?'

'Fifty,' she said, annoyed that he had noticed they were knock-offs. Thanks to her job, she finally had enough cash in the bank to buy the real thing, but they weren't as comfortable as the fakes and her back could only take so much standing around before it started to spasm.

He said, 'We gotta thing later.'

'Kip already flagged me.'

Laslo sipped his champagne. They both watched Kip tossing the basketball in the air. His eyes were on the door to the lobby. He was like a lovelorn schoolgirl. Like Sara Linton waiting for Will to come home.

My heart jumps in my chest every time I hear his key in the door.

'Yo.' Laslo snapped his fingers. 'You in there?'

She took his glass and downed the champagne. 'What does Kip want?'

Laslo shushed his finger to his lips and walked away.

'Ma'am?' A good-looking waiter offered her a tray of champagne glasses.

Angie wasn't old enough to be a God damm ma'am. She snatched a glass off the tray. She walked across the room, picking her way past the Snotleighs and Bratleighs who made up the 110 Sports Management team.

Five months ago, she had tapped Dale Harding for a job. He'd been his usual asshole self about it, but Angie knew how to be an asshole, too. She'd told him that she needed money to pay off her dealer. He'd believed her, because Dale's life was filled with dealers and bookies who took out interest with their fists. Angie had never had a dealer problem. What she had was a Kip Kilpatrick problem. She needed a way into the agent's inner circle, and Dale was ideally equipped to understand the expertise that Angie could bring to the table.

Many of Kip's clients were from the street. They missed the girls they used to have fun with. Angie knew these girls. She understood how their habits were grinding them into the ground. Backing off the pipe or needle a little, cleaning up a little, and letting a rich basketball player show them a good time was a hell of a lot easier on their bodies than throwing down in the back seat of twenty different cars every single day. And if it put a little money in Angie's pocket, all the better.

That had turned out to be the easy part. Kip's inner circle was a harder nut to crack. The agent had kept Angie at arm's length. He had Laslo. He had Harding. He didn't need some broad busting heads for him. All of that had changed the day Angie ran into the bad end of LaDonna Rippy.

The meeting was a fortuitous accident. Angie was sitting across from Kip at the glass table he used as a desk. They were discussing compensation for a girl who'd had it a little rough from one of Kip's players. The negotiation was winding down when LaDonna had slammed open the door. Rippy's wife was an Amazon, the kind of woman who wasn't afraid to pull the loaded gun she kept in her purse. She was mad about something Angie could no longer remember. LaDonna got mad about a lot of things. Angie had suggested a solution, LaDonna had gone away less pissed off, and Kip had asked Angie on the spot if she wanted a more permanent job.

Angie didn't want a permanent anything, but she knew that Marcus Rippy had been charged with rape and she knew that Will was working the other side of the case.

Talk about romantic. Sara could praise him for lifting a stupid bag of dirt but she couldn't hand him evidence on a silver platter that broke open his case.

That had been Angie's initial plan, at least. She had honestly meant to help Will. Then she had seen how much more lucrative it would be to help the case go away. Looking after Will didn't put food on the table. Bribing a few witnesses was nothing she hadn't done before. If Angie hadn't been willing to do it, Harding would have, and if Harding hadn't, then Laslo would've stepped in. When you looked at it that way, it was Angie's patriotic duty to make sure the job went to a woman.

The room started to hush. Marcus Rippy was here. LaDonna was at his side. Her long blonde hair was curled tight, draping over her shoulders. She must have gotten Botoxed this morning. Tiny red dots showed through the almost white powder she used to cover acne scars. She looked pissed, but that could be from a recent plastic surgery. Or it could just be her general disposition. She had a lot to be angry about. Marcus had been her high-school sweetheart. They were married at eighteen. She was pregnant at nineteen. By that time, he was already stepping out on her, drawn to the women who were drawn to his fame.

Of course, LaDonna had been clueless about the other women. At least at that point. She started working as a hotel maid when Marcus attended Duke on a full scholarship. Because of strict NCAA eligibility rules, her paycheck was the only thing that had kept the family afloat. There were a lot of ups and downs in those early years, including an almost-career-ending injury that had cost him his scholarship and kept him out of his first draft.

LaDonna had stood by her man. She had taken on a second job, then a third. Marcus had trained his ass off and come back to what was considered one of the shittiest sophomore seasons in history. He almost got cut from the team, but then something happened. He found his groove. He grew up a little. He'd had another kid by then, and an ailing mother who needed hospice, and a father who wanted to make amends. Marcus Rippy had turned into a superstar and finally LaDonna's hard work had paid off.

Her victory lap had lasted one season. That's how long it took for Marcus to rise to the top again. The magazine covers and endorsements followed, as did all his other shit. Through it all, LaDonna kept up the Tammy Wynette act, standing by her man. She had stood by Marcus when TMZ posted photos of him with various young actresses. She had stood by him when he was accused of rape—both the time Will knew about and the time he did not. And now she was standing by him as the blonde receptionist hung on his arm like taffy at the fair.

Angie put down her glass as she hurried through the crowd. She had her hand around the blonde's waist, her fingernails digging into the skin of the girl's arm, before LaDonna could notice.

Angie told the girl, 'You so much as look at him again, your ass will be on the street. Understood?'

The girl understood.

'Excuse me, please?' Ditmar Wittich tapped his pinky ring on the side of his champagne glass. He looked around the room, waiting for silence. It came quickly. The lawyer had gotten Marcus Rippy off a serious rape charge. His firm had put together the All-Star deal. He made more money than could ever be put on the LED sign, and through the kindness of the Lord Jesus, he was going to let the assembled people share in the making of even more wealth.

He said, 'I would like to propose a toast, please.'

Everyone raised their glasses. Angie crossed her arms.

'First I must say that we are very pleased that Marcus's problems have been dealt with.' He smiled at Marcus. Marcus smiled back. LaDonna looked at Angie and rolled her eyes. 'But today is a celebration of our new collaboration between One-Ten, our international partners, and some of the greatest athletes the world has ever known.'

He kept talking, but Angie wasn't interested. She glanced around the room. Harding was drinking champagne because he wasn't yellow enough already. Laslo was slinking in the corner. Kip was playing with his ball. Two more of the bigger stars had arrived. They stood in the back, towering over the mortals in the room, their gorgeous wives at their sides.

That was when Angie saw them.

Reuben and Jo Figaroa. Fig was not the biggest star, but he was the only one that Angie was interested in. At six feet eight, he was easy to pick out of the crowd. His wife was harder to find, mostly because she worked to stay in the shadows. Jo was petite compared to most of the players' wives. She was built like a ballerina. Not Misty Copeland, but the old-school ballerinas who were such wispy waifs that they could turn sideways and disappear.

That was obviously what Jo was trying to do now. She stood beside her husband, not touching him, her body turned at an angle as she looked down at the floor.

Angie took the rare opportunity to study the girl. Her curly brown hair. Her perfect features. Her graceful neck and elegant shoulders. She had poise. That was what made you notice her. Jo was trying to disappear, but she didn't understand that she was the sort of woman you couldn't take your eyes off of.

'Jesus, Polaski.' Harding elbowed Angie in the ribs. 'Why don't you ask for her number?'

Angie felt her cheeks go hot.

'Sick bitch.' He elbowed her again. 'She's a little younger than your usual.'

'Fuck off.' Angie stalked across the room to get away from him. She could still hear him chuckling his old pervert laugh even with fifty people between them.

She leaned against the wall. She watched Ditmar finish his toast. He did that German thing where he had to look everybody in the eye. He did it with Marcus. He did it with LaDonna. He did it with Reuben Figaroa. He could not do it with Jo. She was staring down into her champagne flute, not drinking.

Her hand was at her neck, fingers playing with a simple gold chain. There was something tragic about her beauty that broke Angie's heart.

Maybe Dale Harding wanted to fuck his daughter.

Angie just wanted to make sure that hers was okay.

MONDAY, 8:00 PM

Angie sat alone on the giant couch in Kip's office. The lights were off. The party upstairs was winding down as people headed off to dinner. Her shoes were on the floor. A glass of Scotch was in her hand. She could hear the steady hum of traffic snaking down Peachtree. Monday night. People still wanted to go out. There were clubs, shopping malls, restaurants. The rich and famous looking to see and be seen.

110 Sports Management was located in the center of Buckhead. Half a mile north, you could find one of the most expensive ZIP Codes in the country. Sprawling mansions with guest houses and Olympic-size swimming pools. Private security. Heavy iron gates. Mega-star athletes. Rap stars. Music people. Drug lords living beside hedge fund managers and cardiologists.

Since the seventies, Atlanta had been a mecca for middle-class African Americans. Doctors and lawyers from the historically black colleges graduated and decided to stick around. A lot of professional athletes from other towns kept homes in the city. They wanted their kids to go to private schools that understood that the only color that mattered was green. That was the great thing about Atlanta. You could do anything you wanted so long as you had the money.

Angie had a lot of money now, at least relative to what she usually kept in her bank account. There were the checks she got from Kip every two weeks, and the pocket change she made off the girls.

None of it made her happy.

For as long as she could remember, Angie had only ever looked at the future. Nothing could be done about the past, and more often than not, the present was too shitty to contemplate. Trapped with her mother's pimp? Temporary. Shuttled to another foster home? Just for now. Living in the back of her car? Not for long. Time is what kept her moving forward. Next week, next month, next year. All she had to do was keep running, keep looking ahead, and eventually she'd turn that corner.

Only now that she'd turned the corner, she found that there was nothing there.

What did normal women want that Angie didn't already have?

A home. A husband. A daughter.

Like everything else, she already had a daughter that she had thrown away. Josephine Figaroa was twenty-seven years old. Like Angie, she could pass for white or black or Latina, or even Middle Eastern, if she wanted to freak out people on an airplane. She was thin. Too thin, but maybe that came with the territory. The other wives on the team were always cleansing or dieting or going to spinning classes or plastic surgeons to get things sucked and filled and pinned back up so they could compete with the groupies who swarmed their husbands. They need not have bothered. Their husbands were not attracted to the groupies because they were hotter than their wives. They were attracted to them because they were groupies.

It was a hell of a lot more fun to be with somebody who thought you were perfect than it was to be with a woman who wouldn't put up with your shit.

Angie didn't know what kind of wife Jo was. Only twice had she been in the same room with her daughter, both times at the 110 offices, both times from a distance, because both times Reuben had been there. He towered over his wife, radiating a quiet confidence. Jo seemed to like this. She leaned into his shadow. She kept her eyes down, demure, almost transparent. The best word that came to mind was *obedient*, which pissed Angie off, because this girl had her blood and that blood had never taken orders from anybody.

Kate.

That's what Angie had thought she would call her daughter. Like Katharine Hepburn. Like a woman who knew how to hold herself. Like a woman who took what she wanted.

What did Jo want? Judging by her demeanor, it seemed like she wished for nothing more than what she already had. A rich husband. A child. An easy life. The painful truth was that Jo was ordinary. She had attended a small high school outside of Griffin, Georgia. She had been smart enough to get into the University of Georgia, but not smart enough to graduate. Angie wanted to believe Jo had dropped out because she was a free spirit, but the math didn't support it. She had left school for a man. Eight years ago, she had married Reuben Figaroa. He was two years her senior and already in the NBA. His reputation was that of a laser-focused player. Off the court, he was often described as reserved, cerebral. He wasn't into flash. He was about doing the job right and going home to his family. Apparently this was what Jo wanted. She'd followed him to Los Angeles and to Chicago and now she had returned with him back to her home state. They had one kid, a boy, six years old, named Anthony.

This was where the publicly accessible information on Jo Figaroa ended. Despite her age, Jo wasn't on social media. She wasn't a joiner. There were no groups with which she was involved. She didn't go to parties unless they were for her husband's work. She didn't meld with the wives. She didn't lunch. She didn't wander around the mall or hang out at the gym. The only way Angie was able to track her at all was through her husband.

One year ago, a Google alert had popped up in Angie's feed. Reuben 'Fig' Figaroa was joining the Atlanta team. According to the article, the move was lateral, the kind of thing that could prolong Reuben's career for another few years.

How had Angie felt when she read the news? Annoyed at first. She didn't want the temptation. Only a raving bitch would show up in Jo's life twenty-seven years after ditching her. Which is why Angie had vowed to leave it alone. No good would come out of trying to insert herself into her daughter's peaceful world.

But then there was a second Google alert: the Figaroas had moved to Buckhead.

And a third: Reuben Figaroa signs with 110 Sports Management.

That was when Angie had finagled a job through Dale Harding, promising him some favors because she knew that favors were the one thing Dale needed.

Why?

Angie wasn't one for introspection. Reaction was more her thing.

And curiosity.

She had been tracking Jo off and on for almost twenty years. Background checks, internet searches and even a couple of private detectives. At first Angie had wanted to know who had adopted her daughter. That was a natural curiosity. Who wouldn't want to know? But like everything else in Angie's life, it wasn't enough. She had to make sure Jo's parents were good people. Then she had to know more about Jo's husband. Then she wanted to know who Jo's friends were, how she spent her time, what she did with all the hours in her day.

Greedy. That was a better word. Angie did all of this because she was greedy. It was the same reason she couldn't take just one pill, one drink, one man.

She wasn't going to blow up Jo's life. That was a promise. For now, for today, all that Angie wanted was to hear her daughter's voice. She wanted to see if the tenor was the same. If Jo shared Angie's dark sense of humor. If she was happy like she should be because she had dodged the biggest bullet of her life the day that Angie had bolted out of her hospital bed.

Twice in the same room. Twice Jo stood silently by her husband.

The girl didn't look at Reuben Figaroa much, and that bothered Angie. After eight years of marriage, there shouldn't be googly eyes, but something was off there. Angie felt it in her gut. She hadn't worked for Kip long, but you didn't need a PowerPoint presentation to understand the athletes' wives. All they had was what their husbands did with a basketball. LaDonna always crowed the day after Marcus did something extraordinary on the court. Likewise, she was hell on heels if Marcus missed an important shot.

Not so much with Jo and Reuben. The more attention the husband got, the more it seemed like Jo wanted to disappear.

And the weird thing was, Reuben Figaroa was getting a lot of attention. Angie didn't understand the terminology, but apparently Reuben's team position wasn't about the glory, more of a grinder than a breakout player. Somehow he had managed to make himself indispensable on the court, the guy who was willing to take a foul or knock some heads or whatever it took to make sure Marcus Rippy scored the basket.

Everybody won when Marcus Rippy scored a basket.

Reuben was the puzzle that Angie needed to figure out. There weren't many pieces to put together. Unusually, he didn't seek attention. He didn't go to clubs or restaurant openings. He actively avoided the press. Interviewers always attributed his shy reserve to a childhood stutter. His background was as innocuous as Jo's. Small-town high school in Missouri, full ride to Kentucky, late-round draft pick to the NBA, middling career until he got dusted with the Rippy magic. None of this afforded great insight. The only thing that made Reuben stick out was that he was white in a sport dominated by black men.

It did Angie no good to know that Jo had married a man who looked like her father.

Angie put her glass on the table. She stared out the window at the dark sky. Ten basketballs were lined up on the ledge. Championship balls, she guessed, but Angie gave not one shit about sports of any kind. The whole concept of men chasing a little ball back and forth bored her to tears. She didn't particularly find the players attractive. If she wanted to fuck a tall, lanky man with perfect abs, she could go home to her husband.

At least she'd always thought she could. Will had waited for her. That was his thing. Angie would go away. She would have a little fun, then a little more fun, then a little too much fun, which would necessitate her going back to Will so that she could recharge. Or hide out. Or whatever she needed to do in order to reset herself. That was what Will was for. He was her safe harbor.

She had never anticipated that a fucking redheaded dinghy would drop anchor in her calm waters.

Angie got it. She saw the attraction. Sara was a good girl. She was smart, if being smart that way mattered. She was corn-raised, from a good family. If a woman like that loved you, then it meant that you were normal too. Angie could see where Will would be drawn to Sara's wholesomeness. He had always been such a freakish goody-two-shoes. Volunteering to help Mrs Flannigan at the home. Cutting the neighbors' grass. He wanted to do well in school. He studied his ass off. He always tried for the extra credit. Except for being retarded, he probably would've been a star student.

It breaks my heart that he's so ashamed of his dyslexia, Sara had told Tessa. *The irony is that he's one of the smartest men I have ever known.*

Angie wondered if Will knew Sara was talking to her sister about his secret. He would not be happy. He was ashamed for a damn good reason.

The overhead lights flickered. Angie looked up at the ceiling. She watched the fluorescent bulbs spark to life. Harding ambled over to the drink fridge and took out a bottle of BankShot. He plopped down on the opposite end of the couch. His eyes were more yellow than white. His skin was the texture and color of a dryer sheet.

'Jesus,' Angie said. 'How much longer do you have?'

'Too long.' He grabbed her Scotch. She watched him top off the glass with the radioactive-looking energy drink.

She said, 'That stuff will kill you.'

'Here's hoping.'

They both heard a basketball bouncing against marble tile. They both scowled.

'Where's Laslo?' Kip asked.

'Here.' Laslo was right behind him. He had a sour look on his face. Angie had tapped a favor for a peek at the guy's sheet. Laslo Zivcovik was small, compact, but he was good with a knife and he had no hesitations about using it. He'd done a stint in jail for slicing up a girl's face, but the heavy time had come from a knife fight outside a bar. Somebody had ended up at the hospital. Somebody had ended up at the morgue.

And now Laslo was in Atlanta with his knife.

'All right, gentlemen.' Kip held the basketball under his arm. He retrieved a black folder from his desk. 'We've got a problem.'

Dale leaned over and helped himself to the bowl of peanuts. 'Rippy rape another squealer?'

Kip looked irritated, but he didn't rise to the bait. 'I don't know if y'all noticed tonight, but LaDonna was more pissed off than usual.'

Laslo groaned. He sat down in the chair opposite Angie. 'What's wound her up this time?'

Angie guessed, 'Her husband cheating on her?'

Harding said, 'You get the bank, you take the spank.'

Everyone but Angie laughed. They never got it, these guys. They thought that the wives only wanted money.

She asked Harding, 'Would you fuck Marcus Rippy for LaDonna's checkbook?'

'Ain't that Kip's job?'

'Shut up, asshole.' Kip was so far in the closet he practically lived in Narnia. 'Remember where we are.'

Harding nodded. 'All right. I get it.'

They all got it. 110's athletes were jet-setting multi-millionaires, but they were also small-town boys whose mamas had dragged them to church every Sunday. Their religion skipped over serial adultery and smoking weed and stopped dead at two guys doing each other.

Laslo said, 'What's she up to?' He meant LaDonna. He was trying to steer things back on track. 'She find out about the girl?'

'What girl?' Harding was paying attention now.

'Marcus has a little play in Vegas. That's not it.' Kip tossed the black file folder onto the couch beside Angie.

She didn't pick it up.

Kip said, 'It's Jo Figaroa.'

Angie's heart did a weird shake. She had never heard anyone say Jo's name aloud before. It had a kind of music to it.

Kip said, 'Polaski?'

She worked to keep her expression neutral as she picked up the folder. The first page had a photograph of Jo. Her hair was shorter. She was holding a small boy in her arms. She was smiling. Angie had never seen her daughter smile before.

Harding brushed peanut dust off his tie. 'She popping pills again?'

'She's an addict?' Angie felt a razor blade pump through her heart. 'How long?'

'Got pulled over in high school for a DWI. They found a stack of scripts in her glove compartment. Valium, Percocet, codeine.'

Angie thumbed through Jo's background check. She found a juvenile arrest record. There was no mention of illegal prescriptions.

Harding explained, 'Her dad had some rhythm with the local force. He got it bumped. She did some community service. Everybody got paid.'

'How do you know?'

'Talked to the AO.'

The arresting officer. Angie checked the address on the report. Thomaston. A small-town cop would be able to hide evidence, but it would take more than one payout.

'Whatever. Drugs aren't her problem.' Kip had traded his basketball for a BankShot. He twisted off the cap and tossed it into the trashcan. 'It's Marcus.'

'Marcus?' Angie looked up from the file. She tried to keep her tone conversational, but the thought of Marcus Rippy sniffing around her daughter made her want to rip his face off. 'What's he got to do with her?'

'They grew up together. He's the reason she met her husband.' Kip said this as if everyone already knew. 'Christ, Polaski, don't you ever read anything?'

'Not if it has to do with sports.'

Harding explained, 'Rippy grew up in Griffin. He and Jo had some kind of summer-lovin' bullshit at junior Bible camp. Fast-forward to his senior year. He was being heavily scouted. Some teams sent players down to woo him. Informal stuff, nothing that wouldn't pass inspection. That's when Jo got her head turned.'

Angie said, 'Reuben Figaroa was one of the players who was sent to woo Marcus.' She had always wondered how Jo had met her future husband. Now she understood. And she also understood that Harding knew a hell of a lot more about her daughter than she did. It made sense. Kip would've wanted Jo seriously vetted before he took on Reuben Figaroa as a client. Wives and girlfriends were always the weakest points.

She asked, 'Have you asked Marcus if anything is going on between him and Jo?'

There was collective guffawing. No one questioned Marcus Rippy. 110 took a paternal relationship with all of their athletes, with the understanding that at any time, their bratty kids could take their toys and leave.

Angie said, 'Let me wrap my head around this. Junior high, Marcus and Jo are sweet on each other. Summer's over. They break up. A few years later, LaDonna hooks up with Marcus. She would've known about his previous girlfriends. I don't see her not getting a full history, even as a teenager.' She asked, 'Why is it a problem now?'

'Because Jo is here, right under her nose,' Laslo answered. 'La D seemed okay with it at first. Brought Jo into the group. Threw a party for her. Took her to lunch. But lately she's been giving Jo the hairy eyeball.'

Angie knew that this would not turn out well for Jo. LaDonna was stone-cold crazy when it came to her husband. Office lore had it that she had taken a shot at a cheerleader who had gotten too close to Marcus at a party. 'What about Reuben? Is he suspicious?'

'Who the hell knows? The guy is a sphinx. He's probably said ten words to me the whole time I've known him. None of them "good job" or "thank you", by the way.' Kip chugged the rest of his energy drink. His throat worked like a goose being fattened up for pâté. Angie didn't know which was worse, watching him play with his ball or listening to him gurgle cherry lime BankShot. Ninety percent of his day was spent doing one or the other. By quitting time, his upper lip was like the red on a beach ball.

'Hey.' Harding tapped Angie's shoulder. 'Nobody calls him Reuben. It's Fig. Didn't you read his bio?'

'Why would I read his bio?'

Kip belched. 'Because he's Marcus's go-to guy. Because he brings in millions of dollars to the firm. Because once his knee gets straightened out, he has the potential to bring in even more.'

Harding asked, 'What's wrong with his knee?'

Kip side-eyed Laslo. 'Nothing's wrong with his knee.'

Angie closed the file. 'Okay, what's the problem we're all here to solve?'

'The problem is that Marcus is getting close to Jo again, and LaDonna doesn't like it, and when LaDonna isn't happy, ain't none of us happy.'

Angie couldn't see it. Reuben struck her as possessive, and Jo seemed to like that just fine. 'What makes you think they're getting close?'

'Because I've got eyes in my head.' Kip opened another BankShot. The bright red liquid spilled onto the floor. 'You can feel it when they're together. Where were you tonight?'

'Not trying to feel things between two adult people.'

'I saw it too.' Laslo started pacing. He was taking this seriously. 'Marcus touched her elbow when he gave her a drink. Intimate-like.'

Harding asked, 'We looking at a Tiger Woods situation?'

Angie asked, 'What does that mean?'

Kip said, 'Tell me you know Tiger Woods is a golfer.'

'Yes, I know who he is,' Angie said, though she had no idea how.

Laslo explained, 'Tiger was at the top of his game, then his family life fell apart, and now he's hit rock bottom. Can't even swing a club anymore.'

'Why did his family life fall apart?'

'Doesn't matter,' Kip said. 'What matters is that Marcus is the same way. If things are bad at home, they're bad on the court. His game is tied to LaDonna.'

Angie still couldn't see it. LaDonna was as erratic as a Ping-Pong ball, but Marcus was having his best season yet. 'How so?'

Kip said, 'Anytime she mentions divorce, you can count on at least five points being shaved from the board. More if she calls a lawyer.'

Angie wanted to laugh, but they were obviously dead serious.

'Five points.' Harding was nodding his head, probably planning how he was going to exploit this information with his bookie. 'Marcus can't play without her.'

Angie asked, 'Does LaDonna know she's got this power?'

'What the hell do you think?' Kip flashed Laslo an incredulous look. 'Does LaDonna know?' He grabbed the basketball. 'She uses it like a God damm guillotine over our heads.'

Harding put down the empty peanut bowl. He clapped his hands clean. 'You want us to plant some Oxy on Fig's wife, call the cops, stick her in the pokey for the night?'

Angie's heart banged into her throat. 'That sounds extreme.'

Harding didn't seem to think so. 'Why use a hammer when you can use an ax?'

She struggled to come up with reasons not to. 'Because Reuben—Fig—is married to this woman. Because she's got a kid—his kid. Because she might not be screwing Marcus.'

'Everybody's screwing Marcus.' Kip said this like it was gospel.

'Look.' Angie leaned up on the couch. She talked to Kip, because this was his decision. 'You told me to handle LaDonna, but handling LaDonna means handling all the wives.' She opened the folder as if she needed to remind herself of something, but the truth was, she was grasping at straws. 'The way you keep the wives happy is you don't cause waves. Sending . . .' she pretended to look for the girl's name, 'Josephine to rehab is a big wave. It's a media thing. It'll get her a lot of attention. There will be interviews and paparazzi. You know what happens when cameras are around. The wives go nuts trying to put themselves in the picture. And then there's the question of whether or not Jo is even using drugs.' She looked at Harding for the answer. He shrugged. She said, 'Walk it out. You plant the drugs, you call the cops, she gets in front of a judge, who puts her in rehab. What happens when they figure out she's not using? Blood tests will show she's clean. She won't go through withdrawal. What if that's the story she tells—that she was framed?'

'Is there a race angle?' Laslo asked. 'I can't tell what she is. Black? White? Latina?'

'She's beautiful,' Kip said. 'That's all that matters. Nobody gives a shit when an ugly bitch complains.'

Harding suggested, 'Jo's mother.'

Kip asked, 'What about her?'

'She was moved up here after the father died. Got some kind of heart condition, so they wanted her to be near a good hospital. The mother's on Fig's dime.'

'Easy,' Laslo said. 'We threaten Jo with the mother. Tell her Mommy is going to end up eating cat food if she doesn't cut it out with Marcus.'

Angie spitballed, 'If Jo's got a line on Marcus, the mother could be looking at an even bigger jackpot. He's got a hell of a lot more money than Reuben does. He could put the mother up in a penthouse on top of the Ritz. Buy her a new heart. Whatever she wants.'

Harding said, 'She's not wrong.'

Angie shot him a look. He hadn't said she was right, either.

Kip said, 'Okay. What's the solution, assholes?'

Angie rushed to answer before anybody else could. 'I'll shadow Jo and see what comes up.' She thought about something else. 'If she's not screwing Marcus, then what's going on between the two of them?'

Kip bounced the ball. 'What else could she want from him if she's not looking to move up the food chain?'

'Could be she's slipping him pills. Could be she's blackmailing him about something from his past. Could be a lot of things.' Angie had to stop to swallow. She couldn't let this get away from her. 'We can't find a solution without knowing what the problem really is.'

Harding said, 'I'm leaning back toward my idea. Jo's the problem. Jo goes away, the problem goes away.'

Angie tried, 'What if Jo isn't the only one who's the problem? What if she's talking to somebody? What if she's working with somebody?'

Harding shrugged, but she could see his mind was swinging back around.

'Don't be stupid about this.' Angie stood up. She knew that Kip responded best to aggression. 'I'll find out what's going on. All I need is time.'

'Time is exactly what we don't have,' Kip countered. 'Training is ramping up. We've got the All-Star ground-breaking in two weeks. I had to cut off my own right nut and hand it to Ditmar to keep Marcus in. This has to be taken care of fast.'

They all went silent again.

Angie stacked the pages in the folder. She had to get out of here before Harding swung back the other way. 'Let me dig a little deeper before we bring down the ax.'

Kip said, 'You've got two days.'

'It'll take that long just to catch myself up to speed.' Angie listed the things she had already done. 'I'll need to follow her around, check her digital footprint, scope out where she spends her time.'

'Clone her phone, read her texts, pull the emails off her computer.' Harding winked at Angie. He was finally on board. 'She's right, Kip. I can get my electronics guy on this pronto, but to drill down what's the what will take at least two weeks.'

'We don't have that kind of time.' Kip tossed the ball in the air. 'You've got one week, Polaski. You know how this works. Either the problem goes away or the wife does.'

WEDNESDAY, 7:35 AM

'You'll have to move along,' an insistent woman in Lululemon warned Angie. She had a fluorescent baton in one hand and a plastic cup of green slush in the other. 'This is the drop-off lane.'

Angie looked up at the elementary school. She had parked at the curb. There was no sign indicating that this was the drop-off lane.

The woman repeated, 'Move along, please.'

A car horn beeped behind Angie. She checked the mirror. Black Mercedes SUV, the boxy, six-bills kind. Just the thing every mother needed to take her kid to school.

'*¿Habla Inglés?*'

Angie swallowed the knives that wanted to shoot from her mouth. Just because she was in a shitty car with a leaking transmission didn't mean she was the fucking maid.

'*Habla* fuck off,' she muttered, jerking the car away from the curb. The coffee cup between her legs sloshed onto her jeans.

'Dammit.' Angie jerked the wheel again, turning out of the school parking lot. She took an illegal left. More car horns blared. She was doing a fantastic job staying undercover.

Peachtree Battle Avenue split in two, a grassy divide separating the north and south lanes. Angie couldn't figure out how to turn back around. She drove over the grass, then parked in the wide mouth of a brick-paved driveway that led to a mansion. Not exactly the best place to hide in plain sight, but better than her vantage point yesterday, which put her too far down from the school to watch Jo drop off her kid.

Kip was getting impatient. Two nights ago he had given Angie a week to figure out what Jo was up to. After a full day of surveillance with no revelations, he was making noises about Dale taking over.

There was no way in hell that Angie would let Dale take over.

She studied the line of traffic on the other side of the street. More black SUVs, some BMWs and the occasional Lexus. E. Rivers Elementary was the Taj Mahal compared to the public school shitholes Angie had attended. The kids were so shiny white that they practically glowed.

Angie had been to the school many times before, but never this early. Usually she parked in the strip mall across the main road and stood on the sidewalk watching the kids on the fenced-in playground. She had wanted to check out Jo's kid. She knew who to look for because there were tons of photos on Reuben Figaroa's Facebook page. Jo wasn't in any of them, but that wasn't why Angie was unhappy about the pictures. No matter how studiously Reuben avoided fame, he was still a public figure. He shouldn't be showing everybody his kid's face. There were nuts out there. Any one of them could figure out where the boy went to school, what time he would be on the playground, just like Angie had.

This was her grandkid, she guessed. Technically, not for real. Angie sure as hell wasn't old enough to be a grandmother. Especially to a kid like Anthony Figaroa.

The name was cumbersome for a six-year-old, but it seemed to fit. Anthony was like a little adult. His brow was permanently furrowed, shoulders rounded, head down as if he wanted to fold into himself. Instead of playing with the other kids at recess, he sat with his back to the wall of the school and stared mournfully out at the playground. He reminded Angie of Will. The lonely aura, the longing mixed with the thing that always held him back.

Will was great at sports, but there was no parent to drive him to games or pay for his equipment. There was also the matter of the roadmap of scars on his body. If Will changed out in the locker room, someone would notice the obvious signs of abuse, and then a teacher would become involved, and the principal and social workers, and suddenly he would be put under a magnifying glass, which was the thing Will hated the most.

Anthony Figaroa clearly shared this same aversion to attention. Then again, so did his mother. Angie saw Jo's charcoal-gray Range Rover inch along the drop-off lane. The same scene played out that Angie had witnessed the day before. Jo didn't wave to the other mothers in the car pool. She didn't speak to the Nazi with the sign who'd shooed Angie away. She made like Anthony. She kept her head down. She stayed in her lane. She dropped off her kid. She drove away. Going by yesterday, or any other day that Angie had watched her daughter, Jo would go home, and she wouldn't go back out again until it was time to pick up Anthony.

Unless it was Thursday or Friday, the days she went to the grocery store and the dry cleaner, respectively. Angie had pictured a lot of things for her daughter, but never that she would turn into a hermit.

Angie's car was pointed in the wrong direction to follow Jo. Another trip through the grassy divide landed her two cars behind the Range Rover, which was stopped at a red light. Jo's blinker wasn't on, which could mean that she was heading straight into the Peachtree Battle shopping center. Angie scanned the shops down the hill. This wasn't Jo's grocery day, and even if it was, she used the Kroger on Peachtree. Her dry cleaner was on Carriage Drive. The only business in the strip mall that was open this early was Starbucks.

The light changed. Jo drove across the intersection and turned into the Starbucks parking lot.

Angie followed at a distance, keeping another car between them. The lot was packed. Angie expected Jo to pull into the line at the drive-thru, but she circled a few times and found a spot.

'Come on.' Angie had to wait out a shuffling woman with her nose in her phone before she could exit the parking lot and find a space in front of the bank across the alley.

She got out of her car and darted toward the Starbucks. She didn't realize what was about to happen until she saw Jo opening the glass door. She was going into a coffee shop. She would place her order at the counter. She would thank the woman behind the register. There would have to be some kind of conversation. Angie would finally hear Jo's voice. This was why she had wanted the job at Kip's in the first place—this moment, this space in time. She would hear her daughter speak. She would divine through some long-snuffed maternal instinct whether or not Jo was okay, and then Angie could get back to her regular life and never think about her lost daughter ever again.

Angie opened the door.

She was too late.

Jo had already placed her order. She was standing with the herd of coffee-buyers, waiting for the woman behind the counter to call her name.

Angie mumbled a curse as she got in line for the register. The guy ahead of her had apparently never been to a Starbucks before. He was asking questions about sizes. Angie pulled a bottle of overpriced apple juice from the fridge. She glanced at Jo, then let herself stare openly.

She wasn't the only person appraising her daughter. Every man in the room had noticed her. Jo was beautiful. She had a way of drawing your eye. What was troubling was that she either didn't notice or didn't care. At twenty-seven, Angie had used her looks like a battering ram. There wasn't a door she couldn't break open.

'Josephine?' the barista called. 'Tall soy latte.'

Josephine, not Jo.

She picked up the cup. She didn't speak. Her smile was stressed, obviously forced. She took the latte to the back of the store. She sat down at the long bar overlooking the parking lot. There was an empty stool one seat down. Angie checked to make sure the cashier wasn't looking. She ducked out of line and took the empty seat before anyone else could.

The bar was narrow, maybe a foot wide. Outside the window, cars snaked toward the drive-thru window. The guy between Angie and her daughter was typing on his computer. She glanced down at the screen and assumed he was writing the great American novel. At a Starbucks. Just like Hemingway.

Angie opened her juice. She had done private eye work off and on for years. There was a go-bag in her trunk with the tools of the trade. Duct tape, a small tarp in case it rained, a good camera, a directional microphone, four tiny cameras that could be hidden inside potted plants and air vents. None of which could help her at this late date. She spotted a newspaper a few seats down. She bumped the woman on the other side of her, nodded at the paper, and it was silently passed her way.

Hemingway, meet Sam Spade.

Angie skimmed the headline on the front page. She chanced another look at her daughter. The cup caught her attention. JOSEPHINE was written in black marker. Angie knew there was a lot in a name. Her mother's pimp had called her Angela. Even now, if anyone said the name, bile would shoot into her mouth.

Angie took a deep breath. She let her eyes travel up.

Jo was staring out the window. Angie followed her sight line to the white stucco wall of the strip mall. The girl was waiting for something. Thinking about something. Upset about something. Her eyes did not move from the wall. She was sitting on her hands. Steam rose from her untouched coffee. Her phone was face up on the bar in front of her. She was tense. Angie felt like she could reach across Hemingway and actually touch the woman's anxiety.

But that wasn't what she was here for.

Angie opened the newspaper. She pretended to be interested in world events. And then she actually got interested in world events, because nothing else was happening. The woman next to her got up and left. The line at the counter thinned, then disappeared. The parking lot began to empty. Finally Hemingway moved to an oversized chair a few tables away.

Angie turned the page in her newspaper. FINANCE.

She glanced at Jo.

Her daughter had not moved. She was still sitting on her hands. Still staring at the blank wall. Still almost shaking with anxiety.

They were the only two people left at the bar. Angie got up and moved a few stools away because that's what a normal person would do. She spread out the newspaper. She wasn't Meryl Streep. She couldn't pretend to be interested in finance. She turned to the LIFE section. She reached for her juice, but so much time had passed that the bottle was warm.

Angie's eyes started to blur from reading the tiny words. She looked out the window and blinked. She watched a car pull into the street. She listened to Hemingway banging away at his laptop.

Out of the corner of her eye, she saw Jo jump. The move was almost imperceptible. A half-second later, Angie heard Jo's phone ring. Not a ring exactly, more like a noise you'd hear from a 1950s sci-fi movie.

FaceTime.

Jo's hands were shaking when she accepted the video call. She held the phone low in front of her face. Angie couldn't see the image of the caller, nor could she hear that person's voice. Jo had slipped in earbuds. She held the tiny mic up to her mouth and said, 'I'm here.'

Angie pulled her own phone out of her purse. She tapped some buttons. She pretended to toss the phone back into her purse, but the move was practiced. The phone landed at an angle, camera facing toward Jo. Angie couldn't look at what was happening live, but she could watch the video later.

'Yes,' Jo said. 'Do you see?'

Angie's vision tunneled on the newsprint. She felt a pain in her ear. She was straining to hear Jo's voice, but it was little more than a whisper.

Jo said, 'Yes. I understand.'

Angie flipped the paper over. She ran her finger down a line of text that she could not read. Jo's voice was still low, but she sounded panicked, afraid.

'I understand.'

Who could make Jo sound scared? Marcus Rippy came to mind. He liked being in charge. Jo was his type. So was Angie, but even at twenty-seven, Angie could handle guys like that. She didn't think little Josephine from Thomaston could handle anything.

'I will,' Jo said. 'Thank you.'

There was a change in the air. Stress draining away. The call had ended. Jo put down the phone. Her elbows went to the bar. Her head dropped into her hands. Relief radiated off her thin body.

Her voice. Angie had been too wrapped up in the whispery hush to analyze the sound.

Jo started to cry. Angie had never been good with emotion. Her options were always to either wait it out or go away. She racked her brain to think how a normal person would behave in a

Starbucks with a woman crying a few chairs away. Angie could reasonably ask the girl if she was all right. That seemed like an appropriate response. Jo's shoulders were shaking. She was clearly upset. Angie could just say the words: *Are you okay?* It was a simple question. People asked variations of it all the time to complete strangers. In elevators. In bathrooms. In line for coffee.

How are you doing?

Angie opened her mouth, but it was too late.

Jo stood up. She unhooked her purse from the back of her chair. Or at least she tried to. The strap got caught. The chair toppled. The sound was like an explosion in the small space. Hemingway rushed over to help her.

'I've got it,' Jo said.

'I can—'

'I know how to pick up a fucking chair!'

She snatched the chair from his hands. She slammed it back in place. The sound echoed like a gunshot. Heads swiveled to see what the problem was. The barista started to walk around the counter.

'I'm sorry,' Hemingway apologized. 'I was just trying to help.'

'Help.' Jo snorted. 'Mind your own fucking business. That's how you can help.'

Jo yanked open the glass door. She stalked across the parking lot. She threw her purse into her car. Her tires burned against asphalt as she streaked out of the parking lot.

'Jeesh,' Hemingway said. 'What was that?'

Angie smiled.

That was her daughter.

WEDNESDAY, 10:27 AM

Angie drove down Chattahoochee Avenue at an old lady's pace. Her transmission was slipping. She didn't have time to top off the fluid. She didn't have time to change her coffee-stained jeans. She was late meeting Dale and his electronics guy. There were a lot of things Angie didn't mind being late for, but everything had changed half an hour ago inside the Starbucks.

'Dammit!' Angie struggled to push the gear into fourth. There was a grinding sound that sent a rattle into the clutch.

Maybe she could talk Dale's guy into topping off her transmission fluid. Or maybe she would torch the car and leave it burning in front of Sara Linton's apartment building. She was the reason Angie had to buy transmission fluid by the case. Normally Angie would spend a few weeks with Will, let him fix the car, then head on her way, but that wasn't an option since Red Riding Hood was sleeping in her bed.

His name is my favorite word, Sara had written to her sister.

'Shit.' Angie hissed out one of *her* favorite words between her teeth. She couldn't dredge up her usual anger for Sara Linton. She was too worried about Jo.

She had to watch the Starbucks video again. Her phone battery was almost gone from playing it so much. Angie kept her palms on the steering wheel and balanced her phone between her fingers. She tapped the arrow for *play*. 'Do you see?' Jo whispered, holding up her iPhone, proving to the caller that she was inside the Starbucks. 'I understand . . . I will . . . thank you . . .'

Before Angie made detective, she had worked as a beat cop. She took nights, because they paid more. Every shift was basically ten seconds of adrenaline sandwiched by eight hours of social work. The old-timers called them chicken bones, because you'd get a call to somebody's shitty apartment and find two rednecks fighting over something stupid, like a chicken bone. Not that the call was ever a cakewalk. You never knew when two neighbors arguing about a barbecue grill could turn into a stand-off with a drunk pointing a loaded shotgun at your chest.

Domestic violence calls were the same, but different. You always went in assuming something really bad was going to happen. Even Angie, who was drawn to confrontation, hated rolling out on a battery call. The men always tried to push her around. The women always lied. The kids always cried, and in the end, all Angie could do was arrest the guy, write up the report, and wait until she got another call to go to the same house over and over and over again.

Jo didn't have any obvious bruises or scars. Her face was perfect. She walked with an even stride, not in the bent-over posture of a woman who'd gotten the hell beaten out of her.

But still, Angie could tell that her daughter was being abused. The way she never looked at her husband. The way she stayed glued to his side, never talking to anybody, never daring to raise her eyes above the floor. The way she never left home except to go to the elementary school, the grocery store or the dry cleaner. The obedient air she assumed around her husband, as if she was not a person but an appendage.

Two nights ago, when Kip was convening a meeting about Jo being a problem, Reuben Figaroa was being flown by private jet to an undisclosed location, where the best orthopedist in the world would perform micro-surgery on his knee. That was all the information Angie could get out of Laslo. An injured player was the kind of news that could tilt the shape of the upcoming basketball season. Jo had stayed at home because things had to look normal. She had to take the kid to school. She had to make people believe that nothing was wrong with her husband.

Angie didn't give a shit about Reuben's surgery. What she cared about was what his absence was doing to her daughter.

Jo was terrified. That was clear. Angie held the evidence in her own two hands.

When Jo said, 'Do you see?' what she meant was, 'Do you see where I am? Exactly where you told me to be.'

When she said, 'I understand,' what she meant was, 'I understand you are in charge and that I can't do anything about it.'

When she said, 'I will,' she meant 'I will do exactly what you just told me to do, exactly how you want me to do it.'

The worst part was at the end of the video. Tears slid down Jo's jaw, her neck. Her fingers trembled around the mic. Still she said, 'Thank you.'

Reuben Figaroa. Angie could clearly see him on Jo's iPhone when she turned the camera to show him the almost empty coffee shop.

Kip had said that Jo was getting too close to Marcus. Maybe that was by design. Jo had known Marcus in junior high. Obviously they were still friends. He was rich. She was desperate. If Marcus was Jo's parachute, then the plan wasn't a bad one. The most life-threatening time for a battered woman was when she tried to leave her abuser. The only thing that shifted the odds was having another man around to protect her. If Jo was getting close to Marcus, it was only because she was pulling away from Reuben. This was what Angie had abandoned her daughter to: a lifetime of being nothing more than a kept woman.

Angie tossed her phone back into her purse. She wiped her eyes. The juice from Starbucks must have gone bad. Her hands were sweating. Her stomach cramped.

Back in her early twenties, Angie had been with a guy who slapped her around. And then punched her around. And then did other things that she thought meant he was desperately in love with her. The violence worked like a magnet. That, and seeing a big, giant man cry like a baby because he was so fucking sorry that he'd hurt you and he was never, ever going to do it again.

Until he did it again.

'Jesus,' Angie whispered. What was the point of staying out of Jo's life? First the pill problem, and now this. Jo had inherited all of Angie's bad choices. 'Fuck!' She banged her hand against the steering wheel, but not because of Jo. She had missed the turn into the parking lot.

Angie struggled with the shifter, trying to force the gear into reverse. The clutch tensed. She heard the gears grinding. Her stomach was still cramping.

'Fuck!' she screamed again. 'Fuck! Fuck! Fuck!' She banged her fists on the steering wheel until the pain shot into her back and shoulders.

She stopped. This was crazy. She had lost it over a stupid missed turn.

Finger by finger, she wrapped her hands around the wheel. She took a deep breath and held it for as long as she could.

Carefully Angie forced the gear into first. She drove to the end of the street, then did a wide U-turn. She had the gear in third by the time she coasted into an abandoned parking lot. She flipped into reverse just to prove that she could and backed into one of the lined parking spaces.

Angie flexed her hand. Banging the steering wheel hadn't been her smartest move. The side of her fist already felt bruised.

Nothing she could do about that now.

Angie looked up at the massive concrete block that was Marcus Rippy's nightclub. The building resembled a mummified robot's head. A cleaning crew was supposed to spiff it up next week, but Angie wasn't sure how they were going to manage it. Weeds shot up from the broken asphalt. Graffiti was everywhere. She had no idea why Dale always wanted to meet here. He must have been a terrible cop. All he wanted was routine. Maybe that's what happened when you got older. Or maybe it was because it didn't matter if Dale kept showing up in the same place over and over again. He'd stopped dialysis a week ago. If what Angie had read on the internet was true, he had a week, maybe two at the most, which meant he'd be dead before anyone figured out the pattern.

Could be he was already dead. Angie looked at the time on her phone. Dale was fifteen minutes late. Sam Vera, his electronics guy, wasn't here either. Why was it that she was the only person who ran on time anymore?

She flipped down her visor and checked her make-up in the mirror. Her eyeliner was melting. Her lips could use a touch-up. She found Sara's lipstick in her purse. Angie twisted the gold case. There was a scratch down the side. You'd think for sixty bucks the thing would be plated in real gold.

Angie looked at the flattened lipstick. She had cut off the tip. She might be a dangerous stalker, but she wasn't unhygienic.

Was she really dangerous?

A few notes left on a car window never hurt anybody. Going through Sara's shit was weird, but that hadn't been on purpose. Or not by design, anyway. Angie had gone to Will's house because she wanted to see him. Not talk to him, but just see him. As usual, he was at Sara's. This had happened many times before. She had used the key Will left on the ledge over the back door. The first thing Angie had seen was his stupid little dog. Betty wouldn't stop yapping. Angie had used her foot to slide her into the spare bedroom and shut the door. She was passing the bathroom when she saw Sara's make-up strewn across the sink.

Angie's first thought was: *Will's not going to like that.*

Her second thought was: *What the hell is Sara Linton doing leaving her shit here?*

Here.

Will's bathroom. Will's bedroom. Will's house.

Angie's husband.

Angie flipped the sun visor closed. She didn't need a mirror to apply lipstick. She'd been wearing it since she was twelve years old. Her hand knew the motion by heart. Still, she leaned up and checked herself in the rear-view mirror. She had to admit that the stuff was worth it. The color didn't bleed. It lasted all day. Rose cashmere didn't exactly suit her, but then again it didn't exactly suit Sara, either.

Angie sat back in the seat. She smoothed her lips. She thought about the other things Sara had left at Will's house. Real Manolo Blahniks. They were too big for Angie's feet, a size more suitable for a drag queen. Black lacy underwear, which was a waste because Will could get turned on by a paper sack. Hair clips, which Angie could use, but she had thrown them away because fuck Sara Linton. Perfume. Another waste. Will couldn't tell the difference between Chanel No. 5 and Dial hand soap.

Then there were the things in the bedside drawer.

Angie's bedside drawer.

She reached into her bag and found a tissue. She wiped off the lipstick. She rolled down the window and threw the tissue on the ground. She could afford to buy her own Sisley now. She could afford to get her car fixed. She could buy her own Manolos, her own perfume.

Why was it that she only ever wanted the things that she couldn't have?

There was a glint of white in her rear-view mirror. Dale Harding's Kia came from around the side of the building. The car slowed to a stop four spaces away. Dale was eating a McDonald's hamburger. The door opened. He shoved the rest of the burger into his mouth and tossed the wrapper onto the ground. His meaty hand clamped onto the roof. The car shook as he wedged himself out.

He asked Angie, 'Where is he?'

Angie was offering an exaggerated shrug when Dale turned toward the street.

Sam Vera circled his van through the parking lot in a lazy figure eight. The idiot probably thought he was doing surveillance, but he was actually drawing more attention to himself. His van was painted a dull gray with a FEEL THE BERN bumper sticker on the back. The gray was a primer coat, broken up by patches of yellowing Bondo. Which Angie only knew about because of Will.

She got out of her car.

Dale asked, 'You find anything out?'

'Fig is beating his wife.'

'No shit.' He obviously already knew. 'I talked to the team fixer in Chicago. They had to make a couple of nine-one-ones go away.'

'You didn't think to share this with me?'

'No big deal. He doesn't strangle her.'

'What a gentleman.' Cops were taught that an abuser who strangled a woman was statistically more likely to kill her. Angie asked, 'Anything else you're hiding?'

'Maybe. How about you?'

Angie dug around in her purse so he couldn't see her expression. Dale had obviously done a good job vetting Jo Figaroa, but her birth certificate would've been a dead end. Angie had given them an alias at the hospital.

The van finally came to a stop. The brakes squealed. She could smell pot. The radio was blaring Josh Groban.

Dale banged his fist on the side of the van. 'Open up, dipshit.'

There was a loud *pop* as Sam Vera threw back the bolt on the van door. His large round eyeglasses caught the sun. He was twenty years old, tops, with a goatee that looked like mange from a squirrel. His eyes squinted behind his glasses. 'Hurry. I hate the sun.'

Angie climbed into the back of the van. The air conditioning was working overtime, but the van was still a giant metal box baking in the sun. Sam's acrid sweat mixed with the sweet odor of pot. She felt like she was in a frat house.

Angie sat on an overturned plastic crate. She kept her purse in her lap because there was greasy-looking shit all over the floor. Dale settled into the front passenger seat, turned sideways so he could see them both. He handed Sam an envelope of cash. Sam started counting the bills.

Angie looked around the cramped space. The van was a mobile RadioShack. Wires and metal boxes and various crap she didn't understand spilled out of the Dewey decimal system he had going on in the back. He specialized in remote surveillance, but not the legal kind. There was a Sam Vera in every major American city. He was paranoid as hell. He had no qualms about breaking the law. He talked a tough game, but he would narc out his own mother if the cops ever leaned on him. Angie used to have her own Sam Vera, but he got picked up by the NSA for breaking into something you weren't supposed to break into.

'M'lady.' Sam offered Angie a bright green phone with black electrical tape holding it together. 'This is a clone of Jo Figaroa's iPhone.'

'That was fast.'

'That's what you pay me for.' He asked Dale, 'Did you get the bugs in place?'

'Planted 'em while the wife was dropping off the kid at school.' Dale's breathing was labored. He looked worse than usual. 'I also plugged in that whatever thingy you told me to put on her laptop. It was in the kitchen. I didn't find any other computers. No iPads. Nothing. Weird, right?'

'Really weird.' Sam told Angie, 'The program Dale put on the laptop is called a shadow tracker, like spyware, but better. I already downloaded every file from the hard drive onto this tablet.' He reached toward a bin and pulled out a scratched-up iPad. Two old-school antennae stuck out of the back that reminded Angie of the rabbit ears on a television. 'I loaded an app to ping the GPS tracker on her car. It's this button here with the car on it. Works exactly like the police model. You're familiar with it?'

'Yes.'

'You can follow her anywhere she goes as long as it's not underground.' He started swiping and tapping the glass. 'The spyware on her laptop acts in real time. Whatever she types on the computer from now on will show up on this iPad, but since I already downloaded all the data, you can also go back and do searches through her hard drive. It's basically her laptop. Not just a copy as of a certain date.'

Dale said, 'You mean not like the thing you gave Polaski before.'

Sam's eyes bulged in his head. 'I didn't—'

'I told him,' Angie interrupted. Dale wouldn't give her Sam's contact information unless Angie told him why. Angie had been a little creative on whose laptop she was breaking into. She told Sam, 'We're cool. Just keep doing what you're doing.'

'All right.' Sam tapped a few more times on the screen. He handed the iPad to Angie. 'Just so you know, the hacker's code is you don't rat out your customers. I'm solid for you, yo.'

'Sure, kid.' Dale pulled a melted Snickers out of his pocket.

Angie looked away so she didn't have to watch him chew. She still wasn't sure what had driven her to copy Sara's laptop. Her patient files were on there, so Grady Hospital had installed some kind of encryption software that took a higher level of espionage than Angie was capable of. Sam had given her something called a dongle that broke Sara's passwords and downloaded all the files. Angie knew this was crossing a line—not with Sara, but with herself. That was the moment at which she had gone from being annoyed to being obsessed to being a full-on stalker.

Was she dangerous?

She hadn't figured out that part yet.

'Get out of the van.' Dale was talking to Sam. 'I need a minute with Polaski.'

Sam balked. 'In the sunlight?'

'You're not going to melt, Elphaba.'

Angie laughed. 'How the hell do you know the Wicked Witch's real name?'

'Look.' Sam tried to talk reason. 'I've got sensitive stuff in here. For other clients. I can't tell you what it is, but it's top-secret stuff.'

'You think either one of us knows what the fuck any of this shit is?' Dale reached back and pushed open the door. 'Get out.'

Sam kept up the hurt act as he jumped out of the van. Dale slammed the door shut. Angie felt her eyes sting at the sudden changes in light.

Dale fished a joint out of the ashtray. He used a plastic lighter to flame it up. He took a long drag and held it. Smoke sputtered out of his mouth when he said, 'I took Delilah to see *Wicked*.'

'Father of the year.'

Dale offered her the joint.

Angie shook her head. She already had three Vicodin on board.

Dale took another drag. He squinted at all the electronic paraphernalia. 'If I knew how to use half this shit, I'd be a billionaire by now.'

Angie knew he'd be exactly where he was, and not just because of his shitty luck at the track. Men like Dale Harding only knew how to hold on to one thing: desperation.

He said, 'Look. I need a favor.'

Angie was familiar with Dale's favors. They all had one theme. 'Did Delilah fall off the wagon?'

'No, nothing like that. She's solid.' He gave her a hard look. 'She's gonna stay clean, right?'

The guy was delusional, but she said, 'Right.'

'It's another thing. My bookie.'

Angie should've expected this. Even the threat of death couldn't stop an addict from taking a hit. Delilah had the horse and Dale had the ponies.

He said, 'I'm into Iceberg Shady for fifteen K.'

'I know you have the money.' Angie knew that Dale kept bricks of cash under the spare tire in the trunk of his car. 'Just peel some off the top.'

He shook his head. 'It's all gotta go to Delilah. She'll need some cash to live off of while the paperwork is moving through. You promised me you'd look after her.'

Angie leaned back against the bins. Wires poked into her back, but she was feeling too claustrophobic to move away. Dale's neediness was eating up all the air. He'd made some kind of side deal with Kip Kilpatrick, his last-ditch attempt to do right by Delilah. There was $250,000 being held in an escrow account. In two weeks, when the All-Star Complex broke ground, the money would automatically flow into a trust fund Dale had set up for Delilah. He was holding on to the promise of the trust fund as his one chance at redemption. Like a big payday could erase the thousands of times Delilah had earned Dale's gambling money between her legs.

Angie wasn't interested in Dale's redemption, and she didn't want the job of wrangling a junkie whore. The only reason she'd said yes was because Dale was dangling the job at 110 over her head. If she had wanted to be responsible for a kid, she would've kept Jo.

Dale dropped the joint back into the ashtray. 'I got this from the lawyer, okay?' He pulled a folded stack of papers out of his inside jacket pocket. A racing form floated to the floor of the van. 'I just need your John Hancock.'

Angie shook her head. 'I'm the wrong person, Dale.'

'I got you the job with Kip. I didn't ask you any questions. You agreed to do this for me, now you're gonna do it.'

She tried to buy some time. 'I need to read it before I sign it, maybe talk to a lawyer.'

'No you don't.' He had a pen in his hand. 'Come on. Two copies. One for you, one for the lawyer to file.' She still didn't take the pen. 'You want me to start asking questions? Like maybe about your husband? Like why do you need to crack the encryption on medical software?'

'That dickslap,' Angie said. Sam had ratted her out after all. She stalled for time. 'How would it work? The trust?'

'The executor, that's you, is authorized to pay out for basic things, like an apartment, utilities, health-care expenses. I want to make sure she always has a roof over her head.' He added, 'I put it in there that you get a grand a month for taking care of it.'

Not chump change, but not enough to retire on, either. Here was the bigger problem: Angie knew Delilah Palmer. She was a selfish, spoiled brat, even without the junkie habit. The first nickel the girl got would end up melted in a spoon and shot into whatever vein she could find.

Which is the reason Angie took the pen and signed the agreement.

Dale laughed at her signature. 'Angie Trent, huh?'

'What about your other problem?' She tucked her copy into her purse. 'I'm gonna guess your bookie, Iceberg Shady, is also a pimp?'

'He runs whores off Cheshire Bridge. That's your old stomping ground, right?'

During her detective days, Angie had worked honey traps out of the Cheshire Motor Inn. 'That was years ago. Those girls are all dead.'

'You don't gotta know their names. You just gotta get them locked up.'

'You want me to get APD to pull a sting on Cheshire Bridge?' She was already shaking her head. She might as well tell them to round up all the sand on Daytona Beach. 'That'll take mountains of paperwork. The girls will be out in hours, arraigned in a week. There's no way they'll do it.'

'Denny will do it if you ask nice.'

Angie hated that Dale's sticky fingerprints were all over her life.

'Come on, Polaski. Give a dying man some peace. Denny would fuck a donkey if you asked him to.'

'Denny would fuck a donkey just because.' She reluctantly took out her phone. Angie only used burners, so she could control who got in touch with her. She pulled Denny's number from the Rolodex in her head and started typing. She asked Dale, 'I guess you want this to happen now?'

'Today is good. Half of Iceberg's bank is on Cheshire. Denny keeps him busy bailing out girls, that should buy me at least a week.'

She studied his watery eyes. Red shot through the whites like yarn. 'Just a week? That's all you've got left?'

'I got it worked out. If my kidneys don't get me, this will do the job.' He pulled a small baggie of white powder out of his jacket pocket. 'One hundred percent pure.'

'Every dealer on the planet says his cocaine is one hundred percent pure.' She finished typing the text. 'It's probably a laxative.'

'It's real,' Dale said, because of course he'd tested it. 'I figure this much coke after all these years, they'll be peeling my heart off the ceiling.'

'Sounds great.' Angie sent the text to Denny. She tucked her phone into her purse. 'Make sure I'm not the one who finds your body.'

'Hand to God,' he swore. 'But lookit, I want you to promise me again, Polaski. You can take your cut of the money, but you'll make sure Delilah is comfortable, right? Not livin' large, but in a nice place, with good neighbors—not like that Asian bitch I gotta deal with. Plenty of healthy food and organic shampoo and all that shit.'

'Sure.' Another promise Angie wasn't certain she would keep. 'But why are you timing it like this? You can eke out another week, make sure it all goes through.'

He shook his head. 'I can't go another couple of weeks. I'm sick of this. Sick of living. I want it over.'

She guessed that he was being honest, but the other part was that Dale knew Delilah would be furious when she learned that the money wasn't going to be handed over in one lump sum. All she would have to do was throw a tantrum and Dale would capitulate, which meant that Angie had to be his posthumous balls. 'Why me? You married Delilah so your ex-wives couldn't get their hands on your windfall. Problem solved. You could hire a lawyer to keep her on a leash. Why do I have to be her banker?'

'Because a lawyer would blow through half the wad before he figured out she was playing him. You don't give a shit about nobody, especially her. She'll beg and cry for more money, and you'll tell her to fuck off.'

Angie couldn't argue with that.

'And because she'll spend it,' he said. 'She's too stupid to plan for the future. She wants everything right now, as much as she can get, as fast as she can get it.'

'Wonder who she gets that from?'

Dale chose not to get her meaning. 'Kids like her, they don't understand the value of a dollar. She's been struggling all her life, and that's on me. The pills. The H. And then Virginia with all her shit . . .' Dale took out his handkerchief. He blew his nose. His tears looked cloudy as they fell from his eyes. 'Jesus,' he said. 'It's the thing.' He meant the fact of his dying, that he was losing control of his faculties. WebMD listed this as a side effect. Vivid dreams. Hallucinations. Memory loss. Lack of coordination.

Dale blew his nose again. He wiped his tears.

Angie watched him struggle to rein in his emotions. She felt cold, even though the van was broiling. Pain could be infectious. She couldn't afford to let it in.

Dale said, 'I just wanna make sure this is done right.'

Angie had never excelled at doing things right. 'What's to stop me from cleaning out all the money and leaving Delilah high and dry?'

'There's oversight from the law firm. You can only write checks to landlords and the power company and places like that, but not like Macy's or McDonald's.'

Angie nodded, but she could think of a thousand ways to get around the restriction. Step one: turn herself into a landlord.

Dale said, 'You promised me, Angie. I've got your word. I'm not saying that means anything, but I will tell you that I'm gonna get downstairs a lot quicker than you are, and if you fuck over my daughter, I'm gonna be waiting for you in hell.'

She didn't want to admit that the warning scared her. 'You don't think I've got a shot at heaven?'

He tossed the used handkerchief onto the floor. 'Tell me why you're so interested in Fig's wife.'

'Because I'm being paid to be.'

'Not a new interest, though.'

Angie smiled. 'Why didn't you ever use that brain on the job?'

'They didn't pay me enough.' He wiped his nose with the back of his hand. 'Stalking can get you ten years in big-girl prison.'

Angie wondered who he thought she was stalking. Sara, sure, but she had been following Jo, too. 'What makes you think I'm stalking somebody?'

'I'm not as stupid as I look, Polaski. You came to me begging for a job. Your husband was trying to make a case against Marcus Rippy. I did some digging.'

Angie felt the hair on the back of her neck go up. She always kept an eye out because of Will. She hadn't even seen Dale coming. 'What do you think you know about me?'

'That you'd fuck over the only guy in the entire world who doesn't think that you're a worthless, cold-blooded bitch.'

'Worthless,' Angie repeated, because that was the only blow that landed. Tanking Will's case against Rippy wasn't about anything else but getting paid. She asked, 'Any more pearls of wisdom?'

'Take care of this thing with Fig's wife. We need Rippy solid for another two weeks. My lawyer says the escrow account is totally legit. Two weeks from now, when those shovels dig into the ground, the two-fifty hits Delilah's trust fund and she's taken care of for the rest of her life. That shovel don't hit, even one day late, then there's nothing and my entire life's been for shit.' Dale pushed open the door. The sun knifed the van in two. 'I can't go to my grave worrying about my deal falling through because that cocksucker Rippy can't keep his dick in his pants.'

'I'll take care of it,' Angie said, but she wasn't sure.

'Good.' The van shook as Dale struggled to get out. He was dizzy. Angie didn't know if it was from the heat or from whatever was killing him. She couldn't force herself to care. All that she knew was that the sooner Dale died, the sooner she would be free of his prying and his sickness and all the other despicable things about him that weighed her down.

'Me again.' Sam took his seat on the other crate. 'Is there anything else?'

She held up the green phone that he'd taped together. 'When is this going to work?'

'She needs to get a text through Wi-Fi or from her network. Once she replies, the phone will activate.'

'Why not just send her a text?'

'Because she'll have to reply or the program can't download. User interface, yo. It's a bitch.'

'Can I listen to her calls?'

'Do people talk on the phone?' He looked puzzled. 'I never really thought about coding for that. I mean, there's text and shit. Isn't that enough?'

Angie was sick of feeling old. 'What about FaceTime? Skype?'

'Yeah, that's trickier. So, with VoIP you—'

'I'm going to shove this thing up your ass if you don't use words that I can understand.'

'I thought I was.' He was being pouty again. 'FaceTime, Skype, that's delayed. There's a program I loaded remotely through an app on her phone. It records any video calls that come in, but you have to wait for the call to be over before you can watch it.'

'How do I access it?'

He gently took the phone from her. He woke up the screen. He pointed to an app showing an old-timey gramophone. 'Press this and it gives you a list. Press the video call you want to see, and it loads. But only after the call is finished.'

'What if I want to see a call that happened this morning?'

'Can't help you. It wouldn't be stored in her phone. All I can access is what's already stored and what happens next, just like the laptop.' He offered, 'I can show you some features on the tablet if you need me to.'

Christ, he was talking to her like she was his grandmother. 'It works like a regular iPad?'

'Well, sure.'

'I'm good.' Angie started to get out of the van.

'I didn't tell anybody,' Sam said. 'About the other stuff I did for you.'

Angie stared at him. 'So when Dale said he knew about the medical decryption software you gave me, he was just taking a wild-ass guess?'

Sam's soul patch twitched.

Angie looked around the van. Dangling wires. Boxes of electronics. Computer monitors. Tablets. Laptops.

Sam asked, 'Are you looking for something?'

'I'm just wondering what the inside of this van would look like if I shot you in the face.'

Sam stuttered out an uncomfortable laugh.

Angie took her gun out of her purse. She rested it on top of the iPad, her hand around the grip. Her finger pressed against the side of the trigger guard, the way she had been taught. Or maybe not. She looked down. Her finger was on the trigger.

'Lady, please.' Sam had stopped laughing. His hands were in the air. 'I'm sorry, all right? Please don't kill me. Please.'

'Think about how you feel right now the next time you're about to put my business on the street.'

'I will. I promise.'

Angie shoved the gun back in her purse. She had gotten carried away. 'Give me whatever you're holding.'

He rummaged around in one of the bins and pulled out a bag of weed. 'This is all I've got.'

Angie took the bag. She gathered up the electronics and climbed out of the van. Sam didn't bother with the door. He streaked out of the parking lot before she could change her mind.

She got into her car. She carefully placed the iPad and the green phone on the seat beside her. She jammed her key into the ignition. The engine rumbled to life. The gears stripped.

Sam was Dale's guy. She had almost shot the kid. Maybe. Who knew what the hell she had been thinking? Angie pulled the Glock out of her purse. She dropped the clip. She ejected the bullet from the chamber. It popped out like a jumping bean and disappeared under her seat. She did a visual to make sure the gun was unloaded. This would at least buy her some space before she pulled her gun the next time.

For right now, she had to get out of here.

Angie fought with the clutch and the shifter. The engine slipped into gear. She pulled out of the parking lot. She couldn't decide which way to go. The green phone wouldn't activate until Jo replied to a text. Angie had to assume Reuben was the only person who ever texted her. According to Laslo, he was in surgery all day. There was no telling when he would come out of anesthesia, but Angie knew the first thing he would do was check in with Jo. Or make her check in with him.

That left Sam's iPad with the antennae jutting up from the back. Angie guessed that whatever shadow program Laslo had planted on Jo's computer would yield very little to go on. Reuben wouldn't let Jo leave for coffee without demanding proof of her actions. There was no way he wasn't monitoring Jo's emails and internet searches too.

Which left this: Jo had a plan. She was up to something that involved Marcus Rippy. Angie had no doubt about that. The girl who had told Hemingway to fuck off at the Starbucks was a girl who was keeping secrets.

Josephine, not Jo.

That was the name she had given the barista.

Angie recognized the sign of a woman trying to reinvent herself. A million years ago, when Angie was dropped off at the children's home, she punched the first person who called her Angela instead of Angie.

Angela was what her pimp called her. Angie was what she called herself.

Reuben called his wife Jo. When Jo was alone, when she managed to pry open a tiny sliver of freedom, she called herself Josephine.

She was planning to get away, probably soon. Reuben would be back on Sunday. That gave Angie less than five days to figure out what her daughter was planning. She looked at her watch. Noon.

There was one source that she hadn't yet tapped: LaDonna Rippy.

If you wanted to know shit about a woman, all you had to do was ask the woman who was pretending to be her friend.

WEDNESDAY, 12:13 PM

Angie punched her brakes as she did the stop-and-start thing up Piedmont Road. Thanks to overdevelopment and geography, there wasn't a time during the day anymore when the narrow street was not clogged. She pushed the gear into first. The shift was smooth now, thanks to a detour to a gas station.

She checked the green phone to see if Jo had responded to a text yet. No luck. There was always the iPad with the rabbit ears, but Angie assumed Reuben policed the laptop the same way he policed Jo's life. She wouldn't be stupid enough to leave anything incriminating on there.

Besides, Angie had learned her lesson about looking at other people's personal files. Sara had thousands of photographs stored on her hard drive, all meticulously organized by date and location. Will and Sara at the beach. Will and Sara camping. Will and Sara climbing Stone Mountain. It was nauseating how happy

Sara always looked—not just in the pictures with Will, but also in much older photos with her dead husband.

Angie wondered if Will had ever seen a picture of Jeffrey Tolliver. His balls would've disappeared inside of his body. Tolliver had been fucking gorgeous. Tall, with dark wavy hair and a body your tongue could never get tired of. He'd played college ball at Auburn. He had been the chief of police. Just looking at him, you could tell he knew his way around a woman.

Angie had to admit, Sara Linton had good taste in cops.

Too bad she didn't know when to keep her greedy hands off them.

Angie ran a red light, crossing onto Tuxedo Road amid a symphony of horns. She let the car coast. LaDonna and Marcus Rippy's mansion was at the end of a gently sloping hill. Where most of the houses had bushes or trees to block the view from the street, LaDonna had made sure the house stood out. A hideously large gold-plated *R* was on the closed gates. The logo was LaDonna's design. She put it on everything, even the hand towels.

Angie pulled up to the gates. She pressed the intercom, gave her name, and waited for the long buzz. She had been to the house a handful of times before to get LaDonna to sign papers from Kip's office. Marcus had his wife on every piece of his business, which was smart or stupid, depending on whether you were LaDonna or Marcus.

The engine rumbled as she snaked up the driveway. There was a dog barking somewhere. Probably the family husky that shit all over everything because no one bothered to take him out. Cars filled the motor court at the top of the driveway. Two Jags, a Bentley, a neon-yellow Maserati.

'Shit,' Angie mumbled. LaDonna was holding court.

Angie had already been announced at the gate, so there was no backing out now. She walked under the portico, past the monitoring room, where a bored ex-cop took a catnap instead of watching live feed from the cameras around the estate. She knocked on the kitchen door. She waited.

The house was shaped like a giant U around an Olympic-size pool. Everything the family needed was on the grounds of the estate, which sounded fun until you realized that you could spend 24/7 on your own property and never see another person. Except for the help. There were dozens of them, all dressed in gray maids' uniforms with white aprons, even though LaDonna had probably despised her uniform back when she was cleaning hotel rooms. Shit always rolls downhill.

Angie couldn't tell if the servants didn't speak English or if they were too afraid to talk. Like all the other times she had visited LaDonna before, the woman who opened the door didn't say a word. She just tilted her head, indicating that Angie should follow her down a long hallway.

The decor gave a nod to LaDonna's Greek heritage—statues and fountains and lots and lots of Greek keys up and down the walls. Just about everything was plated in gold. The faucets in the sinks were giant swans with wings for hot and cold. The chandeliers down the hallway were gold. Angie looked up at the fixtures. The arms were Rippy's logo, curled *R*s dripping with crystals that the sun hit like a laser. She had to look away to keep her retinas from burning. By the time the maid showed Angie into the nail salon, she was seeing spots.

'That you, girl?' LaDonna waved Angie over. Her fingernails were being painted bright red by a slim Asian woman. Four wives were soaking their feet in bath salts, four more Asian women doing their nails. Usher played on the radio. The TV was muted, tuned to ESPN.

LaDonna offered, 'Grab a soak. My girl does a great pedicure.'

'No thanks.' Angie would rip out her nails before she let a stranger touch her feet. She didn't understand the lives these women were living. LaDonna wasn't book smart, but she was smart enough to know that she could be doing more than getting her nails buffed at one in the afternoon. Chantal Gordon had been a professional tennis player before she hung up her racket to have babies. Angelique Jones had been a doctor. Santee Chadwick had been her husband's private banker, a vice president with Wells Fargo. Tisha Dupree was an idiot. This was the best she would ever do.

LaDonna said, 'You got some papers for me to sign?'

'I need to ask you some questions.'

'This about that bitch in Vegas? That shit's been handled.'

Angie waited for the laughter to die down. 'No, it's something else.'

'Sit down, girl. You look beat.'

Angie sat down. She let her purse drop to the floor. She *felt* beat. She didn't know why. Basically all she'd done all day was sit in one place or another. She asked, 'Why isn't Fig's wife here?'

Chantal snorted. 'Girl got her nose too high in the air to slum with us bitches.'

Tisha said, 'She's gonna trip if she doesn't look down at some point.'

There was the inevitable awkward pause.

Angelique asked, 'Is Jo in trouble?'

'I don't know.' Angie studied LaDonna. The woman was waiting for something. If she'd been a cat, her tail would've been twitching. 'Jo seems to keep to herself. Kip is worried that something is wrong. He wants her to be happy.'

'I've never had more than two words with her,' Santee said. 'She's too stuck-up for me.'

Angelique said, 'It's hard to interpret shyness in other people. They tend to come across as aloof.'

'She *is* aloof,' Chantal countered. 'I asked her for coffee. I asked her to go shopping. Each time she says, "Let me check with Fig and I'll get back to you."' She shook her head. 'That was six months ago. I'm still waiting.'

Tisha said, 'I'll go shopping with you.'

Chantal studied the job being done on her fingernails.

'She's too thin.' Angelique was a doctor. She noticed these things. 'I assumed she was stressed out because of the move, putting Anthony into a new school. It's a lot of responsibility moving a household that size.'

'Especially when your man won't lift a finger,' Chantal said. 'When Jameel and I moved here, that man packed one suitcase, and all he put in it was his shit. I asked him what I was supposed to do with his kid's clothes and toys and the kitchen and the bathrooms and he just said, "I'm set, baby. You handle it."'

There were noises of sympathy around the room. Angie didn't see Chantal loading boxes into a rented U-Haul. She had probably paid Jameel back by hiring the most expensive movers she could find.

Santee said, 'Jo married Fig young.'

'Who didn't?' Chantal countered. 'I was nineteen. La D was eighteen. Seems to me she married late.'

Angie looked at LaDonna. She was still watching, but she still wasn't talking.

Santee said, 'Jo has to be happy that Fig's doing well. Marcus has really coached him up.'

Chantal said, 'Jo doesn't care much about basketball.'

There were not-so-fake gasps around the room.

'What does she care about?' Angie asked.

Tisha said, 'She loves Anthony. Her life revolves around him.'

'And her mother,' Angelique said. 'Unfortunately she's in the early stages of congestive heart failure.'

'Maybe that's why she keeps to herself,' Tisha said. 'I lost my mother a few years ago. You don't get over something like that. It just stays with you.'

Angelique told Angie, 'Jo and Fig will be at the party Sunday night. La D and Marcus are hosting a blowout before the season starts. I can talk to her then if you want.'

'I'd appreciate that.' Angie looked at LaDonna again. Nothing good ever came out of the woman's silence. Angie told her, 'I heard you threw a nice party for Jo when she moved here.'

LaDonna blew on her freshly painted nails. She had a glint in her eye.

'You knew Jo before?' Angie tried to tread carefully. 'Back in high school?'

LaDonna waved away the manicurist. 'We didn't go to the same school. She lived in the next town.'

Tisha said, 'I didn't know that.'

'How about church?'

'Yeah, I think she went to my church.'

Tisha opened her mouth, then closed it.

Angie waited. LaDonna never made anything easy. What she didn't understand was that Angie didn't care about her future at 110 Sports Management. All she cared about was Jo. She said, 'Are we going to talk around the fact that Marcus used to date Jo Figaroa, or are you going to get real with me and tell me what's going on?'

LaDonna's lips were still pursed from blowing her nails. 'I wouldn't call holding hands and talking about Bible class dating.'

'What would you call it?'

'None of your God damm business.'

Santee said, 'You want us to boot, girl?'

'Nah, we're gonna take a walk to the pool.' LaDonna stood up. She shoved her feet into a pair of fuchsia stilettos. 'Ostrich skin,' she told Angie. 'My house heels. Custom-made in Milan.'

'Take some sunblock,' Tisha said. 'The sun'll burn you up.'

LaDonna pinned the girl with her steely gaze. She told Angie, 'This way.'

Angie wasn't the type to follow. She walked shoulder-to-shoulder with LaDonna down the corridor. She looked down at the woman's Italian shoes. Gold *R*s were embroidered on the tips. Some threads had started to pull away. There was a tiny stain on the toe. The sight of the defects gave Angie the only sense of pleasure she'd had all day. LaDonna had always reminded her of what pimps called the bottom girl, or the mama in charge—an older whore who kept the girls in line through force or manipulation. She would comfort you or cut you, depending on what it took to keep you earning on the street.

LaDonna slipped on a pair of sunglasses. She pushed open the door. Outside was even hotter and brighter than Angie remembered. She took a breath of humid air. The smell from the nail polish was still in her nose.

LaDonna said, 'Bitch, what're you up to?'

Angie smiled, but only to piss her off. 'I told you. Kip is worried about Jo.'

'She ain't my man's type, if that's what you're getting at.' LaDonna shook her head to make her point. 'Marcus likes a woman with some fight in her. Jo wouldn't say boo to a ghost.'

'She's under Fig's thumb.'

'She's under his fist.' LaDonna snorted at Angie's surprise. 'You think I don't know what that looks like?' She laughed. 'Marcus wouldn't raise a hand to me, but my daddy, he'd get his belt and whoop the skin off my ass.' She pointed to Angie. 'Jo's got the same look my mama did every time she got beat down. Hell, not even when she was beat. He'd just look at her and she'd . . .' LaDonna hunched down and threw up her hands, but she didn't have it in her to look afraid.

Angie asked, 'Did you talk to Jo about this?'

'What would I say? "I know your man is hitting you. Why the fuck don't you leave and take half his money?" Hell, she knows that already. She's known it for near 'bout ten damn years. And what has she done about it?' She walked over to a covered barbecue area. She took a bottle of water from the refrigerator. 'It ain't like it used to be. One picture, one video from an elevator, she'd get the world on her side.' LaDonna laughed. 'Of course, you see how that plays, right? She'll be all over TV and shit and people will feel sorry for her, and then a week later they'll all be blaming her, saying, "Look here in the video where she ain't yelling," and "Look here where she punches him in the chest," and "Why'd she make him mad like that?" and "All she wants is his money."'

Angie shook her head. 'I can't tell if you're saying she should get out or if she's better off staying.'

'I'm saying the girl ain't got no backbone.'

'Backbones come at a price,' Angie said. 'Fig would lose his contract if Jo let the world know what he was doing. There wouldn't be any more money coming in.'

'Fuck the money.' She tossed Angie a bottle of water. 'If Marcus tried that shit on me, ain't enough gold in Fort Knox would keep me here. I still know how to clean a hotel room. Me and my kids would be living out of a box before I let them see me beat down like a dog.'

Angie wondered if that was true. 'Why don't you help her?'

'Shit, I'm not getting that girl's stink on me.' LaDonna drank some water. 'Besides, I got kids to take care of. A household to run. A husband who needs me. I'm not going to throw away my precious time trying to save somebody who don't even wanna be saved.'

A sound came out of Angie's mouth, almost a 'huh.' LaDonna might not be running whores, but she had the mama logic down pat.

'Look at me, sister.' LaDonna took off her sunglasses. 'Watch my mouth. Listen to my words. Take it back to Kip. Jo Figaroa likes what she's got.'

'She likes being hit?'

'Why else is she staying with Fig?' LaDonna added, 'You ain't seen the two of them together when he starts to simmer.

She don't lift a finger to calm him down. Shit, she winds him up. Nags on him. Slaps on him.' She pointed her finger at Angie. 'Right here at this pool, I saw it with my own eyes. Team party a few months ago. We're all lounging, drinking cocktails. Fig tells her something real quiet, like go get me something to drink. Jo don't want to do it. She says, "Get it your damn self." Now, Fig, he don't like that. We can all see him getting riled up. He pushes Jo out of her chair. She still don't get the drink. She mouths off, punches him in the chest, like she ain't afraid of him. We all knew what was coming next. Fig 'bout tore out her hair dragging her inside. Don't know what he did, but she never mouthed off to him again.'

And apparently, none of the collective three thousand pounds of basketball player muscle did anything to keep a one-hundred-pound woman from getting the shit beaten out of her. 'I'm sure Fig was terrified when Jo hit him.'

'Right?' LaDonna said, 'That's exactly what I'm saying, girl. You want out? Take a picture of that shit—the bruises and the fat lip and the black eye. Put it up on TMZ. Call a lawyer.'

'Call a medical examiner,' Angie said.

'Maybe.' LaDonna finished her water. She tossed the bottle into the recycling bin. 'He'll put a cap in her ass if she tries to leave him. And don't even get me started on what Fig would do if she tried to take away his son. That man loves his boy. He'll blow up the fucking world if Jo even thinks about taking him.'

'I thought it was easy. Just take a few pictures and get a lawyer.'

She stared down on Angie. 'Tell me again why you're so worried about Jo.'

'It's my job.'

'Then why are you bringing this shit to me?' LaDonna kept staring at her. 'Why don't *you* help her?'

Angie shrugged. 'Tell me what to do.'

'Don't tell Kip, 'cause he'll put Laslo on your ass if you mess with the team.'

Angie put it back on her. 'So what, then? Wait for Jo's funeral?'

LaDonna gave it some thought. She took out another bottle of water. She twisted open the top. Finally she shook her head. 'Doesn't matter what we do. Even if Jo got away from Fig, she'd just end up back with another asshole doing the same damn thing. That's what my mama did. She finally leaves my daddy, she meets this man who's all sweet on her, gonna take care of her, and the minute they get back from the honeymoon, he's raising his fist to her. That's how it's been happening since Jesus lost his sandals. Some men are born to beat and some women are born to take a beating, and they got these magnets inside of them that always pull them together. Like to like.' She turned to Angie. 'Some people are born with a hole inside them. They spend their lives trying to fill it. Sometimes it's pills, sometimes it's Jesus, and sometimes it's a fist.' She threw the bottle cap into the trashcan. 'We done here?'

Angie knew they were, but she wasn't going to let the other woman have the last shot. 'This girl in Vegas. Do I need to get Laslo to clean that up?'

'It's taken care of.'

She sounded like a Mafia don. 'You make her an offer she couldn't refuse?'

'I broke her God damm teeth out of her face.'

Angie held LaDonna's gaze. She wasn't going to be the one to look away first. 'I'll get out of your hair.'

LaDonna looked out at the pool. 'You do that.'

Angie knew when she was being dismissed. She opened the cold water as she walked back down the corridor. The wives were all atwitter back in the salon, but Angie just grabbed her purse and left. She didn't need an escort to lead her back to her car. She was backing out of the motor court when she remembered the green phone.

'Dammit,' Angie cursed, because of course this was how it had played out.

While she was wasting her time playing patty-cake with LaDonna, Jo had gotten a text. More importantly, she had texted back, downloading the cloning program to her phone.

MR: ITOWN SUITES 1HR.

JOSEPHINE: OK.

The time stamp showed the text had been sent ten minutes ago.

Angie woke up the iPad. She pulled up the GPS tracking software. A blue dot beeped on the map, slowly making its way down Cherokee Drive.

Jo was on the move.

WEDNESDAY, 1:08 PM

Angie stood behind the manager of the OneTown Suites. A monitor sat on the desk in front of him. The screen was split into four perspectives from various security cameras around the motel. The lobby. The elevator. A long hallway. The parking lot.

By sheer luck, the motel was less than fifteen minutes from the Rippy mansion. Or maybe that was by design. Angie had no doubt that Marcus had used the place before. The rooms rented by the week, so you could overpay for a few hours with the understanding that no one would ask questions. The place reeked of bargain-price discretion. Everything was clean and well kept, but downmarket. It was the sort of place a very rich man might take a girl he'd met at one of the strip clubs in the area. Up the street, the St Regis and the Ritz were for more permanent arrangements.

Angie stared at the quarter panel of the monitor that showed the parking lot. Jo was still inside her parked Range Rover, the same as she had been for the last twenty minutes. She was sitting on her hands, just like she had at Starbucks. She stared straight ahead. She didn't move. She didn't get out of the car. Angie looked at the time. The text from Marcus had come in fifty minutes ago. Anthony's school would let out in another hour. If Marcus Rippy had scheduled a tryst, it would have to be a fast one.

The manager tapped the keyboard and scrolled through more angles of the parking lot and hotel. He asked, 'How much longer?'

'As long as it takes.'

'I guess you paid me enough,' the man said, a vast understatement considering the five grand Angie had put in his pocket. He probably would've done it for a thousand, but Angie had been in a hurry and she didn't have time to negotiate.

There were two adjoining rooms at the back of the motel, separated by a locking privacy door. Everything Angie needed was in her go-bag. The directional mic was slim enough to fit under the door. The transceiver plugged into the wall. The headphones plugged into the jack. Since Angie had gotten to the motel so quickly, she'd had plenty of time to plant the cameras, but she hadn't done this kind of work in months. There was no charge left in the batteries.

The desk phone rang. The manager picked up. Angie gathered a guest was having problems with the television.

She started pacing. She didn't want to think about how this could go wrong. Meeting at a motel didn't mean meeting in a motel room. Marcus Rippy drove a Cadillac Escalade. The back was more than adequate to accommodate two people.

The manager hung up the phone. He asked Angie, 'This who you're waiting for?'

She looked at the monitor. Marcus's black Escalade had pulled into the space beside Jo. Angie held her breath, waiting for her entire plan to go sideways. Jo stayed in her car. Marcus got out of his. Angie followed his progress across the parking lot. His gait was slow, casual, but he scanned left and right as if he was making sure no one was watching him. He did another scan before he opened the door to the lobby.

A bell rang.

'Showtime.' The manager stood up and left the room.

Angie toggled through the security cameras to find the one that covered the front desk. The manager was there, tucking his polo shirt into his shorts. Marcus wore a baseball cap low on his head. Sunglasses covered his eyes. His clothes were nondescript, the chunky three-hundred-thousand-dollar watch missing from his wrist. He seemed to know where the cameras were. He kept his head down. He didn't look up. He passed the manager a wad of cash, because LaDonna monitored every penny that went in and out of their accounts.

Angie heard the manager talking, but she couldn't hear Marcus. A key was passed across the counter. Maps of the city and the Wi-Fi password were offered. Marcus shook his head to both. The camera lost him as he headed toward the door.

The bell rang again.

Angie toggled the switch to get back to the parking lot. Marcus was standing outside the front doors. He waved for Jo to come in.

Initially Jo didn't move. She seemed to be deciding something. Was she really going to do this? Should she go into that room with Rippy? Should she drive away?

Finally Jo decided. Her door opened. She got out of the car. She tucked her hands into the pockets of her jeans as she jogged across the parking lot.

The manager knocked on the door. Angie opened it.

He said, 'Is that who I think it is?'

'Not for five thousand dollars it's not.' Angie started randomly pulling plugs from the back of machines. She had already taken the CD-R out of the video recorder.

'Hey.' He held up his hands. 'I know how to take a pay-off. I work at a motel by the interstate.'

Angie thought about the gun in her purse. Unloaded. Probably a good thing. She cracked open the office door. Jo and Marcus were getting into the elevator. She ducked down behind the counter as the doors closed.

Angie waited until she heard the motor sending the elevator up. She took the back stairs slowly, because she couldn't beat them up to the second floor. She heard them talking as she got to the top landing. A key was put into a lock. A door opened. A door closed.

Angie went into the hall. She walked briskly toward the adjacent room. She'd oiled the lock with a can of WD-40 from her go-bag. The key silently slipped in. The tumblers engaged. She pushed open the door on oiled hinges and held on to the knob so that the automatic arm would not slam it shut.

The door between the two rooms was thin. Marcus and Jo were already talking in the other room. His deep baritone vibrated the air. Jo's voice was softer, more like a hum.

Angie sat on the floor by the transceiver. She held one of the headphones to her ear.

'. . . anymore,' Jo said. 'I mean it.'

Marcus said nothing, but Angie could hear his breath, a steady in and out. Angie adjusted the sound. She cursed herself for not keeping the batteries charged in all the cameras.

Marcus said, 'What do you want me to do, Jo?'

'I want you to look at this.'

There was a rustling sound, then a tinny whine that Angie thought was feedback. She adjusted the knobs on the transceiver. It wasn't feedback. It was a woman's voice, chanting the same word over and over again.

'No-no-no-no-no . . .'

Angie turned up the volume. The chant was faint, distant, as if it was being filtered through a cheap speaker. Had Jo turned on the television?

Marcus said, 'Jesus, Jo. Where did you get this?'

'Just watch.'

Watch.

Not the TV. Maybe a video. Angie closed her eyes, focusing on the ambient sounds. A wind noise, someone breathing, a rhythmic tapping.

The woman's voice again.

'No-no-no-no-no . . .'

'Fuck.' A man's voice, out of breath.

'No-no-no . . .'

'Fuck.' The same man again, excited.

A second man, even deeper voice: 'Shut her up.'

The first man: 'I'm tryin'.'

Angie sat back on her heels as it dawned on her what she was listening to.

Jo had a video of two men fucking a woman who kept saying no.

Marcus said, 'Turn it off.'

The first man. Marcus Rippy was the first man.

'Please,' Marcus said. 'Turn it off.'

Angie listened to the silence, her stomach clenched like a fist. What the fuck was Jo doing? She was all alone. Nobody knew she was here. She'd just shown a two-hundred-pound slab of muscle a video of him forcing himself on a woman who kept saying no.

Marcus asked, 'Has LaDonna seen this?' Jo must have shaken her head, because he said, 'You better be damn glad.'

Jo said, 'I'm not trying to hurt you.'

Angie heard footsteps across the room. A curtain was raked across a rod. Silence. More silence. Angie quietly upended her purse onto the floor. She had to load her gun. She had to be ready.

Marcus said, 'What are you going to do with that?'

Angie froze, waiting.

'I just want out.' Jo's voice sounded frail. 'That's all I want. I don't want to hurt you. I don't want to hurt anybody.'

'Jo-jo.' Marcus sighed. He didn't say anything else. He was trying to figure out how to handle this.

Angie tried to put herself in Marcus Rippy's shoes. He was a smart man. He had probably been blackmailed before. He had used the motel before, too. He knew to look for the security cameras. He knew that the footage would show Jo and he knew that the manager had recognized his face.

Angie took her hand off her gun. She kept waiting.

Marcus said, 'Fig's not gonna let you take his son.'

'He will if he knows I have a video showing him raping a girl.'

No. Angie mouthed the word through the closed door. Marcus was in the video, too. Jo couldn't be this stupid. You couldn't show a man a video of him gang-raping a woman alongside your husband and expect for either of them to let you walk away.

'If Fig sees that . . .' Marcus gave a heavy groan. 'Jo, he'll fucking kill you.'

Jo didn't answer. She didn't need anyone to tell her that her husband was going to kill her.

'You want money?' Marcus sounded angry. 'That's what this is about? You're trying to blackmail me?'

'No.'

'You show me a video of me and Fig having a little fun and—'

'That girl was raped. She was almost beaten to death. She had the GBI investigating—'

'You know that ain't on me.' He was obviously trying to control his temper. 'Come on, girl. We were just having some fun. That's all.'

'She looks drugged.'

'She's a junkie. She knew what she was doing.'

Jo was silent again. Angie's ears hurt from straining so hard. All she could hear was her own heartbeat. Fast. Scared. This was too dangerous. The girl on the tape had to be Keisha Miscavage. This was Will's case that Angie had made go away. She'd paid out hundreds of thousands of dollars in bribes. If there was a video, then Jo was sitting on a gold mine.

If she made it out alive.

Marcus said, 'I can give you money.'

'I don't want money.'

'Then what the hell do you want?'

'My son.' Jo's voice wavered. 'I want my mother to be safe. I want to get a job somewhere and make an honest living.'

'How are you gonna do that without money?'

Jo started crying. Angie couldn't tell if the sobs were for real.

'Come on,' Marcus said.

'You can talk to Reuben. Tell him he'll be off the team if he doesn't let me go.' Jo's voice had cracked on the last word. 'Please, Marcus. We have a history together. We have love between us. I know that. I'm not trying to exploit you or take advantage of you. I'm asking as a friend. I *need* you as a friend.'

Silence.

'Marcus—'

'You know that isn't my decision.'

Angie waited for the girl from Starbucks to show up, to tell him that he was full of shit, that he was Marcus Fucking Rippy, that he could do whatever the hell he wanted to do.

Jo said nothing.

'Come on now,' Marcus said. 'Sit down, girl. Let's talk about this.'

Angie heard the springs in the bed flex.

Shit. He could rape her. The security footage showed Jo willingly going into the motel. Marcus could call it cheating. He could threaten to tell Reuben Figaroa, and Jo would be even more trapped than she already was.

Marcus said, 'All that video shows is me having a little fun.'

'I saw the end. She was begging for her mama.'

Marcus didn't respond.

Jo said, 'I heard her say it, Marcus. "Mother."'

'That's not what you think it is.' His voice had an edge to it that Angie prayed her daughter noticed.

'Marcus—'

'I couldn't even finish, okay? I had too much to drink. There was a lot going on that night. I just left. Whatever happened next, that ain't on me.'

Jo didn't respond.

He asked, 'Is this the only copy?'

Angie tensed. She silently willed words into Jo's mouth: *I made copies. I sent them to a friend. If anything happens to me, the police will get it.*

Jo said, 'The only other copy is on the laptop at home.'

Fuck.

Jo said, 'Reuben's laptop. He leaves it in the kitchen. He wanted me to find it.'

Marcus muttered something she couldn't make out. Or maybe Angie was distracted. She had the rabbit-eared iPad in her car that contained a copy of every single file from the kitchen laptop. Why hadn't she looked at it before?

Jo said, 'Reuben doesn't care what I see, because he knows I'm too scared to do anything about it.' She gave a sad laugh. 'I *am* too scared. I was terrified to come here. Those two times we were together, I couldn't think about anything but him coming into the room and shooting us both in the head.'

Marcus kept silent.

'I can't get a cup of coffee without showing him on my phone where I am. I can't drink water at night because I'm not allowed to leave the bed to go to the bathroom. I can't leave the house without his permission. I can't eat food that he doesn't approve of. He checks the logs on the treadmill to make sure I run my three miles every day. He's got cameras inside the house, the bedrooms, the bathrooms. I cut myself shaving my legs the other day and he knew about it before I even got out of the shower.' Her voice sounded raw, desperate. 'I'm kept like a damn animal in a cage, Marcus.'

'Come on. It can't be that bad, Jo-jo. He loves you.'

'He's going to love me to death.'

'Don't talk that way.'

'I'm halfway dead already.' Jo's tone of voice indicated that she meant what she was saying. 'This video is my only chance to get away with Anthony. If I don't leave soon, then I'll end up dead by Reuben's hand or by my own.'

'Aw, girl, don't say that. Suicide is a sin.'

Angie bit her tongue so she wouldn't scream.

Marcus asked, 'I guess you told your mama about all this?'

Jo didn't answer. Was she shaking her head?

'How long have you been carrying all this on your shoulders?'

'Too long.'

'Jo—'

She started to cry in earnest. Angie pressed her hand to the door. She could feel Jo's sadness pressing back.

She said, 'It started back in college. I had to drop out because he beat me so bad. Did you know that?'

Nothing from Marcus.

'My dorm mate reported it, and the cops were called. The only way to keep Reuben out of jail was to marry him. The minute that ring went on my finger, it was over.' She gave that same dry laugh from before. 'Eight years I've been walking toward my grave. The only thing I can control is how fast I jump in.'

Marcus said, 'Jo-jo, let's talk about this. We can figure it out.'

'I need to pick up Anthony from school. Reuben makes me call as soon as he's in the car.'

'Don't leave. Not like this.'

'If I'm late—'

'You'll be on time,' Marcus told her. 'Let's talk about what you're going to do.'

'I don't know.' Jo sounded torn. 'I can't show anybody that video without implicating you, and I won't do that, no matter how bad you were.'

'On my life, Jo, on my kids' lives, it's not what you think it is.'

Jo didn't answer at first. She was obviously conflicted. Whatever tied her to Marcus Rippy ran deeper than LaDonna realized.

Jo said, 'I want to care about that girl. I want to want justice for her, but all I see is a way out.' She gave a sharp laugh. 'What does that say about me? What kind of person am I that I'm willing to trade one woman's life for my own?'

Marcus said, 'You know me, Josephine. You know me better than anybody else. We got a history, going back to when I was a boy and you were my girl. I ain't never been rough like that. Not with you. Not with nobody. You know me.'

'That's not what I thought when I saw the video.'

'I was never like that with you.' He added, 'Not back then, not last month. Not right now, if you'll have me.'

'Marcus.'

They were kissing. Angie recognized the sounds. She felt herself shaking her head. What the hell kind of Russian roulette was her daughter playing?

'No.' Jo had obviously pulled away. 'I can't do this.'

'Play the video again,' he challenged. 'Show me where I hurt that girl.'

Angie waited for her daughter to remind him that even doped up, the junkie in the video had kept saying no.

Instead, Jo told him, 'Take my phone. Destroy it. I can't hurt you. Not like this.'

Angie tasted blood in her mouth from biting her tongue.

He said, 'What happens if Fig calls and you don't pick up?'

Jo didn't answer. Angie prayed her daughter was seeing through this. Marcus knew that Fig kept track of her through the phone. He also knew that there was a copy of the video on Fig's laptop. Telling Jo to keep her phone built trust, and there was only one reason that Marcus needed Jo to trust him: he was going to fuck her over.

Marcus asked, 'What are you going to do, Jo? I want to help.'

'Nobody can help. I was just venting.' Angie heard footsteps as Jo walked across the carpet. 'I need to pick up Anthony.'

'Put this problem on my shoulders,' Marcus said. 'I've always taken care of you. Stood up to that teacher who was trying to get free with you. Made sure your mama knew you were a good girl.' He paused, and Angie hoped to God Jo wasn't nodding.

Marcus said, 'Let me figure out how to take care of Fig in a way that gets you what you need.'

'There's no way, Marcus. Not without hurting you, and I won't do that.'

'I appreciate that, but you deserve better.' He paused again. 'La D has this party on Sunday. Fig already said y'all would be there.'

'God, I can't take a party.'

'You gotta show face, girl. Make him think everything is okay.'

'And then what?'

'Give me some time to get a plan. I'm going to figure this out, and I am going to take care of you, even if it means moving you and Anthony into one of my houses, putting a guard outside the door, to buy you some space to think about this.'

'Oh Marcus.' Jo sounded heartbreakingly hopeful. 'Would you really do that? Could you?'

'Just give me some time,' he said. 'I need to pray on it a bit, figure out the right thing to do.'

'Thank you!' Jo's voice was almost euphoric. 'Marcus, thank you.'

There was more kissing.

Again Jo pulled away first. 'I need to pick up Anthony. Thank you, Marcus. Thank you.'

The door clicked open then shut as Jo left the room.

Angie heard her soft footsteps out in the hall.

'Shhiiiit,' Marcus whispered from the next room. The mattress squeaked. There were ten beeps as he dialed his phone.

Marcus Rippy might very well pray on the situation, but Angie knew exactly who he was going to call on to fix it.

'Kip,' Marcus said. 'We got a big fucking problem.'

WEDNESDAY, 3:18 PM

Angie rode the elevator up to the twenty-seventh floor of the Tower Place office building. Not the twenty-eighth or -ninth floor, where 110 was located, but the one below that Angie had never been to. Dale had texted her to meet him there. He'd told her to come as soon as possible.

Paranoia teased up the hair on the back of her neck as she watched the lights announce the floors. Had Dale figured out that Angie was on Jo's side? He had a weird sixth sense, especially where Angie was concerned. She didn't like surprises. She held her purse tight to her body. She should've loaded her gun. This didn't feel right. There was no reason for Dale to text her to meet him on a different floor.

No good reason, anyway.

The elevator doors slid open. Angie hesitated before stepping out. The floor was under construction. Lights dangled from their cords. Stacks of building materials and buckets of paint created a maze. Outside, the windows showed blue sky. Inside was ominous, filled with shadow.

If Angie was going to kill somebody, this would be as good a place as any.

She walked around the room, picking her way past the stacks of paint cans and rolling scaffolding. She thought about the iPad with the rabbit ears, the one that held a download of everything on Reuben Figaroa's kitchen laptop. Angie hadn't had time to search for the video that Jo had shown Marcus Rippy. She assumed that Marcus had told Kip about the backup and she guessed that Kip would find a way to wipe the machine clean. Whether or not that meant the iPad would wipe clean, she had no idea. Angie couldn't call Sam Vera for help. He was Dale's guy, like just about everybody she knew. In the end, all she could think to do was tear off the antennae, shut the thing down, and leave it in the safe at the OneTown Suites.

For five thousand dollars, she hoped like hell the manager really did know how to take a pay-off.

'Progress,' Dale said.

Angie almost jumped out of her skin. 'You scared the shit out of me.'

Dale seemed to enjoy the effect. 'Kip's upstairs with Rippy.'

'Then why are we down here?'

'Because there ain't no security cameras down here.'

Angie swallowed to clear the dust from her throat. She made herself walk toward him, open, nothing to hide. 'Why the cloak-and-dagger?'

'Something with Rippy. That's all I know.'

Angie let go some of her tension. Of course that's why they were here. She'd heard Marcus call Kip with the problem. She should've anticipated that Kip would call in Dale, who would call in Angie.

She glanced around the room, pretending like she hadn't already scoped out the exits and hiding places. 'What's going on here?'

'Progress,' Dale repeated. 'One-Ten is expanding. Now that the All-Star deal is going forward, they need a whole team to manage the branding, make sure the athletes are out front and center, keep all of their noses clean. Laslo's gonna run it.'

Angie nodded, because that made sense. Sports management didn't just mean negotiating contracts. They managed every aspect of the athletes' lives.

'You hear back from Denny?'

Angie had forgotten about Dale's bookie problem. She looked at her phone. Denny had texted her back three hours ago. She scrolled through a long explanation about how much trouble he was going to get into for rounding up every whore on Cheshire Bridge before she got to the only part that mattered. 'He says they'll do it tonight.'

'Good.' Dale said, 'I gave the lawyer that paperwork for the trust. It's official.'

'Have you told Delilah yet?'

He shook his head. 'I want you to tell her.'

The last thing Angie wanted to do was tell a junkie she'd hit the mother lode. Then again, he could be lying just for the sake of lying. Dale liked to fuck with people. She asked, 'How do I get in touch with her? Is she staying at your place?'

'She's moved into her mama's old place. I figured Kip would clean out my pad at the Mesa the minute I'm gone.' He coughed into his hand. 'If the job falls on you to turn it over, don't go into the attic. There's just a bunch of papers up there. Old cases and shit.'

Angie wasn't going anywhere near Dale's house. 'Sure.'

'You'll wanna stay out of the bathroom, too. Different reasons.'

The elevator dinged. Kip and Marcus were talking in low murmurs that drained away when they saw Angie and Dale. She tried not to think about the hope in Jo's voice when Marcus mentioned putting up Jo and Anthony in one of his houses, protecting them from Reuben Figaroa with an armed guard if necessary.

The only person Marcus Rippy was ever going to protect was himself.

Dale asked, 'Where's Laslo?'

'Not here.' Kip told Marcus, 'You should go back upstairs, bro. Let me handle this.'

Marcus shook his head. 'This ain't like those other situations, man. I'm not going to let you hurt her.'

Angie studied Marcus Rippy's face. He looked conflicted, which made a sort of sense if you didn't already know how this was going to end. Angie had spent most of her professional life talking people into doing things they knew were wrong, whether it was getting a suspect to flip on his buddy or bribing someone into changing their testimony before a trial. Without exception, everybody's weak spot always ended up being some combination of self-preservation and money.

Dale asked, 'Who are we supposed to not be hurting?'

Kip gave Marcus another chance to leave. When he didn't, Kip answered, 'Jo Figaroa has a video.'

'Of what?' Dale asked.

Marcus said, 'None of your fucking business.'

Dale glanced at Angie. She kept her expression as still as she could.

'It doesn't matter what's on the video.' Kip crossed his arms. Angie realized this was one of the rare times she'd seen him without a bottle of BankShot or a basketball. He said, 'Jo has the video on her phone. That's all you need to know.'

Angie asked, 'Are there copies?'

'We're taking care of that.'

That explained Laslo's absence. Kip would've sent him to get the laptop before Jo could get home from school with Anthony.

Dale said, 'There's a computer—'

'The copy isn't on a computer,' Kip interrupted. 'Laslo has it handled. End of discussion.'

Angie considered the lie. Marcus would have already told Kip that the incriminating video came from Reuben's laptop. The first question out of the agent's mouth would've been to ask about copies. Kip was holding back as much information from Dale and Angie as he could, which actually benefitted Angie. Dale knew the laptop had been cloned onto the iPad. Apparently Kip did not.

Angie said, 'I can hire a skell to apple-pick the phone right out of her hand. Problem solved.'

'You can't take the phone,' Marcus said, his voice strident. He was thinking about Jo, and the fact that Reuben made her check in. Which on the surface was laudable, but if he were really concerned about Jo, none of them would be here.

'It's not just the video,' Kip said. 'It's that Jo's seen it. We can't trust her not to blab. She's got to be taught a lesson about keeping in line.'

Dale asked, 'Time to use the ax?'

Angie felt her stomach tighten.

'No.' Marcus sounded alarmed. 'You can't hurt her. Not physically.'

'It's a euphemism. We won't hurt her.' Kip said, 'We've got an alternate plan.'

'Alternate plan?' Marcus repeated. 'How'd you come up with that so fast? Who you been telling my business to?'

'We're your team, Marcus.' Kip explained, 'We've known for a while that Jo might be a problem.'

Angie waited for someone to point out that Reuben Figaroa was the problem. When it didn't happen, she asked, 'What about the husband?'

'Fig can't know about this.' Marcus asked Kip, 'When's he coming home?'

'He isn't cleared to fly until tomorrow night.' Kip held up both his hands, like a traffic cop trying to stop an oncoming bus. 'And I understand—Fig can't know about the video, or Jo meeting you alone. Trust me, Marcus, I know Fig has a temper. We don't need him stuck with a murder charge when we're less than two weeks away from the biggest jackpot of our lives.'

Marcus gave a slow nod, seemingly sad about the fact that money trumped everything. Angie was the only person in the room who didn't accept the trade-off. Jo's life was worth more than a basketball game or yet another glorified shopping mall.

Marcus asked, 'What's the alternate plan?'

Dale answered, 'Long time ago, Jo was arrested with a bunch of scripts in her car.'

'Back in high school?' Marcus shook his head. He was back to playing Jo's savior again. 'Naw, man, those were for me. I hurt my back, had to keep playing. Jo took the weight. She knew they'd go easy on her.'

Angie thought about Jo sacrificing herself for Rippy. Was this what her daughter was like, always lying down for a man?

Kip said, 'Details on the arrest are still out there. We can use it.'

'Use it how?'

Dale said, 'I'll put some Oxy in her car, call in a buddy of mine, and she'll spend a few days in jail. Give her time to reflect on her problems.'

'Nuh-uh.' Marcus shook his head. 'You can't send Jo to jail. I won't allow it. You work for me, man. All of you—you work for me, and I say no.'

In any other situation, Angie would've laughed in Rippy's face. He had convinced himself that he was a good man backed into a tight corner. She wanted to look at her watch and time how long it took for him to capitulate. Her best guess was three minutes.

'Marcus.' Kip sighed a heavy breath, feigning frustration at this awful dilemma that he, too, had no taste for. 'I don't want to send her to jail either. But this is serious stuff. We've got to figure out a way to put Jo in her place without alerting Fig. She needs an ax, not a hammer.'

'What the fuck does that even mean?'

Dale said, 'It means that she needs to understand this is a business.'

Kip took over. 'The next ten days are precarious for all of us. You saw what happened to the investors when that Keisha Miscavage bullshit came up. What do you think is gonna happen if you and Fig get embroiled in a new scandal? We're not just talking about Jo blowing up your career, your home life, your family. This could blow up the entire project.' He shrugged, helpless. 'Someone has that much power, you don't shut her up, you shut her down.'

Marcus shook his head, but Angie could tell he was close to breaking. 'That ain't right, man. She came to me for help.'

Kip shot Dale a look of desperation. Angie looked away so she didn't get the same. Jo in jail for a few days wouldn't be a bad thing. She'd be safe from Fig. Two days would give Angie some time to figure out a plan. If she could juggle the right balls in the air, Jo would be on a plane to the Bahamas on Sunday morning instead of scuttling off to rehab.

Kip said, 'Marcus, tell me our other options. This isn't like Chicago. We can't twist arms and throw around some money. Jo gets away with blackmailing you once, she'll try it again. And people will listen to her, man. You want a *Rolling Stone* cover about that shit? Or worse, for her to go to LaDonna with some bullshit story about video this and video that?'

Marcus physically recoiled at the mention of his wife. 'She wouldn't bring LaDonna into this.'

'You sure about that?'

Marcus didn't look sure of anything.

Kip saw an opening. 'There's no telling what else Jo is planning. We need to make it clear that she's not the one with the power. It's not like I enjoy the prospect of backing her down.' He shrugged, helpless. 'But if we scare the shit out of her, let her sit in a five-by-nine cell for a few days, eat shit on a shingle and watch the clock tick with no idea when it's going to stop.' Kip shrugged again. 'It's the best way to handle it, Marcus. You know that.'

Marcus asked, 'What's Fig gonna do when he gets home tomorrow night and finds out his wife is in county lock-up?'

'I can handle Fig.'

'Bull. Shit.' Marcus spat out the two words. 'Ain't nobody can handle him. Dude's a freak when he's pissed off. Something like this, Jo pulling jail time? He won't put her in the hospital. He'll put her in the grave.'

Kip said, 'He'll be in a knee brace. Doc says he can't bend his leg for another week.'

Angie watched Marcus trying to concoct a fairy tale where Jo was safe. He asked, 'What else did the doc say about Fig?'

Kip said, 'A month in the brace, another month of physical therapy. He's got at least five more years in him. But the point is, there's nothing to worry about this weekend. Once Fig gets back from Texas, if Jo wants to get away from him, all she has to do is walk fast.'

Angie didn't know if Jo had it in her to walk away from anything unless Anthony was at her side. She grabbed at straws. 'Send her to rehab. It'll look good for the judge. It'll buy her thirty days away from Fig. That'll get us past the ground-breaking, and it will help Jo.'

Marcus asked, 'How does that help Jo?'

Angie wasn't going to make this too easy for him. 'Nobody's going to beat the shit out of her in rehab. That'll happen when she gets out.'

Dale said, 'Rehab means therapy. What if one of them shrinks talks her into turning on Fig?'

'We can't deal with what-ifs,' Kip said, though that was exactly what they were doing. He told Marcus, 'Look, I like Jo too, but we can seriously undercut her credibility with the arrest, right? Nobody listens to a junkie. Just ask Keisha Miscavage. Plus, you know Jo's not going to leave Fig. She's tried at least five times before, and that's only the times we know about.'

'I dunno.' Marcus was obviously convinced, but he had to make like his arm had to be twisted just a little more.

Dale said, 'I don't know if I've got enough juice to keep her in past Sunday. Saturday is a stretch.'

'La D is throwing a team party Sunday night,' Marcus said. 'Even if Fig could move around, he wouldn't mess her up before the party. People would ask too many questions.'

Dale said, 'So, we keep her in jail two days, we get her through the party Sunday, we whisk her off to rehab the next morning.'

Marcus scratched his chin. He still wasn't going to make this easy.

Kip said, 'The tabloids will be all over this. You know Fig hates the press. He'll be on his best behavior. He's fucking nuts, but he's not stupid. This isn't five years ago. You can't get filmed beating the shit out of a woman and expect to keep playing.'

Marcus didn't disagree. 'I don't know about jail, man. Jo's sensitive. She ain't that kind of girl.'

'It's no big deal. It's like going to a spa.' Kip's eyes lit up with an idea. 'Actually, this could work in Jo's favor. We'll get publicity on it. They can turn it into a story about Jo's recovery, getting clean for her kid, whatever. She'll get a photo shoot, have her hair and make-up done. She'll love it.'

'No she won't,' Marcus said. 'Jo hates being photographed. She never wants to be the center of attention.'

'Even better,' Kip said. 'She'll do it because she won't have a choice. Good press for Reuben. Good press for the team.'

Marcus looked genuinely worried. 'I can buy Fig waiting it out for a couple of days because of his knee, but then what? Dude packs some serious heat. He keeps an AK by his front door.'

'He's had guns for years. He hasn't used them yet.' Kip seemed to think there was some safety in his logic. 'Jo will be fine.'

Dale said, 'I'll make sure they take care of her in jail. She'll get her own cell. She'll be in solitary. None of the other inmates will talk to her. I've got a gal who's been working there since dirt. She knows how to keep girls safe.'

Marcus stared at him. 'Who the fuck are you, man?'

'He's a fixer,' Kip said. 'He gets shit done.'

'He looks like a fucking corpse.' Marcus sniffed. 'Damn, man, clean your shorts. You smell like piss.'

Angie said, 'He was a cop for twenty-five years. He knows how the system works. If he says he can make sure Jo is protected inside, then she will be.'

Marcus looked at Angie like he had just noticed she was in the room. His eyes traveled up her legs, followed the curve of her waist to her breasts. She knew that she was his type, even with a few years on her.

Angie tried to work the advantage. She could feel at least part of a plan coming into focus, even if it was just to buy Jo some time. 'Jo goes to the grocery store on Thursdays. That's tomorrow. We can plant the pills then, make sure that her kid isn't with her. That keeps her safe for two days while she's in jail. Marcus, you'll make sure Jo is all right during the party. Then Monday morning, she's off to rehab, and we've bought ourselves thirty days. Meanwhile, the All-Star Complex breaks ground. The press stays good. Everybody wins.'

Marcus chewed the side of his lip. He was finally letting himself come around. 'What about her kid?'

Angie said, 'They'll give Jo one phone call. She can ask her mother to pick up Anthony from school and watch him until Fig gets home.' Her mouth was so dry she could barely make enough saliva to speak. The plan looked good on paper, but it was risky as hell, mostly because it depended on a guy with an uncontrollable temper keeping himself in check. She told Kip and Marcus, 'You guys have to be clear with Fig that Jo needs to look good for the cameras. All it will take is one bruise, or her walking funny, and some idiot with a blog is going to break the story. If Fig hates the press as much as you say he does, then make it clear that they're going to be watching Jo like a hawk, especially once she's out of jail.'

'This works,' Kip said. 'Two days in jail. Thirty days in rehab. Jo sees how easily we can turn her life upside down. Fig will be fine by the time she gets out. You know his temper burns off if you give him some time.'

Marcus was nodding already. 'Might wake the dude up, make him think she's taking pills 'cause maybe she can't take what he's giving anymore.'

Angie bit her lip so she wouldn't call him on his bullshit.

'Okay, good.' Kip turned to Dale. 'The video on the phone can be wiped when Jo is in jail, right? Some kind of government mistake, blah-blah-blah.'

Dale said, 'My guy can do that remotely.'

'Good,' Kip repeated. 'So, Dale plants the Oxy. I'll get one of Ditmar's people to shuttle Jo through the arraignment, tell them not to make a stink when she's held over to Saturday.'

'Naw, man. Get her to plant the Oxy.' Marcus nodded toward Angie. 'This guy looks like he'll be dead before I leave the room.'

Dale's lips went into a tight white line. He was dying, but he still had his pride.

'Fine. Done. We're out of here.' Kip told Marcus, 'Let's head back upstairs. I've got some last-minute details to go over with you about the ground-breaking.'

Marcus took another look at Angie before he let Kip lead him back toward the elevator.

Dale waited until they were gone before he spoke. 'Fucking piece of shit fucker.' He kicked over a ladder. 'Who does he think made his rape charges go away? And the two that didn't even get filed?' He kicked the ladder again. 'I put blood on my hands so that dickwad could keep dribbling a fucking basketball.'

Angie guessed she had figured out how Dale had finagled the money for the trust fund.

He said, 'Do I look like a fucking corpse?'

'You look like you've got the flu,' she lied. 'You could always go back on dialysis.'

Dale leaned against the wall. He was winded from kicking the ladder. 'Sitting in that fucking hospital room for four hours a day, three days a week, everybody talking about how they're gonna get a kidney soon.'

Angie couldn't listen to his sob story. She had to figure out how she was going to take care of Jo. 'I need to get going.'

'Hold on. Where's that iPad? The clone thing? I don't trust this bullshit about no copy on the laptop.'

'I didn't see any movies. Just a bunch of pictures, emails with her mother.'

Dale stared at her, trying to suss out the truth.

Angie rolled her eyes. 'I'll smash it with a hammer. Problem solved.'

'Fine. But bring me the pieces.'

Shit, now she had to buy another iPad and pound it into parts. 'Anything else, Your Majesty?'

'You know this jail and rehab thing is only temporary.' Dale raised his eyebrows. 'Kip's paranoid, Marcus is terrified of LaDonna. You think they're gonna be cured of that when Jo gets out of Hotel Junkie in thirty days?'

'What are you saying?'

'I got you this job. You wanna keep it, you're gonna have to take over for me.'

'You mean I gotta get blood on my hands?'

'Don't put on an act with me, Lady Macbeth.' Dale's yellow teeth flashed. 'Mark my words, even if Jo keeps her mouth shut, these guys are gonna get paranoid. They're gonna start losing sleep. They're gonna start worrying about what Jo will say. Eventually they'll come to you to solve the problem on a more permanent basis.'

'What the hell does that mean?'

'You know what it means.'

Angie did. He thought that Kip would hire her to murder Jo, which confirmed in her mind that Kip had hired Dale to kill for him before. She hoped to God that he'd gotten more money than the measly quarter of a million that he was leaving Delilah.

'Listen to your Uncle Dale,' he advised. 'Make it look like a suicide. She's got a drug problem. Jail and rehab would depress the hell out of anybody. Some pills, some booze, a bathtub with the water left running, and she slips down and drowns peacefully in her sleep.'

Angie started to shake her head, but then she remembered that Dale wouldn't ever find out what happened. 'Thanks for the advice, Uncle Dale.'

'Wait.' He stopped her from leaving. 'Seems strange that you know Jo goes to the grocery store on Thursdays. Especially since you only started following her this week.'

'I asked around. You're not the only person who knows how to be a detective.'

'Right.'

'Is that all?' Angie tried to walk away, but he grabbed her arm.

'You'll need these for tomorrow.' Dale reached into his pocket. He pulled out a Ziploc bag that contained around a dozen green pills. OxyContin, 80 milligrams. Enough to land Jo in jail, but not enough so that she could get hit with distribution.

He said, 'I know you prefer Vicodin.' His yellow teeth showed under his wet lips. 'Maybe a little too much.'

'What shot out your kidneys? Rainbows and sunshine?' Angie wasn't going to let him use her habit against her. Dale had blown through enough coke over the years to powder the Alps. 'At least I know when to pull back.'

'Doctors ever get that hole in your stomach to close up?' Dale had a smug look on his face. 'It's the coating on the pills, right? Eats through the stomach lining.'

Angie snatched away the bag of Oxy. 'Take a shower, Dale. Marcus was right. You reek of piss.'

'Why don't you lick it off me?'

Angie could hear him laughing as she walked away.

THURSDAY, 10:22 AM

Angie pushed an empty cart through the Kroger, looking for Jo. The store was too clean. Her eyes hurt from the fluorescent lights. Everything was aggressively tidy. The last time Angie had been in an actual grocery store, she was with Will. Domesticity was his only fetish. He bought things in bulk, always the same brands with the same logos because he was too stupid to read about anything that might be new or better. Angie loathed domesticity. She had gotten bored with the whole process, sneaking crap into his cart: some root beer, then peach sorbet, then a different kind of butter, and five minutes later, he was freaking out like the robot from *Lost in Space*.

Sara probably did all of his shopping now. Ironed his shirts. Made his dinner. Tucked him into bed at night. Changed his diaper.

Angie pushed her way through the deli and spotted her daughter in the produce section. Jo held a peach in her hand, testing it for softness. There was a distant look in her eyes. Maybe she was thinking about her plan to escape from her husband. That was why Jo had shown Marcus the video. She thought he would take care of her, make all the bad things go away. What she didn't understand was that Marcus Rippy wasn't going to jeopardize any part of his life to help Jo.

Even if he wanted to, Kip wouldn't let him.

The video was their only leverage. Angie had to copy the file off Jo's phone before the police scooped her up. She didn't trust the backup iPad, even turned off and locked in a motel safe. Sam Vera was too good at his job, and Angie wasn't willing to roll the dice with Jo's life.

Dale wasn't a fortune-teller, but he understood how these things worked. Jo was an uncertainty. People hated uncertainty, especially when money was involved. It would only be a matter of time before Marcus got paranoid and Kip got desperate. Laslo had stabbed a man to death in Boston. There was other dirty work she knew about in Atlanta. His job was to keep the trains running on time. Angie didn't see him having any qualms about neutralizing Jo. Which meant there wasn't much time left for her daughter to get away.

'Let me call my mother.'

Angie felt her stomach flip. Jo was talking to her. She was standing ten feet away. She held a peach in her hand. Her voice was raised just loud enough to carry.

Jo said, 'My son is at school. Let me call my mother before you take me.'

Angie looked around, making sure no one could hear them. 'What are—'

'I know Reuben has you following me.' Jo put down the peach. 'I saw you at the Starbucks. You were at my son's school last month.'

'It's not what you think.'

Jo was trying to sound like she wasn't afraid, but the muscles in her neck stood out with tension. 'I won't come willingly unless you let me take care of my son.' Her composure started to break. She was clearly terrified. 'Please. He's Reuben's boy, too.'

Angie felt a sharp pain in her chest, a physical response to the helplessness that her daughter was obviously experiencing. 'Your husband didn't send me. I'm here to help you get away.'

Jo laughed.

'I'm serious.'

'Fuck off, woman. Don't waste my time.' She pushed her shopping cart to the next aisle. She tore off a produce bag and started loading it with oranges.

Angie said, 'You're in danger.'

'No shit.'

'Marcus went to Kip about the video.'

Jo laughed again. 'You think I didn't figure something like that happened? The laptop crashed this morning. Won't even boot up. Everything on my phone got erased.' She opened her purse. She took out her phone. She offered it to Angie. 'You want it? Take it. I don't even have pictures of my boy anymore.'

Angie slapped her hand away. 'Listen to me. I'm trying to help you.'

'You can't help me.' Jo turned around. She pushed her cart over to the juice section.

Angie followed her. 'You're going to be arrested.'

Jo looked confused, then angry. 'For what?'

'They planted Oxy in your car.' Angie left out the part where she'd been the one to do it. 'The cops are going to be waiting outside when you leave. They're going to keep you in jail for two days.'

'But—' Jo had the look that Angie had seen before when rich, entitled people found out they were going to have to bend to the law. 'I didn't do anything.'

'It doesn't matter,' Angie told her. 'They have it all planned out. They want to teach you a lesson.' Angie gave her a moment to let reality sink in. 'You'll get out of jail Saturday night, you'll go to LaDonna's party with Fig on Sunday night, then Monday morning, you'll go to rehab.'

'I won't be able to walk Monday morning.'

'Reuben's knee will be in a brace.' Angie felt the words rush into her mouth like water. She had to make Jo believe that she could keep her safe. 'He'll be effectively crippled.'

'You think that matters?' She shook her head again. 'You can't outrun a bullet to the back.'

'The press will be everywhere. If he hits you, they'll see it.'

'If he leaves a mark.'

Angie struggled to convince her. 'You tell him if he touches you, you'll go out into the yard and take off your clothes and let the photographers record exactly what he's done.'

'What photographers?' She looked even more panicked. 'Reuben doesn't like the press.'

'They'll be following you the minute you get out of jail.'

'Oh God.' Jo put her hand to her neck. Her breathing was shallow. 'Marcus told Reuben I met with him. Alone.'

'No. Reuben doesn't know about the motel, the video, any of that.' Angie watched the relief pass through Jo's body like a muscle relaxer. 'Marcus took the problem to Kip. This is how Kip's handling it.'

Tears filled Jo's eyes. She was clearly terrified. 'Do you know what my husband's going to do to me for bringing attention down on him?'

Angie couldn't stand her distress anymore. 'I'm going to help you get away.'

'What?' Jo sounded disgusted. 'Are you crazy?'

'I'm going to help you,' Angie repeated, and she realized that she had never spoken truer words in her life. She had abandoned Jo once before, but she was going to do everything she could today, right now, to guide her daughter to safety.

She said, 'Let me help you.'

'Fuck off, lady.' Jo turned furious, the same as you would expect from any trapped animal. 'You ambush me at the grocery store and tell me you're my savior, and I'm supposed to believe you, risk my life for you, risk my son's life for you? Where do you get off, bitch? Who the hell do you think you are?'

Angie didn't have the words to tell her. *I'm your mother. I'm the teenager who didn't want to raise you. I'm the woman who abandoned you.*

'I'm a friend,' Angie said.

'Do you know what happened to the last friend who tried to help me? He ended up in the hospital. Probably won't ever walk again.'

'Do you know what happened to the last woman who threatened Marcus Rippy?'

Jo looked away. If she didn't know, she had a good idea. The despair was back, the helplessness. 'Why would you risk your life to help a stranger?'

'I had a daughter who was in your situation.'

'Had,' Jo repeated. 'She got killed?'

'Yes,' Angie said, because she knew that's how most of these stories ended. 'She was killed because I didn't help her. I'm not going to let that happen again.'

'Jesus.' Jo saw through the lie. 'You think you can get me on your side, make me trust you? I've seen you at One-Ten. If you're not working for Reuben, you're working for Kip Kilpatrick.'

'You're right. I work for Kip,' Angie admitted. 'And I do a lot of bad shit for him, but I'm not going to do this.'

'Crisis of conscience?' Jo gave a hard laugh. She knew what fixers did. She'd been wrapped up in professional sports for her entire adult life. 'Reuben keeps a knife by our bed. His gun is two inches from his hand when he takes a shower. He beats me.' She realized her voice was too loud. People were starting to stare. 'He beats me,' she repeated, softer. 'He rapes me. He makes me beg for him to keep doing it. I have to apologize afterward for making him lose control. He makes me thank him when I'm allowed to get a fucking cup of coffee or take my son on a playdate.'

'Then leave.'

'You don't think I've tried?' She looked away, shaking her head. 'The first time, I went back home. I stayed at my mama's. Three days away from him. Three days of freedom. Do you know what he did?' She glared at Angie. 'He dragged me out of my mother's house by my hair. He near about beat the life out of me. He locked me in a box and he kept me in his garage and you know what the cops told my mama when she called, telling them that her daughter had been kidnapped by a madman? "Domestic problem." That's all I am—a domestic problem.'

Angie wasn't surprised. The small-town cops who had arrested Jo with those prescriptions were probably the same cops who had looked the other way on Jo's abduction. If you were willing to take one pay-off, then it was just a matter of time before you took another.

'There is a wall of money backstopping these men. They don't lose things. They don't lose their wives. They don't lose their children.' She told Angie, 'I tried in California. I tried in Chicago. Each time, Reuben came and dragged me back. He used my mama against me. He used Anthony.' Jo's tone changed at her son's name. 'My birth mother abandoned me. I know how that feels. I'm not going to do that to my child.'

Angie felt her stomach clench. 'Do you know anything about her?'

'Does it matter?' Jo asked. 'I can't run to her for help, if that's what you're asking. She's probably dead by now. Even back then, she was a prostitute. A junkie. Exactly the kind of trash you'd expect to give up a baby.'

Angie took a deep breath.

'I'm not going to leave my boy. If Reuben was father of the year, I still wouldn't leave Anthony. That kind of damage, it rots your soul.'

Angie had to get away from the subject. 'What was your plan when you showed Marcus the video? What did you think you'd get out of him?'

'Money. Protection.' She slowly exhaled. 'Without the video, I've got nothing.'

'It doesn't matter. It's what you've seen. It's your ability to open your mouth.'

'Nobody cares what I have to say.'

'You know too much,' Angie told her. 'As far as Kip and Marcus are concerned, your mouth is a loaded gun.'

Jo took a deep breath, just like Angie had. 'So here I am again, trapped right back where I started.'

Angie couldn't abide the resignation in her voice. 'I've got a plan to buy you some time, get you away from your husband.'

'What are you going to do?' Jo's mouth twisted into a scowl. 'You think you can take on Reuben Figaroa? Shit. You'll get a gun in your face. That man doesn't back down and he does not give up control.' She counted down on her fingers. 'I'm not on the bank accounts. I'm not on the investments. I'm not on the pensions. I'm not on the house. I don't own my car. I signed a prenup before we got married.' She laughed, this time at herself. 'I was in love, baby. I didn't want money. I willingly signed myself into slavery.'

'I can get you out,' Angie said. 'I can keep you safe.' She had thought through some of this already. Dale's trust fund for Delilah. Angie was authorized to pay for an apartment and living expenses. She could use the money for Jo instead. 'I can get an alias for you. I'll help you hide out. Once you're safe, I'll find a lawyer who can negotiate with Reuben.'

'How're you gonna get me out?' Jo asked. 'That's the hard part. You might as well be saying to me that you're gonna hide me out on Mars, and we'll figure out how to fly me there later.'

She was right. Reuben would be waiting for Jo outside the jail. He wouldn't let her out of his sight until she left for rehab. *If* he let her leave for rehab.

'You don't get it, do you?' Jo seemed genuinely perplexed. 'Reuben doesn't care about basketball. He doesn't care about Anthony. He doesn't really care about me. He wants control.' She closed the space between her and Angie. 'I'll do whatever that man wants. *Anything*, you feel me? He just says the word. Snaps his fingers. And he still holds a knife to my face. He still wraps his hand around my throat. He can't get off unless I'm terrified.'

Angie couldn't think about all the ways her daughter had been shamed. 'Tell me something, what's it going to be like when Anthony gets older? How are you going to protect him?'

'Reuben wouldn't hurt his son.'

Angie wondered if she could hear herself. 'He's going to see how his daddy treats you. He's going to grow into that same kind of man.'

'No,' she insisted. 'He's sweet. He's got nothing of his daddy in him.'

'Wasn't Reuben sweet when you first met him?'

Jo pressed her lips together. She looked down at her hands. Angie thought that she was going to come up with another excuse, but she said, 'What's your plan?'

'You'll bail out Saturday. I know Reuben will be waiting for you outside the jail. So will the photographers. I'll make sure of that. You can go with me instead.'

'That's your plan?' She looked more dejected than before. 'Step two of that is Reuben either pulls out his gun and shoots me in the head, or I get a call from his lawyer saying I'm a junkie with a record and I'm never gonna see my son again.' She laughed. 'And he still shoots me in the head.'

She was right, but Jo had spent years trying to think of a way out. Angie had spent two days. 'What about when you go to the party on Sunday?'

Jo started to shake her head, but then she stopped. 'Anthony will stay with my mother. She's the only one Reuben allows to keep him.'

Angie asked, 'Can you get away from Reuben at the party? Go to the bathroom or something?'

'He'll be with the guys. With Marcus.' She explained, 'That's when they made the video. It was that girl, the one who charged Marcus with rape.'

'Keisha Miscavage?'

'Yes.' She wiped her eyes. She couldn't wipe away the fear. 'You should know what you're up against. What they do to women who don't matter. That girl was drugged. I know they put something in her drink. An hour later, she's in that bedroom, arms flopping around, out of her mind, telling them no. And they just laughed while they took turns with her.'

Angie knew what a gang rape looked like. She wasn't shocked by the details. 'Sunday night, as soon as you're on your own, slip out of the house. Go down the driveway. Take a left. There's a turn-off for an alleyway that the gardeners use. I'll be parked there waiting for you.'

Jo didn't answer. This was happening too fast. 'Why?'

'I told you about my daughter.'

Jo shook her head, but she was still desperate enough to listen to a complete stranger. 'I meet you at this turn-off. Then what?'

Angie said, 'I'll go to your mother's and pick up Anthony.' She talked over Jo's protest. 'That's the first place they'll look for you. I can handle them better than you can.'

'Why not get Anthony first, then meet me at the party?'

Angie could tell she needed something to push her over the line, to make her take that first step. 'What happens if you don't get away and I've got your kid in my car? How do I explain that? How do you explain it?'

Jo looked down at the floor. Her eyes tracked back and forth. She chewed her lip. Angie recognized the signs of negotiation. Jo's escape from the party would set the plan in motion. That was the point at which there would be no turning back. If she didn't slip away, if she changed her mind at the last minute, then Anthony would stay at her mother's and Jo would take a beat-down and everything would go back to normal.

Jo asked, 'What am I supposed to do while you're kidnapping my son?'

'I'll rent a car under an alias.' She'd have to get Delilah's driver's license, but that shouldn't take more than a dime of heroin. 'Sunday night, I'll leave the car parked down the street from the Rippy's. Once you leave the party, I'll drive you to the car. You go to the OneTown motel and wait for me. I'll go to your mother's and pick up Anthony. Once I bring him to the motel, you jump on the interstate and drive the car west. I'll stay here and make sure your tracks are covered.'

'And then what?'

'We find a lawyer to negotiate with Kip to get you out of this mess.' She stopped Jo before she could throw up obstacles.

'Remember that you can testify that you saw Marcus in that video, too.'

'Testify?' She turned skitterish again. 'I'm not going to—'

'It won't come to that. All that matters is the threat.'

Jo pressed her lips together again. 'Why should I trust you?'

'Who else are you going to trust?' Angie waited for an answer that she knew would never come. 'What do I gain from tricking you?'

'I'm trying to figure that out.' Jo picked at the gold chain around her neck. 'I thought Reuben sent you to fetch me. That's what he usually does. But he doesn't let the fetcher take care of me. He does that himself.'

'Who does he send to fetch you?'

'A man,' she said. 'Always a man.'

Angie gave her time to think.

'Do you want money?' Jo asked. 'That's what you get out of this, a piece of whatever I get from Reuben?'

'Would it make you feel better if I asked for something?'

'I don't know.' She was still thinking about it, trying to find the holes. 'My mother can't travel. She has a heart condition. She can't be far from the hospital.'

'Look at me.' Angie waited until her eyes were locked with her daughter's. The same brown irises. The same almond shape. The same skin tone. The same hair. The same voice, even.

She told the girl, 'If I was your mother, I would tell you to take Anthony and leave and never look back.'

Jo swallowed. Her perfect neck. Her straight shoulders. Her anger. Her fear. 'Okay,' she agreed. 'I'll do it.'

SATURDAY, 4:39 AM

Angie yawned as she drove down Ponce de Leon Road. The dying moonlight made everything look chalky white. She was exhausted, but she couldn't sleep. Jo's arrest two days ago was still all over the news. The predicted press scrum had gathered around the jail waiting for her release later today. Kip had warned Reuben to stay in line. Rehab had been arranged for Monday. Marcus had held a press conference last night where he talked about how Jo and Reuben's marriage was strong, that they would get through this, that they just needed people to keep them in their thoughts and prayers. A blurred photo of Jo with her head down, sitting on the floor during one of Figaroa's games, was the only image anyone could find of her.

She was safe for now. That's what Angie kept telling herself. Jo just needed to be safe for another day and a half.

From the outside, it seemed like Jo had a good chance of escaping. The plan didn't feel complicated. There were just a lot of moving pieces. Angie had spent the last two days doing her part. Stealing Delilah's ID. Renting the car. Driving the escape routes back and forth. Buying a used iPad out of the back of a van. Smashing it with a hammer. Delivering the pieces to Dale. Acting like she was fine so that he didn't get too close or too curious.

As always, money was the hard part. Angie had thirty thousand dollars in her checking account, but she couldn't use it to help Jo. At least not if Dale was still alive. He could access her account. There could not be any recent hefty withdrawals. Angie's only option was to peel off some of the cash Dale kept in the trunk of his car and hope that he didn't notice. He'd always kept pay-off money under his spare tire, especially when his bookies were chasing him down. Angie would take the cash tomorrow, right before the party. She wouldn't be greedy. Jo didn't need to stay in five-star hotels while she made her escape. For a few grand, she could drive out west and find a dirtbag motel with HBO to keep the kid occupied.

Stealing Delilah's identity had been comparatively easy. Angie had cased out a convenience store down from where Delilah was living. She knew the girl would show up eventually. Staying off H was hard, even with the Suboxone. It made you fidgety. It made you hungry. Angie had paid a kid to hang around the store. When Delilah had finally shown up, he'd picked her wallet out of her purse. He'd snatched her driver's license, cloned one of her credit cards, and was gone before Delilah got to the cash register.

Angie had been in the store when it happened, hiding behind a Coke display. A risky move, but she couldn't stop herself. She had always been fascinated by Delilah. At least as fascinated as you could be by someone you despised. What made her so special? It had to be more than blood. Dale had other family he barely gave a shit about. So what made him protect Delilah all those years, make it his dying wish that she was taken care of? It had to be more than pussy. Dale could buy that off anybody.

Angie had to admit that the girl wasn't bad looking—if you were into cheap and trashy. She'd managed to put on some weight. She no longer looked like a skeleton. She'd stopped coloring her hair. Apparently she still wasn't washing it. Even standing fifteen feet away, Angie could see that the brown was more of an oily black. The split ends tapped at her shoulders as she loaded her purchases onto the counter. A 40 of malt liquor. Two bags of Cheetos. A can of Pringles. Snickers bar. Skittles. She asked for two packs of Camels, because watching her father die from Type 2 diabetes and kidney failure was not the cautionary tale you'd expect it to be.

Delilah never looked at consequences. She didn't even look at next week. What mattered was today, right now, what she could get her hands on, who she could exploit, and how she was going to make money off it.

Did she know about Dale's trust fund? Angie wasn't sure, but she knew that Dale would have a fail-safe. Someone else would know about the trust. Someone else would make sure that the girl knew Angie was holding.

There was only one other person Dale trusted, and Angie hoped like hell she never found herself face-to-face with that vicious motherfucker ever again.

Angie stopped for a red light. She yawned again. She rubbed her face. Her skin felt rubbery. Not enough Vicodin. She was trying to taper off for tomorrow night. The next few hours would be excruciating, but her mind had to be sharp. She went over the plan again, trying to see the holes, trying to anticipate the snags before they happened.

The iPad was the key. It was inside Angie's private-eye bag, locked in the trunk of her car. The thing felt radioactive. It was also an open question. Jo had said that Reuben's laptop had been wiped clean. Jo's iPhone had been remotely erased, too. Did that mean the iPad would be erased if Angie turned on the power? The technology eluded her. The value did not.

She hadn't told Jo about the iPad because she didn't trust Jo. She recognized the girl's equivocation in the grocery store. Jo had only agreed to Angie's plan because she saw that there would be a last-minute way to stop it: don't leave Reuben at the party.

What would Jo decide?

Another open question. Angie wasn't sure her daughter would leave. And even if she left, would she stay gone? Jo had left Reuben before. Five times before, that Kip Kilpatrick knew of. Angie felt the truth gnawing at her gut. Even if Jo left, she would go back to Reuben as sure as Angie was sitting in her car. The only way to stop that from happening was to make certain there was no Reuben to go back to.

Will worked at the GBI. They had computer people. If there was a video on the iPad, he'd find a way to access it. He would throw Marcus and Reuben in jail and Jo could work with a lawyer to break the prenup. Or not break it. Reuben's career would be finished. His life would be over. Jo could disappear. She could take her monthly draw from Delilah's account and go back to college. Meet a nice guy. Have another kid.

Angie laughed out loud. The sound echoed in her car. Who was she kidding? Jo didn't like nice guys any more than Angie did. There was a reason Angie couldn't live with her husband.

She wasn't even sure she was going to live past tomorrow.

Dale Harding had blood on his hands. Laslo had killed before. Kip didn't mind pulling the trigger from behind the safety of his big glass desk. If any of them found out Angie had helped Jo, then there was no amount of running that would get her away.

Maybe that was why she wanted to see Will one last time. Or even if she couldn't see him, see his things. Touch his clean, starched shirts hanging in the closet. Mix up his perfectly matched socks in the drawer. Put his toothpaste in the wrong hole in the porcelain holder. Carve an *A* in his soap so the next time he showered, he touched his body and he thought of her.

Angie downshifted the gear into first. She had almost driven by Will's house. She pulled over to the curb, parking across the street in front of a fire hydrant.

Will lived in a bungalow that used to be a crack house and was probably worth half a million bucks by now, if only for the land. The inside was meticulously restored, decorated entirely in neutrals. His desk was pushed up against a wall in the living room. A pinball machine took pride of place in the dining-room. The spare room was full of all the books he had read with his painstaking slowness, determined to get through the classics because he thought that's what normal people did.

In the summer, he mowed the lawn every other weekend. He cleaned the gutters twice a year. Every five years, he painted the trim around the windows. He pressure-washed the decks and porches. He planted flowers in the little garden outside the front door. He was a regular suburban dad except that he didn't live in the suburbs and he didn't have a kid.

At least not as far as he knew.

The driveway was empty, as usual. Will spent most of his free time at Sara's. Angie couldn't get past the security system in Sara's building without spending some serious money, but she had found old photos of the apartment archived on a real-estate site. Chef's kitchen. Two bedrooms. An office. Master bath with soaking tub and a shower with ten body jets.

Apparently she liked to keep the body jets to herself.

I took a page from Mama's book, Sara had written three weeks ago. *I had the painters tackle the guest bathroom while we were at work. I changed out the towels to match. Will was so pleased to have his own bathroom in my apartment, but honestly, I was going to kill him if I had to keep sharing.*

Angie wondered if Will was stupid enough to fall for the trick. She assumed he was. He fell for a lot of Sara's crap. He probably had a T-shirt that said, HAPPY WIFE, HAPPY LIFE.

She smiled, because the only way Sara could marry Will was if she pried him away from Angie's cold, dead hands.

If for that reason alone, Angie would survive tomorrow.

She checked for curious neighbors before walking around the side of the house. With any other owner, the back gate would squeak, but Will kept everything well oiled. Angie found the spare key over the door frame. She slipped it into the lock. She opened the door and found two greyhounds staring back at her.

They were curled into a sleepy pile. They blinked in the faint light, looking more surprised than scared. Angie wasn't afraid. The dogs knew her.

'Come on,' she whispered, clicking her tongue. 'Good boys,' she coaxed, petting them as they stood and stretched. She held open the door. They went outside.

Betty barked.

Will's dog was standing in the kitchen doorway, protecting her territory.

Angie scooped up the mutt with one hand, clamped her mouth shut with the other, and tossed her outside. She had the door closed before Betty could get her bearings. The little asshole tried to get back in through the dog door, but Angie blocked it with her foot until she could put a chair out front.

Betty barked again. Then again. Then there was silence.

Angie looked around the kitchen.

Dogs meant people.

Will and Sara were here. They must have walked from her apartment. They walked all the time, even in the summer heat, like cars had never been invented.

Angie took a moment to consider what she had done. What she was still doing. This was a little crazy-stalker, a little more dangerous than usual.

Was she dangerous?

She had locked her purse in the car. The gun was still unloaded. Something had told her to leave the clip out, make herself walk through those extra steps—jam in the clip, pull back the slide, load a bullet into the chamber, curl her finger around the trigger—before she did something that she couldn't get out of.

Angie looked down at her foot. The toes were up, heel down, about to take a step. She rocked back and forth. Leave? Go? Stay here until someone woke up?

He drinks hot chocolate in the morning, Sara had written to Tessa. *It's like kissing a Hershey bar when I wake up.*

The iPad was in Angie's trunk, too. She had told herself on the drive over that she was going to hand over the movie to Will. His golden ticket back into the Marcus Rippy rape charge. He would be ecstatic. So why had Angie left the iPad locked in her trunk if the plan was to give it to Will?

She looked down at her foot. Toes still raised, undecided.

In all honesty, Angie never knew exactly what she wanted to give Will. A good time. A hard time. A bad time when Sara came into the kitchen expecting to suck chocolate off his lips and found Angie instead.

She smiled at the thought.

The clock on the stove read five in the morning. Will would wake up for his run in half an hour. He had an internal alarm that you couldn't silence no matter what you did to entice him into staying in bed.

Angie's toes pressed to the floor. Her heel raised up. Her toes went down again. She was walking. She was in the dining-room. She was in the living room. She was in the bathroom. She was in the hall. She was standing outside Will's bedroom.

The door was cracked open.

Will was on his back. His eyes were closed. A sliver of light played across his face. His shirt was off. He never slept with his shirt off. He was ashamed of the scars, the burns, the damage. Apparently that had changed. The reason why was between his legs. Long auburn hair. Milky white skin. Sara was propped up on her elbow. She was using her hand with her mouth. It was her other hand that Angie couldn't stop looking at. Will's fingers were laced through Sara's. Not gripping the back of her head. Not forcing her to go deeper.

He was holding her fucking hand.

Angie pressed her fist to her mouth. She wanted to scream. She was going to scream. She turned around, forcing herself into an unnatural silence. She was in the living room, the kitchen, the backyard, the driveway, her car. It wasn't until she was locked inside her car that she let it out. Angie opened her mouth and screamed as loud as she could. She yelled so long that she tasted blood in her mouth. She banged her fists on the steering wheel. She was crying, aching so bad that every bone in her body felt charred with rage.

She got out of the car. She opened the trunk. She grabbed her purse. She found her gun. The clip was out. She shoved it back in. She started to pull back on the slide, to put a bullet into the chamber, but her hands were too slick with sweat.

She looked at the gun. The Glock had been a gift to herself when she got the job with Kip. She should've cleaned it better. The metal looked dry. Will used to oil her gun for her. He used to make sure her car had enough gas, that her transmission wasn't leaking like a sieve, that she had enough money in her bank account, that she wasn't out there in the world alone.

He was doing those things for Sara now.

Angie got back into her car. She tossed the gun onto the dashboard. This wasn't right. She was trying to do good, to help Jo, to help Will with his case against Marcus Rippy, to risk her fucking life to save her daughter. This was the thanks she got? She could already have a target on her back. Dale was clearly suspicious. He knew more than he was letting on. Angie thought she was playing them, but maybe they were playing her. Or Jo could be the weak link. Fuck not showing up outside Rippy's house tomorrow night. Jo could've already told Reuben what was going on. Chain reaction. Reuben would tell Kip, Kip would tap Laslo, and Angie would have a knife sticking out of her chest by the time Jo bonded out of jail.

Let Will identify her body. Let him see the knife in her heart. Let him experience the horror that came from realizing he had failed her just like every other time he had let her down. Let him hold her lifeless, bloody hand while he cried.

And let that cunt Sara Linton see all of it.

Angie found a notebook in her purse, clicked her pen. She started writing in big capital letters:

You fucking piece of—

Angie stared at the words. The pen had torn through the paper. Her heart was pounding so hard that she felt it pushing into her throat. She tore the page out of the notebook. She tried to regulate her breathing, to stop her hand from shaking, to calm the hell down. This had to be done right. She couldn't hurt Will with her words if she didn't sharpen her tongue with a razor.

She pressed the pen to the blank sheet of paper. Cursive. Crooked, sloping lines. Not for Will, but for Sara.

Hey, baby. If someone is reading this to you, then I am dead.

She filled the page front and back. She felt like a dam had broken inside of her. Thirty years of having his back. Taking care of his problems. Comforting him. Letting him fuck her. Fucking him back. Will might not find the letter soon, but he would find it eventually. Either Angie would be dead or Sara would nag him into finally making a break. Will would go to the bank. He would find Angie's post office box. And instead of finding a way to track her down, he would find this letter.

'Fuck you,' Angie mumbled. 'Fuck you, and fuck your girlfriend, and fuck her sister and her fucking family and her fucking—'

She heard a door close.

Will stood on his front porch. He was dressed in his running gear. He stretched up his arms, leaned one way, then the other. His 5:30 run. One thing that would never change. Angie waited for him to see her car, but instead of looking out into the street, he knelt down on the front walk and plucked a flower from the garden. He went back into the house. Almost a full minute passed before he returned to the porch, hands empty, smile on his face.

Angie could take care of his silly grin. She got out of her car. She stared at him, waiting for him to see her.

At first, he didn't. He stretched his legs. He checked the water bottle that fit into the small of his back. He retied his shoes. Finally, he looked up.

His mouth gaped open.

Angie glared at him. Her fingernails itched to claw out his eyes. She wanted to kick him in the face.

He said, 'Angie?'

She got into the car. She slammed the door closed. She cranked the engine. She pulled away from the curb.

'Wait!' Will called. He was running after her, arms pumping, muscles straining. 'Angie!'

She could see him in her rear-view mirror. Getting closer. Still screaming her name. Angie slammed on the brakes. She grabbed the gun off her dash. She got out of the car and pointed the weapon at his head.

Will's hands shot into the air. He was fifteen feet away. Close enough to catch up to her. Close enough to take a bullet to the heart.

He said, 'I just want to talk to you.'

Angie's finger was resting just above the trigger. Then it was not. Then she felt the safety lever under the pad of her finger, then the trigger, and then she pulled back hard.

Click.

Will flinched.

The bullet didn't come.

Dry fire. The chamber was empty. Angie's hands had been too slick to pull back on the slide.

Will said, 'Let's go somewhere and talk.'

She stared at her husband. Everything was so familiar, but different. The lean cut of his legs. The tight abdomen under his T-shirt. The long sleeves that covered the scar on his arm. The mouth that had kissed her. The hands that had touched her. That touched Sara now. That held her fucking hand.

She said, 'You've changed.'

Will didn't deny it. 'I need to talk to you.'

'There's nothing to say,' she told him. 'I don't even recognize you anymore.'

He held out his arms. 'This is what I look like when I'm in love.'

Angie felt the cold metal of the gun against her leg. The air had left her body. Acid ripped apart her stomach.

Pull the slide. Load the bullet into the chamber. Press the trigger. Make the problem disappear. Make Sara a widow again. Erase the last thirty years, because they didn't matter. They never mattered. At least they didn't to Will.

Angie got back into the car. The gun went back onto the dash. She pressed the gas all the way to the floor. Her body hurt. Her soul ached. She felt like Will had beaten her. She wished that he had. Bloodied her mouth. Bruised her eyes shut. Kicked her bones to pieces. Railed against her, screamed at her, seethed with rage . . . Anything that would prove that he still loved her.

SUNDAY, 11:49 PM

Angie fired up a joint. The moon was full overhead, almost like a spotlight. She looked in her rear-view mirror. Clear. It wasn't yet time for Jo to leave the party. They had settled on midnight because it seemed like as good a time as any. LaDonna's party had started at nine. No one who mattered showed up until ten. Two hours to mingle. Two hours for Jo to extract herself from Reuben. Or to take the coward's way out and stay with her husband.

Midnight.

Jo would either turn into a pumpkin or she would turn into Angie's daughter.

Angie blew on the tip of the joint. She honestly had no idea what Jo would do. The stark truth was that she did not know Jo Figaroa. Angie was here because she had made a promise to herself that she would see this through. What happened next was up to Jo. The only certain outcome was that Angie was going to leave town either way.

She looked down at the yellow plastic ring on her finger. The sunflower leaves had been crushed in her purse. All of her purses. Angie changed out her bag every other day, but she always transferred the ring, because . . . Why?

Because it meant something?

A child's toy, bought from a bubble gum machine to signify a relationship that had begun almost thirty years before. Angie always pretended that she didn't remember that first time with Will. Mrs Flannigan's stuffy basement. Mouse shit on the floor. The stained futon mattress. The smell of spunk. He had been so vulnerable.

Too vulnerable.

Like fear, vulnerability was contagious. That day, Will had been distraught, but Angie was the one who felt inconsolable. She had shown him a side of herself that no one else had seen before or since. She had told him about her mother's pimp. She had told him about what came after. Will had never looked at Angie the same way again. He took on the job of savior. Of superhero. He risked his life to protect her. He constantly bailed her out of trouble. He gave her money. He gave her safety.

What did he want in return?

Nothing that Angie could see. This was not the kind of transaction she could live with. In many ways it would've been better if Will had held it over her head or punished her. A feeling of pity was his only reward. Will never asked her for the things that he knew other men had paid for. He clearly wanted it. He wasn't a saint. But there was too much knowledge, too much of a clear-eyed understanding of the pain that had bonded them together in that dank, lonely basement.

Angie was ten years old when Deidre Polaski stuck a needle in her own arm and took a three decades long nap. For weeks, Angie sat beside the woman's comatose body and watched soap operas and slept and bathed Deidre and combed her hair. There was a roll of cash in a Sanka jar behind the radiator. Angie used the money for pizza and junk food. The cash ran out before Angie could. Deidre's pimp came knocking on her door, looking for his piece. Angie told him there was nothing left, so he took a piece of her instead.

Her mouth. Her hands.

Not her body.

Dale Harding knew better than to shit where another man would pay to eat.

Everyone always said Dale was a bad cop. No one ever figured out how bad. They thought it was booze and gambling. They didn't know that he had a stable of underage girls supplementing his paycheck from the city. That he took pictures. That he sold the pictures to other men. That he sold the girls. That he used the girls for himself.

He had tricked out Delilah, his own daughter. He had tricked out Deidre, his own sister. He had tricked out Angie, his own niece.

Thirty-four years ago, Dale was the one who knocked at the door. Angie's uncle. Her savior. Her pimp.

This was how Angie knew about the bricks of cash Dale kept under the spare tire in his trunk. Escape money, he always called it, for the time when the detectives he was working with turned their detecting his way. They never figured him out, and meanwhile, Dale had earned and gambled away fortunes. There were always more abandoned girls to exploit. There was always more cash to be made. And there was always Angie on the periphery, waiting for him to notice her.

He was the closest thing to a father that she had ever had.

Every home the state placed her in, no matter how good or bad, Angie always found a way back to Dale. She became a cop for him. She took care of his problems. She looked after Delilah when most of the time all she could think about was wrapping a bag around the girl's head and watching her suffocate.

Will had no idea that a cop had pimped Angie out. He was as good as Dale Harding was bad. Will did things the right way. He followed the rules. But he also had that same feral, animal side to him that Angie did. Will could dress in a suit and keep his hair cut over his collar, but she saw through the disguise. She knew how to push that button that brought out the beast. Over the years, Angie had toyed with telling him about Dale. There was a time when Will would've tracked Dale down, put a bullet in his gut, if he found out what the man had done to Angie.

She wondered what he would do if he found out now. Probably talk to Sara. Discuss how tragic Angie's life was. Then they'd go out to dinner. Then they would go home and make love.

That's what bothered Angie the most. Not the blow job, not even the hand-holding, but the ease between them. The sensation had permeated the room.

Happiness. Contentment. Love.

Angie couldn't remember ever having that with Will.

She should let him go. Give him permission to have the normalcy that he had yearned for his entire life. Unfortunately, Angie never did the right thing when she felt wounded. Her inclination was to lash out. Her inclination was to keep hurting Will until he finally hurt her back.

Angie stubbed out the joint in the ashtray. Everything she hated about Jo was everything that was inside of Angie.

She looked at her watch. 11:52. The clock felt like it was moving backward.

Angie got out of her car. The sweltering heat almost pushed her back inside. The temperature hadn't dropped with the sun. Her thin cotton shift was little more than a handkerchief, but she was still sweating. She leaned against the trunk. The metal was too hot. Angie walked down the side of the road, careful not to go too far. Her nerves were rattled. She had tapered off the Vicodin too quickly. She was concerned about Jo. She was scared of Laslo. She was terrified of Dale. She was worried that her plan to neutralize Kip Kilpatrick would come back to bite her in the ass.

Dale always said you had to use an ax, not a hammer. Angie figured she might as well use it to cut off the head of a snake.

A woman screamed.

Angie's head jerked toward the street. Toward the Rippys' driveway. Toward the sound of a woman begging for help.

'Please!' Jo screamed. 'No!'

Angie popped open her trunk. She didn't take her gun. She found the tire iron. She kicked off her heels. She ran down the street, arms pumping, neck straining, the same as Will when he had chased her car yesterday morning.

'Help!' Jo screamed. 'Please!'

Angie rounded the corner to the driveway. The gates were open. The house glowed with lights. Music thumped. There was no security guard. No one was watching the cameras.

'Please!' Jo begged. 'Help me!'

Reuben Figaroa was dragging his wife by the hair. Jo's bare feet scraped across the grass. He was taking her to the woods, away from the house. He wanted to have some privacy.

'Help!'

Angie didn't give him a warning. She didn't tell him to stop. She held the tire iron over her head as she ran toward him. By the time Reuben realized she was there, Angie was swinging the heavy metal bar at his head. She felt the iron shudder in her hand, vibrate down her arm and into her shoulder.

Reuben dropped Jo. His mouth was open. His eyes rolled back in his head. He fell to the ground, unconscious. Angie raised the iron again, this time aiming for his knee. The one with the brace. The one he'd had surgery on. Time was moving slow enough for her to register the fact that the best orthopedist in the world had given him five more years of playing basketball and with one swing of her arm Angie was going to take that away.

'No!' Jo stopped Angie's hand. 'Not his knee! Not his knee!'

Angie struggled, trying to free her arm, to take that final swing.

'Please!' Jo begged. 'Don't! Please!'

Angie looked at the tire iron. Saw her daughter's hand gripping her own. The first time Jo had ever touched her.

'Let's go,' Jo said. 'Let's just go.' She was begging. Her eyes were wild. Blood poured from her nose and mouth. She looked like she didn't know who she was more afraid of: Angie or her husband.

Angie forced the muscles in her arm to relax. She jogged down the driveway, ran down the street. Her shoes were still in the road. Angie scooped them up as she walked by. She was throwing the tire iron in the trunk when Jo caught up with her.

'I need him to play,' she said. 'His next contract—'

'Get in the car.' Angie threw her shoes into the back seat. She didn't want to hear excuses. Even as Jo left, she was planning her way back.

The engine was already running. Angie strapped on her seat belt. Jo got into the car. Angie pulled away before she could close the door.

'He saw me,' Jo said. 'I was trying to—'

'It doesn't matter.' Reuben had recognized Angie. She had seen it in his eyes. He knew she worked for Kip. He knew that she was his fixer. And now he knew that Angie had taken his wife.

Jo reached for her seat belt. The buckle clicked. She stared ahead at the road. 'Do you think he's dead?'

'He passed out.' Angie looked at her watch. How long before Reuben came to? How long before he called Kip and Laslo and Dale?

'What have I done?' Jo mumbled. It was sinking in now, the price she would pay for her disobedience, the cost of returning to her life. 'We have to stop. We can't do this.'

Angie told her, 'I've got the video.'

'What?'

'I have the video of Marcus and Reuben raping that girl.'

'How?' Jo didn't wait for an explanation. 'You can't use it. They'll go to jail. LaDonna—'

'I'm not afraid of LaDonna.'

'You damn well should be.'

Angie swerved into a parking lot. She pulled into a space beside a black Ford Fusion. 'Here's the key.' Angie dropped the sun visor and let the key fall into Jo's lap. 'Go to the motel. Wait for me.'

'We can't do this,' Jo said. 'The video. They'll kill me. They'll kill you.'

'Don't you think I know that?' Angie's fists were clenched. She was overwhelmed with the desire to punch some sense into her child. 'It's over, sweetheart. This is the end of the line. There's no going back to Reuben. There's no going back to anything.'

'I can't—'

'Get out.' Angie leaned over and pushed open the door. She fought with the seat-belt buckle. 'Get out of my car.'

'No!' Jo clawed at Angie's hands. 'He'll find me! You don't understand!' She scanned Angie's face, looking for compassion. When she didn't find it, her face contorted in agony. She covered her eyes with her hands. Sobs came out of her mouth. 'Please don't make me.'

Angie watched her daughter cry. The girl's thin shoulders were shaking. Her hands trembled. The act might be heartbreaking to someone who actually had a heart.

Angie said, 'Cut the shit. I'm not buying it.'

Jo looked up at her. There were no tears in her eyes, just hatred. 'You can't make me do anything.'

'Was he sweet to you?' Angie asked, because that was the only thing that made sense. 'You got out of jail, and instead of beating you, he said everything was going to be okay? That it was going to be different from now on?'

Jo's nostrils flared. Angie had hit the mark.

'Is that how he roped you back in? "Oh baby, I love you. I'll take care of you. I'll never let you go. I'll never abandon you like your mama did."'

'Don't you throw my mama back in my face.'

Angie grabbed Jo's chin and jerked her head around. 'Listen up, you dumb bitch. Reuben saw me. He knows that I'm helping you. You think your mama didn't give a shit about you? That's not even half of what I'm feeling right now.'

Jo's tears were real now.

Angie tightened her grip on the girl's face. 'You're gonna get in that car and you're going to drive to the motel and I'm going to pick up your son and we are both going to get the hell out of here. Do you understand me?'

Jo nodded.

Angie pushed the girl's face away. 'Give me your phone.'

'I dropped it when—'

Angie patted her down. She found the iPhone tucked into Jo's bra. 'Did you tell your mother that I'm going to pick up Anthony?'

Jo nodded again.

'If you're lying to me—' Angie stopped, because there was nothing to do if Jo was lying. 'Get out of the car.'

Jo was too afraid to move. 'He'll find me. He'll find us.'

Angie grabbed the front of her dress and slammed her against the seat. 'You do this right now or I will cut your son into little pieces and mail him back to you.'

'Reuben will give you whatever you want.' Her voice was a shriek. 'He'll pay whatever—'

'Anthony will pay.'

Tears streamed down Jo's face. She had realized that she was out of options. Slowly she nodded, just like Angie knew she would. Women like Jo only ever responded to threats.

Angie said, 'Don't stop to use a pay phone. Don't go back to Rippy's. Get in the car. Drive to the motel. Wait for me.'

Jo got out of the car. She opened the door to the rental. Angie waited for her to drive off, to make sure she went down Piedmont instead of back toward Tuxedo Drive.

Angie rolled down the window. She tossed Jo's iPhone onto the pavement. She resisted the urge to get out of the car and stomp it into the ground.

'I knew it,' she mumbled to herself.

She had known that her daughter was weak. She had known that Jo would try to back down.

Angie ran over the phone with her car three times before she took a left out of the parking lot. She headed toward Peachtree. Jo's mother lived in a fancy condo near Jesus Junction, paid for by Reuben Figaroa. Angie had to be calm when the old woman opened the door. And she had to hurry, because she had no idea whether or not Reuben had regained consciousness.

The first place he would look for Jo was at her mother's.

Angie checked her reflection in the mirror. Her hair was a mess. Her eyeliner was smudged. She used her finger to straighten the line. She couldn't look dangerous when Jo's mother opened the door.

Was she dangerous?

Hell, yes, she was dangerous.

Angie's cell phone rang. The noise filled the car. She reached around to the back seat. She blindly fished her phone from her purse. Too late. The ringing had stopped. She looked at the screen.

MISSED CALL FROM HARDING, DALE.

'Shit.' She'd wasted too much time in the car with Jo. Ten minutes? Fifteen? Reuben was awake. Kip had been notified. Laslo was on the hunt. Dale thought he could talk her in, that she was still a ten-year-old girl he could trick with candy while he rammed his cock up her ass.

Angie's phone made a whistling sound. Dale had sent a text.

She swiped her thumb. A photograph loaded.

Anthony.

Eyes wide. Back pressed up against a blank wall. The long, sharp blade of a hunting knife pressed to his neck.

The word underneath read: GRANDSON.

Angie gasped. She had to pull over. Her heart had stopped beating. Her blood ran cold. Jo's child. Her grandchild. What had she done? Why was this happening?

Another whistle. Another text. Another photo.

Angie's hands were shaking so hard she could barely hold the phone.

Jo.

A hand around her neck. Her back to the window of a car door. Her mouth open, screaming.

Dale's text read: DAUGHTER.

Acid filled Angie's throat, shot up into the back of her nose. She pushed open the door. Her mouth opened. A stream of bile splattered against the pavement. Her stomach turned inside out. She tasted blood and venom.

What had she done? What could she do to stop this?

She sat back up. She wiped her mouth with the back of her hand.

Think, she told herself. *Think.*

Dale had taken Jo. He had taken Anthony, or had someone else do it for him. He had sent Angie two photos, proof of life. The backgrounds were different. Jo was in a car. Anthony was against a painted wall. This was coordinated, planned, because Dale was always two steps ahead of Angie. He had looked into Jo. He had looked into Angie. He had obviously taken a great deal of time to build the web she now found herself trapped in.

She clicked on her phone.

She could already guess the answer, but she still texted the question.

WHAT DO YOU WANT?

Dale responded immediately: IPAD.

Dale had never trusted Angie. Not even with the little things. He must have taken the pieces of the smashed iPad to Sam Vera for examination. Sam had discovered it was not the clone. Dale had asked himself why Angie would go to the trouble of swapping them out. And then he had realized that a video Marcus Rippy wanted to get rid of was worth a hell of a lot more than a quarter of a million dollars in an escrow account.

Nothing had changed since Angie was a child. She thought she was in control, but all the while, Dale was pulling her strings.

Her phone whistled again.

Dale had written: NIGHTCLUB. NOW.

MONDAY, 1:08 AM

Dale's Kia was already parked in front of the club. Delilah leaned against the hood smoking a cigarette.

Angie was out of her car before it came to a full stop. The asphalt was hot against her bare feet. She raised her arm. The gun was in her hand. She pointed it at Delilah and pulled the trigger.

There was a bullet in the chamber this time.

'Fuck!' Delilah doubled over, clutching her leg. Blood squeezed out between her fingers. 'You fucking bitch!'

Angie struggled against the need to pull the trigger again. 'Where is Jo?'

'Fuck you!' Delilah screamed. 'She's fucking dead if you don't do what you're supposed to do!'

'Where is she?' Angie repeated.

'You mean your daughter?' Dale struggled to get out of the car. In the moonlight, his face looked almost completely white.

There were flecks of dried skin around his mouth. His eyes were golden. He leaned heavily on the car. He had a revolver pointed at her across the roof.

'Kill her!' Delilah screamed. 'Blow her fucking brains out.'

'It's just a flesh wound,' Dale said. He was out of breath from getting out of the car. His skin was shiny, but not with sweat. 'Take her gun.'

Angie pointed the Glock at Delilah's head. 'Try it.'

Dale told Angie, 'You shoot her, I shoot you, I still get what I want because I got your daughter and you know what I can do to your grandson.'

Angie's determination wavered. Jo. She had to think about Jo. If she thought about what Dale would do to Anthony, she wouldn't make it through the night.

Dale said, 'Dee, take the gun away from her.'

Delilah limped over. Her hand reached out, but Angie threw the Glock across the parking lot.

'Shit,' Dale said. 'Go get the gun.'

'I don't need no gun.' Delilah flicked open a switchblade and pointed it at Angie's cheek. 'You see how sharp this is, bitch? I can slice open the side of your face like a watermelon.'

'Do it.' Angie looked her cousin in the eye. The same color iris. The same almond shape. The same fiery bluster, except Angie had the balls to back it up. 'If you don't cut me now, then the next time you see that knife, I'll be cutting your eyes out of your head.'

'None of you is doing shit. Put the fucking knife away.' Dale's tone of voice should've been a warning, but Delilah knew he would never hurt her. He said, 'Search the car.' When she didn't move, he said, 'Dee, please. Search the car.'

Delilah slapped the handle against the back of her hand and worked the blade closed.

'Hey.' Dale banged on the roof, waiting for Angie's attention.

She looked at him. Her heart stopped. For just a moment, she forgot why they were here. Dale was dying. Not eventually. Not soon. He was dying right now. She could see the effects of his organs shutting down. His lips were blue. He wasn't blinking. He had stopped sweating. The color of his skin reminded her of the thick, yellowed wax that she had to scrape off the coffee table if she left the candle burning too long. There was no spark in his eyes, just a dull, weary acceptance. Death shadowed every crevice of his heavily lined face.

Angie looked away so that he wouldn't see the tears in her eyes.

He said, 'Deidre Will?'

The alias Angie had written on Jo's birth certificate under MOTHER.

Dale said, 'You didn't think I'd start snooping when you asked for the job at One-Ten?'

Angie wiped her eyes with the back of her hand. Will's ring was still on her finger. She turned it around so that Dale couldn't see it. 'Where is Jo?'

'Good as dead.' Delilah was rummaging around inside Angie's purse. 'I'm gonna stick my knife in that bitch's chest.'

Angie snatched the bag away. She asked Dale, 'Where is Jo? What did you do to her?'

'She's safe for now.' His eyelids were heavy. Saliva pooled into the corners of his mouth. The gun in his hand was held at an angle. 'Whether or not she stays safe depends on what you do.'

Angie repeated, 'Where is she?'

Dale nodded toward the club. The chain on the door had been cut. The only thing that kept Angie from running was Dale's revolver. He would use it. He wouldn't kill her, but he would stop her.

'Dammit!' Delilah yelled. She was rooting around the trunk. She found the go-bag, the bottle of transmission fluid. 'It's not here, Daddy.'

Angie said, 'Is that what you call your husband?'

'Shut up, bitch.'

'Both of you shut up.' Dale asked Angie, 'Where's the iPad?'

'Nowhere you'll ever find it.' Angie had used some of the cash from Dale's trunk to bribe the motel manager again. She remembered thinking if things went sideways, she wanted to make sure Will never found the video.

Dale said, 'You forgetting I have your daughter trussed up like a steer?'

Angie didn't buy the bluff. 'You won't hurt her. She's too valuable.'

'Fig doesn't want her back. Tainted goods. She made her choice.'

Angie knew this wasn't true. Jo had said it herself. Reuben Figaroa didn't lose.

Dale asked, 'What's on the video?'

'More money than you could imagine,' Angie answered. 'We can figure this out together, Dale. People don't have to get hurt.'

He smiled. 'You want to share the cut.'

'Fuck that,' Delilah said. 'Bitch ain't gettin' none of my money.'

'Baby, shut your mouth.' Dale didn't have to raise his voice. Delilah knew there were some things she couldn't get away with.

He told Angie, 'Go get the iPad. Bring it back to me. Then we'll talk.'

Angie tried to bargain with him. 'You're close to the end. I can see it, Dale. You're going to need my help.'

He shrugged, but he had to know he had hours, maybe just minutes, before he was gone.

She said, 'Delilah won't be able to negotiate with Kip. You said it yourself. She'll take a handful of magic beans.'

Delilah started to protest, but Dale stopped her with a look.

'She can't deal with Kip Kilpatrick. He'll eat her for lunch.'

'You think I'm going to leave it to her?'

Angie tasted bile in her mouth. 'Who has Anthony?'

'Your grandson?' Delilah laughed. 'You decrepit old bitch. Got a twelve-year-old grandbaby.'

'He's six, you idiot.' Angie asked Dale. 'Where is he?'

'Don't worry about the kid,' Dale said. 'Worry about yourself.'

'You didn't . . .' Angie's pulse drummed in her throat, pounded in her head. There was only one other person who scared her more than Dale. 'Who did you give him to?'

'Who do you think?' Delilah started to laugh again. Angie kicked her in the knee. The girl screamed as she dropped to the ground.

Dale said, 'Angela,' but it was too late.

She didn't care that he had a gun pointed at her head. Angie ran toward the building. She couldn't move fast enough. Every step seemed to take her farther away. She yanked open the door.

The blackness of the building engulfed her. She couldn't get her bearings. Shadows grew out of the floor.

'Jo?' she yelled. 'Jo, where are you?'

Nothing.

She looked over her shoulder. Delilah had gotten back up. She was running at an awkward gait, her injured leg slowing her down.

Angie went deeper into the building. Trash was everywhere. Shards of glass cut open her bare feet. Her purse snagged on something. The leather tore open. Her eyes started to adjust. Dance floor. Bar at the back. Balcony above. Two darkened windows filtered the moon. There were rooms upstairs.

The front door banged open. Delilah. She was an outline against the shadows. She had the switchblade in her hand.

'Dee!' Dale's voice was faint behind her. 'We need her alive.'

'Fuck that,' Delilah whispered, not to Dale, but to Angie.

Angie crouched down. She searched in vain for something to use against the girl. She was numb to the sensation of her hands being sliced open. Crack pipes. Pacifiers. Condoms. Useless pieces of nothing.

Delilah's shoes crunched across the floor.

Angie looked up. The balcony. The rooms. All of them with doors. Only one of them closed.

She ran toward the stairs. She tripped. Her knee hit the concrete edge of the tread, but she kept going. She had to get to Jo. She had to save her daughter. She had to tell her that she would never threaten Anthony, that he was precious, that she would do whatever she could to protect him, that she would not abandon her grandson to the same fate that Angie had been abandoned to herself.

She was almost to the top of the stairs when her foot slipped out from under her. Angie fell hard against the concrete. Delilah's hand was around her ankle, dragging her down. Angie rolled over, kicking, screaming, trying to shake the girl off.

'Bitch!' Delilah pounced on top of Angie. A sliver of moonlight caught the glint of the switchblade. Angie grabbed Delilah's wrists. The blade was inches from her heart, long and skinny, surgically sharp. Delilah pressed her weight into the handle. Angie felt the tip of the blade touch her skin. Her arms started to shake. Sweat poured off both of them.

'Stop it,' Dale said, his voice still faint.

They couldn't stop. This feud had been going on too long. One of them was going to die. Angie was going to be damned if it was her. Delilah was younger and faster, but Angie had twenty more years of rage inside of her. She pushed Delilah's hands down, moving the blade away from her heart.

It wasn't enough.

Delilah summoned up her last bit of strength and plunged the knife into Angie's belly.

Angie groaned. She had managed to twist at the last minute, taking the blade into her side. She felt the cold hilt of the knife, then Delilah wrenched away the blade and held it over her head, aiming for Angie's heart.

'Stop!' Dale ordered. 'We need her alive!'

Delilah stopped, but she wasn't finished. She slammed the back of Angie's head into the concrete, then ran the rest of the way up the stairs.

Angie couldn't follow her. She saw stars. Literal stars. They exploded behind her eyelids. She threw up in her mouth. She felt the vomit slide back down her throat. She was going to pass out. She couldn't fight it. This was how her life was going to end. Delilah killing Jo. Anthony taken by a monster. Angie choking to death on her own vomit.

Will. She wanted Will to find her. The look of anguish on his face. The knowledge that she had died alone, without him.

A sudden piercing scream shook Angie out of her stupor.

'No!' Jo screamed. 'Stop!'

The sound was visceral, not the way she screamed when Reuben hit her. It was the scream of someone who knew that they were dying.

Angie rolled over. She pushed herself up from the stairs. The sharp pain in her side did not stop her. Dale's staggering footsteps on the stairs below did not stop her. She bolted up the last few steps. She ran across the balcony.

A gun fired. The sound was delayed for a split second. Angie felt the bullet whiz past her head. She heard a chunk of concrete fall to the floor. She turned around.

Dale was sitting on the stairs. His gun was in his lap. Even from twenty yards away, Angie could hear him panting for breath. 'Stop,' he said, but Angie wasn't afraid of him anymore. You only feared for your life when you had something to lose.

Delilah came out of the room. She was covered in blood. She was laughing.

'What did you do?' Angie asked, but she knew what the girl had done.

Delilah clapped together her hands as if she could clean them. 'She's dead, bitch. What're you gonna do now?'

Angie looked at Delilah's empty hands. She had left the knife inside of Jo.

Her only weapon. Her only defense. 'You stupid cunt.' Angie grabbed Delilah by the arm and swung her toward the open balcony.

There was no sound.

Delilah was too terrified to scream. She teetered, almost catching herself, but then she lost her balance. Her hands shot out. She clawed at the air. She finally screamed as she plummeted down.

Her body hit the ground with a sickening crunch.

Angie looked at Dale. He was still sitting. He held his revolver with both hands, taking the time to aim, because he wasn't going to warn her this time. He was going to kill her.

Angie darted into the room. She closed the door behind her. The knob came off in her hand. She pushed against the door. It was latched closed.

'Angie?' Dale said. He had managed to stand. She could hear his feet scuffing the stairs. 'Don't drag this out.'

Angie closed her eyes. She listened. He was out of breath, but he wasn't shuffling. She had locked herself in this room. He had four more shots in his revolver. Four more chances at close range to hit a target a blind man could hit in his sleep.

There was only one thing to do.

Blood cupped Angie's bare feet as she blindly searched the room. She found Jo in the corner. Her body was propped up against the wall. Gently Angie felt for the knife. She found the handle sticking out of Jo's chest.

'Angie,' Dale said. He was closer. He knew he didn't need to rush.

Angie sat down beside her daughter. Cold concrete curled up through the blood-soaked floor. Dale had been killing Angie every day of her life since she was ten years old. She wouldn't let him have the final blow. The knife that killed her daughter would be the knife that killed Angie. She would drive it into her own chest. She would bleed out in this dark, empty room. Dale would open the door and find her already gone.

Slowly Angie reached for the switchblade. Her fingers wrapped around the handle. She started to pull.

Jo groaned.

'Jo?' Angie was on her knees. She was touching Jo's face. Stroking back her hair. 'Talk to me.'

'Anthony,' Jo said.

'He's safe. In my car.'

Jo's breathing was shallow. Her clothes were slick with blood. Delilah had stabbed her over and over again, yet somehow Jo was still breathing, still talking, still fighting to survive.

My daughter, Angie thought. *My girl.*

'I can stand up,' Jo said. 'I just need a minute.'

'It's okay.' Angie reached down for Jo's hand.

It wasn't there.

She felt smooth bone, an open joint. 'Oh God,' Angie breathed.

Jo's hand was nearly severed from her wrist. Only tendon and muscle kept it attached to her body. Angie felt the steady spurt of blood pulsing out of her open artery.

'I can still feel it,' Jo said. 'My fingers. I can move them.'

'I know you can,' Angie lied. A tourniquet. She needed a tourniquet. Her purse had ripped off her shoulder. There was nothing in the room. Jo would bleed to death if she didn't do something.

Jo said, 'Don't leave me.'

'I won't.' Angie took off her underwear. She wrapped the thong around Jo's wrist and pulled as tight as she could.

Jo groaned, but the pulsing blood slowed to a trickle.

Angie tied off the knot. She listened for Dale. She tried to hear his footsteps. There was a low keening. Angie didn't know if it was coming from Jo or from her own mouth.

'Please.' Jo leaned into her. 'Just give me a minute. I'm strong.'

'I know you are.' Angie held her as close as she dared. 'I know you're strong.'

For the first time in her life, Angie cradled her daughter in her arms.

All those years ago, the nurse had asked her if she wanted to hold her baby, but Angie had refused. Refused to name the girl. Refused to sign the legal papers to let her go. Hedging her bets, because that's what she always did. Angie could remember tugging on her jeans before she left the hospital. They were still damp from her water breaking. The waist was baggy where it had been tight, and she had gripped the extra material in her fist as she walked down the back stairs and ran outside to meet the boy waiting in the car around the corner.

Denny, but it didn't matter that it was Denny because it could've been anybody.

There was always a boy waiting for her, expecting something from her, pining for her, hating her. It had been like that for as long as Angie could remember. Ten years old: Dale Harding offering to trade a meal for her mouth. Fifteen: a foster father who liked to cut. Twenty-three: a soldier who waged war on her body. Thirty-four: a cop who convinced her it wasn't rape.

Thirty-seven: another cop who made her think he would love her forever.

Will.

He had said forever in Mrs Flannigan's basement. He had said forever when he put the sunflower ring on her finger.

Forever was never as long as you thought it was.

Angie touched her fingers to Jo's lips. Cold. The girl was losing too much blood. The handle of the blade sticking out of her chest pulsed against her heart, sometimes like a metronome, sometimes like the stuck second hand on a clock that was winding down.

All those lost years.

Angie should've held her daughter at the hospital. Just that once. She should've imprinted some memory of her touch so that her daughter didn't flinch the way she did now, moving away from her hand the way she would move away from a stranger's.

They *were* strangers.

Angie shook her head. She couldn't go down the rabbit hole of everything she had lost and why. She had to think about how strong she was, that she was a survivor. Angie had spent her life running on the edge of a razor—sprinting away from the things that people usually ran toward: a child, a husband, a home, a life.

Happiness. Contentment. Love.

All the things Will wanted. All the things Angie had thought she would never need.

She realized now that all of her running had led her straight to this dark room, trapped in this dark place, holding her daughter for the first time, for the last time, as the girl bled to death in her arms.

There was a scuffing noise outside the closed door. The slit of light at the threshold showed the shadow of two feet slithering along the floor.

Angie closed her eyes again. Dale had done the same thing when she was ten years old. Stood outside the closed door to Deidre's apartment. Waited for Angie to open up. Deidre never hesitated to open the door. She didn't care who was on the other side so long as he could bring a needle full of heroin closer to her arm.

Her daughter's would-be killer?

Her own murderer?

Open the door and let him in.

'Angela,' Dale said, the same now as he had then.

The door rattled in the frame. There was a scraping sound. Metal against metal. The square of light narrowed, then disappeared, as a screwdriver was jammed into the opening.

Click-click-click, like the dry fire of an empty gun.

Gently Angie eased Jo's head to the floor. The girl groaned with pain. She was still alive, still holding on.

Angie crawled around the dark room, ignoring the chalky grit of sawdust and metal shavings grinding into her knees, the stabbing pain beneath her ribs, the steady flow of blood that left a trail behind her. She found screws and nails and then her hand brushed against something cold and round and metal. She picked up the object. In the darkness, her fingers told her what she was holding: the broken doorknob. Solid. Heavy. The four-inch spindle stuck out like an ice pick.

There was a final click of the latch engaging. The screwdriver clattered to the concrete floor. The door cracked open.

Angie stood up. She pressed her back to the wall beside the door. She thought about all the ways she had hurt the men in her life. Once with a gun. Once with a needle. Countless times with her fists. With her mouth. With her teeth. With her heart.

The door opened a few more careful inches. The tip of a gun snaked around the corner.

She gripped the doorknob so that the spindle shot out between her fingers, and waited for Dale to come in.

'Angela?' he said. 'I'm not going to hurt you.'

The last time he would ever tell her that lie.

She grabbed Dale's wrist and pulled him into the room. He stumbled, twisting around. Moonlight played across his face. He looked surprised. He should've been surprised. Forty years of tricking out little girls and not one of them had ever turned on him.

Until now.

Angie drove the doorknob into the side of his neck. She felt the resistance as the rusty spindle tore through cartilage and sinew.

Dale's breath hissed out. She tasted the decay from his rotting body.

He fell back onto the floor.

Blood splashed the front of her legs.

His arms flopped open. His lips parted. His eyes were closed. One last breath seeped out, not a snake hissing, but a tire slowly deflating. The moon had shifted outside the windows. A long shadow crept into the room, caressing Dale's body in darkness. Hell had sent a minion to claim his miserable soul.

'Angela.'

The name snapped Angie out of her daze. She had never told Jo her name. She was using the name that Dale had called her.

'Angela,' Jo repeated. She was sitting up. She held the knife steady with her hand. 'I want to see my boy.'

Anthony. Christ, what was she going to do about Anthony?

'Help me up.' Jo struggled to stand.

Angie rushed over to help. She couldn't believe the strength left in the girl.

Jo said, 'I need to see my boy. I have to tell him—'

'You will.' Angie ignored her own pain as she helped raise Jo up. They both staggered a few steps before Jo walked forward on her own. Angie could see the knife now, pushed in to the hilt. Jo's hand was dangling from her arm. The tourniquet had slipped. Blood spurted out, flicking across Dale's body. More blood covered the floor. Jo slumped against the wall.

Jo said, 'Just give me a second. I can do this.' She couldn't do it. She slid to the floor. Angie ran to catch her, but it was too late. Jo slumped to the ground. Her eyes closed. Her face went slack. Her lips still moved. 'I can do this.'

Angie made her cop training take over. Basic triage. No time for an ambulance. She had to find a way to slow the bleeding again or Jo would never make it down the stairs. There was the tarp in her car. Duct tape. She took a step, then stopped. This was a crime scene. Two sets of footprints, two suspects. Angie had her HAIX police boots in the car. Reuben Figaroa would be looking for his wife. His son. Angie needed to cover Jo's tracks. Dale's car. The bricks of cash in the trunk. Delilah's credit cards. The APD. The GBI.

Will.

Rippy was his case. He would be called here. He would find Dale. He would find a lake of blood. Angie knew him. She knew how his mind worked. He wouldn't stop digging until he had buried them all in a grave.

'Angela,' Jo whispered. 'Is it Anthony?'

Zzzt. Zzzt.

Dale's phone was vibrating in his pocket.

Jo said, 'Is it my boy? Is he calling?'

Jo's boy was being held by someone who had him pressed against a wall, a hunting knife to his neck.

Angie flipped open Dale's phone. She pressed it to her ear. There were sounds: a child crying, a cartoon playing too loud.

A woman said, 'Hey, asshole, I'm losing my patience here. You want this little boy or should I sell him for parts?'

Fire burned its way into the pit of Angie's stomach. She was ten years old again. Frightened, alone, willing to do anything to make the pain go away.

'Dale?' The woman waited. 'You there?'

'Mama?' Angie's ten-year-old voice came back into her mouth. 'Is that you?'

She laughed her low, husky laugh. 'Yeah, it's me, baby. Did you miss me?'

Present Day

NINE

Will pressed his phone tight against his ear. He heard Angie's voice echo in his head.

It's me, baby. Did you miss me?

Was this the Xanax? Will looked at his phone. CALLER ID BLOCKED. He sat up. He looked around the chapel like Angie might be there. Watching him. Laughing at him. He felt his mouth moving. He didn't hear any words coming out.

'Will?' Her teasing tone was gone. 'You okay, baby? Take a breath.'

Take a breath.

Sara had said the same thing to him downstairs. Except this time, he wasn't having a panic attack. He was filled with a blinding, uncontrollable rage. 'You fucking bitch.'

She laughed. 'That's more like it.'

Rippy's club. Angie's purse. Her gun. Her car. Her blood. And now the body in the funeral home with her wedding ring.

She had set him up. She had gotten herself into trouble, and whatever way she'd managed to claw her way out had presented an opportunity for her to fuck with his head.

He said it again. 'You fucking bitch.'

She laughed at him again.

Will would've punched her in the throat if she were standing in front of him. He would find her. He would do whatever it took to track her down and strangle the life out of her worthless body.

The chapel door opened. Faith walked in.

Will took in gulps of air, trying to swallow down his fury. His outrage. His resentment.

Faith opened her mouth to ask him what was wrong.

He motioned for her to be quiet, saying into the phone, 'Angie, why did you do this to me?'

Faith's jaw dropped. She froze in place.

'Why?' Will demanded. 'You faked that scene at Rippy's club. You made me think you were dead. You made me think it was your body in the basement. Why?'

Angie was silent, though she'd had an entire day to contemplate her answer.

'Angie—' Will's voice cracked. He felt raw, desperate to hear an explanation. 'Tell me, God dammit. Why did you put me through this? Why?'

Angie drew out a long, exasperated sigh. 'Why do I do anything?' She rattled off some familiar answers. 'I'm a fucking bitch. I want to ruin your life. I make you miserable. I don't know what you look like when you're in love because you've never been in love with me.'

Will turned away from Faith, afraid to show her how much he could hate somebody. 'That's not good enough.'

'It'll have to do for now.'

He couldn't handle this. He was going to crack, end up dead on the floor, if he let himself feel all the things that were boiling up inside of him. He tried to think like an agent, not a human being who had just been skull-fucked by a psychopath. 'Whose body is in the basement?'

'Not yet,' Angie said. 'First tell me what it felt like when you thought I was dead.'

Will forced his fingers not to crush the phone. 'What do you think it felt like?'

'I want you to tell me.' She waited for him to speak. 'Tell me how you felt, and I'll tell you who's in the basement.'

'I can find out myself,' he said. 'We're running her prints right now.'

'Too bad her finger pads are cracked open.'

'We can get DNA.'

'She won't be in the system.' Angie said, 'You've been working this case. Other cases, too. What if I told you I could break everything wide open right now, only all you have to do is tell me how you feel?'

'I don't want your help.'

'Sure you do. Remember how I helped you the last time? I know you were grateful then.'

Will couldn't have that conversation in front of Faith. 'Did you kill Dale Harding?'

'Why would I confess to murder now?'

Will felt exhaustion pulling at him like a sickness. 'Now, as in not like the other times?'

'Careful, baby.'

He covered his face with his hand. This wasn't happening. She had hurt other people like this, but never him. He couldn't stop asking, 'Why? Why did you do this?'

'I wanted you to know what it would feel like to really lose me.' She was silent for a few beats. 'I saw you today. Don't ask me where. The look on your face when you thought I was really dead. I bet you wouldn't miss Sara that way.'

'Don't say her name.'

'Sara,' Angie repeated, because she would not be told what to do. 'I saw you, Will. I know that look. I saw it when you were a kid. I saw it last year. I know who you are. I know you better than anybody else on earth.'

The letter. She was quoting from her own letter. 'Who's in the basement?'

'Does it matter?'

Will didn't know what mattered. Nothing mattered. Why had she done this to him? He had only ever loved her. Taken care of her. Made sure she was safe. She had never done that for him. Not now. Not ever.

She asked, 'Has Faith managed to get a ping on me yet?'

Will turned around. Faith was on her phone, probably requesting a trace.

'Josephine Figaroa,' Angie said.

'What?'

'The girl in the basement. Josephine Figaroa. My daughter. Your daughter. Our child, together.' She paused. 'Dead.'

Will felt his mouth open. His heart was shaking so hard that he had to sit down. A child. Their child. Their baby. 'Angie,' he said. 'Angie.'

There was no response. She'd ended the call.

He put his hand to his mouth. His breath was cold against his palm. Angie had killed him from the inside, slicing into his heart with a surgeon's precision. A child. A daughter. His fucked-up genes inside of her.

And now she was dead.

Faith knelt beside him. 'Will?'

He couldn't speak. He could only think about a little girl sitting at the back of a classroom struggling to follow what the teacher said because her stupid father couldn't teach her how to read.

She would have ended up trapped in the system, the same as Will. Abandoned, the same as Will.

How could Angie be so cruel?

'Will,' Faith repeated. 'What did she say?'

'Josephine Figaroa.' He had to force the name out. 'In the basement. Angie's daughter. Josephine Figaroa. That's her name.'

'The basketball player's wife?' Faith rubbed his back. 'We'll deal with that in a minute. Do you need me to get Sara?'

'No,' he said, but Sara was already coming through the door behind them. Amanda was with her. They both looked worried.

And then Faith told them about Angie's phone call and they looked furious.

'What?' Sara demanded. 'What?' She couldn't stop saying the word.

Amanda gripped the side of the podium. She spoke through gritted teeth. 'Did you run a trace?'

Faith said, 'We couldn't lock in. She must've timed it.'

'God dammit.' Amanda looked down at the floor. She took a shallow breath. When she looked back up, her game face was on. 'Did we get a phone number?'

'It's blocked, but we can pull it on—'

'I'm on it.' Amanda started working her BlackBerry. 'Was Charlie able to match the fingerprints?'

'No,' Faith said. 'Her finger pads were too—'

'Cracked,' Will said. 'Angie knew that. She said the DNA won't be in the system.'

Sara said, 'Angie's blood type was at the scene.' She kept shaking her head, completely baffled. 'Her purse. Her gun. I don't understand. Why would she do this?'

Faith asked, 'Would Angie's daughter have the same blood type?'

Sara didn't answer. She was shell-shocked, the same as she'd been this morning.

'Daughter?' Amanda asked.

Will couldn't answer.

Amanda asked, 'In the interest of futility, did Angie mention why she did all of this?'

'She's a monster,' Will said, the same words that people had been saying about her for over thirty years. At the children's home. At foster homes. At the police station. Will never argued them down, but he never believed them either. They didn't know

Angie. They didn't know the hell she had been through. They didn't know that sometimes the pain was so bad that the only thing that made you feel better was lashing out at other people.

She had never lashed out at Will before. Not like this.

'If it really is Josephine Figaroa, we'll have fresh prints in the system,' Faith said. 'She was arrested last Thursday. She had Oxy in her car. I saw it on the news.'

Amanda asked, 'Angie said this woman is her daughter?'

'Yes.' Will couldn't tell them that Josephine was his daughter too. He had to get some clarity. He needed time to think. Angie had lied about so many things. Why should he trust her now?

'Figaroa,' Amanda said. 'Why does that name sound familiar?'

'Her husband is Reuben Figaroa. He's a basketball player.'

'Marcus Rippy.' Amanda spat out the name like a bad taste in her mouth. 'This entire day has been a giant circle leading directly back to him.'

Will stood up. 'The patrol car can access footage from the street cameras.'

He didn't wait for a response. He jogged up the aisle. He was outside and in the parking lot by the time they exited the building. Will pulled open the cruiser's passenger-side door and got into the car. The uni gave a startled bark.

Will pointed to the laptop mounted on the dash. 'I need the footage from every camera in the area.'

'I was just pulling that up for your boss.' The uni punched some keys. 'These are the ones you want to see. I got two different angles, one from the street that runs in front of the funeral home, one that runs along the back.'

Faith opened the back door and slid into the car.

Amanda knelt beside Will. She told the uni, 'Dunlop, tell me you found something.'

'Yes, ma'am.' Dunlop pointed to the screen. 'This is right after the funeral van left at eight twenty-two.'

The prank call for a bogus body pick-up. Not a joke from another mortuary student, but a ruse to get Belcamino out of the building.

'This is where the car first comes in.' Dunlop turned the laptop around. Will saw the street corner, the rear entrance to the service alley. The night vision was fuzzy. The street lights weren't helping. At 8:24:32, Angie's black Monte Carlo SS turned into the alley that ran behind the funeral home. The driver's face was a blob. A flash of blonde hair under a black hoodie. The car disappeared from the camera's view as it rolled up the paved alley.

Will hit the arrow key, fast-forwarding the video to pick up the car again. Six minutes passed before the Monte Carlo drove back down the service alley and turned onto the street.

Faith said, 'She went to the back door where the elevator is. She came back out. Six minutes is enough time to put a body in the freezer.'

Dunlop reached over and tapped some keys. 'It picks up again here on the front street view.'

The Monte Carlo turned into the lot, using the entrance that was fifteen feet away from where they were. Angie's car glided into the handicapped parking space. The driver got out. The roof of the car was about four and a half feet off the ground. The woman was around five-eight, close to Angie's height. She was overweight, not like Angie, or maybe she had bulked up her clothes. The long-sleeved hoodie must have been sweltering, but she kept the hood on, head down, hands deep in her pockets as she walked up the street.

Faith asked, 'Is it Angie?'

Will shook his head. He was out of the identifying Angie business.

'Could be Delilah Palmer,' Faith guessed. 'Blonde hair, but Delilah changed her hair a lot.'

Amanda said, 'Dunlop, where do you pick her up next?'

'Nowhere. She's either lucky or she knows the cameras.' He tapped another few keys. He fast-forwarded and reversed through several different street angles before giving up. 'She could've walked under the bridge, jumped into a car on the interstate. Headed up to Tech. Downtown. There are lots of blind spots where she could'a parked another car or had somebody waiting for her. Hell . . .' He shrugged. 'She could've jumped on a bus.'

'Check the buses,' Will said, because that sounded like something Angie would do. Or maybe not. He was the last person who could predict her behavior.

Amanda's knees popped as she stood up. 'Tell me about this Josephine Figaroa.'

'Basketball wife.' Faith got out of the car. 'Oxy. That's all I know.'

Will said, 'The husband. Reuben "Fig" Figaroa, one of Marcus Rippy's alibi witnesses for the night of the rape. He's a power forward. Very physical. Rebounds well on defense. Kip Kilpatrick's client.'

'This hole just keeps getting deeper,' Amanda said.

'Here's her DL.' Faith showed them her phone. She had pulled up Josephine Figaroa's driver's license.

Will studied the photo. Dark hair. Thin and tall. Almond-shaped eyes. Olive skin. She looked like Angie from twenty years ago.

Did she look like Will? Did she have his height? Did she have his problems?

Amanda said, 'Inasmuch as you can tell anything, the photo resembles the woman in the basement.'

Faith said, 'She's a carbon copy of Angie.'

Will said nothing.

'You two.' Amanda waved over Collier and his partner. They had been so quiet that Will had forgotten they were there. 'Ng. Take off those stupid sunglasses. I put you on missing person reports. Josephine Figaroa. Did she come up?'

'Fig's wife?' His face was small without the glasses. 'No, she wasn't in any of my searches. I would recognize the name.'

Amanda told Faith, 'You'll come with me to talk to the husband. See if we can get an ID, figure out whether or not the wife is missing in the first place. I don't trust Angie as far as I can throw her, and believe me, if she was here, I would throw her.'

Collier said, 'The wife's a pill popper. She did a two-day stint in the Fulton lockup. Got out Saturday. Supposed to be going to rehab this morning.'

'And now she's at a funeral home with knife wounds in her chest.' Amanda tucked her hands into her hips. 'I don't trust any of this. Angie's misdirecting us for a reason. She's buying time so she can make her play.'

'What's the play?' Collier asked. 'This is a lot of dead bodies for a game.'

Amanda said, 'It's only a game to *her*.'

'Josephine has a kid.' Faith held up her phone again. 'I found the husband's Facebook page. Anthony. Six years old.'

Anthony. Jo Figaroa's son. Angie's daughter. Will's grandson?

The picture showed a small boy with a furtive smile.

'Look at the shape of his eyes,' Faith said. 'Those are some strong genes.'

Were they Will's genes, too?

1989. Angie was stuck in a group home with over a dozen other kids.

Except for that time when she wasn't.

Faith said, 'There's not a missing six-year-old white boy on the wire. We'd know about it immediately.'

Ng said, 'That's for damn sure.'

'Collier,' Amanda said. 'What's your progress on locating Delilah Palmer?'

'I was gonna tell you before. We found her rental car abandoned in Lakewood. Wiped clean.'

'Dammit, Collier!' Faith slammed her hand on the trunk of the cruiser. 'You found her car? I have to hear about your God damm gas station hot dogs but you can't text me when—'

Will realized that Sara had disappeared.

He scanned the front of the building, the lawn, the parking lot. He walked toward the street. She was behind her BMW, leaning against the bumper, staring into the distance. The overhead light put a halo around her. Her expression was unreadable. He didn't know if she was upset or concerned or afraid or furious.

They were ending the day exactly the same way they had started it.

Will walked away from the noise and the screaming and maybe even his job, because he didn't care about any of them anymore.

He told Sara, 'Let's go home.'

She gave him the keys. He opened the passenger door for her, then walked around the front and got behind the wheel. He was backing out of the space when she took his hand. Will felt his heart lift in his chest. This wasn't the Xanax. Sara's presence soothed him. Earlier tonight, she had been willing to walk away from him—not to hurt him, but because she only ever wanted what was best for him.

He said, 'I don't think I can talk about any of this right now.'

She squeezed his hand. 'Then we won't.'

Tuesday

TEN

Faith paged through her notebook as Amanda drove them to Reuben Figaroa's house. Her columns were hardly worth reviewing. Will had been right when he'd told her there wasn't a case to be built. Faith saw what he had seen: a bunch of arrows, a bunch of unanswered questions. Nothing added up, even when you threw in the name Josephine Figaroa. The dead woman was just another arrow that indirectly led back to Marcus Rippy.

Maybe she should try to link them to Angie.

Her eyes started to blur. She looked up, blinking to clear her vision. The streets of Buckhead were deserted. It was almost one in the morning. Faith had been dead asleep in front of the television when Amanda had called her to the funeral home. She could barely recall dropping Emma off at her mother's house. She was so exhausted that her brain hurt, but this was the job. There was no such thing as a reasonable hour to notify a man that his wife was dead.

Not that Faith was absolutely certain that the woman at the funeral home was Jo Figaroa. She certainly *could be* the woman in the driver's license photo, but Angie's involvement skewed everything. Faith's policy toward liars was to always discount everything they said, no matter how much sense their story made. It wasn't easy. The human brain had an annoying need to give people the benefit of the doubt. Especially people you cared about.

For instance, Faith was trusting Will when he said that Angie hadn't told him anything else important, even though he had spent a hell of a lot of time on the phone with her just to be told a victim's name.

Amanda said, 'Your mother used to pin her notes up on the wall so that we could see all the moving pieces.'

Faith smiled. The pinholes were still there. 'Do you think that Jo Figaroa is Angie's daughter?'

'Yes.'

'Who's the father?' She didn't get an answer, so she suggested the obvious one. 'Will?'

'I'm not so sure about that.' Amanda slowed the car. She pulled over to the side of the road. She put the gear in park. She turned to Faith. 'Tell me what you know about Denny.'

'Denny?' Faith shook her head. 'Who's Denny?'

'Short for Holden,' Amanda explained. 'Though Denny is two syllables. Holden is two syllables. I suppose that means it's not short, just less pretentious.'

Faith was too tired for semantics. 'Let's just stick with Collier.'

'Start from the beginning. What did he do? How did he present himself?'

Faith had to pause for a moment so that she could put together her day. It seemed like an eternity had passed since she'd picked up Will at the animal clinic this morning, which was technically yesterday morning because it was past midnight.

She told Amanda about the first meeting with Collier and Ng outside Rippy's club, the interminable amount of time she'd spent with him at Dale Harding's, the texts that told her nothing, the tedious observations about his personal life, the constant sexual innuendo, the reluctance to carry on an adult conversation about the case.

'I don't trust him,' Faith admitted. 'He keeps pushing this Mexican heroin cartel angle. He didn't tell me about finding Delilah's car, but he told me about every useless whore he talked to in Lakewood.'

Amanda confirmed, 'Ng said that they were handling a domestic call when they got routed to the nightclub?'

Faith strained to recall his exact words. 'He said it was pretty violent, which means they were probably at the hospital. Grady is close to Rippy's club, about a ten-minute drive at that time of morning. It would make sense for them to take the call.'

'The nine-one-one came in at five AM,' Amanda reminded her. 'Would you volunteer to investigate a dead body at a warehouse at the end of your shift?'

Faith shrugged. 'Dead cop. The unis recognized Harding. You'd push your shift for a cop.'

'True,' Amanda agreed. 'What else is bothering you about him?'

Faith struggled to articulate her gut feeling. 'He keeps showing up. He was with Will when he found the Jane Doe in the office building. He drove him home. He was there tonight at the funeral home. What was he doing there?'

'Collier and Ng are our APD liaisons. They're working parts of the case. It makes sense that he'd get the call about the car.'

'I guess.' Faith tried to pluck out the obvious answer. 'Maybe Collier's just an idiot who keeps falling up. His dad was on the job. He's obviously got some juice.'

Amanda said, 'Milton Collier was on the job for two years. He took a fifty-one off a twenty-four, lost two fingers before he could call a sixty-three.'

Faith accessed her arcane knowledge of ten-codes from Amanda's soup-can-and-string days. Collier's dad had been stabbed by a crazy person and lost some fingers before backup arrived. She asked Amanda, 'And?'

'Milton clocked out on a medical disability. The wife was a schoolteacher. They made ends meet by taking in foster kids. Dozens at a time. Collier was one of them. Eventually they adopted him.'

'Huh,' Faith said, because Collier had overshared just about everything, down to his twisted nut sack in high school, but he hadn't mentioned that he'd been in the system the same as Delilah Palmer.

The same as Angie, too.

Faith asked, 'Were Collier and Angie ever in the same home together, like when she was sixteen years old and pregnant?'

'That's an interesting question, isn't it?' Amanda didn't give the answer, but Faith knew she would find out. Amanda asked, 'What else did Angie say on the phone call with Will?'

'It was brief,' she lied, because the call had lasted just under three minutes. 'I'm sure she spent some time taunting him.'

'Why is that, do you think?'

'Because she's a terrible human being.'

Amanda gave her a sharp look. 'She's cunning is what she is. Look at our day. Angie had us running around in circles. East Atlanta. Lakewood. North Atlanta. Will was all over midtown. You were stuck at Harding's. I was at Kilpatrick's. What's more, Angie has knocked Will out of the equation, which shows brilliant strategy. Will knows her intimately. He could be our best ally in helping us figure out what Angie is really up to, but she has rendered him completely useless. You saw how he was in the basement.'

Faith had seen how broken Will had been, and what's more, she hadn't been able to take it. He had been making a weird whooping sound, like he couldn't catch his breath. Faith ran from the room so that he wouldn't see her crying.

She asked Amanda, 'You think Angie's fucking with him so that he won't figure out what she's really up to?'

'If I were teaching a class on mind games, that play would be part of my curriculum.'

God knew Amanda could play some mind games. 'Okay, Angie's screwing with him. To what end?'

'She's buying time.'

'For what?'

'That's the sixty-four-thousand-dollar question, isn't it? What exactly is Angie Polaski up to?'

Faith didn't think she would ever find the answer. She was so tired and so stressed out that she doubted she could tie her own shoes right now, let alone figure out why Angie Polaski did the awful things she did.

Amanda said, 'Walk me through it.'

Reluctantly, Faith looked down at her notes again. 'Harding is murdered Sunday night. Angie stages the scene to make it look like she, Angie, was murdered, but it's actually Jo Figaroa, who probably shares her mother, Angie's, rare blood type, B-negative.'

'Hm.' For once, Amanda hadn't been ahead of her. 'Do you think Angie murdered Jo?'

Faith wasn't sure. 'She's a monster, but I can't see her killing her own child.'

'Neither can I, but Harding could have killed Jo, then Angie killed Harding. Or tried to, with the doorknob.' Amanda asked, 'What happened next?'

'Angie takes the body out of the club. She torches Dale's car, which sounds like something Angie would do if she was pissed off, and she'd be pissed off if Dale killed her kid.' Faith couldn't even contemplate a real-life scenario with her own children. There would be salt in the ground for a thousand years. 'The nine-one-one comes in Monday morning at five. Then Monday night, Angie hands us Jo's body at the funeral home and calls Will to torture him.'

'Sara puts Josephine's time of death around noon to one.'

'That's un-Sara-like specificity.' Faith scribbled the time in the margins. She realized, 'If Josephine died between noon and one, that means Angie had her in the trunk of her car until she left the body at the funeral home just before eight thirty PM.'

'There was a lot of blood in the back seat, all type B-negative, and a little blood in the trunk that Sara says could have been left post mortem from the chest wound.'

Faith shivered at the coldness it would take to drive around with your own child bleeding to death in the back of your car.

'It's a timing issue,' Amanda said. 'Angie is dragging out the clock. That's why she waited so long to get rid of the body.'

'Or something changed in her plan,' Faith guessed, but she really had no idea. She saw Amanda's earlier logic, because Will was the one person who could probably figure out what Angie was thinking. He knew her motivations. He knew what she was capable of. But it wasn't just Will she was fucking with. 'Angie's worked murder cases before. She knows what it's like. All the blood and violence freaks you out no matter how many times you've seen it. You're panicked you're going to miss something. You can't turn off your brain. You can't sleep, even when there's time. Throw in the emotional angle and she's basically put us in Gitmo.'

Amanda said, 'I'll say what I said this morning: we're missing something big.'

'Maybe Reuben Figaroa can offer an explanation.' She closed her notebook. All of the sense was gone. Her notes looked like one of Emma's coloring projects. 'I'll never get back to sleep after this. I could use one of your Xanax.' She looked up at Amanda. 'What are you doing carrying around Xanax, anyway?'

'Just a little trick from the old days.' Amanda turned back to the steering wheel. 'You have a suspect who's too jumpy to talk, you crush half a pill into his coffee. He gets a little loosey-goosey and you have him sign on the dotted line.'

'I can think of sixteen different ways that's illegal.'

'Only sixteen?' Amanda chuckled as she pulled back onto the road. 'Talk to your mother. She's the one who came up with it.'

Faith could see her mother doing this in the seventies, but she couldn't see Amanda doing it now, which meant that she'd dodged another question. Pressing her was not a mountain Faith was prepared to climb. 'How are we going to approach Reuben? Is this a death notification or an interrogation? His wife has been missing since at least Sunday night. He hasn't filed a report.'

'We should handle this just as we would handle any suspicious death of a spouse.' Amanda reminded her, 'The husband is the first suspect. More women are murdered by their intimate partners than by any other group.'

'Why do you think I stopped dating?'

The comment was meant as a joke, but Amanda cut her a side-look. 'Don't let this job turn you off men, Faith.'

Faith studied Amanda. This was the second time in as many days that she had tried to give her dating advice. 'Where is this coming from?'

'Experience,' Amanda said. 'Take it from a woman who has been doing this job for a very long time. It's simple statistics. Men commit the most violent crimes. Everyone knows that, but not everyone sees it played out in the real world every single day like you and I do. Remind yourself that Will is a good man. At least when he's not being pig-headed. Charlie Reed is exceptional—not that you should repeat that. Your thing with Emma's father didn't work out, but he's still a good guy. Your father was a saint. Your brother can be an ass, but he would do anything for you. Jeremy is perfect in every way. Your Uncle Kenny is—'

'A cheater and a womanizer?'

'Don't miss the forest for the trees, Faith. Kenny adores you. He's still a good person. It just didn't work out for us. But there's someone out there who could work out for you. Don't let the job tell you otherwise.' She tapped her foot on the brake. 'What was the street number?'

Faith hadn't realized they were already on Cherokee Drive. She pointed to a large stone mailbox a few houses down from the country club. 'There.'

Amanda turned into the driveway. An enormous black gate blocked her progress. She pressed the button on the security key-pad. She waved at the security camera discreetly mounted in the tall bushes that blocked the view of the house from the road.

The Figaroas obviously valued their privacy. Faith guessed there was enough front yard for a football field. Still, she could make out the glimmer of lights on the bottom floor. 'They're already awake. Do you think the press got wind of this?'

'If they did, we have a small pool of suspects who could've leaked the news.'

Collier again. He was the proverbial bad penny. If he knew Angie, did that mean he knew Dale Harding? And if Harding and Angie were the types of cops that Holden Collier kept company with, what did that say about Collier?

Faith was a big believer in guilt by association.

She asked Amanda, 'Have you ever heard of a woman named Virginia Souza?'

Amanda shook her head.

'Collier mentioned her before.' Faith found her phone in her pocket. She read back through his texts, looking for the woman's name. 'Virginia Souza. Collier tracked her down because she worked Delilah's corner, so they probably had the same pimp. Family said she OD'd six months ago, but that's from Collier, and I don't trust Collier because he's a lying liar.'

'You sound so much like your mother sometimes.'

'I wish I could tell whether or not that was a compliment.' Faith searched the state database for Virginia Souza's rap sheet. 'Here we go. Fifty-seven years old, which is a bit long in the tooth for a whore. Prostitution times a thousand, going back to the late seventies. Child endangerment. Child neglect. Accessory to the exploitation of a child. None of which Collier mentioned.' Faith felt a cramp in her thumb as she paged through the woman's sordid criminal history. 'Several drunk and disorderlies. Shoplifting. No drug violations, which is odd since the family said she OD'd six months ago. Or Collier said the family said she OD'd six months ago. Two assaults, both on minors—Collier told me about those. Suspect in the kidnapping of a minor. Suspect in another exploitation. She really has a thing for kids. Known aliases: Souz, Souzie, Ginny, Gin, Mama.'

'Mama in charge,' Amanda said, using the colloquialism for a pimp's right-hand woman. 'She's a bottom girl.'

'Makes sense, considering her age and her sheet. All these assaults on kids, that could be her doing the pimp's job, keeping the stable in line.'

'What is taking these people so long?' Amanda pressed the buzzer on the gate a second time, keeping her finger down long enough to make it clear she wasn't going to go away. 'Do you have a phone number?'

Faith was about to look when the gates started to open.

'Finally,' Amanda said.

The driveway curved to the left, leading them toward a detached six-car garage at the rear corner of the house. Amanda pulled into the motorcourt, parking beside a Tesla SUV. Striping had turned the pavement into a miniature basketball court with a goal set low enough to indicate Reuben Figaroa had built out the space for his six-year-old son.

'Kip Kilpatrick,' Amanda said.

Faith saw the agent standing in an open doorway. His suit was so shiny that it caught the security lights. He had a bottle of bright red sports drink in his hands that he tossed back and forth as he watched the car pull up. Will had underestimated the man's doucheness. Faith could smell it coming off him like damp in a basement.

Amanda said, 'Here we go.'

They both got out of the car. Amanda walked toward Kilpatrick. Faith glanced through the windows in the garage doors. Two Ferraris, a Porsche, and in the last bay a charcoal-gray Range Rover, the same type of vehicle that was leased to Jo Figaroa.

Amanda said, 'Mr Kilpatrick, what a pleasure to see you twice in the same day.'

He looked at his watch. 'It's technically two days. Any particular reason you're out this late visiting another client of mine?'

'Why don't we discuss that inside with Mr Figaroa?'

'Why don't we discuss that outside with me?'

'I find it odd that you're even here, Mr Kilpatrick. Are you making a late house call?'

'You've got five seconds to either explain why you're here or to get off Mr Figaroa's property.'

Amanda paused a moment to let some of the power shift. 'I'm looking for Josephine Figaroa, actually. She seems to be missing.'

'She's in rehab,' he said. 'Left this morning. Packed her into the car myself.'

'Can you tell me the name of the facility?'

'No.'

'Can you tell me when she'll return?'

'Nope.'

Amanda seldom hit walls, but Faith could see that she had found herself flat against Kilpatrick's denials. She finally laid down the truth. 'Two hours ago, a body was found that was identified as Josephine Figaroa.'

Kilpatrick dropped the bottle, which exploded against the pavement. Red liquid splashed all over the ground, his feet, his pants. He didn't move. He barely registered the mess. He was genuinely astonished.

Amanda said, 'We need Mr Figaroa to positively ID the body.'

'What?' Kilpatrick started shaking his head. 'How did . . . What?'

'Do you need a minute?'

He looked at the ground, noticed the spilled drink. 'Are you sure?' He shook his head, and Faith could practically hear him coaching himself into putting his lawyer face back on. 'I can do the ID. Where should I meet you?'

'We have a photo, but it's—'

'Show me.'

Amanda already had her BlackBerry out. She showed him the picture she had taken of the woman's face.

Kilpatrick flinched. 'Jesus Christ. What happened to her?'

'That's what we're here to find out.'

'Christ.' He wiped his mouth with his sleeve. 'Christ.'

A shadow passed over the doorway, impossibly ominous, like a monster in a storybook.

Reuben Figaroa came outside, careful not to get his shoes wet. He wore a badly wrinkled gray suit with a blue shirt and black tie. Shaved head. Dark mustache and goatee. He was shockingly tall, his head nearly brushing the door frame. He also had a paddle holster with a striker-fired Sig Sauer P320 clipped to his black leather belt. He wore the gun to the front and looked more than capable of using it.

Amanda said, 'Mr Figaroa, could we please speak with you?'

Reuben held out his hand, which was three times the size of Amanda's. 'Let me see the picture.'

'No, man,' Kilpatrick warned. 'You don't want to see that. Trust me.'

Amanda gave Reuben her BlackBerry. The phone looked as small as a pack of gum in his enormous hand. He held the screen close to his face, head tilted as he studied the image. Faith was used to Will's height, but comparatively, Reuben was a giant. Everything about him was bigger, stronger, more threatening. He had only said five words to them, but Faith felt every part of her being telling her that this man was not to be trusted. He was looking directly at a photograph of his dead wife, yet his face showed absolutely no emotion.

Amanda asked, 'Is that your wife, Josephine Figaroa?'

'Jo. Yes, it's her.' He handed the phone back to Amanda. He seemed positive about the ID, but his affect remained as flat as his tone of voice. 'Please come in.'

Amanda could not hide her surprise at the invitation. She glanced back at Faith before entering the house. Kip Kilpatrick indicated he would take up the rear. He wasn't being a gentleman. He wanted to keep an eye on her. Fine by Faith. She made sure he saw her clock the Ruger AR-556 propped up against the door. The rifle had every bell and whistle. Magazine grip. Flash suppressor. Rear-folding battle sight. Laser. Thirty-round magazine.

Reuben led them down a long tiled hallway. He was limping. There was a metal brace on his leg. Faith appreciated the slow pace because it gave her a chance to look around. Not that there was much to see. The house was spotless—literally. There were no photographs on the stark white walls. No sneakers by the door. No clothes piled in the laundry room. No toys scattered into every corner.

Faith didn't care whether or not a person lived in a mega-mansion or a box, if you lived with a six-year-old child, you lived with his shit. She saw no greasy fingerprints or scuffed baseboards or the scattered sticky Cheerios that inexplicably trailed every child like breadcrumbs.

The living room was just as bare. This was not open-concept. There was no line of sight from the kitchen, just a series of closed doors that could lead anywhere. No curtains softened the floor-to-ceiling windows. No artwork or plants warmed up the space. All of the furniture was raw steel and white leather, built to a basketball player's scale. The plush rug was white. The floor was white. If there was a kid living here, he was hermetically sealed.

'Please.' Reuben indicated the couch. He didn't wait for the women to sit down. He took the chair that kept his back to the wall. Sitting, he was roughly Faith's height. His eyes were a weird, almost Confederate gray. There was a long Band-Aid on the side of his shaved head. The bump underneath was the size of a golf ball.

She asked, 'What happened to your head?'

He didn't answer. He just stared at her with a look of mild disinterest, the way a lion might look at an ant.

Amanda said, 'Thank you for talking with us, Mr Figaroa. I'm so sorry for your loss.' She sat on the couch beside him. She had to teeter on the edge so that her feet would touch the ground. Kilpatrick was slumped into another chair, his feet dangling like Lily Tomlin playing Edith Ann. He seemed more upset than Jo's husband. His face had not fully recovered from the shock.

Reuben was still looking at Faith, waiting for her to sit.

'I'm fine, thanks.' She didn't want to be scrambling to stand if something went wrong.

There were a lot of things that could go wrong.

She had spotted another assault rifle by the front door, an AK-47 that looked like it had been retrofitted with a bump fire stock, which effectively made the weapon a legal machine gun. There was a second handgun inside a heavy-looking hinged glass box on the coffee table, another Sig Sauer, this one a reverse two-tone Mosquito.

Amanda had a five-shot revolver in her purse that she kept inside a Crown Royal bag. Faith had her Glock in her leg holster. They would be no match for Reuben Figaroa. He was turned in his chair, his elbow resting on the back corner, so that his hand was less than two inches from the Sig on his hip.

Reuben said, 'What happened to Jo?'

'We're not sure,' Amanda admitted. 'The autopsy has yet to be performed.'

'When will that be done?'

'Later this morning.'

'Where?'

'The morgue at Grady Hospital.'

He waited for more details.

'The medical examiner for the Atlanta Police Department will perform the procedure, but someone from the GBI will be on hand to offer assistance.'

'I want to be there too.'

Kilpatrick sat up. 'He's in shock,' he told Amanda. 'Of course he doesn't want to be there when his wife is autopsied.' He shot Reuben a look of warning. 'When did she die?'

'Perhaps Mr Figaroa can tell us first how he spent yesterday, Monday?'

'Don't—' Kilpatrick said, but Reuben held up a hand to stop him.

'I was at my doctor's office first thing Monday morning. As you can see, I've recently had surgery on my knee. I had to do a follow-up appointment. After that, I had a business meeting with Kip, then we had another meeting with my lawyer, Ditmar Wittich. Then I was with my various bankers for the rest of the day. City Trust. Bank of America. Wells Fargo. Kip can give you their numbers.'

Kilpatrick said, 'Obviously none of the people Fig met with can tell you what they talked about, but I can get the times verified. The banks will have security footage. You'll probably have to get a warrant.'

'There's still late Monday night and into this morning.' Amanda told Reuben, 'Forgive me, but it seems odd that it's two in the morning and you're still dressed in a suit.'

'That's why I delayed you at the gate,' he said. 'I felt it would be inappropriate to answer the door in my pajamas.'

Amanda nodded, but she didn't point out that his suit looked like he'd been wearing it all day.

Reuben asked, 'Where was she found?'

Amanda didn't answer the question. 'I was hoping you could help us with the timeline.' She turned to Kilpatrick. 'You said that you packed Jo into her car Monday morning?'

'Figure of speech.' Kilpatrick saw that he'd painted himself into a corner. 'I packed the car for her Sunday night. I don't know what time she left Monday morning.' Kilpatrick's eyes kept nervously going to Reuben. 'So the last I saw her was Sunday night. We were at a party.'

Faith asked, 'She drove herself to rehab in her own car?'

Kilpatrick had seen Faith looking in the garage at Jo Figaroa's Range Rover. 'I don't remember.'

'And you?' Amanda asked Reuben.

'Sunday night,' Kilpatrick answered before his client could. 'Reuben was at the party too. So was Jo. She left early. Had a headache, wanted to pack, I don't know. Reuben took some pain pills when he got in. This is Sunday night, after the party. He woke up Monday morning and assumed Jo had left for rehab. In a town car, because her Rover was still here.' He was just making this up as he went along. 'You know with rehab, they don't let the patients make any calls home for the first two weeks, so we had no way of knowing whether or not she arrived at the clinic.'

Amanda could've punched all kinds of holes in the story, but she only nodded.

Reuben asked, 'Who killed her?'

'We're not sure that she was murdered.'

'The picture,' Reuben said. 'Someone hit her face. Beat her.' He looked away. His clenched fists were the size of footballs. It was the first time he had registered any emotion about his wife. 'Who killed her?'

'Ms. Wagner,' Kilpatrick interjected. 'I feel that you should know that Jo had an Oxy habit. Pretty serious. Fig had no idea until she got busted. That's why she's in rehab. Was going to rehab.' He stopped to swallow, clearly flustered. 'You should be looking for her dealer. Underworld people.'

Faith remembered what Will had said about Angie supplying drugs to young girls. Her way of helping them stay off the streets. Had she supplied drugs to Jo Figaroa, too?

'You have an impressive gun collection.' Amanda looked around the room, pretending that she hadn't noticed the arsenal before. 'Is it a hobby, or are you worried about your family?'

Reuben fixed his steely gray eyes on her. 'I take excellent care of my family.'

Kilpatrick said, 'Ms. Wagner, I'm sure you're familiar with Georgia HB60 section one through ten. Law enforcement officers are not allowed to ask private law-abiding citizens about guns or permits, or any other weapons, concealed or visible. Especially inside a private home.'

Faith asked, 'Did Jo say goodbye to Anthony?'

Reuben's eyes narrowed. 'Yes.'

Faith waited, but he obviously wasn't going to offer more. 'Is Anthony here?'

'Yes.'

'Can we talk to him? Maybe his mother—'

A phone rang, a piercing bell that for some reason made Faith's hand move toward her gun. Reuben's hand moved too. Very slowly, he reached into his pocket and pulled out an iPhone. Faith looked at Kilpatrick. He had moved to the edge of his seat, tensed, waiting. Reuben's eyes were no longer so steely. His almost stone-like demeanor cracked just a little bit.

They all watched him put the phone to his ear.

'No,' he mumbled. He waited. 'No,' he mumbled again. He ended the call. He shook his head once at Kilpatrick. He kept the phone in his hand, which was all right by Faith, because she wanted his dominant hand to stay occupied. 'Sorry,' he apologized. 'Private matter.'

'Reuben?' An older woman had pushed open one of the doors. She was African American, impeccably dressed, with a choker of pearls around her neck. 'Would you like me to bring your guests some tea or coffee?'

'No, ma'am. We're fine.' Reuben smoothed down his tie. 'Thank you. Everything is fine.'

She hesitated, then backed out of the room.

The exchange had taken seconds, but Faith had caught a glimpse of the woman's face. Her bottom lip was quivering.

Kilpatrick explained, 'That's Jo's mother. She's got a heart condition. We'll wait to tell her the news when she can handle it.'

'Forgive me,' Amanda said. 'But was Josephine adopted?'

Reuben had regained his composure. The flat affect was back. 'Yes. She was an infant when it happened. She never knew her mother.'

'How sad.' Amanda coughed into her hand. She patted her chest and coughed again. 'I'm sorry to trouble you. Could I have some water?'

'I'll get it.' Faith walked toward the kitchen.

Reuben started to stand, but Kilpatrick said, 'It's cool.'

Faith saw why it was cool as soon as she entered the kitchen. Bullet head. Tight black clothes. Laslo Zivcovik was sitting at the kitchen island. He was eating ice cream from the carton. The woman who had to be Miss Lindsay stood on the other side. She was wringing a white towel in her hands, clearly unsettled by what was going on in the next room. The pearls hadn't been Faith's only tip-off. The older woman's lip quivered the exact same way Will had described it.

Faith said, 'What a beautiful kitchen,' even though the kitchen more closely resembled a padded room at an asylum. The cabinets were white. The appliances were all hidden behind white panels. The marble countertop waterfalled onto the marble floor. Even the open staircase in the back of the room was a painfully bright white.

'Thank you.' Miss Lindsay folded the towel. 'My son-in-law designed it.'

That explained a lot. Reuben might as well be a slab of marble himself. 'It must be a chore keeping it clean, especially with a little boy. Your daughter must have a lot of help.'

'No, she does it all on her own. Cleans the house. Does all the cooking. The laundry.'

'That's a lot of work.' Faith repeated, 'Especially with a little boy.'

Laslo's spoon clattered onto the counter. He asked Faith, 'You need something in here?' His Boston accent made him sound like he had cotton shoved into his cheeks.

Filling a glass of water wouldn't take long enough, so she said, 'I volunteered to help with the tea.'

'I'll get the kettle.' Miss Lindsay opened and closed cabinet doors, which told Faith she didn't visit much.

'Yo.' Laslo tapped his spoon on the counter for attention. He pointed to a hot-water dispenser, which meant that Laslo had been here a lot.

'All these new-fangled gadgets.' Miss Lindsay started taking down mugs. White. Gigantic. Built for Reuben Figaroa, like everything else in the house.

Faith started filling the mugs with hot water. The kitchen counter was so tall that she felt the need to lean up on her toes. She asked Miss Lindsay, 'Are you here to watch your grandson?'

She nodded, but didn't speak.

'Six years old, so he must be in first grade?' Faith filled another mug. 'That's such a wonderful age. Everything is exciting. They're so funny and happy all the time. You just want to hold on to them forever.'

Miss Lindsay missed the counter. The mug shattered like ice against the marble floor, white flecks shooting everywhere.

At first, no one moved. They stared at each other in some kind of Mexican stand-off until Laslo told the old woman, 'Go upstairs, sweetheart. I'll clean this up.'

Miss Lindsay looked at Faith. Her lip was quivering again.

Faith said, 'I think you met my partner yesterday. Will Trent.'

Laslo stood up. His boots crunched the broken ceramic on the floor. 'Go upstairs and take care of Anthony. All this noise down here. You don't want him to wake up and get scared.'

'Of course.' Miss Lindsay bit her lip to stop the quiver. She told Faith, 'Good evening.'

Her cane clunked against the floor as she walked toward the back staircase. She turned to look at Faith, then she started the arduous climb. What felt like an eternity passed before her feet disappeared.

Laslo's boots pulverized the broken mug as he took his place back at the kitchen bar. He gripped the spoon. He scooped some ice cream into his mouth and smacked his lips. His eyes were on Faith's breasts. He said, 'Nice tits.'

She said, 'You too.'

Faith used her shoe to kick open the swinging door, knowing it would leave a mark. Amanda was already off the couch, her purse in her hands. She said, 'Thank you, Mr Figaroa. We'll be in touch. Again, I'm so sorry for your loss.'

Kilpatrick showed them out. He let them take the lead down the hallway like he was afraid they would dart off and find something he couldn't explain away.

At the back door, he told Amanda, 'If you have any more questions for Fig, call my cell. Number's on my card.'

'We'll need him to positively ID the body. A DNA sample would be helpful, too.'

Kilpatrick smirked at the suggestion. No lawyer willingly gave up a client's DNA. 'Take another picture once you have her cleaned up. We'll go from there.'

'Wonderful,' Amanda said. 'I look forward to seeing you in a few hours.'

Kilpatrick wouldn't stop smirking. 'Yeah, that on-the-record interview with Marcus that you talked Ditmar into agreeing to yesterday—that ain't gonna happen. Call Ditmar if you don't believe me.'

He didn't slam the door, because he didn't have to.

Amanda gripped her purse like she wanted to strangle it as she walked to the car.

Faith walked backward, looking up at the second-floor windows. There were no lights on. No Miss Lindsay peering out from behind the curtains. Faith had the same feeling that Will had described before: something wasn't right.

They both got into the car. They were both silent until the car was turning onto Cherokee.

Amanda asked, 'Nothing from the mother?'

'Laslo was there.' Faith asked, 'What about that phone call? Kilpatrick almost jumped out of his skin.'

'Curiouser and curiouser.' Amanda said, 'Reuben Figaroa is an angry man.'

Faith would've said 'duh' to anyone else. The guns lying around the house. The operating room aesthetic. Reuben Figaroa was a human checklist for a controlling husband. Whether or not that crossed into violence was an open-ended question. At the very least, it made sense that his wife would be popping pills on her way to the grocery store.

What didn't make sense was why she had been murdered.

Amanda said, 'His alibi will hold. You know that. And I find it very convenient that his entire day was filled with people who are professionally bound by one legal standard or another to keep their mouths shut.'

'Angie got her killed,' Faith guessed. 'That's what this is about. Not Marcus Rippy or Kilpatrick or Reuben or any of that. Angie did one of those Jerry Springer "Surprise, I'm your mother!" things and trapped Jo into doing something that ended up getting her murdered.'

'Don't let the tail wag the dog,' Amanda warned. 'I'm worried about the son—Anthony. Even I know there should be some toys, or at least a few smudges on the glass coffee table.'

'Backpack, shoes, coloring books, crayons, Matchbox cars, dirt.' Faith had forgotten how much dirt boys dragged in. They were like lint traps to every particle of dust in the atmosphere. 'If a six-year-old boy lives in that house, then his mother spends all day cleaning up after him. And she does it on her own, by the way. Miss Lindsay confirmed that Jo doesn't have help. She does the cooking, the cleaning, the laundry, just like a real housewife.'

'Jo disappeared Sunday night. For all intents and purposes, it's now Tuesday morning. We'll assume the husband doesn't scrub toilets. Did Miss Lindsay take over the cleaning?'

'I don't see how. She could barely lean down with her cane. But you're right that something is going on with Anthony. I kept pressing her buttons on the kid, and she would've cracked if Laslo hadn't been there.' Faith said, 'We can call the school. They'll give out truancy information. I'm assuming he's at E. Rivers. It's basically a publicly funded private school for rich white kids.'

'It's too early. No one will be there until six.'

Faith yawned reflexively at the mention of the late hour.

Amanda said, 'I want to talk to that Jane Doe that Will found in the building. She must have seen something. Where did she get all that coke?'

Faith was still yawning. Too much information was coming at her too fast. Her brain felt like a spinning top. 'Figaroa seemed unequivocal about the identification from the photo. How could he be sure? Her head is the size of a watermelon. Someone beat the shit out of her.'

'Here's another problem.' Amanda pointed to the clock on the radio. 'We got there at one in the morning. They were all awake, dressed. Kilpatrick was there in a suit. Reuben was in a suit. Laslo was there. The mother-in-law still had her pearls on. All the lights were on in the house. They were staying up for a reason.'

Faith said, 'Kilpatrick didn't know that Jo was dead.'

'No,' Amanda said. 'He was shocked when I told him. You can't fake that.'

'Figaroa was in a knee brace. But he had that bump on his head. Someone took a heavy swing at him.'

'Jo?'

Faith laughed, but only out of desperation. 'Angie? Delilah? Virginia Souza?'

'The AK by the front door looks retrofitted for automatic.'

'The AR by the back door has a slide fire. That's one hundred rounds in seven seconds.' Faith shook her head, trying to clear it. 'What the hell is going on in that house?'

'Concentrate. Kilpatrick is a fixer. Laslo is a fixer. What problems were they there to fix?'

'If we're buying that Kilpatrick didn't know Jo was dead, then that's not the problem they were fixing.' Faith reminded her, 'Miss Lindsay was at Kilpatrick's on Monday afternoon. That's when she saw Will. She was upset about something.'

'Her daughter was arrested for possession of drugs.'

'Yeah, last Thursday. Jo was out of jail by Saturday. Her mother was at Kilpatrick's with a new problem. A Monday problem.

An after-Harding-was-killed problem. An after-her-daughter-disappeared-but-we're-saying-she's-in-rehab problem.' Faith thought of another red flag. 'She went to Kilpatrick, not Reuben.'

'That phone call Reuben got a few minutes ago. That was strange.'

'It seemed like they were all waiting for a call, even Miss Lindsay. The minute the phone rang, she stuck her head out of the kitchen to find out what was happening.' Faith turned to Amanda. 'If the call wasn't about Jo, then the only thing I can think of that would upset Miss Lindsay that much is Anthony.'

'Put it together, Faith. Reuben Figaroa went to Kilpatrick's office Monday morning. Next, they both met with his lawyer. Reuben spent the rest of the day visiting three different banks, and now they're all at the house, early in the morning, fully dressed, waiting for a phone call. What does that tell you?'

'Ransom,' Faith said. 'Angie kidnapped her grandson.'

ELEVEN

Will paced outside Jane Doe's hospital room while her doctors did their morning rounds. He stuck his hands in his pockets as he paced. He felt weirdly exhilarated, almost giddy, even though he hadn't slept last night. He was thinking more clearly now than he had in the last thirty-six hours. Obviously Angie thought she could wind him up with her mind games, but all she had done was laser-focus his desire to bring her down.

And he was going to bring her down hard, because he knew exactly what she'd been doing.

'Will?' Faith said. 'What are you doing here?'

He didn't stop to explain himself. Everything that had been knocking around his head for the last seven hours exploded out of his mouth. 'I looked back at my notes from the Rippy rape investigation. Reuben Figaroa was Rippy's main alibi at the party, and Jo Figaroa was her husband's main alibi. Angie knew this.

She also figured out that Jo was a junkie, and junkies are really easy to control. She manipulated Jo into blackmailing her husband. If Jo broke Reuben's alibi, then that broke Rippy's alibi, and the whole thing came crumbling down. But instead of caving in and paying them off, Reuben went to Kilpatrick. Kilpatrick put Harding on to solving the problem. Harding called the cops in to bust Jo, and when that didn't shut her up, he solved it by killing her.' He felt himself smiling, because all the clues had been there right from the beginning. 'Angie called me to clean up the mess, because that's what she does.'

Faith didn't say anything for a few seconds. Finally she asked, 'How would Angie know about the witness statements?'

'They were in my files at home. She must've seen them. I know she saw them.' He realized he was talking too fast and too loud. He slowed himself down. 'She mixed up the witness statements. She knows my system, the color coding, and she mixed them up to let me know that she'd seen them.'

'Where's Sara?'

'Downstairs, watching the autopsy.' He gripped Faith's arms. 'Listen to me. Angie lost her leverage when Jo died. She's trying to get us—'

'We think Angie kidnapped her grandson.'

Will felt his grip loosen on her arms.

'He wasn't at school yesterday. He didn't show up this morning.'

Will scanned her eyes, trying to understand where this was coming from. 'He could have a cold, or—'

'Come over here.' She led him to the chairs across from the nurses' station. She made him sit down, but she stood in front of him, stood over him really, and told him what she and Amanda had found.

Will's earlier elation over cracking the case started to dissipate the moment she mentioned Miss Lindsay poking her head out when the phone rang. By the time she had finished recapping the last few hours, Will was leaned over in the chair, his hands clasped between his knees, completely deflated.

Everything she said made perfect sense. The lawyers and bankers made sense. The expectation around the phone call made sense. Angie getting her daughter murdered and still trying to pull some cash out of it made sense.

What was wrong with him? How had he loved such a despicable person?

Faith said, 'You could be right about the blackmail plan going sideways, only when Harding took out Jo—'

'Angie saw Anthony as the perfect stand-in.' Will rubbed his face with his hands. Survival of the fittest. Angie always kept moving forward. She didn't worry about consequences because she never stuck around long enough to deal with them.

He said, 'I hit Collier.'

'I figured that out. I wish you'd hit him harder.' She covered a large yawn with the back of her hand. 'We're going to have to rework Collier's side of the case. He lied about Virginia Souza's death by OD. She's alive and kicking as of last week. We've got footage of her at the jail posting a cash bail on an eighteen-year-old picked up for solicitation. Delilah Palmer is still our only solid lead. She could be a victim. She could be a perpetrator. Either way, the first person she'd go to for help is her pimp. We need to find Souza. If she really is the mama in charge, then she'll know who Delilah's pimp is. We get the pimp, we get Delilah.'

'Agent Trent,' the doctor said. 'You can talk to the patient now, but keep it brief and try not to excite her any more than she already is.'

Faith asked, 'What's she excited about?'

The doctor shrugged. 'Free food, clean sheets, nurses to wait on her, cable TV. We replaced all of her blood, so this is probably the first time in decades she's been clean. She's been on the streets for twenty years. We're like the Ritz here.'

'Thanks.' Faith asked Will, 'Ready?'

Will wanted to stand, but he felt like he was weighted down with lead. Yesterday's numbness had returned. Every lost minute of sleep slammed into him like a pile driver. 'We can't do anything, can we? About Anthony. His father hasn't reported him missing. We can't demand to see him because we don't really have any proof that something's wrong. Reuben's got a wall of lawyers telling him his rights, and if he's as much of a control freak as you say, he's going to insist on handling all of this on his own.'

Faith said, 'Amanda's working on a warrant to tap his phones. She's got four cars outside his house. If anyone leaves, they'll be followed. But you're right, you and I can't do anything right now except work our end of the case.'

Will felt the elephant from last night take a tentative step onto his chest. He shook it off. He wasn't going to humiliate himself again the way he had at the funeral home. 'Angie said that Jo was my daughter. Sara says my blood type doesn't rule me out.'

'Do you believe Angie?'

He told Faith the only truth he knew. 'All I can think about is punching her in the throat until her windpipe collapses so that I can see the panic in her eyes while she suffocates to death.'

'That's disturbingly specific.' Faith got that expression on her face that told him she was going to try to mother him. 'Why don't you go home and get some rest? It's been a tough couple of days. I can interview Jane Doe. Amanda should be here any minute. You probably shouldn't be talking to a potential witness anyway.'

'It's already tainted. I'm the one who found her.' Will stood up. He straightened his tie. He had to take a cue from Angie and keep moving forward. If he let the stress get to him, if he had another stupid panic attack, he'd never be able to hold up his head again. 'Let's do this.'

He let Faith lead the way. Jane Doe 2 was one of three Jane Does on the ward. Jane Doe 1 was in a quiet room at the end of the hall. Jane Doe 3 had a cop outside her door. Grady was Atlanta's only publicly funded hospital. There were a lot of Does here.

Their particular Jane Doe was in a tiny room sectioned off by a glass window and a heavy wooden door that wouldn't close all the way. Machines pumped and hissed. A heart monitor tracked beats. The lights had been left on. Both of Jane Doe's eyes were blackened, because that's what happened when your nose collapsed into your face. Heavy bandages were wrapped around the top two-thirds of her head, leaving her mouth and chin exposed. Greasy brown hair puffed out between the gauze. Two surgical drains, basically clear bags that caught excess fluid and blood from the wound, were dangling down either side of her face. She reminded Will of the colo claw fish from the bad *Star Wars*.

Jane stopped eating her Jell-O mid-bite when Faith and Will walked in. 'Leave that door open. I don't wanna end up being another black woman who dies mysteriously in police custody.'

Faith said, 'First, you're not in police custody, and second, you're not black.'

'Shit.' Jane rubbed at her white arms. 'How'd I manage to fuck up my life so bad, then?'

'I'm assuming personal choice had something to do with it.'

Jane put down the empty cup. She sat back in bed. Her voice was raspy. She was older than Will had first thought, closer to fifty. He had no idea why he'd ever thought she might be Angie.

Jane said, 'Whaddaya want? I gotta sponge bath in a few minutes, then *Judge Mathis* is on.'

'We want to talk to you about Sunday night.'

'What's today?'

'Tuesday.'

'Holy shit, that was some blow.' The drain bags flopped against her cheeks as she laughed. 'God damm, bitch. Sunday, I was on the moon.'

Faith gave Will the look that said she didn't have the patience for this.

He told Jane, 'I feel like we got off on the wrong foot. I'm Special Agent Trent with the GBI. This is my colleague, Faith Mitchell.'

'Call me Dr Doe, on account'a I'm in a hospital.'

Will doubted the woman was carrying an ID and he couldn't fingerprint her without arresting her, which brought its own problems. He said, 'All right, Dr Doe. Someone was murdered Sunday night in the building across the street from where we found you Monday morning.'

She asked, 'Shot?'

'We're not sure. Did you hear a gunshot?'

Jane leveled him with a gaze. 'Do you know that at least once a year, a dog shoots somebody?' She seemed to think this was useful information. 'You ask me, people should be real careful about keeping dogs in their homes. Aha.' She looked past Will. Amanda was in the doorway. Jane said, 'The captain always commands from the back of the ship.'

Amanda accepted the compliment with a nod of her head. 'Agent Mitchell, why hasn't this suspect been transferred to the prison ward downstairs?'

Faith said, 'You mean the one with no TV or sponge baths?'

'Damn, bitches, you don't gotta go DEFCON so fast.' Jane struggled to sit up in the bed. 'All right, I got information. What's in it for me?'

Amanda said, 'You've got one more day in the ICU, then you'll be transferred downstairs to the regular patient wards. I can get you a couple of extra days on the ward. After that, you'll be enrolled in a treatment program.'

'Nah, I don't need no program. I'm back on the coke as soon as I get outta here. I'll take the extra two days, though. And you'll give it to me because I was in the building when it happened.'

'The office building?' Will asked.

'No, the whatsit, the one with the balcony.' Her brown teeth showed in a smile beneath the bandages. 'Now I got your attention.'

Faith crossed her arms. 'What time did you get there?'

'Aw, shit. They stole my Rolex.' She patted her wrist. 'What time? How do I know what time it is, bitch? It was dark outside. There was a full moon. It was Sunday. That's what I know.'

Faith stepped back so that Amanda could take over. She knew when a witness had turned against her.

Amanda said, 'Start with the gunshot.'

'I was across the street in the office building, bedding down for the night, right? Then I hear this gunshot and I'm like, "What the fuck?" Like, could it be a backfire from a car? Could it be a gangbanger, which, holy shit, that ain't my jam.' She coughed to clear some phlegm from her throat. 'Anyway, so I'm lying there thinking about what can I do. Then I decide I need to check it out in case there's some kind of gang thing going down, get my ass outta there, ya know?'

Amanda nodded.

'I'm on the third floor, tucked up in my crib, so it takes me a little while to get down. Place is a goddam deathtrap. Before I'm out the door, I hear a car streak off, like burning rubber.'

Will bit his lip so a curse wouldn't slip out. Jane Doe had gotten there too late.

Amanda clarified, 'You heard a car leaving the scene?'

'That's right.'

'Did you see the car?'

'Sort of. Looked black, with some red along the bottom.'

Angie's car was black with red stripes.

Jane said, 'But there was another car in the parking lot. White, kind of foreign-looking.'

Dale Harding's Kia.

'And, so, I go back up to my crib, right? Don't need to get involved in that shit with cars running off in a hurry. I been out there on the street long enough to know a deal gone bad when I see it.'

Will felt a moment of disappointment, but then Jane started talking again.

'So I'm back up in my crib, just lyin' there, and I get to thinking, well, shit, you know what I'm thinking. Maybe I got it wrong. This is a transactional kind of neighborhood. I got some scratch in my pocket. There's a car outside that building, another car just screeched off, it seems like there's gonna be a dealer inside, right? Simple economics.' She pushed herself up in the bed again. 'So I mosey on back across the parking lot, go inside the building, and it's dark as shit. Windows are tinted or something. I'm walking around blind and then my eyes get with the program and I see there's this gal on the floor. At first I thought she was dead. Started checking her pockets, but then she moved and I was like, "Whoa."'

Amanda asked, 'This is the bottom floor, not the upper level?'

'Correct-o-mundo.'

'Where was she lying on the floor, exactly?'

'Shit, I dunno. I'd need a map, right? Not like I was paying attention. I just walked into the building and boom, there she was.'

'What did she look like?'

'Dark hair. White gal. She's laid out on her side. Can't move her arms and legs, can barely move her head, but she's making this moaning sound so I'm like, "All right, that's it. I'm gettin' the fuck outta here," only I can't because there's another car pulls up in the parking lot.'

'The same car?'

'Yeah, but I seen it for real this time. Square nose like an older car. But I ain't no car expert, right?'

Angie's Monte Carlo was black with a square nose. Why had she returned to the scene? Why had she left in the first place?

Amanda asked, 'How much time had passed since the car first peeled off?'

'Mebbe 'bout thirty minutes? I dunno. Don't have to punch a clock in my line of business.' Jane continued, 'So, the car is out front, so I booked it to the back. Hid behind that bar thing. Peeking out, like . . .' She elongated her neck. 'And I see this second bitch comes in. Tall. White. Long hair like the first one. Thinner. Don't ask me what her face looked like because who the hell can see in that place? Like a fucking tomb.' She pointed to the pitcher on her bedside table. 'Gimme some of that, will ya, honey?'

Will was closest, so he poured some water into a Styrofoam cup.

Jane took a drink, drawing out the tension with a loud gulping sound. 'Okay, so the second bitch comes in, and she's just fucking furious, right? Kicking things around. Cursing. Motherfuck this. Motherfuck that.'

Definitely Angie. But why was she mad? What had she screwed up?

'She goes upstairs like she's marching against Hitler, you know what I mean? Feet just pounding.' She put down her cup. 'I hear her upstairs, doing what, I don't know. Throwing shit around. Going in and out of rooms. Leaving shit. Moving shit.'

Staging the crime scene.

'She's got a flashlight. Did I tell you that?'

Amanda said, 'No.'

'One'a them little lights that's real strong. That's why I'm not leaving my cover, right? Didn't want that light shining on me. Who knows what the bitch would do?'

She went silent.

Amanda repeated, 'And?'

'Oh, well eventually the bitch came back downstairs. She says another couple'a three motherfucks, kicks the chick on the floor. Real hard. And the chick, she moans loud-like: "Uhhhhhn." That's when it got interesting.'

Again Jane went silent.

Amanda warned, 'Don't draw this out.'

'All right, I'm just trying to have some fun here. I don't get to talk to people much.' Jane took another drink of water. 'So, bitch just stands there listening to her moan for a coupla minutes. Staring down at her like "You piece of shit." Then, wham, bitch just grabs the chick by the leg and starts dragging her out of the building. And man . . .' She shook her head. 'That chick was moaning before, but when the bitch yanked on her leg, that's when the screaming started.'

Will felt a pain in his jaw. Had Angie dragged her own mortally wounded, paralyzed daughter out of the building?

'Then, bitch comes back in *again* and starts kicking things around again.'

Hiding the fact that she'd dragged a body across the floor.

'She leaves for real this time. Next thing I hear something like a car door slamming. Lots of car doors slamming.'

Faith asked, 'Could it have been a trunk?'

'I don't got, like, radar ears, bitch. It was just lots of things slamming shut on a car.' She looked exasperated. She didn't like Faith asking questions. 'Anyway, then there's this *whoosh!* like I don't know what. Big *whoosh.* And I look up at the windows—now the windows are blacked out, right, but I see these flames shooting up like a Viking funeral. Just . . .' She waved her arm around. 'All over the place.' She dropped her hand. 'That's it. The car pulled away.'

Amanda asked, 'Did you see anyone else?'

'Nah, that's the truth. Just the bitch and the chick and the fire.'

'No children?'

'What the hell would a kid be doing there? It was the middle of the night. Should be tucked up in bed.'

Amanda asked, 'You didn't go upstairs to see what the first woman did up there?'

Jane licked her lips. 'Well, I might'a. Just out of curiosity.'

Amanda rolled her hand, indicating she could continue.

'There was a dude up there. Not dead, but just as good as. The light was better on account of the windows are right across from the balcony.'

'And?'

'Bastard was a fucking whale. Sleeping real sound, but like I said—not dead. But close. You could tell. Or at least I could. I seen some people die in my time. Pissed himself already. Had a doorknob in his neck. Like that guy from TV. You remember that show?' She snapped her fingers twice, like in *The Addams Family*.

Will provided, 'Lurch, but I think you mean Frankenstein.'

'That's right.' She winked at him. 'I knew you were the smart one, honey.'

Amanda said, 'I'm waiting to hear where the coke came in.'

'Dead guy's jacket pocket.' She patted her chest. 'If I squatted down, stretched my arm real far, I could take it without getting blood all over me. Two fucking grams. I ain't seen that much blow since I was a kid.'

'So you went across the street because . . .'

'I couldn't stay in there with that guy dying. That's just weird. And who knew if the bitch would come back? God damm, she already left and came back once.' Jane started breaking off pieces of Styrofoam from the cup. 'So I moseyed back across the street, partied until the sun came up. Then the cops rolled in, so I was like, shit, I better cheese it up the stairs. Once I started climbing, I couldn't stop until I got to the top. That blow was fucking pure, man. One hundred percent.'

Will saw Faith roll her eyes. Every dealer said his blow was pure.

Amanda asked, 'Is that it? You're not leaving anything out?'

'Hell, it don't seem like it, but you never know, right?'

Amanda typed on her BlackBerry. 'I'm going to have another agent take your statement. He'll bring a sketch artist who will talk you through the night, try to jog your memory.'

'That seems like a lot of trouble to go through.'

'Consider it part of your get-out-of-jail-free card.' Amanda motioned for Will and Faith to follow her out of the room. She walked a few feet down from Jane's room, stopping in front of the nurses' station.

Faith asked, 'Do we believe her?'

Amanda said, 'Charlie found a bloodstain on the lower level. He thought it came from a nosebleed.'

Will said, 'Angie could know how to stage a crime scene.'

'I'm trying to wrap my head around this.' Faith tried to talk it out. 'Somehow Jo bled out in the room upstairs, then she made her way to the bottom floor, where she collapsed. Angie leaves for some reason. She comes back for some reason. She drags Jo to her Monte Carlo, blows up Dale's Kia, then drives off again?' She added, 'And leaves her own daughter marinating in her trunk for six hours?'

Will stifled his impulse to say that Angie wouldn't do something like that.

Amanda said, 'I'm getting a lot of pushback on that warrant for Figaroa's telephone. We got the street surveillance approved, but just barely. No one has left the Figaroa house except Laslo. He was sent to McDonald's for breakfast. He bought three cups of coffee and three breakfast platters.'

'Three, not four, which means that they didn't get anything for Anthony.' Faith said, 'Let me get my notes. I need to talk this out again.'

Will didn't want to listen to another recap.

He looked past Faith's shoulder, pretending that he was listening. He watched the nurse typing something onto a tablet computer. All of the patient files at Grady were digitized. The whiteboard behind the nurses' station was still low-tech. They hand-wrote patient names and updated their status so that they could keep track of the ward. As Will watched, the nurse went to the board and erased Jane Doe 1. She wrote in a new name with a red marker. All caps, which was easier for him to read. And it helped that he had seen the name several times before.

He said, 'Delilah Palmer.'

Amanda asked, 'What about her?'

He pointed to the board.

The nurse had overheard him. She explained, 'Domestic abuse. They can't find the boyfriend. She walked into the ER with a knife sticking out of her chest.'

'When?' Faith asked.

'Early Monday, right before my shift.'

Will said, 'I thought we checked the hospitals for stabbing victims.'

'*We* didn't.' Faith sounded furious. She told the nurse, 'Olivia, the patient's been Jane Doe One since I was here last night. What changed?'

'The orderly checked her clothes before he took them down to the incinerator. He found her driver's license.' Olivia capped the marker. 'She's still in an induced coma, so you can't interview her. Anyway, I thought this was being handled by the APD.'

Amanda asked, 'Who caught the case?'

'I can look it up here.' Olivia referenced the tablet computer. Her face broke into a smile. 'Oh, it was Denny. Denny Collier.'

TWELVE

'Subarachnoid hemorrhage,' Gary Quintana said. 'That sounds like spiders.'

'It's a spidery area,' Sara told him. 'But basically it means she had bleeding in that part of the brain.'

'Oh, wow. Weird.' Gary continued reading Josephine Figaroa's preliminary autopsy report. Whatever Amanda had said to the young man yesterday morning had clearly left a mark. His shirt-sleeves were rolled down. He wore a knit tie in place of his heavy gold necklace. Even his ponytail had been neutered. Instead of jutting proudly from the back of his head, the hair had been gathered into a neat bun.

She was sad to see the ponytail go.

'Okay.' Gary read aloud from the conclusion. 'Cause of death is an epidural hemorrhage. What's that?'

'It's another type of intracranial bleed.' Sara could tell he wanted to know more. 'She experienced an external trauma to her head. The skull fractured, tearing her middle meningeal artery, which branches off the external carotid and helps supply blood to the brain. Blood filled the space between the dura mater and the skull. The skull holds a fixed volume, meaning it can't expand. All of that extra blood put too much pressure on her brain.'

'What happens when that happens?'

'In general, the patient loses consciousness transiently. At the time of injury, they're typically knocked out for a few minutes. Then they wake up and exhibit a normal level of consciousness. That's why these bleeds are so dangerous. There's a severe headache, but they're lucid until the bleed progresses enough to shut down the brain. Left untreated, they slip into a coma and die.'

'Wow.' He looked at the gurney that held Figaroa's body. They were standing in the hallway outside the APD morgue, which was located in the sub-basement of Grady Hospital. The gurney was pushed up against the wall, awaiting transport. Thanks to a batch of bad meth, the medical examiner had a full house.

Gary said, 'She sure went through some hell.'

'She did.'

He returned to the report. 'What about "fracture of the cervical vertebrae?" That's the neck, right? That sounds really bad, too.'

'It is. She would've likely been paralyzed.'

'Her heart was bruised, too.' He frowned, disturbed by the findings. 'Somebody whooped the hell out of her.'

'Not necessarily.' Sara explained, 'The skull fractures are evenly distributed. The ribs and cervical vertebrae are fractured, as you said, but the thoracic vertebrae and long bones aren't. She's not really bruised except on one side. Did you notice that?'

'Yeah, what's that mean?'

'That it's very likely that she either fell or was pushed from a great height. The cervical fractures are a tip-off. You don't get those from being beaten. She fell from at least twenty feet up. She hit the ground on her side. Her skull fractured, the artery tore, and then a few hours later, she died from the brain hemorrhage.'

'That balcony inside the club was about thirty feet up.' Gary looked at Sara with a sense of awe. 'Wow, Dr Linton. That's pretty cool how you scienced that out.' He handed her the report. 'Thank you for sharing all this with me. I really want to learn.'

'I'm glad Amanda assigned you to my division.'

'Yeah, she got me to slick up my look.' He patted his tie. 'I gotta represent, you know? The focus should be on the victims, not on me.'

Sara supposed this was reasonable advice. 'I should track them down to let them know about the findings. Do you have any more questions?'

'Yeah, she's just, like, out here in the hallway. You think it's okay if I put her back in the freezer?'

'I think that would be very nice.' Sara patted him on the shoulder as she walked toward the stairs. The ICU was six floors up, but the elevators at Grady worked on their own time and she needed to find Amanda sooner rather than later.

Of course, finding Amanda meant she would also find Will. Sara was shaken by an unwelcome reticence. She still wasn't sure how she felt about last night. Will hadn't wanted to talk in the car, but then he wouldn't shut up once they got home. He hadn't slept. He had been almost manic, spouting theories that were the equivalent of a snake eating its own tail. He was furious with Angie. He was deeply hurt, whether he would admit it or not. Everything that came out of his mouth was either talking around Angie or talking about her. Sara looked at him as a doctor and wanted to medicate him, and this time make sure he didn't palm the pill. She looked at him as his girlfriend and wanted to wrap her arms around him and make everything better. Then she had looked at him as a woman who'd been married, who knew how to be in a healthy relationship, and wondered what the hell she had signed up for.

Sara pulled open the door to the ICU just as a man was yelling, 'So fucking what?'

Holden Collier threw his hands into the air. His boyish affability was gone. It was no wonder why. Amanda, Faith and Will were crowding in on him. Two of the Grady security guards were standing close by, their hands resting on their guns.

Collier demanded, 'Why would I report a domestic when we're looking for an unexplained stabbing?' He threw up his hands again. 'It's explained. The boyfriend did it. She won't name him. What am I going to do?'

'Tell me again.' Amanda's tone was hard as steel. 'From the beginning.'

'Unbelievable.' Collier threw up his hands a third time.

Sara had no idea what he was being accused of, but his innocent act was filled with textbook overreaction.

He said, 'I was already at the ER with a perp. I took the domestic. She was bleeding out, but I got her story. Boyfriend came after her with a knife. She won't tell me his name. Where she lives, whatever. Same bullshit as usual. She went into surgery. I wrote the report. I told them to call me if her status changed. That's my job.' He wasn't finished. 'You're so fucking hell-bent on jamming me up, you don't even see what this case is really about.'

'Tell me what it's about.'

'Rippy's club is a shooting gallery. Gang tags are everywhere. Harding has a shit bucket in his closet. He was running drug mules up from Mexico and it got him killed, end of story.'

Amanda asked, 'What about your relationship with Angie Polaski?'

Sara bit her lip. Angie. She would give her entire life savings to never, ever have to hear the woman's name again.

Amanda said, 'Sunday night into Monday morning, you had three calls back and forth with a burner phone. One of them lasted twelve minutes.'

'I was talking to an informant. He uses a burner. They all use burners.'

'Who's the informant? I want his name.'

'I'm not doing this here.' Collier had finally realized he couldn't bluster his way out of the problem. 'If you want to question me, I've got a right to have my union rep in the room.'

'Give him a call, Denny. This is happening.'

'Can I go?'

'We'll be in touch.'

He stomped off, barely acknowledging Sara as he bumped open the door to the stairs.

Faith had her hands on her hips. She was furious. Amanda was furious. Will looked the same as he had for the last twenty-four hours, like a deer caught in the headlights.

Amanda said, 'Dr Linton. What do you have?'

'Nothing you're going to like.' Sara felt sorry to again be the bearer of bad news. 'According to the preliminary autopsy report, Josephine Figaroa died of a brain bleed. The stab wounds in her chest were very shallow, post mortem, so there wasn't any bleeding. The cut on her cheek was post mortem, so no bleeding. Her fingertips didn't crack from the heat. Someone sliced them with a razor, probably to hide her identity, which doesn't make sense, but that's your department. Speaking from my department, I can tell you the finger cuts were post mortem too, because there was no bleeding.'

Amanda clarified, 'You're saying that the blood at the crime scene did not come from the woman who was autopsied downstairs.'

'Exactly. All of her bleeding was internal. My guess is that she fell, probably from the balcony. Charlie said there was some blood on the ground floor. I'm assuming it came from her nose. She was alive for several hours, probably paralyzed, before the bleed killed her.'

Amanda didn't seem surprised, which was not unusual, because she had a good poker face. What was puzzling was that neither Faith nor Will seemed surprised either.

Amanda asked, 'Could it be possible that there was a second victim at the crime scene?'

'Absolutely. The club was heavily trafficked over the last few months. Someone with even a rudimentary knowledge of crime scene investigation could temporarily pull the wool over our eyes. At least until the labs, fingerprints and analysis came back, which could take weeks, maybe months.'

'Did you see any signs of a child?'

'A child?' Sara was confused. 'You mean a toddler? Infant?'

'Six years old,' Faith said. 'We have a missing kid. We think Angie took him.'

Sara's hand went to her chest. She looked at Will, expecting him to be staring at the floor, but instead he looked back at her. There was a hardness to his expression that she had never seen before. His manicness was gone. Anger had enveloped him body and soul.

He said, 'We think Angie had a blackmail plan going with Jo. Jo ended up dead, so Angie thought she could leverage the grandson.'

'But she told you that Jo was dead. You had no idea that Jo even existed, let alone that she was Angie's daughter. Why would she tell you anything?'

'Something went wrong with the plan.' Will had to be guessing, but he sounded certain that Angie had yet again risked someone else's life for her own reward.

Amanda said, 'Come with me.' She took Sara into a room with a cop standing outside. The lights were low. Sara scanned the equipment by the bed: cardiac monitor, central line, catheter, NG tube, test tube. The patient's right arm was elevated, propped on pillows—not too low so that the blood rushed into her fingers, not too high so that there wasn't enough circulation. Surgical gauze and drains ballooned around the hand. O_2 sat measures were on the tips of her fingers.

Sara said, 'Her hand was reattached.'

'Yes.'

Sara studied the woman's face. Brown hair. Olive skin. The eyes were swollen, but they still had the distinctive shape.

Amanda said, 'She was admitted as a Jane Doe, but they found her ID this morning. Delilah Palmer.'

That name sounded familiar. Instead of asking Amanda more questions, Sara went back to the nurses' station and asked to borrow a tablet computer. She still had her admitting privileges at Grady. The nurse, Olivia, knew her from before.

Olivia said, 'The waiting room should be empty.'

Sara got the hint. Four people blocking the ICU hallway was never a good idea.

They all walked down to the empty waiting room. Will stayed at Sara's side. His shoulder touched hers. He was trying to make sure the connection was still there. She couldn't find it in herself to let him know this was true.

Sara sat down on one of the chairs. She logged into the system and scanned the woman's CT, X-rays, MRI and surgical notes.

Finally something made sense.

Faith asked, 'Well?'

Sara relayed the information from the chart. 'She was stabbed sixteen times, mostly in the torso, twice in the head. The tip of the knife broke off in her collarbone, minimizing the reach of the blade, which is probably why it just missed the heart and liver. The bowel was punctured. Her left lung collapsed. What remained of the knife was left imbedded in her sternum. The first slash must have been to her arm.' Sara held up her own arm, the same as she had done yesterday morning. 'The attacker came straight at her. She took a defensive posture. The knife sliced her wrist, nearly severing the joint. She would've been flailing her arms, trying to stop the attack, which would spray blood everywhere, like a hose. Fortunately for the victim, the blade severed the radial and ulnar arteries. I say fortunately, because the arteries contract when they're sliced in two. That's why suicides tend to fail. You sever the artery, it rolls up into the arm and stops the blood almost like when you pinch the end of a garden hose to stop the pressure.'

Will asked, 'That's where all the blood came from, right?'

'That volume of blood could definitely come from this type of injury.' Sara studied the X-rays again. 'This isn't the first time she's been attacked. She's got several older, healed fractures to the face and head. Two breaks in her arm, probably separated by a few years. These are classic signs of abuse.'

Amanda asked, 'Does the chart give Palmer's blood type?'

'They typed her when she came into the ER. It's B-negative. Type is inherited. You would need either a B mother or B father to have it.'

'Like Angie,' Faith said.

Amanda asked, 'Can you pull up Delilah Palmer's past admits?'

Sara went back to the home screen. She found Delilah Palmer's medical history, which hadn't been ported into the ICU chart yet. 'Palmer was born here twenty-two years ago. Ward of the state. Overdoses. PID times five. Bronchitis. Skin infections. Needle abscesses. Heroin addict. She had a baby two years ago. Hold on.' Sara went back to the belly scans from two nights ago. 'Okay, according to the most recent chart, the one that was started Sunday night, the woman lying in the bed at the end of the hall has a scar for a C-section.' She flicked back through the screens. 'But the older chart says that Palmer had a natural childbirth two years ago, which would fall in line with an episiotomy scar, which is what the body downstairs, the one Angie left at the funeral home, has.' She looked up. 'The body downstairs showed signs of long-term IV drug use, but there's no indication of drug use in the woman at the end of the hall, who is supposed to be Delilah Palmer.' Sara felt slow on the uptake. 'The body downstairs is Delilah Palmer. Jo Figaroa is here in the ICU. Angie switched their identities.'

'That's what we think.' Faith showed her two photographs on her iPhone. 'The one on the right is Jo Figaroa. The one on the left is Delilah Palmer.'

Sara studied the two women. There was an eerie similarity. 'Are they related?'

'Who knows?' Faith asked. 'They both had the shit kicked out of them. Figaroa's own husband couldn't tell them apart.'

Sara didn't point out that Will hadn't been able to, either.

Faith said, 'We have a witness who puts Angie sticking Palmer in her trunk. I've gotta assume that Angie mutilated the body so we couldn't get a positive ID off the fingerprints.'

Sara asked, 'Why would Angie want us to think that Jo Figaroa was dead?'

Will said, 'She's working a scam. That's the only explanation. Our Jane Doe put together the night of the attack for us. Harding's dying. Josephine is bleeding to death. Angie rushes Josephine to the hospital, then instead of leaving town or lying low, Angie drives back to the club to remove Delilah and stage the scene. That's a lot of work for somebody who doesn't like to do a lot of work. I guarantee you there's some kind of payday at the end of this.'

Sara felt overwhelmed with disgust. She dropped the tablet on the chair beside her. She was sick of Angie's games, and she was the only one in the group who actually had the luxury of walking away.

Will seemed to sense that she was at the end of her rope. 'I'm sorry.'

Sara didn't want to blame him. If ever there was a victim of Angie's machinations, it was Will. 'Do you have any idea where she is? Where she might be keeping a child?'

He shook his head, and she saw the idiocy of her question. If they knew where Angie was, they would be breaking down her door.

Faith said, 'We can only hope that because he's her grandson, she'll . . . *Motherfucker* . . .' Faith's voice trailed off. 'She's here.'

They all turned in unison.

Angie had just stepped off the elevator. She looked up. Her mouth formed an 'O,' a perfect reflection of their shock. She tried to get back onto the elevator, but the doors closed. She scrambled toward the stairs.

She wasn't fast enough.

Will had bolted the moment he'd seen her.

In seconds he'd closed the gap between them. His arm shot out. His fingers snagged the back of her collar. Angie was wrenched back by the neck. Her feet flew out from under her. She hit the floor. He picked her up and threw her into the waiting room. Chairs clattered, crashing into each other, tipping over. He snatched her up again, his fist went back. The only thing that kept Will from shattering her into pieces was the two security guards jumping on his back like they were taking down a charging bull.

'Will!' Faith yelled, leaping into the fray. She pushed him against the wall. 'Stop it!' She was panting, out of breath. She said, 'Stop it,' quieter, still making it clear she wasn't going to let him do what he obviously wanted to do. 'Calm down, okay? She's not worth it.'

Will shook his head. Sara knew what he was thinking. Killing her was worth it. Hurting her was worth it.

Sara said, 'Will.'

He looked at her, his eyes on fire.

'Don't,' she said, though she wanted him to.

The fire abated. The sound of her voice seemed to relax some of the tension from his body. He held up his hands in surrender, telling Faith, 'I'm okay.'

Faith stepped back, but she made sure that she stayed between him and Angie in case he changed his mind.

'Shit, baby.' Angie slumped onto the floor, chuckling like this had all been great fun. She wiped blood from her mouth and nose. There was more blood on her shirt, but it hadn't come from her face. 'Last time you came at me like that, we were both naked.'

Amanda said, 'Arrest her.'

'For what?' Angie asked. 'Getting beat up by a cop in front of a bunch of witnesses?' Angie lifted the tail of her shirt to survey the damage. Her side had been stitched up, crudely, to close a wound. Will had broken open the sutures. 'Anybody know a doctor?'

Sara said, 'I'm not touching her.'

Angie laughed again. She shook her head. 'Jesus.'

Will said, 'Where's Anthony? Who's watching him?'

Angie pressed her hands to the floor, pushing herself up to standing. Her purse fell down her shoulder, another cheap knock-off bag. 'Who's Anthony?'

Will ripped Angie's purse from her arm.

'Hey . . .'

He held her back with one hand. He threw the purse at Faith.

Angie reached up for his hand, but Will pulled away as if she'd burned him with acid. He was clearly trying to keep his temper under control. The God's honest truth was that Sara still didn't want him to.

'iPhone. iPad.' Faith laid out the contents of Angie's purse across two chairs. 'Flip phone. Five-shot revolver, fired once. Prescription.' She tossed the bottle to Sara. 'Tissue. ChapStick. Change. Business cards. Purse crap.'

Sara looked at the bottle. The script was from a vet clinic off Cascade Road, prescribed to a pet named Mooch McGhee. Keflex, which was fine if you were a dog and couldn't get MRSA. Sara put the bottle back on the chair. Angie could figure that out on her own.

'Unlock it.' Faith held out the iPhone to Angie. 'Now.'

'Go fuck yourself.'

Will took the phone. He unlocked it in two tries. He handed it back to Faith, who immediately went to the call log.

She said, 'Collier's number is on here. Twice last week. Three calls early Monday morning that match the times on his phone.'

That explained Collier. Yet another man whose life Angie had ruined.

Faith said, 'She's got a lot of calls back and forth from a 770 number.' Faith hit the callback button. She let it ring for a full minute before hanging up. 'No answer. No voicemail.' Again she scanned the log. 'This is all with the 770 number. Incoming at one forty Monday morning. Outgoing thirty-two seconds later. Then outgoing half an hour later. Incoming at four AM, then another incoming at one fifteen yesterday afternoon. Then seventeen outgoing calls over the rest of yesterday and into today.'

Will asked Angie, 'Who are you trying to get in touch with?'

'My mother.'

Amanda had her own phone out. 'I'll do a reverse trace.'

Faith went to the texts. 'This was between the flip phone and Angie's phone, twelve twenty Sunday night. She writes: WHAT DO YOU WANT? The flip phone writes back: IPAD. Then a few seconds later: NIGHTCLUB. NOW.' She scrolled up and waited for a photo to download.

Faith's mouth dropped open. She showed them the phone, stunned.

At 12:16 Sunday night, Angie had been sent a picture showing Josephine Figaroa with her back pressed against a car window. A man's hand gripped her neck. She looked like she was screaming. Beneath it was the word DAUGHTER.

Faith scrolled up again. There was another photo, this one sent at 12:15 Sunday night. It showed a young boy with the blade of a large hunting knife pressed into his throat. The word below read GRANDSON.

Sara put her hand to her own heart. The boy's terror cut through her like she was holding him in her own arms. 'Where is he?'

Angie raised an eyebrow, as if this was yet another mystery.

'Where—' Sara made herself stop talking. Angie fed off pain.

Faith checked the flip phone, going through the sent messages. 'The first photo I showed you, the one of Jo Figaroa, was taken with this flip phone. The second photo, of Anthony, was forwarded to the flip phone by the same 770 number that Angie has been trying to call.'

'The 770 number is from a burner.' Amanda had obviously heard back on the reverse trace. 'We're working with the phone company to find out which tower it's pinging from.'

Will asked, 'Who sent that picture of Anthony? Was it Delilah Palmer? Was it Harding?'

Angie ignored him.

Faith picked up the iPad. She pressed the home button.

'Don't,' Angie said, for the first time registering concern. 'You can't turn it on.'

'Why not? This is why your grandson was taken, right? For whatever is on this iPad?'

Angie pressed her lips together. She watched Faith's finger on the button.

Will said, 'Turn it on.'

'No.' Angie reached out to stop her, but Will pushed her away. She said, 'If you turn the power on, then the files will be erased.'

'What files?'

Angie said nothing.

Will said, 'She's lying. Turn it on.'

'Go ahead,' Angie dared. 'The files will be gone and we'll never see Anthony again.'

Faith asked, 'Should we risk it?'

Amanda sighed. 'It's an hour in traffic to get it to the computer lab. We don't know where the boy is. We don't know if she's telling the truth. The files might already be wiped clean. Or we turn it on and we wipe it clean.'

Will said, 'Schrödinger's cat.'

Angie clearly didn't get the reference, which gave Sara a sense of victory because she did.

'All you need is a Faraday cage,' Sara said. 'It's a grounded metal screen that blocks electrical fields. That's why your phone won't work in an elevator. Go down to the sub-basement, stay inside the elevator and you can turn on the iPad without any signal interference.'

Angie snorted. She asked Will, 'This is what gets you going?'

'Yeah,' he told her. 'It is.'

Angie rolled her eyes. She still had her hand pressed to her stomach. Blood was seeping between her fingers. 'What are you looking at?'

Sara couldn't answer. She was gripped with the same low-level fury that had followed her around since Charlie told them that the Glock was registered to Angie. Every good moment Sara had with Will was always going to have Angie's shadow lurking over it.

'Aw.' Angie pouted her lip. 'Little Sara's upset. Are we going to have another Bambi incident?'

Sara slapped the shit out of her.

Angie raised her hand to retaliate, but Faith caught her wrist, twisted her arm behind her back and forced her into the wall. 'Don't forget how many people were happy to hear that you were dead.'

'Don't forget how many weren't.' Angie wrenched her arm away. She rubbed her wrist. 'Give me my shit back. I'm leaving.'

Will said, 'You're not going anywhere. Who has Anthony? I know you don't have him.'

She shook her head, laughing like he was too stupid to understand.

'You've never called anybody seventeen times in your life. You fucked this up, right? You lost Anthony and now you're trying to get him back. That's why you told me it was Jo in the funeral home instead of Delilah. You wanted me to go to Reuben Figaroa's so that he was forced to put out an Amber Alert.' He was standing close to her, crowding her space the way he would any suspect. 'Your plan went sideways and you needed me to figure out that his son was gone.' He stepped closer. 'We're here now. We know Anthony is gone. We know Reuben's being blackmailed to get him back. Tell me what you know. Let me help make this right.'

'What the fuck do you care, Will?' She slammed her palms against his chest, pushing him away. 'I can handle this, all right? I can take care of myself and my family the same as I've been doing all my fucking life with no fucking help from you.'

Will's jaw jutted out like a shard of glass. 'Your grandson's life is at stake.'

'You're the one stopping me from doing what I've gotta do.'

'Angie, please. Let me help you. I want to help you.' He sounded desperate. 'If that's my grandson out there, then I deserve a chance to know him.'

'Nice try.' She pulled away. 'Jo isn't yours. Not unless you got my hand pregnant.' She gave Sara a pointed look. 'Which, if that was possible, your girlfriend would have a load of fetuses pouring out of her mouth.'

Sara tensed every muscle in her body so that she wouldn't lash out again.

Angie asked her, 'Did you read the note I left for Will?'

'Yes.'

Angie was clearly thrown that there wasn't more.

'Please,' Will said. 'Angie, there's a little boy out there. Your family. Maybe your only family. Tell us how to help him.'

'Since when do you care about helping family?' She gave a derisive snort. 'I'm your family. I'm fucking bleeding and you don't even care.'

Will took out his handkerchief. He pressed it to Angie's side.

Sara felt her heart start to wither at the sight of him touching her so gently.

'I'm sorry,' he told Angie. 'I didn't mean for it to get like this. You're right. It's my fault.'

Angie glanced at Sara. Real or not, she wanted to make sure that Will's obsequience had an audience.

Will said, 'I know I hurt you. I'm sorry. Please, Angie. I'm sorry.'

Angie looked away from Sara, but only so she could soak up Will's misery.

'Please,' Will repeated. Sara wanted to snatch the word out of his mouth. She hated the sound of his begging. 'Please.'

Angie let out a short breath. 'Do you know how bad things have been for me?' Angie covered Will's hand with hers. Sara couldn't tell if she was breaking down or just playing Will like she always did. 'Do you know the things I've had to do? Not just this week, but before?'

'I'm sorry I wasn't there.'

'Harding was him, Will. When Deidre checked out, Harding was the guy on the other side of the door.'

Will took the words like a blow. This wasn't an act. 'You told me he was dead.'

'He is now.'

Shock had almost rendered Will speechless. 'Angie—'

'What he did to me . . .' Angie's voice was low, troubled. She could see the effect her words were having on Will. 'He did it to Delilah. He did it to a lot of girls. For years. I couldn't stop him.'

'Why didn't you tell me?' His hand reached out. He stroked back her hair. 'I could've done something. Protected you.'

'I fucked up so bad, baby.' Angie inhaled sharply. She was crying. 'I know I fucked with you, but it was only to protect Jo. I had to buy her some time in the hospital, some time to heal, while I worked on getting Anthony back.'

'I get it now,' he said. 'I understand.'

'I don't know how it all went so bad . . .' She swallowed hard. 'Dale was always smarter than me. Always stronger. He got inside my head again. Him and Mama, like they always did. I never saw it coming.'

'We can still get Anthony back,' Will said. 'Let me help you.'

'I just needed six more days. Then I could get Anthony, take care of Jo, make sure she got her happy-ever-after.' Angie sniffed. 'Somebody deserves a happy-ever-after, don't they? Somebody needs—' Her voice broke. 'I can't lose him, baby. I already abandoned her once. I can't lose her kid.'

'We're not going to lose him.' His hands went to her shoulders. He looked her in the eyes. 'When you said your mother sent you the photo of Anthony, you meant Virginia Souza, right?'

Angie stiffened.

'Right?' he repeated.

Angie jerked away. 'You fucking asshole.'

Will's face registered a deep satisfaction. For once, he'd managed to be the one doing the manipulating.

He told Amanda, 'Dale Harding was Angie's pimp. Virginia Souza was his bottom girl.' He wiped his hands on his shirt like they were dirty. 'Virginia has Anthony. She's the one who took the picture. She's the one who has him.'

Angie glared at him. 'I fucking hate you.'

He stared at her with a look of utter contempt. 'Good.'

Amanda asked Angie, 'Where is Virginia Souza?'

'Go fuck yourself, you dried-up old bitch.'

'All right. You've outspent your welcome.' Amanda told Faith, 'Take her down to the prison ward. Get her some medical attention.'

'No!' Angie panicked. 'Leave me up here. Handcuff me to Jo's bed if you have to.'

Amanda tried again, 'Where is Virginia Souza?'

'She's not gonna hurt him. The father's the highest bidder.' She had her arms crossed low on her belly. She was pressing into the wound, making the blood run. She tried again with Will. 'There's a video on that iPad. Something that's worth a lot of money. Virginia knew I had it. She said she'd trade Anthony for the iPad. I was supposed to meet her yesterday morning, but she double-crossed me.'

He was still unmoved. 'Virginia called Reuben Figaroa directly. That's why you wanted me to intervene. I get Anthony back for you, and then what? You sell whatever is on the iPad?'

'I don't give a shit about the money. You know that, baby.'

Amanda asked a third time, 'Where is Virginia Souza?'

'You don't think I've been looking for her?' Angie demanded. 'She's lying low. Not in her usual places. Nobody will tell me where she is. They're scared of her. They should be.' Angie wiped her eyes again. She always saved her tears for herself. 'You can't trust her. She's a cold bitch. She doesn't care who gets hurt, especially kids.'

Sara chewed at the irony.

'There's something else.' Faith asked Angie, 'Why did you come here?'

'To say goodbye to Jo, in case . . .' Angie looked out into the hall. 'I kept waiting for the Amber Alert, but it didn't come.'

Faith said, 'Reuben won't report him missing. He's trying to handle it on his own.'

'I figured.' Angie took one of the tissues from her purse. 'I was going to go to his house and shoot him in the head.'

The casual way she detailed her plan to murder a man sent a shiver of cold through Sara's veins.

Angie blew her nose, wincing at the pain in her side. 'Without Reuben, the iPad matters again. I could do what I was going to do in the first place. Trade the iPad for Anthony.'

'With Kip Kilpatrick?' Faith guessed.

Angie was still trying to get Will's attention. He was deliberately looking away from her. She said, 'I know I fucked this up, baby. I was just trying to help my daughter. She doesn't even know who I am.'

Will's face was stone. Angie had no idea what she had done to him. Sara's only hope was that this new-found clarity would last longer than the crisis at hand.

Amanda's phone rang. She listened for a beat, then told them, 'Reuben Figaroa left his house. Laslo Zivcovik is in the car with him. They're going west on Peachtree. Just crossed over Piedmont. We've got three cars on chase. The other stayed at the residence.'

Faith said, 'He's going away from downtown, toward the malls. Public place. Lots of people. That's where I'd do an exchange.'

Amanda looked at her watch. 'The mall just opened. There won't be much of a crowd yet.'

Angie said, 'He's doing reconnaissance. That's why he brought Laslo. Reuben is a control freak. He thinks his wife has been murdered. Somebody stole his son and is demanding money. This is why I wanted to go through Kip. I told Virginia that Reuben would shoot her in the head if he ever got the chance.'

Amanda said, 'I don't know how fast I can get SWAT there. The Buckhead precinct can do deep backup. We've got three agents in three cars. We're at the end of rush hour. It'll take an hour for us to get up to Buckhead. We can go lights and sirens part of the way, but—'

Sara said, 'There's a helicopter on the roof.' She had flown in the air ambulance for emergency transports. 'The Shepherd Spinal Center has a heliport. That'll cut your travel time to fifteen minutes.'

'Perfect,' Amanda said. 'Faith, handcuff Angie to the bed, get someone from APD to sit on her. Make sure they're not connected to Collier. Will goes with me in the chopper. He's the better shot and Reuben hasn't seen his face.' She tossed her keys to Will. 'My rifle is in the back of the car. The magazines are in the lockbox. Get my speedloader and a pack of ammo.'

Instinctively Sara grabbed Will's arm. This was happening too fast. Amanda was talking about shooting people. People shooting back. Sara didn't want him to leave. She didn't want to lose him.

Will cupped his hand to Sara's face. 'I'll see you back home when this is over.'

THIRTEEN

Will studied the map on the wall inside the security offices at Phipps Plaza. There were a thousand ways the hand-off between Reuben Figaroa and Virginia Souza could spin out of control. Deshawn Watkins, the chief of security, outlined a few of them for Amanda.

'There are four possible points of approach directly into level three.' Deshawn pointed out three different escalators and the elevator that serviced all three levels inside the main atrium. 'Then there's another set of escalators if you go through the Belk department store. One up, one down. Then there's this elevator here inside Belk, and another elevator here at the street entrance. None of the main elevators go to the parking garage except this one here and here.'

Amanda said, 'So we're effectively inside a sieve.' She looked at her watch. They were assuming that the meet would take place on the hour or half-hour. She told Will, 'It's eleven sixteen. If we get past noon, we're going to have to rethink this. There's no telling how many people will turn up here for lunch.'

Deshawn said, 'You're talking most of the people who work in the stores, a lot more kids. This place is filled by twelve thirty.'

Will rubbed his jaw as he studied the map on the wall. The layout was familiar. He'd been to Phipps with Sara more times than he would've liked. The mall was three levels, stacked like a wedding cake, with the smaller top tier pushed to the front. There was a round open atrium that ran through all three floors. The railings were glass with polished wood and gold handrails. The elevator had a glass back. Will couldn't help but be reminded of Marcus Rippy's nightclub, though the ambience was the exact opposite. The floors were sparkling clean. Skylights brought in ample sunshine.

Reuben Figaroa sat in the food court area on the third level, the same as he'd been the entire time. He had picked a good location to trade off his son. Or maybe Virginia Souza had chosen the spot. Even on a Tuesday, the top level was a mecca for pre-school children. The Legoland Discovery Center hosted Toddler Time every Tuesday morning. The movie theater was running a cartoon marathon. Kids weren't the only problem. There was a large open food court with several fast-food restaurants. Scattered through the rest of the mall were elderly mall walkers and shoppers perusing the over one hundred stores.

If Will was going to trade off a kid for money, this is where he'd do it.

Then again, they didn't know whether or not Reuben Figaroa meant to make a trade.

A public place. A controlling man who owned a lot of guns. A terrified little boy. A woman who had built her life around hurting kids.

This could go like clockwork or it could go like hell.

Will mentally walked through the best-case scenario: Souza walks into the mall with Anthony. The good guys scoop up the kid and return him to his father. Second-best: Souza manages to give them the slip as she makes her way to the food court, she trades Anthony for the money, the good guys isolate her on the second level, then make an arrest.

Will didn't want to think about the worst-case scenario, the one where Reuben, who didn't mind hitting women, demanded payback. The one where Virginia Souza had a gun or a knife and a kid in her hands. The one where they went to a second location that there was no way to control.

Then there was Laslo.

Then there was the possibility that Souza had an accomplice.

As the mama in charge, she had her pick of young girls who would do her bidding. Any one of them—any two or three of them—could be posing as one of the young mothers in the food court.

Souza's girls were street savvy. They would know what a cop looked like. They could warn Souza. They would have her back if the trade went south. They were all as feral as Angie, hardened and mean and desperate to do whatever it took to protect their family.

Amanda said, 'She won't take the elevators. That's not a quick getaway.'

'It wouldn't make sense to go down to the parking garage.' Deshawn pointed to the map again, the glass elevator in the atrium. 'She'd have to go down two levels, then this is the closest exit. But we can keep the elevators from going down to the garage if you want.'

'Do that.' Will told Amanda, 'Reuben has the knee brace. He won't be able to move fast.'

'Let's hope it's not Reuben we're following out of this mall.' Amanda asked Deshawn, 'How would you get out of here? Down the escalators to the second level, then what?'

'Level one is the only way out.' Deshawn was still at the map. 'If we take out the parking garage, there are twelve street entrances. Three each at Belk, Saks and Nordstrom. Then we've got two more entrances off Monarch Court and one more entrance off the Avenue of the South. Either one can take you to Peachtree or the interstate. I'd go this exit at the valet parking station.'

'Makes sense,' Amanda said. 'Reuben's car is parked in front of Saks. He takes a right, he's in the car, then onto the interstate.'

'Or home,' Will said, but Amanda's look told him that she didn't think it was likely.

Her radio clicked. She walked to the other side of the room, checking in with the team. Twelve uniformed cops from the APD's Buckhead precinct were scattered around the mall. SWAT was on the roof and staked out across the buildings on the corner. Mall security was keeping to its regular rounds so as not to raise suspicion. Three of the GBI agents from the chase cars outside Reuben's house were spread out near the escalators. The fourth was trailing Laslo, who had been casing the mall for the last hour and a half.

Angie was right about Reuben Figaroa. He had come early to give himself a tactical advantage. Which was good, because it had given Amanda time to set up her people too.

Will's biggest concern was, had Virginia Souza done the same?

All they had to identify the woman by was her last booking photo, which had been taken four years ago. Her long, stringy brown hair and smeared make-up made her look like central casting's idea of an old whore. If Souza was as smart as Angie said, she'd know that she couldn't walk into Phipps Plaza looking like herself. The mall was too high-end for her to go unnoticed.

Deshawn said, 'We can call in maintenance, maybe put up a barrier on that escalator, make it look like it's broken down.'

Will said, 'I'm worried that might tip him off.'

'He doesn't look jumpy.'

'No,' Will said, but that wasn't necessarily a good thing. A composed man was a man who had made up his mind.

They could detain Reuben. You didn't need cause to do that. But then Souza might have a spotter who warned her off, and the next time they saw Anthony he would be in a gutter or on the internet.

Will looked at the bank of high-definition monitors on the wall. The displays were in full color. There was no need to toggle through the different security cameras. There were sixteen screens. The largest monitor, the one in the center of the wall, showed Reuben Figaroa.

He was sitting at the back of the food court, one level up from where Will stood. The open atrium was at his shoulder. There was no way he could escape over the side. Even a basketball star couldn't survive a three-story fall. Fortunately, the tables immediately around him were vacant. The other shoppers were keeping a wide berth. The mothers seemed especially suspicious of a man sitting alone in the place where they had brought their children.

Reuben had come incognito, a Falcons hat tight on his bald head. A laptop was on the table in front of him. He was slumped in the chair in an attempt to conceal his height. His mustache and goatee had grown into a full beard, because he was one of those guys who needed to shave every four hours. He was wearing a black T-shirt and black jeans, not exactly combat gear, but close enough. A large duffel bag was at his feet. Because of the T-shirt, they knew he wasn't wearing a gun, but the duffel bag was easily large enough to accommodate a rifle or an automatic machine gun or a handgun, or all three.

Amanda was off the radio. She told Will, 'Laslo just left the mall. He moved the car to the Ritz-Carlton. He's parked in the valet lane. This is about to happen.'

Deshawn said, 'He'll leave out the Nordstrom side to get to the Ritz.'

'I'll let SWAT know.' Amanda gave Will the radio, then headed toward the door. 'Faith is on her way up. I'll take my place. Will, be ready to move wherever you're needed. Belt and suspenders.'

Deshawn picked up a desk phone. He told Will, 'I'll tell Nordstrom security we think they're going to see some action.'

Will watched the monitors. The security office was right outside a single escalator that led to the top floor. Amanda held on to the handrail as she climbed. Like Reuben, she was in disguise, dressed in a pastel-blue tracksuit and white T-shirt that she had picked up at one of the stores. Her big purse was empty except for her revolver and three speedloaders. She was wearing glasses. A floppy white old-lady hat was on her head. Like everyone else on the team, she wore an earbud that worked as a two-way radio, picking up her speech through a vibration in her jaw.

Instead of walking toward Reuben, she sat down at one of the tables outside Belk, about sixty feet away. She kept her back to him. Phil Brauer, one of the agents from the chase cars, was already at the table with two cups of coffee. They blended in well, passing for an old retired couple with time on their hands.

Amanda said, 'We're in place.'

Deshawn asked Will, 'You sure we don't just clean this place out?'

'It'll tip her off.'

'That's a big risk.'

'We've got someone inside the Legoland, another at the theater. We'll lock down everything the moment there's any sign of trouble.'

'What about the pedestrians?' He pointed to the monitor showing the food court. 'There's at least a dozen people there.'

Will had counted nine, including a table of four young mothers with babies in strollers. Amanda had placed herself between the women and Reuben Figaroa. 'If we don't get this kid today, then the woman who has him will trick him out to the nearest pedophile.'

'Jesus.' Deshawn let that sink in. 'What's your plan if she tries to run off with the kid, takes him hostage or something?'

Will tapped the rifle on his shoulder.

'Jesus.'

Faith entered the room. She was wearing the black suit she kept in the trunk of her car instead of her usual GBI blue shirt and khakis. Her gun was on her hip. She nodded at Deshawn, asking Will, 'What've we got?'

'Amanda is here with Brauer. She put herself between Reuben and this table.' He pointed to the four young mothers. They were laughing. One of them was feeding her baby. Another was on her phone.

Faith said, 'They can take cover inside the Belk if they need to.'

Will said, 'We've got one of our guys inside Legoland. Store security knows to bring down the gate if there's trouble. They've been keeping the kids to the back where there's a birthday party. The gift store is at the front so there aren't a lot of potential problems there. Same with the movie theater. The cartoon lets out at noon, but we've got APD inside, behind the concession stand and at the mall exit, ready to lock them in place.' He showed her the map on the wall. 'We've got the escalators covered here, here, here and here.' He pointed to the corresponding areas. 'Laslo is parked across the street from here. SWAT is outside.'

'They're good. I didn't see them.'

'We gave all the store managers Souza's booking photo. They've been told not to approach her. We didn't want to pass the photo to the clerks and start a lot of chatter.'

'She's not going to look like her booking photo.'

'It's all we have.'

Faith stared at Reuben Figaroa. 'I don't like that duffel bag. Even with a million bucks in cash, it doesn't need to be that big.'

Will followed her gaze to the monitors. Reuben was still sitting at the table staring at his laptop. 'We had one of our guys sitting near him, but Reuben got spooked, so we had to pull back.'

'He couldn't tell what was in the bag?'

'No, but Reuben's been looking at pictures of the wife and kid on the laptop, scrolling through them over and over again.'

'Who's that?'

Will looked at the big monitor. A young woman was walking toward Reuben. She sat down three tables away. Her head was bent toward her phone. White earbuds disappeared into her hair. She was wearing what most of the other mothers were wearing, some variation on a gym outfit.

Reuben stared at the woman for a long while before turning back to his laptop.

Faith said, 'Her shoes are wrong.'

Will looked at the red shoes. They were slip-ons. 'You mean because she's not wearing sneakers?'

'A woman who can sit around a mall on a Wednesday morning in her workout clothes doesn't buy her shoes at Walmart.' She added, 'Also, why is she here if she isn't with a kid?'

Will studied the other women on the periphery of the food court. Invariably they had some form of child attached to them, whether they were holding a baby or dragging a toddler away from Legoland.

Deshawn said, 'It's eleven twenty-eight.'

'Green jacket.' Faith stepped closer to the monitors. 'That's a woman, right?'

An androgynous-looking woman was waiting outside the elevator on the first level. She was wearing dark sunglasses and a Braves baseball cap with the brim pulled low. Her jeans were dark blue. The dark green jacket was zipped almost to her neck. Her hands were tucked into the pockets.

Deshawn said, 'She doesn't work here. At least not so that I've noticed.'

'Is that Souza?' Faith asked. 'She could have the kid somewhere else, maybe in a car downstairs.'

A second location. The worst of the worst-case scenarios.

Will got on the radio. 'We need a quiet sweep of the garage. Check for Anthony in a parked car.'

The woman pressed the elevator button again. Her hand went back into her jacket pocket. There was something furtive to her movements. She was clearly nervous.

Will clicked on the radio again. He told Amanda, 'We might have someone in the elevator. Green jacket. Stand by.'

'Ten-four,' Amanda said.

'She doesn't look young, right?' Faith practically had her nose touching the monitor. 'The way she carries herself. She's not talking on her phone or listening to music. It's too hot for that jacket.'

Deshawn said, 'We'll see her face when she gets on the elevator.'

The doors slid open. Green Jacket didn't look up as she got on. She kept her head down, hands still tucked deep into her pockets. The doors started to close, but her arm shot out, stopping it.

'Shit,' Faith said. Yet another woman was getting onto the elevator. Tall, blonde ponytail, dressed in a V-necked T-shirt and running shorts. She was trying to wrangle a two-seater baby stroller onto the elevator. An infant was in the front seat. A little girl dressed like a character from the Lego movie slept in the back.

'I don't like this,' Faith said. 'That's two kids. Two hostages.'

As they watched, Green Jacket leaned down, gripping the front of the stroller and pulling it onto the elevator. There was an exchange of pleasantries before the doors closed. They silently rode up to the third level.

'She's still not looking at the camera,' Faith said. 'Nobody keeps their head down all of the time like that.'

Will held the radio to his mouth. 'Green Jacket, getting off the elevator.'

Phil Brauer stood up from the table. He threw away his coffee cup in the trashcan. Green Jacket helped the blonde maneuver the stroller out of the elevator, then walked toward the movie theater. Brauer sat down at another table. He put his phone to his ear. Will heard the man's voice on the radio. 'Can't tell with the hat. She's got dark hair. Looks about the right age.'

They all leaned closer to the screens. Green Jacket stood in front of the box office. She looked up at the board that showed the movie times.

'Is it her?' Faith asked. 'I can't—'

'Contact,' Amanda said.

Reuben Figaroa was standing up.

The blonde with the tandem stroller stood on the other side of his table.

Virginia Souza.

The bottom girl had cleaned up well. She had dyed her hair honey blonde instead of bleaching it. Her make-up was understated. Her clothes accentuated her body but didn't show off too much. The ponytail gave her a more youthful look. She had been here before, taking time to study the other women to make sure she would blend in.

'It's Anthony,' Faith said.

She was right. Anthony was in the back of the stroller. He was dressed in pink. His legs were folded up underneath him. He was too big for the seat. His eyes were closed. They were shaped like Angie's. His skin was Angie's. His jeopardy was Angie's.

Will clicked the radio. 'It's her. She has Anthony and an infant in the stroller. There's a second woman, probably backup, three tables over, red shoes.'

Amanda said, 'Alpha team, Delta team, lock down.'

She was closing off Legoland and the theater.

Faith asked, 'What are they saying? They're just standing there.'

There was obviously a terse exchange going on between Reuben and Souza. Will saw that the man's fists were tightly clenched. He kept looking at his son, then at Souza, like he couldn't decide whether or not losing Anthony was worth the pleasure of killing her.

'She told him about her backup,' Faith guessed. 'That's the only reason he's not on top of her. Red Shoes has to have a gun.'

'The iPad,' Will said, because he knew how these women worked. 'Souza wants to put Reuben on the hook for more money. She thinks she can get the iPad from Angie.'

Amanda cut in. 'Brauer texted. He can't hear them. He can't see what Red Shoes is doing. Can anyone see her hands?'

Will told her, 'She's got her phone in her lap.'

'The purse,' Faith said, because like almost every woman there, Red Shoes had a purse that could easily accommodate a handgun.

Phil Brauer moved his chair, turning sideways. He was holding out his cell phone like he needed glasses to read something, using his peripheral vision to check on Green Jacket.

She was still looking at the box office times. She still had her hands in her pockets.

Faith said, 'They're sitting down.'

Reuben was in his chair. He didn't slump like before. His shoulders were straight. His legs were so long that his knees reached the other side of the small table. Souza had to keep her chair pulled back so that she could face him. Her mouth kept moving. She seemed blind to the effect her words were having.

Faith said, 'This is taking too long. She's worked men more than half her life. Why can't she see that he's about to explode?'

'Just go in.' Deshawn sounded desperate. 'Why aren't you guys moving? Nobody's armed.'

'You don't need a gun to throw a baby over the side of that balcony.'

'Jesus.'

Will squinted at the infant in the front seat of the stroller. 'Can you tell if the baby is moving?'

Faith shook her head. 'Where's the diaper bag, the sippy cups, the extra blankets, the wipes?'

'You think it's fake?'

'Why would she bring a baby? They're too much trouble.' She said it again, 'This is taking too long.'

Reuben Figaroa seemed to be thinking this same thing. He had his hands clasped together in his lap. He wasn't reaching for his duffel bag. He wasn't talking. He glared at Souza as she lectured him. His anger was like a third person at the table. Will could almost see the crank on his back winding tighter and tighter. Souza either had no idea what she was doing or she assumed that she had all of the power.

Reuben Figaroa didn't like women with power.

'Red Shoes is getting up.'

The young woman stood and walked toward the escalator. Her phone was pressed to her ear.

Will kept his eyes on Virginia Souza. She was warning Reuben about something, giving him an ultimatum. Her finger jammed into the air. She didn't seem to notice that her chair was moving, sliding her closer and closer to the table.

Will said, 'He's got his feet hooked around the chair legs.'

'What's he doing under the table?'

Reuben's hands were working on something, peeling at something.

Will put the radio to his mouth.

It happened so fast that he didn't have time to press the button.

Souza's chair yanked forward, pinning her to the back. Reuben plunged a large knife straight into her throat. Her hands went up. He grabbed her wrists, holding them with one hand while with the other he stabbed her belly again and again underneath the table.

'Shit!' Faith hissed.

Blood poured down Souza's chair. She slumped over.

Reuben stood with the duffel bag. He reached for Anthony.

'Watch out!' Deshawn screamed.

Green Jacket was drawing down on Reuben. Double-barrel stainless-steel Snake Slayer. Two shots from the derringer would send ten .38 special-sized projectiles flying through the air.

Phil Brauer ran toward the woman, but it didn't matter.

Reuben pulled a Sig Sauer out of his duffel and shot Green Jacket in the head.

'Lock down!' Amanda ordered. 'Now!'

Will ran from the room, his rifle slamming into his back. Faith was on his heels. They were fifty yards from the atrium, one level below the food court. He felt like he was running on a treadmill as he circled the large opening. Every step forward took him two back. Faith bolted up the escalator to the third floor. Will rounded the far side of the atrium. He slung around his rifle, slid across the floor on his knees and took up position across from where Reuben Figaroa stood.

The barrel of Will's rifle rested on the railing. His eye was to the scope. The safety was off. His finger stretched along the trigger guard.

He took a breath.

Forty yards.

He could make the shot in his sleep, but Reuben held Anthony to his chest, his giant arm crushing his son's ribs. The muzzle of the Sig Sauer was pressed against Anthony's temple.

Amanda said, 'Drop it!'

Her stance was wide. She had her revolver out, fifteen feet from her target. Faith had stopped the escalator. She was lying flat to the stairs. Phil Bauer was kneeling behind a table. They had formed a triangle, trapping Reuben inside. Like Will, they were all looking for a shot. Like Will, they were all coming up short. Anthony covered his father's heart, his lungs, his belly, any place that a bullet could stop him.

Reuben screamed, 'Back the fuck up!'

Will looked through the rifle scope. Reuben's finger was wrapped around the trigger. One single twitch and Anthony's life would be over. Will knew that Amanda was going through the same checklist that he was. If she hit Reuben's leg, he could still pull the trigger. If she aimed for his head and missed, he could still pull the trigger. If she hit his head, he could still pull the trigger. If she miscalculated by even the smallest fraction, she could end up killing a six-year-old boy.

Amanda said, 'You're surrounded. There's no way out.'

'Get the fuck out of my way.'

Will tensed. Reuben had an athlete's reflexes. In seconds, he could flick his wrist and shoot Amanda, and Will would be left with the same bad choices.

Reuben walked toward Amanda. He limped in his knee brace. 'Get back, bitch.'

'You don't want to do this.' Amanda backed up. Will's view was obstructed as she passed in front of the elevator. 'Put the gun down and we can talk.'

Reuben kept walking, Anthony tight to his chest. Will moved counter to him, rifle up, praying for a clean shot.

Reuben punched the button on the elevator. 'I'm walking outta here.'

'Put the boy down,' Amanda said. 'Put him down and we'll talk.'

'Shut the fuck up!'

The sound of his father shouting was enough to wake Anthony from his stupor. His eyes went wide as he realized what was happening. He started screaming, a high-pitched sound like an animal caught in a trap.

The elevator doors opened. Reuben got on. Will had a straight line through the glass wall of the elevator. He still couldn't shoot. Even from this distance, he wasn't sure the bullet wouldn't pass through Reuben and kill Anthony.

The doors closed.

Will jogged back around the atrium. The elevator car passed the second floor. He ran toward the next escalator. The stairs were going up. Will shuffled down, his feet tripping on the metal treads. He grabbed on to the rails, lifted his legs and hurled his body the rest of the way down.

His feet hit the floor just as the elevator doors opened.

Anthony was crying. He squirmed to get out of his father's arms. Reuben struggled to hold on to the kid and the gun. He was yelling at the boy to be quiet. Will ran at a crouch, using the back of the escalator for cover. The butt of his rifle was jammed into his shoulder. He kept one eye on the sight.

Anthony kept flailing, arms wide. His feet kicked, landing a blow on his father's bad knee. Reuben dropped him.

Will swung around and pulled the trigger.

The world stopped spinning.

The butt of the rifle recoiled into Will's shoulder. There was a flash at the end of the muzzle. The cartridge ejected out to the side. The bullet sliced the dense air like a knife cutting open a bag of flour.

Reuben Figaroa's shoulder jerked back. He slammed against the elevator doors and slid to the floor.

Will followed him down, going to one knee. His trigger finger started to pull back again, but Anthony stopped him.

Reuben had the Sig pointed at his son's back. His aim was steady. Will had put the bullet in the wrong shoulder.

Reuben said, 'Come here, boy.'

Will was fifteen feet away from Anthony. Reuben was less than two.

'Anthony,' Will said. 'Run.'

Anthony didn't move.

Will slid his knee across the floor, trying to get a better angle. Reuben's flanks were protected by the deep elevator alcove. The only shot that could take him out would have to come from the front.

'Stop.' Reuben's eyes tracked back and forth between Anthony and Will, and then Faith.

She was on the other side of the escalator. Another triangle, again with Reuben at the center. Will heard footsteps as more officers approached, but he didn't dare take his eye off Reuben Figaroa.

'Anthony,' Reuben ordered. 'Get over here, boy.'

Faith said, 'Anthony, sweetheart. Come to me. It's okay.'

Will slid over a little bit more. His finger tensed on the trigger.

Reuben screamed, 'Now, God dammit!'

Anthony stepped back.

Will took his finger off the trigger.

Reuben wrapped his injured arm around his son. Anthony fell into him, his head blocking his father's face. The Sig pressed at the boy's temple. Anthony didn't struggle. He didn't speak. He had learned to be still when his father was angry. All of his fear channeled into his lip, that quivered like his adoptive grandmother's, and the look of resignation in his eyes that he'd inherited from Angie.

When she talked to Will about the abuse, she never talked about it. She only gave advice: *All you have to do is wait until it's over.*

Anthony was waiting for the inevitable. The screaming. The hitting. The black eye. The split lip. The sleepless nights as he waited for the door to open.

'Back away.' Reuben had to rest the side of his hand on his son's shoulder. He was panting hard. Blood poured from the bullet hole just below his clavicle. They were at the same impasse as the one upstairs, only now, Reuben was even more desperate.

Will said, 'Put down the gun. You don't want to do this.'

'Shit.' Reuben's hand started shaking. Blood slipped down his other arm. The muscles were spasming, tensing his chest and shoulders. 'What'd you hit me with?'

'Hornaday sixty-grain TAP URBAN.'

'Tactical Application for Police.' Reuben's eyelids were heavy. His face was slick with sweat. 'Reduced penetration for urban environments.'

Will used his back foot to push his knee forward. He couldn't come from the side. He had to get closer. 'Sounds like you know your ammo.'

'You see that Snake Slayer that bitch pulled?'

'Probably had .410 Bonds in the chamber.'

'Lucky I stopped her.' Reuben blinked sweat out of his eyes. Will wondered if the man's vision was blurring. There were a lot of important things near the clavicle. Subclavian arteries. Subclavian veins. Sara would know. She would record the damage in Reuben Figaroa's autopsy, because if the man hurt Angie's grandson, he would not walk out of here alive.

'Let's talk this out,' Will said. 'You're gonna need surgery. I can help you.'

'No more surgery.' Reuben shook his head. He was blinking more slowly now. His arm was not so tight around Anthony. The muzzle of the Sig had tilted upward, but he could still put a bullet in his son's brain.

Will moved closer.

Faith made a noise. Anthony looked at her. Will did not. He knew she was trying to wave the boy over.

'Don't.' Reuben straightened the gun.

Will asked, 'What's the trigger pull on that Sig? Five and a half pounds? Six?'

Reuben nodded.

'Why don't you move your finger? You don't want to make a mistake.'

'I don't make mistakes.'

Will slid closer. Ten feet. If Reuben moved just a little to the side, Will was close enough for the head shot. To make one. To receive one. Will couldn't trust the gun in Reuben's hand. It was upstairs all over again. Reuben could flick it out and kill Will. He could flick it back and kill Anthony.

Will said, 'You're not doing too well, man.'

'I'm not,' he agreed. The arm around Anthony started to relax again. The boy could pull away, but Reuben could still shoot the gun. At Anthony. At Will.

'Let's talk this out,' Will repeated. He pushed a few inches closer. The rifle was out in front of him. Thirty-nine inches of weapon. One hand on the grip, the other on the stock. Will slid his hand farther down the barrel. His shoulder would dislocate if the gun went off. He curved his back, buying the illusion of extra space.

Reuben said, 'I can't leave my boy alone.'

Will couldn't look at the kid. He couldn't see Angie's eyes looking back at him. 'You don't have to take Anthony with you.'

'There's nothing left for him,' Reuben said. 'Jo's gone. My career is gone. That video gets out, and my freedom is gone.'

Will said, 'Do you see how close I am?'

Reuben's eyelids fluttered. He straightened the Sig.

Will said, 'I can pull the trigger right now.'

'So can I.' Reuben's breathing was shallow. His skin had no color. Will could see every single pore in his face, every single follicle of hair. 'I'm not going to leave my boy alone.' He swallowed. 'Jo wouldn't want that. Her real mother left her. She would never leave her son.'

Will pushed himself closer. He thought about why Reuben was doing this, how the loss of control had spun out his life. He asked, 'How do I stop this, Reuben? Tell me how to save your son.'

'Who killed her?'

Will tried to think of the best lie to tell him, the one that would keep him from murdering his son. That Jo was still alive, that Reuben had something to live for? That Jo was dead, but the woman behind her murder was in police custody? That she was Jo's mother? That she had tried to ransom her own grandson?

Reuben was out of patience. 'Who, man? Who killed Jo?'

'The woman upstairs.' He couldn't tell if he'd made the right choice, but he had to keep going. 'Her name is Virginia Souza. She's a prostitute who met Jo in jail. They argued. Souza took out her revenge.'

To Will's great relief, Reuben started nodding, like that made sense. 'Was it over drugs? What they fought over?'

'Yes.' Will moved another millimeter, then another. His hand slid farther down the barrel. Too far to safely hold on to the stock. There was no way he could safely fire the rifle now. 'Souza knew that Jo was rich, that she had money. She followed her to the party. She kidnapped her. She took Anthony.'

Reuben nodded again. The reason was obvious. His wife had hidden her addiction. She would hide other things. 'Bitch is dead now.'

'That's right,' Will said.

'Jo too.' He stopped to swallow. 'She betrayed me. Betrayed everything we had. She didn't listen to me.'

'That's what women do.'

'They just take and take and spit you out like you're nothing.'

The muzzle of the Sig had tilted up again, but again not enough to clear Anthony's head. Reuben was faltering. His muscles were twitching. His nerves were in disarray. His finger could pull the trigger by mistake or by design. Whether it was pointing at Will or at Anthony when it happened was going to be a delicate dance.

'Stop moving,' Reuben said.

'I'm not moving.' Will moved up.

Reuben's throat flexed as he swallowed. 'She kept it from me. The pills. She stole that video. I know she's the one who stole it. Ruined my life. My son's.' He swallowed again. 'My son.'

Will was close enough now. He could only grab one thing: the gun or Anthony.

Anthony or Will.

All it came down to was which direction the gun was pointing.

'It's okay.' Reuben was looking at Will now, a flatness to his eyes. His mouth gaped open. His lips were blue. He was having trouble getting air. He blinked, slow. He blinked again, even slower. He blinked a third time and Will lunged forward, his arm swinging through the air, backhanding Anthony out of the way.

Reuben's head exploded.

Hot blood splattered Will's face and neck. Bone was inside his mouth, up his nose. His eyes were on fire. He fell back, dropped the rifle. He clawed at his face. Strings of muscle and tissue caught in his fingers. He sneezed. Blood sprayed onto the floor. He could barely see it. He was standing, walking backward like he could get away from the carnage, but the carnage was all over him.

'Will!' Amanda yanked him forward by his arm. He stumbled, tripping over his own feet. She kept pulling him, then dragging him across the atrium, down a corridor, where he bounced off the wall. He was completely blind. Carpet was under his feet. He tried to open his eyes, but he couldn't. Splinters were ripping apart his eyeballs—shards of Reuben Figaroa's bone and teeth and cartilage.

'Lean over.' Amanda pushed him down.

Cold water streamed into his mouth, his face. Chunks of gray matter slid down his skin. He saw light. He blinked. He saw white porcelain, a tall faucet. They were in the bathroom. He was leaning over the sink. Will reached for the soap dispenser. It ripped off the wall. The bag burst. He took handfuls of soap and scrubbed his face and neck. He ripped off his shirt. He scrubbed his chest until the skin was raw.

'Stop,' Amanda said. 'You're going to hurt yourself.' She grabbed his hands. She made him stop before he peeled the skin off his body. 'You're okay,' she told him. 'Take a breath.'

Will didn't want to take a breath. He was sick of people telling him to take a breath. He stuck his head under a different faucet in a clean sink. He rinsed out his mouth. The water was pink when he spat it into the bowl. He rubbed his face, scratching the skin, making sure there were no more pieces of Reuben Figaroa in his eyes and hair.

'Drink some more water.'

He picked something out of his ear. Red grit, part of a molar.

Will threw the tooth against the wall. He leaned his hands on the basin. His breath was like fire in his lungs. His skin burned. Phantom drops of blood slid down his face and neck.

'It's all right,' Amanda said.

'I know it's all right.' He closed his eyes. It wasn't all right. Blood was everywhere. In the sinks. Pooling onto the floor. The bathroom was freezing. He was shaking from the cold.

'Anthony?' He clenched his teeth to keep them from chattering.

'He's safe. Faith has him.'

'Jesus,' Will mumbled. He tried to regulate his breathing, to get back some sense of control over his body. He squeezed his eyes shut. 'I wasn't sure Faith had a line.'

'She did. I did. All of us did. But he beat us to it.' Amanda started pulling paper towels from the dispenser. 'Reuben Figaroa killed himself.'

Will's head jerked up in surprise.

'The second Anthony was gone, Reuben put the gun under his chin and pulled the trigger.'

Will stared at her in disbelief.

She nodded. 'He killed himself.'

Will tried to play it back in his head, but all he remembered was the fleeting concern as he shoved Anthony out of the way that the kid would fall and hurt himself.

Amanda said, 'You did everything right, Will. Reuben Figaroa made a choice.'

'I could've saved him.' Will wiped his face with a paper towel. The rough paper was like a cat's tongue. He looked down expecting to see blood but finding only the dark stain of water.

Was Faith wiping Anthony's face in another bathroom?

When the gun had gone off, the boy had been standing as close to Reuben as Will had been. For how many years would Reuben's son feel the slick fibers of his father's brain dripping down the side of his face? How many nights would he wake up screaming, scared that he was suffocating on the gray matter and bone that he'd sniffed up into his nose?

'Will,' Amanda said. 'How could you have saved him?'

Will shook his head. He had made the wrong choice. He'd felt it in his gut even as the lie had come out of his mouth. 'Reuben would've put down the gun if I'd told him the truth about Jo. That she was alive. That he had something to live for.' He wadded up the paper towel into a ball. 'You heard what he said about not leaving Anthony alone, that Jo wouldn't want that. No way he would've pulled the trigger if he'd thought there was still a chance that his family was intact.'

'Or he would've shot you instead. Or been shot by any one of us, because he stabbed a woman to death two floors above us. He shot another woman in the head. He beat his wife for nearly a decade. He threatened to murder his own son. Where are you getting this notion that there was some romantic bond between Reuben Figaroa and his wife that you could magically invoke and make everything better?'

Will chucked the paper towel into the trash.

'If you love someone, you don't go out of your way to hurt them. You don't torture them. You don't terrify them or make them live in constant fear. That's not how love works. It's not how normal people work.'

Will didn't need Amanda to point out that there wasn't much daylight between Angie and Reuben. 'Thanks, but I think I'm going to pass on today's parable.'

Amanda didn't respond. She was looking at his bare chest. The round, perfect *O*s that the cigarettes had seared into his flesh. The black tattooing left by the electrical burns. The Frankenstein stitches around the skin graft from when a wound refused to close.

Before Sara, he would've scrambled to cover himself. Now, he was just intensely uncomfortable.

Amanda unzipped her jacket. 'I used to come watch you on visitation days.'

Visitation days. She meant at the children's home. Will had always looked forward to the visits, until he started dreading them. All the kids were bathed and trotted out for prospective parents. And then the kids like Will were trotted back in.

'I couldn't adopt you. I was a single woman. A career gal. Obviously I was unfit to take care of anything more than a pet rock.' She wrapped her jacket around his shoulders. Her hands stayed there. She looked at him in the mirror. 'I stopped visiting because I couldn't stand the longing. Not my own, which was hard enough, but *your* longing broke my heart. You wanted so badly for someone to pick you.'

Will stared down at his hands. There was blood crusted into his cuticles.

'I picked you. Faith picked you. Sara picked you. Let that be enough. Let yourself accept that you're worth it.'

He used his thumbnail to scrape out the blood. His skin was still pink. He shivered again from the cold. 'She's going to be alone.'

Amanda helped him into the jacket. 'Wilbur, women like Angie are always going to be alone. No matter how many people surround them, they will always be alone.'

He knew that. He had seen it all of his life. Even when Angie was with him, she still held herself apart. 'Do you think we have a case against her for letting Delilah die in the trunk of her car?'

'With Jane Doe as our only witness? No security footage, no DNA, no incriminating fingerprints, no smoking gun, no corroborating testimony, no confession?' Amanda laughed at the futility. 'It's Denny who's going to suffer. I can keep him out of jail, but he'll lose his job, his pension, his benefits.'

Will didn't want to feel sorry for Collier, but he did. He knew too much what it felt like when Angie threw you to the wolves.

'Let me get this.' She tried to zip the jacket. She couldn't get it closed past his chest. The bottom was too short. The waist hit him above his navel. 'I'll have to buy you another shirt before you go back out there. You look like a Filipino sex worker.'

She meant it as a parting shot, but he couldn't let her go yet.

'It's never going to catch up with her, is it?' He said, 'The people she hurts. The damage she does.'

'Trust me, Will. Life always makes you pay for your personality.' Amanda gave him a rueful smile. 'It catches up with her every single second of the day.'

Eleven Days Later—Saturday

FOURTEEN

Sara stood in her kitchen watching the noon news as she ate a bowl of ice cream. After eleven days of speculation, Ditmar Wittich was finally giving an interview. He sat with a scaled model of the scuttled All-Star Complex behind him, delivering a diatribe about how the project was still a good idea. He might as well have been speaking gibberish. The reporter clearly only cared about sentences that contained the words *Rippy* or *Figaroa*.

Wittich said, 'The complex would bring thousands of jobs to the city.'

Sara muted the TV. Other than the German accent, she had no idea where Will got the Goldfinger reference. Wittich was much more of a Stromberg.

She dumped the rest of the ice cream into the sink. Probably not the best choice for lunch, but it beat daytime drinking. When she glanced back at the TV, the screen was split between Wittich and that video that was being called the Rippy Rampage. Sara wanted to look away, but she couldn't. Hardly anyone in the world could. Someone at the GBI had leaked the file from Angie's iPad. Amanda was on the warpath, which to Sara's thinking meant she was probably the culprit.

Angie had been right that the video was damaging, though probably not for the reason she had assumed.

The film that Reuben Figaroa had made of himself and Marcus Rippy raping a drugged Keisha Miscavage had shattered internet viewing records. Unfortunately, all people could talk about was the last three seconds of footage when, off camera, a door is slammed open, a hand reaches out to swat Reuben's iPhone away, and a woman screams the beginning of what is obviously the word *motherfucker*.

The blur of pink before the video goes black is almost lost to the naked eye, but slow down the frames and you can see the custom-crafted Italian leather stiletto kicking Keisha Miscavage's head. The ostrich-skin shoe is dyed bright fuchsia. There is a gold *R* embroidered on the toe.

Will had recognized the shoe immediately. He had a thing for shoes. He remembered that LaDonna Rippy had worn the stilettos to the one and only interview her husband had submitted to during the rape investigation.

Marcus Rippy was freely giving interviews now. He'd turned on his wife, insisting that he and Reuben had just been having a little fun with Keisha Miscavage. The video backed him up. Keisha was drugged but showing no outward signs of injury before LaDonna entered the room. According to Marcus, it was LaDonna who had done the real damage.

So here was Will's new case: LaDonna had beaten Keisha. LaDonna had choked her, punched her, strangled her over the course of five hours. LaDonna had left the bruises on Keisha's back and legs and put her into a coma that had kept her in the hospital for a week.

The forensic evidence backed this up. LaDonna's DNA had matched the sweat and saliva found on the victim's body. Keisha's DNA was found in the spots of blood on LaDonna's pink shoes. The prosecution wasn't open and shut—with the Rippys' money, nothing was ever a sure thing—but there was also a documented pattern of behavior.

LaDonna Rippy was a jealous woman. Will had found three previous out-of-court settlements where victims had been paid for their silence. A woman in Las Vegas was still managing to tell her story despite LaDonna breaking her jaw and busting out her teeth. Another woman in South Carolina from fifteen years ago was shopping a tell-all book. There would be more, because there was always more. It seemed like Marcus Rippy's wife was looking at serious prison time.

Whether or not Marcus was looking at the same was up to a jury to decide. The world could come up with all kinds of excuses when a man raped and beat a woman. Not so much when a woman was the one doing the damage.

Sara couldn't let herself sink into this depressing quagmire again. She turned off the TV. She called up her song list and put on Dolly Parton. She kicked the vacuum into the kitchen. She rolled up her proverbial sleeves and started taking everything out of her cabinets so she could clean them.

This was back to her normal level of stress management, though Sara had spent plenty of time watching *Buffy* on the couch and drinking way too much alcohol. Will had been tied up closing the Reuben Figaroa case and opening new ones against LaDonna and Marcus Rippy. His late nights and early mornings had him staying at his house so he wouldn't deprive Sara of her sleep. They were depriving each other of much more than that. Yet another thing that was going wrong. Sara knew from her first marriage that the only sure-fire way to stop having sex was to stop having sex.

Not that sex would be any more than a temporary solution. There was still the larger issue of what had happened with Angie and Will and Will and Sara, and Sara couldn't fix that on her own.

The phone rang. She bumped her head on a drawer. Sara let out some choice words as she reached for the phone on the counter.

'It's me,' Tessa said. 'I'm in a phone booth. We've got four minutes before my money runs out.'

Sara turned off the music. 'Why are you calling from a phone booth?'

'Because your precious niece dropped my cell phone down the hole in the outhouse.'

Sara covered her mouth to muffle the laughter.

'Yeah, it's really funny that my phone is encased in shit and I'm going to have to stick my hand down there and fish the fucking thing out.' Tessa's missionary work was more about helping people and less about watching her language. 'I am literally in the middle of nowhere. I can't just walk up to a Verizon store and buy a new one.'

'Where is she now?'

'Probably scribbling in my books and cutting up my clothes.' Tessa sighed. 'She's with her father, who is making sure I don't kill her. And don't tell me I was just as bad when I was her age. I already got an earful from Mama.'

Tessa *had* been just as bad, but mentioning their mother was enough to drain away any desire to tease. 'I got an earful, too.'

'She's worried about you.'

Sara pushed herself up onto the counter. 'There's a fine line between being worried and being self-righteous.'

'What's that, Kettle? Pot can't hear you.' Tessa changed the subject before Sara could come up with a snappy retort. 'Have you had the Talk with Will yet?'

The Talk. The reckoning. Sara was dreading it as much as Will.

She told her sister, 'I've been giving him some space. All that stuff with Reuben Figaroa and Anthony and . . .' She didn't have to remind Tessa of the details. The story of the hostage stand-off in the mall had made it all the way to South Africa. 'I just didn't want to pile onto him: "Sorry you witnessed a horrific suicide, but let's talk about our relationship."'

'You'll have to get around to it eventually.'

'What's the point?' Sara asked. 'What'll happen is, I'll say what I have to say and he'll nod a lot and look down at the floor or past my shoulder and he'll rub his jaw or pick at his eyebrow, and at the end of the day he won't tell me anything about how he's feeling because he thinks he can just pretend it away and we'll be fine.'

'Ohhh.' Tessa drew out the word. 'You didn't tell me Will was a man. Now all of this suddenly makes more sense.'

'Ha ha.'

'Sissy, you keep saying to me again and again that he won't talk, but what are you saying to him?'

'I told you I was giving him space.'

'You know what I mean,' she countered. 'I can see you being all stoic and logical and letting him think this is some sort of math problem that has an *X* or *Y* solution, when inside you're about to die, only you can't let him know that because you're worried about looking like some damsel in distress.' She stopped for a breath. 'Lookit, there's nothing wrong with being a damsel. It's not a man/woman thing. It's a human thing. *You* like taking care of him. *You* like feeling needed. There's no sin in letting Will have the same thing with you.'

Sara knew what was coming next before Tessa even said it.

'You need to show him how you feel.'

'Tess, I just—' She had to tell the truth, if only to her sister. 'I know this sounds petty, but I don't want to feel like I'm his second choice.'

Tessa's response was not immediate. 'Will is your second choice.'

She meant Jeffrey. 'It's not the same.'

'In a lot of ways, it's worse for Will. There's no question that you'd still be with Jeffrey if he were alive. But in Will's favor, Angie's still alive but he's choosing to be with you. So it's really more like a divorce, and you have to put up with his bitchy ex-wife, which puts you in line with exactly half the female population.'

Sara leaned her head back against the cabinets. She stared out the windows in the living room. The sky was an almost painfully clear blue. She wondered how Will was spending his Saturday. Their perfunctory phone call last night had been filled with a lot of noises about future plans that neither one of them seemed too excited about.

Tessa said, 'Every person has baggage. You've got all your shit with Jeffrey. Lord knows I've got my shit. People have baggage. The next guy, if you move on, will have baggage. The pope has baggage. Jeffrey had baggage. You didn't hold that against him.'

'Because he belonged to me,' Sara said, and she understood that this was what hurt most. She was jealous. She didn't want to have to share any part of Will with anybody else. His mind. His heart. His body. She wanted him all to herself.

'Sissy, don't cry.'

'I'm not crying,' Sara lied. Fat, stupid tears were rolling down her face. In the abstract, she could logic out all of the reasons why Will was wrong for her. But then she thought about losing him and she could barely find a reason to get out of bed.

The phone started beeping, giving them their thirty-second warning that time was running out.

Tessa said, 'Look, you know your choices. You can go find Will and tell him that you love him and that you want him in your life and that you're miserable without him.'

'Or?'

'You can turn Dolly Parton back on and finish vacuuming out your kitchen cabinets.'

Sara looked around the kitchen. She really should stop being so predictable. 'Is there a third option?'

'Fuck the hair off his balls.'

Sara laughed.

They both silently waited for the three quick beeps on the phone before the line was cut.

Sara hung up the phone. She looked out the windows again. A bird floated through the air. Its wings fluttered in the breeze. Sara missed having bird feeders in her backyard. She thought about the open houses she had looked at with Will a lifetime ago. She had pictured her weekends spent filling up hummingbird feeders and doing laundry and reading on the back porch while Will worked on his car.

When they were all standing in the waiting room in the Grady ICU, Angie had told Will that she wanted to give her daughter a happy-ever-after.

Sara could give that to Will. She could give him everything if he would only let her.

The dogs stirred from the couch. They wandered toward the door. Their tails wagged, because they knew the person on the other side.

Sara's first thoughts were purely instinctive. Her hair was packed into a granny bun. She was sweating from being inside of the cabinets. Her face was red from crying. She was wearing a ratty T-shirt and cut-off jeans. Even her bra was baggy. They had not been in a relationship long enough for Will to see her this way.

She jumped down from the counter with the hope of making it to the bathroom before he opened the door.

She made it to the living room.

'Hey.'

Sara turned around.

He had a bunch of takeout menus in his hand. 'These were in the hall.'

'My neighbor is out of town.'

He dropped the menus on the dining-room table. He held up his key to her apartment. 'Is using this still okay?'

'Of course.' Sara pulled at the cut-offs. She straightened her shirt. Will had obviously come from home. He was in jeans and one of his running shirts. Tessa's third option flittered through her mind.

He said, 'Faith just called me. Kip Kilpatrick died about twenty minutes ago.'

Sara knew the man had been in the hospital for the last twenty-four hours. His symptoms were all over the place. 'Did they ever figure out what was wrong with him?'

'He ingested high amounts of ethylene glycol. It's found in antifreeze and—'

'Transmission fluid.' Sara remembered the distinctive red bottle in the back of Angie's trunk. 'She'll get away with it, won't she?'

'I don't care. I mean, I care because a man died. Even though he was a prick.' He shrugged. 'Faith says it was the sports drink. It's red, the same as the transmission fluid, and apparently the taste is sweet, so Kilpatrick wouldn't have noticed it. Half the bottles in his office mini-fridge were spiked.'

'Clever.'

'Yeah.'

They both went silent.

Sara felt like she had had some variation on this conversation for the last week and a half. They talked about something terrible that Angie had done. They talked about work. One of them said something about grabbing a meal, over which they would have an even more stilted conversation, then Will would make an excuse about needing to go home so that he could finish some paperwork and Sara would go home and stare at the ceiling.

She said, 'So, what else? It's lunchtime. Are you hungry?'

'I could eat.'

'There's nothing in the house. I'll need to shower if we go out.'

'I miss you.'

Sara was shocked by his directness.

'I miss your voice. I miss your face.' He walked toward her. 'I miss touching you. Talking to you. Being with you.' He stopped a few feet away. 'I miss the way you rock your hips when I'm inside of you.'

Sara chewed her lip.

'I've been trying to give you some time, but I feel like that's not working. Like I should just start kissing you until you forgive me.'

If only it was that easy. 'Babe, you know I'm not mad at you.'

He put his hands in his pockets. He didn't look at the floor. He didn't look past her shoulder. 'I've got a court date at the end of next month. There's something called a divorce by publication. You put a notice in the newspaper, and if you don't hear back in six weeks, the judge can grant you a divorce.'

Sara felt her brow furrow. 'Why didn't you do this before?'

'My lawyer said it would never happen. Judges don't like to do it that way. They rarely sign off on it.' He said, 'I asked Amanda to pull in a favor and find me a judge who would.'

Sara knew how hard it was for Will to ask for help.

He said, 'I'm sorry I kept things from you. I know my not telling you stuff is a big thing. And I'm sorry.'

She didn't know what to say except 'Thank you.'

He wasn't finished. 'The way I grew up, you had to hide the bad things. From everybody. It wasn't just about people liking you or not liking you. If you acted out or said something wrong, it got passed on to your social worker and your social worker put it in a file and people—potential parents—they wanted normal kids. They didn't want problems. So you had a choice. You either let yourself be really bad, like to let them know that you didn't care whether or not they chose you. Or you kept your problems to yourself and hoped.'

Sara didn't dare answer. He so rarely talked about his childhood.

He said, 'With Angie, anything I told her, she would find a way to throw it back in my face. Find a way to hurt me with it or make me feel stupid or—' He shrugged, likely because the possibilities were endless. 'So I kept it all inside, no matter how important or inconsequential, because that was how I protected myself.' He still did not look away. 'I know you're not Angie, and I know I'm not a kid living at the home anymore, but what I'm saying is that it's a habit I have, the not telling you things. It's not a character trait. It's a flaw. And it's something I can change.'

'Will.' Sara didn't know what else to say. If he had told her all of this two weeks ago, she would've thrown herself into his arms.

'I got you this.' He took a key out of his pocket. He slid it across the counter. 'I changed the locks. I installed an alarm. I changed the combination on my safe. I took myself off everything that has to do with Angie.' He paused again. 'I understand that you need time, but you need to understand that I am never, ever going to let you go. Not ever.'

She shook her head at the pointlessness. 'I appreciate the sentiment, but there's more to it than that.'

'There really isn't,' he insisted, the same as he always did. 'We don't need to hash it out, because all that matters is how we feel about each other, and I know that you love me, and you know that I love you.'

All that Sara could see was a giant circle. He was apologizing for not talking about things, then saying that they should not talk about things.

'Anyway,' he finally said. 'I'm gonna leave now, give you some time to think about this, maybe start missing me too.' His hand rested on the doorknob. 'I'll be here when you make up your mind.'

The door clicked shut behind him.

Sara stared at the door. She shook her head again. She couldn't stop shaking her head. She was like a dog with a tick in its ear. He was so infuriatingly elliptical.

I'll be here when you make up your mind.

What did that even mean?

Here, as in the general 'I'm here for you,' or *here*, as in actually physically waiting right now in the hallway for her decision?

And why was it solely her decision in the first place? Shouldn't the future of their relationship be something they decided together?

That was never going to happen.

She turned back to the kitchen. Pots and pans were scattered on the floor. The vacuum hose was full of dog hair. She would have to clean it out before she let it touch the cabinets. Or she could just give up on today, take a shower, get on the couch, and wait for a reasonable hour to drink.

The dogs followed her to the bathroom. She turned on the shower. She took off her clothes. She watched the water fall, but didn't get in.

Will's words played on an endless loop in her head. The memories worked at her irritation like a match striking flint. All that he'd offered her were Pyrrhic victories. He was finally divorcing Angie, but Angie would still be around. He had changed his locks, but Angie would find a way inside just like she had before. He had gotten an alarm. Angie would know the code, just like Will had known the code to unlock her cell phone. He'd said that he was never going to leave Sara. So what? Neither was Angie. This was just more of Will's fairy-tale thinking that all he had to do was wait it out and everything would magically be okay.

Sara turned off the shower. She was so frustrated that her hands were shaking. She put on her robe as she walked back into the bedroom. She picked up the phone to call Tessa, but then she remembered the outhouse. And then she realized that calling her sister was pointless, because Tessa would only say the obvious: that in his usual roundabout way Will had just offered Sara everything that she had wanted from him for the last year and her response was to let him walk out the door.

Sara sat down on the bed.

Dumbass, she thought, but she didn't know whether she meant herself or Will.

She had to look at this logically. Will's earlier declarations could be interpreted one of two ways. One: he was going to try to be more open, but he would rather stick needles in his eyes than talk about their relationship. Two: why would they talk about what they wanted when they already had everything that they needed?

One and two. *X* and *Y*.

'God dammit,' Sara muttered. The only thing worse than her mother being right was when her little sister was.

Sara stood from the bed. She cinched her robe tight as she walked back up the hallway. She passed through the living room. The dogs followed her to the door. Their ears perked when Sara wrapped her hand around the knob.

Her resolve started to slip.

What if Will wasn't standing there when she opened the door?

Too much time had passed. Five minutes? Ten? He wouldn't still be out there.

What if *here* meant somewhere else?

Logic had failed her, so she had to rely on fate. If Will wasn't in the hallway, she would take his absence as a sign. That it wasn't meant to be. That she was a fool. That Angie had won. That Sara had let her win because she was too busy obsessing about what she thought she wanted rather than stopping and appreciating what she had.

Show him how you feel.

Tessa had told her to be more vulnerable. There was nothing more vulnerable than opening a door without knowing what would be on the other side.

Sara loosened her robe.

She unpinned her hair.

She opened the door.

Epilogue

Angie sat down on a wooden bench in the park. The slats were ice cold. She should've worn her coat, but the January weather was that weird mix of freezing in the shadows and burning hot in the sun. Angie had purposely chosen a bench shaded by the trees. She wasn't hiding, but she didn't want to be seen.

Her vantage offered a clear view of Anthony on the other side of the park.

Her grandson. Not for real, but technically.

He was on the swingset, surrounded by at least ten other kids. His legs were straight out, his head leaned back. He was giggling as he tried to climb higher and higher. Angie was far from an expert, but she knew that this was how a six-year-old was supposed to behave. Not sitting against the wall watching other kids have fun, but out there in the middle of it, running around, happy like the rest of them.

She hoped the boy would hold on to his happiness for a good long while. Six months had passed since Reuben Figaroa had killed himself. Anthony's mother had almost died. He had been held by a stone-cold bitch for two days. They had moved away from Atlanta, back to Thomaston, where his mother's people were. He was in a new school. He had to make new friends. His father was still in the news as more and more of Reuben Figaroa's sins emerged.

But here Anthony was, kicking it on the swing. Kids were like rubber bands. They snapped back quickly. It was only when the years started to roll by that they retracted from the memories.

Was Jo still retracting?

Angie looked past the swingset. She studied the group of mothers at their usual picnic table.

Jo was sitting with them, but on the periphery. Her arm was in a sling strapped low on her waist. Angie didn't know the prognosis, but she took it as a good sign that Jo's hand was still attached. She also took it as a good sign that Jo had finally joined the other women. The park was a regular afternoon event. Jo had held herself apart for months, politely smiling, nodding over a newspaper or a book from several picnic tables away. That she was actually sitting at their table now, that she was looking at them, talking to them, had to be progress.

Angie hadn't talked to her daughter since the night Delilah had tried to murder her. At least not so Jo could hear. The last thing Angie had told Jo as she dropped her off at Grady was a list of instructions. Angie had already called Denny on the way to the hospital. Ng was there too, so they had to come up with a script for Jo that would pass for credible: that Jo's boyfriend had hurt her, that he had disappeared, that she would not give his name, that she didn't want to press charges, that her name was Delilah Palmer.

Jo had played her part well, but she didn't know about the other things that Angie had done, like cleaning up the mess at the crime scene, using her cop training to hide everything in plain sight. Like taking Delilah on the last, most miserable ride of her life.

Angie still shuddered if she thought too long about the things she had done to Delilah's body. Not letting her die, because the bitch deserved that, but the cutting.

Sure, Angie was dangerous, but she wasn't sick.

The important thing was that the ends justified the means. Jo was living proof of this. Literally—she was living. The rest of it, Angie didn't know. Jo's hand would hopefully heal, but some wounds stayed open no matter what balm you tried.

Angie could only guess what was going on in her daughter's head right now. Jo would still be feeling guilty about Reuben. Guiltier still that she was relieved to have him gone. She would be worried about Anthony, the short-term damage, the long-term damage. She wouldn't yet be worrying about herself, but she would be feeling exposed, because the entire world knew what her husband had done to her. To Anthony. To Keisha Miscavage. To other women, because in the ensuing months, victims had started coming out of the woodwork. Marcus Rippy and Reuben Figaroa had taken their show on the road, drugging and raping women across the country. There might be as many as thirty victims.

Angie wondered if Jo took some kind of comfort in knowing that Reuben never beat the women he raped. That was only something special he saved for Jo.

If you were keeping score, and Angie was the type to do just that, Keisha Miscavage was the real winner. The fact that any person with a computer could Google her gang rape had not cowed the girl. Angie had followed Keisha's story in the news. She was back in school. She was staying clean. She was on the lecture circuit, talking to other students about assault. People believed her now, or at least more people did than not. One woman accusing a man of rape was a crazy bitch. Two women, three women, a few dozen women—they might have a point.

Anthony jumped off the swing. His feet landed wrong. He fell flat on his ass. Jo sprang to her feet, but so did Anthony. He wiped the sand off his butt. He hopped four times in a jagged line, and then he was off.

Jo didn't sit back down until her son had settled on the rope climb. She had her hand to her chest. The other mothers were clearly teasing her about her concern. Jo smiled, but she kept her head down, wary of even this small amount of attention.

Angie wanted Jo to be more like Keisha. To go out into the world. To tell everybody to fuck off, to stand up, to be strong like her mother. To do something other than hide herself away.

Was it shyness? Was it fear?

For the last few months, Angie had been mentally composing a letter to Jo. The content wasn't always at the forefront of her thoughts. She wasn't obsessing over it. What happened was, she was packing up her shit to move to a new place or she was driving down the road in her new car and she would think of a line that would work in the letter:

I should've kept you.

I should've never let you go.

I loved you the moment I saw you yell at that asshole in Starbucks, because that was when I understood that you are my daughter.

Angie knew that she could never actually write the letter. Not if she wanted to give Jo her happy ending. The temptation was still there, though. Angie was selfish enough, she was cold-hearted enough, and she certainly had proven that she didn't mind leaving a few casualties in her wake, but for now, she was content to do what she had always done: watch her daughter from afar.

Jo seemed like she was going to be okay. She was going out more. Sometimes she'd wind up at the coffee house near Anthony's new school, where she'd sit for hours just because she could. Other times she'd go to church and sit in the back pew, hands clasped in her lap as she stared at the stained glass behind the altar. There were aunts and cousins and all sort of boisterous, happy people that Angie could not imagine having to spend Thanksgiving and Christmas with. Anthony was attending a private school two counties over. They were financially secure. Jo hadn't been on any of Reuben Figaroa's accounts, but she was still married to him when he had taken the coward's way out, and she had inherited all of his investments, the properties, the cars, the money.

Angie had her own inheritance, too. From her uncle, which had a certain kind of irony, since Dale had never claimed her until Deidre was gone and he could trick her out. The bricks of cash that Angie had taken from his Kia totaled eighteen thousand dollars. Together with the money in her bank account, she had about fifty grand to live on before she figured out what to do with the rest of her life.

Back to being a private eye? Back to running scams? To running girls? To running pills? Back to Atlanta?

Not once since Deidre had drugged herself into a coma had Angie felt like she had choices. From the age of ten, Dale was always there, pushing Angie, pulling her, slapping her around. Even when she managed to get away, Virginia always connived her back into the fold.

In her imaginary letter to Jo, Angie would explain how Dale and Virginia had gotten their hooks into her. That she had only been four years older than Anthony when it happened. That she had been vulnerable. Terrified. That she had done anything and everything to keep them happy because they were all she had in the world. Maybe she would even quote LaDonna Rippy. The bitch was going to spend some hard time in prison for holding on to those shoes, but she hadn't been wrong about the nature of damage. Some people had holes inside of them that they spent their lives trying to fill. With hate. With pills. With scheming. With jealousy. With a child's love. With a man's fist.

Angie had created the hole inside of Jo. She had to own that truth. Jo had her adoptive parents. She had a normal life. But the second Angie had abandoned her baby in that hospital room, Jo had started to tear. The old saying was that women married their fathers. Angie had a sinking feeling that Jo was attracted to men who were more like her mother.

There weren't a lot of excuses to make, but this is what Angie would have told her daughter: badness doesn't come all at once. The dominoes fall over time. You hurt someone by mistake and they let you get away with it. Then you try hurting them on purpose and they still stick around. And then you realize that the more you hurt them, the better you feel. So you keep hurting them, and they keep hanging on, and the years roll by and you convince yourself that the fact that they still stand by you means that the pain you cause is okay.

But you hate them for it. For what you do to them. For what they do to you.

A sudden strong breeze cut through Angie's thin shirt. She looked up at the tree. American sycamore, she guessed, maybe one hundred feet tall. Tiny dots of dead leaves and twiggy tendrils gave the canopy the appearance of a hairnet. Massive trunk, shallow roots. The kind of tree that, for all its grandeur, would eventually topple during a bad storm.

'Anthony!' Jo yelled, loud and clear.

He was running up the slide. He guiltily ran back down, waving an apology. Jo slowly returned to the bench. She shook her head. She was smiling. Not a big grin that showed her teeth, but a smile that said things might end up okay.

Would Angie end up okay?

She was doing all this thinking about writing a letter when the only letter that mattered was the one that Will had left for her.

The minute she had been released from police custody, Angie had rushed to her PO box. She needed to cash her last check from Kip Kilpatrick before his account was closed.

The check wasn't there.

She had found a letter from Will instead.

Not a letter, really. More like a note. No envelope. Just a folded sheet of notebook paper. He hadn't used his computer. He had used a pen. Will never wrote anything but his signature anymore. He was too ashamed. The last time Angie had seen his handwriting was in high school, before computers, before anyone knew what dyslexia was and just thought his childish, backward letters and bad spelling signified a low IQ.

Typical Will, his note was succinct, as brief as anything Angie had ever left Sara on the windshield of her car.

It is over.

Three words. All underlined. Unsigned. Will had always avoided contractions. She could picture him sitting at his desk in his house, studying the note, sweating over the spelling, unable to tell if he'd gotten it right and too proud to ask anyone to check it for him.

Sara wouldn't know about it. This was between Will and Angie.

'Mommy!' The piercing scream made her flinch. Three little girls started running around, shouting their heads off. There didn't seem to be a reason why, but the sound was contagious. Pretty soon all the kids were screaming.

Her cue to leave.

Angie walked toward the parking lot. The sun quickly warmed her. Her car was an older model Corvette she'd bought off Craigslist. The money had come from an advance she'd taken off Delilah Palmer's credit card. It's not like the little bitch would get stuck with the bill. Weirdly, the car reminded Angie of Delilah. The tires were bad. The paint was chipping. Still, the engine had a threatening rumble when she turned the key.

The interior had the lingering odor of perfume. Not from the previous owner, but from Angie. She still had half a bottle of Sara's Chanel No. 5. The scent didn't exactly suit her, but then it probably didn't suit Sara, either.

Angie was still keeping an eye on her place-holder.

She had gotten Sam Vera to hook her up with the same technology he had used to clone Reuben Figaroa's computer. The contents from Sara's laptop were updated in real time now. She was still writing sickly sweet emails about Will to her sister.

When he holds me in his arms, all I can think is that I want this to last forever.

Angie had laughed when she'd read the line.

Forever was never as long as you thought it was.